WHILE NOBODY IS WATCHING

by

MICHELLE DUNNE

Copyright © 2020 by Michelle Dunne
Cover and jacket design by 2Faced Design
Published by arrangement with Bad Press Ink

ISBN 978-1-951709-39-6
eISBN: 978-1-951709-55-6
Library of Congress Control Number: available upon request

First published June 2020 by Bad Press Ink
First North American edition published in May 2021
by Polis Books, LLC
44 Brookview Lane
Aberdeen, NJ 07747
www.PolisBooks.com

POLIS BOOKS

For Dominic & Emily

CHAPTER ONE

The high-pitched ringing in her ears was enough to drown out the rest of the world almost completely although she was becoming vaguely aware of the dirt in her throat and the metallic taste of blood. A lot of blood. She forced her eyes open and stared straight up at the beautiful clear blue sky, oblivious for now of the carnage all around her. Her arm weighed a ton when she tried to move it and before she could, someone closed in on her. He was hovering above her, casting a long shadow as his body blocked out the sun. She shifted her gaze to see that it was Lenny Jones, but he didn't look like Lenny Jones. He was wearing a thick outer layer of grey dust and he was shouting, though no sound was coming out. She couldn't tell if he was shouting at her or not, because he kept looking from her to something else, and then back to her again. She turned her head to see who else was there, but whoever it was, she could only see his back over the mound of dirt between them. He was using his right hand to steady himself against what used to be a car as he hunched over something, and he too seemed to be shouting. But he didn't hold her attention for long as her eyes drifted to the large jagged metal fragment that was jutting up out of her shoulder. The world was still silent except for the ringing, which suddenly intensified as a white-hot pain flashed in her head and she realised that she was screaming. So hard in fact that suddenly she had no air left in her lungs and like her head, they burned. Lenny's face was right next to hers now, nudging her, licking her cheek...

Lindsey jolted awake and grabbed the nearest thing to her. When she realised that it was Frank, she let go and swung her legs out of bed, and with her elbows resting on her knees, she lowered her head into her hands. Frank moved with her and nudged the side of her head until she looked at him and finally hugged him in thanks for waking her. It wasn't the first time that someone or something in her dreams had turned out to be Frank doing the job that he was born to do. As if her seven-year old German Shepherd didn't have enough problems of his own. The poor dog hadn't had a full night's sleep in weeks.

She turned towards him and scratched his ears with her shaking hands. 'You're too old for this shit, aren't you buddy?'

He held perfectly still as she rested her head against him. Her heart was beating a tattoo in her chest but his warmth, and the rise and fall of his chest calmed her like it always did.

He whined as she got up and headed for the wardrobe, but he came and stood beside her, his body pressed against her bare legs as she rested her forehead against the wardrobe door. Her T-shirt was drenched in sweat even though her body shook with the cold, but she couldn't bring herself to move for what felt like an hour. It was more like ten minutes, but when she finally got dressed it was in a tracksuit pants and a vest despite the weather. It was four in the morning, still pitch dark and raining hard, which was the only time she dressed like this; when she was certain that no one would see her, and when she knew that going back to bed would be futile.

'Remember the days when one little Benzo would do the trick, Frankie?' she asked the dog, in a voice that struggled to make its way out. But she still managed a wry smile for his benefit.

He looked up at her and waited for her to continue.

'I know, I know,' she replied, as if Frank was the one who'd reminded her that one little pill soon led to two, which soon led to half a bottle. Eventually, no matter how many she took, they failed to make a dent in her sleep problems. However they did a good job of ensuring she couldn't remember her own name, so these days she did the only other thing that could possibly help.

'Get some sleep, sweetheart.' She kissed Frank one more time before heading for the door and minutes later she was running full tilt through the almost deserted city streets in the driving wind and rain.

Most Cork people didn't know the side of the city where Lindsey preferred to run. They knew the streets of course, but not how she knew them. They knew the vibrant, friendly, bustling Cork City that was portrayed in The Lonely Planet guidebook as one of the top ten cities in the world to visit. But Lindsey stuck to the side streets and alleyways, which at this time of night she shared only with the heroin addicts, hookers, teen gangs and drunks. She weaved her way through them and around them with her heart racing, her scars on full view, breathing in perfect rhythm with her stride. Any one of them could take her eye out without a second thought, but she didn't worry about that, because she knew they'd never catch her. Most of them didn't even see her.

But someone did. She knew that for a fact too. By now Lindsey had come to assume that she was never alone, no matter how things might seem to the contrary. Someone was watching her, maybe even now, as she sprinted with the noise of the wind rushing in her ears and a deluge of rain bouncing off the ground around her. She could still feel it. She'd been feeling it for weeks; at work, at home and even here, in the middle of the night when the rest of the world was sleeping, she could feel eyes on her. At first she assumed that it was her unreliable imagination. It was to blame for so much these days and it seemed to take pleasure in torturing her. But then the notes started to arrive. Someone was *telling* her that they saw her. That she wasn't always alone when she thought she was and as her heart hammered against her chest, a part of her hoped they'd show themselves tonight.

As she turned down another side street into the wind, she picked up the pace even more, so the five miles to where she was headed passed in the blink of an eye. Finally, she stopped and bent over with her hands on her knees in front of the old thick metal door with the flaking grey paint, barely visible through the collage of spray paint depicting everything from Bob Marley's joint smoking face to an, *I fucked your mother* confession. To the naked eye the tiny laneway looked deserted, but the derelict buildings on either side of the metal door hid a lot. On the far end of the lane was Angel's adult store, open 24/7. Behind this street was the bus station, which always attracted a select crowd at night, and the street opposite was the city's red light area.

'S'you again,' mumbled the gaunt, bleary eyed man who was sitting in the opposite doorway. 'Are you real?' He stared right through her for a few seconds and then he laughed, like something truly hilarious was happening in his head.

He was young enough and looked relatively clean considering, but was clearly off his head. As he was every time she saw him. He was as familiar to her as the metal door was, but this was the first time he seemed to notice her. It was the first time she'd seen him notice anything.

'You speak,' she replied, despite telling herself not to.

She kept her eyes on him as she worked the key off the rubber band knotted around her wrist. Her heart was still pounding, partly from the run and partly because of this guy, yet she took her time. The laughing soon subsided and all that remained was a slight grin. His eyes weren't focused on anything and he didn't look like he was about to move anytime soon.

'Give's a few bob?'

'What for?'

'Jam,' he grinned.

She took a step towards him and studied his face. He didn't look like he'd been on the streets for too long. His pale, freckled skin was still in relatively good nick, but he wasn't dressed for the outdoors. He never was, with his denim jacket and jeans.

'How long have you been here?'

He shrugged. 'I'm always here. What I can't figure out is, why are *you* here?' He wagged his finger with a smile that said, *I know exactly why you're here.*

'You think you know me?' She took another step towards him. Could he be the one?

'The girl who plays with knives,' he grinned, looking at her scars. 'How about that few bob?'

8

She didn't have a few bob and if she did, she wasn't about to pump it into this man's veins, so she didn't reply. She doubted very much this guy could get it together for long enough to insert himself into someone's life without being seen, so she was done talking to him. She turned her back on him and headed towards the metal door.

'Stuck up bitch,' he mumbled.

She ignored him as she let herself in, quietly closing the door behind her.

The building was once upon a time a small bag factory, but now the concrete shell of the ground floor was home to Street's Boxing Gym. Street himself lived upstairs on the second floor and above that was a disused attic space with a leaky roof. Street's was nothing like the swanky, air-conditioned gyms that were dotted all over the country these days. Here, the smell of stale sweat and dampness permeated the air, not helped by the fact that the tiny windows just below ceiling height hadn't been opened in years; not since the bars went up on the outside. The concrete floor was painted red and the walls had been whitewashed sometime in the distant past. The ring took up the most space and there was a heavy bag and a speed bag on either side of it. Medicine balls and weight plates were lined up neatly near the pull up bar. Ropes and gloves hung from various hooks, a long bench ran along each wall, and a locker filled with spare gear and first aid equipment stood in the far corner next to Street's tiny partitioned office, and that was about it. One shower, one toilet, and no mirrors. That was Street's. This wasn't the first time she'd found herself there in the middle of the night and it wouldn't be the last.

Drenched to the skin, Lindsey didn't waste time gloving up, nor did she wrap her hands, which she knew she'd probably regret later. But for now she wanted to feel it all. She wanted enough pain to eliminate the images burning in her brain, so after a short series of deep breaths she charged at the heavy bag, putting her whole body into every punch until she couldn't feel her knuckles any more. Her wrists screamed in pain and her shoulders felt like they were about to leave their sockets. Thirty-two minutes exactly left her spent, at which point something moved upstairs.

She grabbed the bag to stop it from swinging on its chain and she stood still, listening, but all she could hear was blood rushing in her ears.

There was an old rubbish bin filled with ice water in the corner, behind the heavy bag. There always was. Most of the ice was melted, but it was still cold enough to burn as she lowered her hands in, clenching and unclenching her fists as she slowly dipped her arms, up as far as the shoulders. She got on her knees, submerged as far as she could in the bin, as her face contorted in pain and her stomach clenched, but she made no sound. This would be her saving grace for today. She knew it and soon her body relaxed. Her stomach unclenched and as a board creaked overhead, she stood up, shook off the water and left quietly, locking the door behind her.

Outside, she leaned against the wall while she slipped the key back onto her rubber wristband. As she did so, she watched her new friend for a moment as he slept fitfully in his doorway and while she studied him, she thought briefly about the day ahead. She expected a certain amount of pain, but she was OK with that. In fact she welcomed it as a distraction, for distractions were what she craved more than anything these days. Anything that could take her out of her own head for a while was a good thing.

She took another minute to mentally cross the junkie off her list of possible menaces before jogging away and minutes later he was gone from her mind.

Home for Lindsey Ryan was a tiny one-bedroom cottage which looked like it belonged in the heart of the countryside, instead of on the outskirts of Cork city. But then it literally was the outskirts. The nearest suburb was Blackpool and the road from there continued on towards Limerick. Lindsey's house was one of the last to be seen on the way and despite being hers for over four years, it was still in a state of disrepair. In fact, to the naked eye it probably looked unlived in. The previous owners lived to be ninety-eight and ninety-two respectively, and following their deaths, the house sat idle for more than six years. Something to do with a lack of kin and a lack of deeds. During this time it made quite a nice home for some homeless, some addicts, some dealers, some rats, and a family of ferrets who were stubborn about leaving. She got a good deal on the place and in that first week she hired people to make the plumbing and electrics function, but that was it as far as professional tradespeople went. Since then she'd gone through phases of working on what had become her longest-running project. In one particular phase, she barely left the house for six months, during which time she replastered the entire place. She then realised that she'd made a balls of it and spent nearly two months hacking it all back down. She then bought sheets of insulation board and nailed them to the walls in each room, to give a more level surface, and then started again with the plastering; just a light skim this time. A shoddy job no doubt, if someone took a trained eye to it, but a few coats of paint and she was happy with it. After that she ripped up the faded and cracked old lino from the hall and kitchen floors and the moth eaten and badly stained carpets in the sitting room and bedroom, which she replaced with a cheap but not bad looking laminate floor which she laid herself. It was slightly warped in places and the knots in the wood didn't quite meet where they should, but some strategically placed rugs worked well. This house helped her whenever she needed it and she loved it, but as she opened the rusty gate and made her way up the short garden path with her muscles burning from the run home, she stopped short before going inside. Frank was barking just inside the door and she knew why.

It was the fourth note in as many weeks that she'd found stuck to her front door with a thumb tack and each word was made up of individual letters cut out of magazines, exactly like you'd see in movies. She pulled out the tacks and checked the door. Four tiny little holes grouped close together. The faded and scratched condition of the door was barely visible to her, but those four holes might as well have been a burst from a .50 calibre machine gun. They were all she could see when she looked at the front of her house. The faded and dirty pinkish paint that she swore she'd paint over. The small white sash windows on either side of the front door; the garden that was becoming overgrown again. She saw none of it. Only those four damn holes.

She walked around the outside of the house through the long wet grass, her fists clenching and unclenching again and her wrists protesting each movement. Someone else had walked there before her and now she was walking in the flattened path they'd made all the way around. There was a larger flat patch near both windows at the back of the house. Other than that, they left nothing else behind. Except of course for the note. She looked at it one more time, more closely now. It was a plain A4 sheet of paper. The kind that everyone and anyone had access to and she could only assume that, whoever it was, would be a big enough CSI fan, that they would also have worn gloves and used tweezers to construct each note. She folded it and brought it inside with her.

'Hey handsome,' she painted on a smile and was greeted with the same enthusiasm one might expect from an elderly parent who hasn't seen you in a while. She gave Frank a good scratch behind the ears and then slapped her leg once, which was enough for him to follow her anywhere.

'Don't you worry about them, Frankie,' she maintained the smile as she prepared a healthy mixture of dog food and crushed up joint health supplements for his breakfast. 'We both know who it is, don't we?' She put his bowl on the floor and started fitting his back and hip brace. 'It's nobody. Anyone who hasn't got the balls to deal with someone to their face is a nobody, isn't that right?' She tied the last straps on his brace before mumbling, 'And it'll take more than some god damn nobody, eh?'

Lindsey scratched him once more and headed for the shower, but not before checking each room on the way. She knew she wouldn't find anything. After all, there's no way Frank would be happily munching on his breakfast if someone was in the house, but she checked everything anyway, and as she showered she stood facing the frosted glass window, waiting to see some kind of movement where there shouldn't be any.

Lindsey kept a weapon of some sort in each room. A baseball bat in her bedroom, a hurley in the sitting room and another one in the kitchen.

An iron bar was leaning against the end of the bath right now. It was a habit she'd formed a few months earlier when she really started hearing things and now, before settling into any spot, she knew exactly how she would reach it if needed, and as she stood in the bath under the stream of hot water, she knew for a fact that one bound and her hands would be on it. There was no one there of course. But there had been.

The shower did little to relax her so she spent no time wallowing in it. She dried off quickly and dressed in jeans and a hoodie. She tied her hair in the usual unkempt ponytail, but as always her fringe was sleek and smoothed down in such a way that it almost fully covered the S shaped scar running from her forehead, down along her temple. The rest were easy enough to hide. Long sleeves, round necks, no problem. But this one she hated. This one was the reason why she had to keep her hair long and her fringe shaped. This was the one that prompted the questions.

She sat for a minute at her tiny kitchen table beside Frank, who was sitting patiently beside his now clean bowl. The chair under her had one leg that was slightly shorter than the other three, so it wobbled nicely as she sat down and kept wobbling as she put on and tied up her converse sneakers. The other two chairs had defects of their own, so it made no difference which one she chose to sit on.

'You done?'

Frank looked up at her and she smiled.

'Well then, let's go.' She headed for the door, with Frank close behind her.

Tús Núa was the name of the Centre where Lindsay had worked for over a year now. It translated as 'new beginnings', which was a nice idea. In reality, it was where the troubled youth of Cork spent their days when they were under court order to do so. Most didn't want to be there and had no interest whatsoever in new beginnings. But there were some. And some were better than none.

Theirs was like any other community centre. The ground floor was a basketball court, with line markings for several other sports including soccer and tennis. Their nets were stolen a few years ago and were never replaced, like most other things that went missing or got broken. Upstairs was the kitchen and a small, cluttered dining area. A long corridor housed four rooms used for all sorts of things and at the top of the stairs, just beside the kitchen, there were two toilets and what was once a shower room that had been converted into a very small office for Lindsey and one other youth worker by the name of Mike Hastings. There was one desk, one computer, three chairs which had to be stacked in order to open or close the door on account of the old and awkward filing cabinet taking up more space than everything else put together. Floating shelves on the walls were jam packed with folders, all bursting at the seams and this was where Lindsey spent as much of her time as she possibly could.

'What are you doing here?'

'I work here, remember.' Lindsey smiled at Sheila, who was a part of the minimal furniture in the kitchenette where she'd worked for almost twenty years. She cooked, she cleaned, she made tea like there was no to-morrow. She still threatened kids with the wooden spoon, but somehow they loved her. Now she was standing inside the large serving hatch, hands on her bony hips with a disapproving look on her prematurely wrinkled face.

'You've been in for twelve days straight. When the hell are you going to take a day off?'

'When you do. Besides, the alternative is to stay at home and paint my house.'

'Of course you could hire a nice young fella to paint it for you, like a sane woman would do. All you'd have to do is sit there and admire him.' Sheila barked out her infectious laugh. The kind that only a lady with a sixty a day smoking habit could produce and Lindsey couldn't help but join her.

'Wouldn't that be nice.' she was happy to pretend. 'But there's a new guy coming in to teach a bit of carpentry today. We have to make a good impression.' She grinned and rolled her eyes, but the sad fact was that it was true.

Places like theirs relied heavily on funding and volunteers and neither was easy to come by. Volunteers in particular had a lot to put up with. The last carpenter came to the end of his wick almost six months ago and left in a hail of foul language and indignation. It was around the same time that Lindsey acquired her set of wonky dining room chairs, courtesy of the kids who'd rather die than take enough pride in their work to bring them home. She was happy to declare her love for their chairs and the pride that she'd feel in having them in her home until such time as they wanted them back. Not that they'd listened, or necessarily cared.

'What's his name again?' She walked past Sheila's hatch, into the tiny office that she shared with Mike.

She picked up the diary on the desk, flicked through it to today's date and ran her finger down the page, over the barely legible scribble and doodles that filled it. 'Ray Allen.'

'Never heard of him,' Sheila replied as she sneaked a piece of bacon into Frank's mouth. A piece she'd cooked especially for him.

'Will you please not feed him that shit?'

Although her back was turned to Sheila, she knew that she was pulling a face and mimicking her good naturedly. Lindsey made the same request every time, but she'd have a better chance of training food loving Frank to say no.

According to her own notes, their new volunteer was a retired Garda. That was good. Most of the good ones were. If they hadn't been scared off by now, then chances are they wouldn't be.

Lindsey went back to the kitchen and poured a bowl of cereal and she sat down with Sheila. She ate while Sheila drank coffee and chain smoked John Players. The smoking ban didn't apply to Sheila and Lindsey had no interest in forcing it upon her. Not while it was just the two of them there. When the kids arrived it was different, which was why she inhaled as many as she could between now and then. Today was the first day of school holidays, so things were about to get hectic.

'How many have we today?' Sheila asked between puffs.

'Fourteen.'

'You OK?'

'Yeah… why?'

'No reason,' she shrugged. 'You just have bigger than normal bags under your eyes.'

'You're saying I look like shit?' Lindsey grinned.

'And your hands are swelling.'

Lindsey stretched and flexed her wrists, which were killing her now. 'What time is it?'

Sheila continued to look directly at her, the pair locked in a silent standoff that lasted no more than ten seconds, before Sheila finally answered. 'Well according to that clock on the wall, right next to your big thick head, it's half eight.'

'Better get to work then.' Lindsey stood up, startling Frank who was dozing at her feet. Sheila shook her head as she too got up and started fanning the smoky air towards the open window.

Frank looked from Sheila to the frying pan and back to Sheila.

'Don't you give me those eyes,' Sheila scolded him with a soft smile on her face. 'It'd be more in your line to have a chat with your Mammy. Tell her she needs to get a life for herself, like a normal thirty whatever-year-old woman. Maybe she'll listen to you.'

Lindsey patted her leg and Frank trotted out the door behind her, leaving Sheila with an audience of zero.

CHAPTER TWO

'I did in my fuck.'

The voice broke into a high-pitched squeak half way through the word *fuck,* which echoed around the indoor basketball court. It belonged to Jamie Cussons, a thirteen-year-old from Blarney. Lindsey knew this because she'd heard his pre-pubescent voice enough times over the course of the past two months. However she could no longer see Jamie as he was buried under Greg Patterson, also known as Choppers because of the size of his teeth. But his teeth weren't the only part of Choppers that were oversized. At just sixteen years of age, he was six foot two and built like a barge. Aside from using his nickname, which he appointed to himself before anyone else had the chance, no one dared mention his bucked teeth. Even a glance in their direction was enough to earn a kid a black eye and today, Jamie was the unlucky one.

'Hey, hey, break it up!' Lindsey shouted, as she covered the length of the court in seconds and grabbed Choppers by the shoulders and dragged him off Jamie. He strained against her, making Lindsey really regret her decision not to strap her hands earlier that morning, as her wrists once again screamed in pain. He was bulling to get at the scrawny thirteen-year-old again, so she jammed herself between the two of them. Jamie's fists were bundled around the back of her hoody as he made himself as small as possible and clung to her back, while Lindsey's fists were balled around the front of Greg's T-shirt.

Choppers was all but foaming at the mouth, his eyes wild. His breathing was as erratic as he was and his breath in her face was pungent.

'Calm down, Greg,' she kept eye contact with him while she spoke to Jamie. 'Jamie, go on upstairs.'

Jamie bolted and when he was far enough away, he turned and gave the middle finger to Choppers' back.

'Come on,' Lindsey let go of Greg's T-shirt and motioned towards the stairs and by the time they reached her office, there were two steaming cups of tea sitting on the desk thanks to Sheila. As always, hers would be perfect; black with a dash of cold water and Greg's would be milky with four sugars, just the way he liked it. Not that he *liked* anything per se, but it was as close as he'd get.

'Close the door.' She squeezed around to her side of the desk, past the two stacked chairs and instructed Choppers to sit on the third. She pushed the cup towards him and he duly ignored it, as he slouched onto the chair and crossed his ankle over his knee, which given their confinement, took more effort and discomfort than it would have if he just sat straight. But the impression that he wanted to give, as always, was that he didn't give a fuck.

'Go on then, get it over with,' he rolled his eyes with a grin.

'Get what over with?'

'The *Now Greg, you know you shouldn't be fighting,* bla, bla, fucking bla, speech,' he spoke in a sing song voice, loaded with sarcasm.

'I would, but I don't like to waste my time.'

'So scream at me then.'

'Would it do any good?'

He shrugged, still with a grin on his face.

'How's your mother?'

'Fuck you, bitch,' the anger was back and the grin finally disappeared.

Greg's mother worked as a prostitute, so he took any reference to her as an automatic insult. During his lifetime, she'd been brutally gang raped, robbed numerous times, addicted to heroin, clean of heroin and addicted to heroin again. She'd been beaten numerous times and once went missing for eleven days, and that was just the stuff in his file. He had an older brother with a long list of convictions, currently serving time in Portlaoise prison for his involvement in a tiger kidnapping and he didn't know who his father was. To say that the kid had it tough was an understatement.

'I saw her with her arm in a sling last week. That's why I'm asking.'

'That's none of your fucking business, bitch.'

'Bitch eh? That's four times today that I've been called that and twice was by you.'

He smiled again. 'Who were the others?'

'So what did Jamie do to you?'

'He put his stupid fucking face where I could see it.'

'And that was a good enough reason to beat up someone half your size?'

He rolled his eyes again and Lindsey could feel her own temper rising, though she kept it in check.

She leaned across the desk towards him and spoke in a low, slightly menacing tone. 'You know there are men like you all over this city, Greg. Your mother has probably met a few of them.'

'Mention my mother one more time and...'

'And what? You hate those fuckers, don't you?'

He inhaled and exhaled loudly, his nostrils flaring, but he didn't answer.

'Those men who think it's OK to beat your mother, to break her arm, to rape her...'

He slammed his fist down on the table, but Lindsey didn't flinch.

'Where do you think they started out? Do you think they just woke up one day and decided to be bastards? Or do you really think that your mother did something each and every time to deserve what she got?'

'Shut the fuck up!' he roared.

'They started with the little guy with the stupid looking face, Greg. In fact, your mother is no different from Jamie Cussons. She's smaller, she's weaker. She's more vulnerable and you're none of those things,' except vulnerable, she thought but didn't say. 'Does that mean that the only thing you can be in life is a bully who preys on the weak? Is that all you want to be? One of the so-called *men* that people like your mother and Jamie

Cussons have to watch out for every day of their lives?'

'You can't say this shit to me. You...'

'Why not? You're man enough to hear a bit of truth, aren't you?'

He rolled his eyes yet again and shook his head, but had nothing to say except, 'Can I go now? Are you finished?'

Lindsey gestured towards the door. 'Stay away from Jamie.'

'Tsss, whatever.'

Lindsey took a gulp of tea and brought both cups with her to the kitchen where Sheila was just finished patching up Jamie's split lip.

'Jamie, give me a hand finding Frank will you? I haven't seen him for a while.' Of course Lindsey knew exactly where Frank was. If he wasn't within ten feet of her, then he'd be outside chasing a ball around with Mike and the kids. Jamie had been coming to the Centre for about eight weeks now. He was thirteen-years-old and the shyest they'd ever had there by far. Because of the fact that he didn't talk much, Lindsey didn't know a lot about him, other than what was in his file. His mother died of cancer when he was ten. He had an aunt who couldn't or wouldn't take him on, but she did help to track down his biological father. Jamie was the result of a one-night stand and his father had no more interest in him than his aunt did. According to his file, Jamie was picked up for shop lifting time and time again.

Frank was pretty much the only individual that Jamie was truly comfortable with, so he was happy to help look for him.

'You OK?' Lindsey asked, putting her hand on his shoulder and leading the way out of the kitchen and down the stairs.

He nodded but didn't look at her and didn't speak, as he gently shrugged her off.

'How did the woodwork go this morning?'

He shrugged.

'Ray seems nice?'

Another shrug.

As soon as they got outside, Jamie called out Frank's name. He was on the outdoor basketball court, where he would once have been tearing through the legs of the players, trying to get the ball from them. But he was getting too old for that now, so instead he trotted up and down the sidelines, waiting for the ball to come to him. As soon as he heard Jamie's voice he changed direction and crossed the court, causing a small pile up of bodies as those playing had to stop short of tripping over him, but Frank didn't care. His objective was Jamie and he took the shortest route to get to him. Jamie reached in his pocket and pulled out a strip of bacon.

Lindsey laughed. 'Did Sheila give you that?'

Jamie smiled and nodded.

'She's trying to give my dog a bloody heart attack.' She tapped her leg and headed for the bench that was built into a little shelter. Frank followed her and Jamie followed Frank. They sat in silence, watching the kids playing basketball for a few minutes. Frank had his muzzle in Jamie's lap and he was quietly rubbing him.

'How are you getting on, Jamie?'

'Fine.'

'Do you like coming here?'

He shrugged.

'You know what my job is?'

Shrug.

'I'm a sounding board.' She smiled and looked at him. 'You probably heard Greg shouting at me a few minutes ago?' He was after all, in the kitchen right next door.

'I heard him.'

'That's kinda why I'm here.'

'So people can shout at you and call you a... bitch?'

There's that word again, although Jamie seemed uncomfortable using any swear words. They didn't come naturally to him.

'Sometimes,' she nodded. 'People need to vent their frustrations every now and then. Sometimes they need to scream in anger, but that doesn't mean that I'm the one they're angry at. Obviously there are other ways to express yourself, but some people just don't know how.'

He didn't reply. His gaze was still firmly on Frank who as always, did his job like the pro that he was.

'You know Frank there has seen me at my angriest and my most scared.' She smiled. 'He's *my* sounding board.'

He looked up at her now with a look of mild surprise. 'Why are you angry?'

'Everyone has some reason, Jamie. Even you I'll bet.'

He shrugged again. 'What are you scared of?'

She couldn't answer for a minute, while she tried to control her breathing which was becoming slightly ragged, as a dull ache spread across her chest. What the hell was wrong with her? Frank jolted his head up off Jamie's lap and came to her. She forced a smiled and scratched his head. 'Things I can't change,' she mumbled.

'I heard you say last week that you can change anything.'

Now she was the one surprised. 'When?'

'You said it to that girl with the glasses after Mike caught her smoking dope out here.'

She nodded. 'Oh yeah. Well… what I meant by that, was that a person can change the path that they're on. What you *can't* change is your past.'

'Obviously.'

She smiled.

'So what'd they do to you?'

'Who?'

'Your family.'

'That's why we're all here isn't it? Fucked up families?'

She still hated hearing things like that from kids like Jamie. Thirteen-year-olds shouldn't know hardship like these guys did. She shook her head. 'Not necessarily. We have no control whatsoever over what other people do, Jamie, and that obviously includes your family. But we can control what *we* do. We all make bad decisions at some stage and we can blame whoever we want for them. But at the end of the day, they're our decisions. It's what we do next that counts.'

'What'dya mean?' He reached for Frank again and Frank duly switched sides, now that Lindsey's meltdown hadn't gone full blown.

'Why does anyone do anything?' She shrugged. 'For attention? For approval? To get someone to notice them?' His eyes were on Frank, but he was listening. 'But what if the best way to get all of those things was to tell yourself that you don't need them? You think all the people who don't notice you now, won't notice you a few years from now when you finish school *despite* them? When you get a college degree *despite* them? When you go places and achieve things that they could only dream of? You think people won't notice you then? The right people?'

There was silence for a minute and Lindsey was happy to let the question settle on him until he was finally ready to answer.

'Do we have to talk about this?'

Lindsey shook her head.

'Then I don't want to.'

'OK. But you have my attention, Jamie. Now, what do you want to talk about?'

'Can I just play with Frank?'

Lindsey reached over and patted the dog. 'Sure. But no more bacon,' she smiled.

Jamie returned a wan smile and Lindsey got up and left them to it.

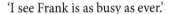

'I see Frank is as busy as ever.'

Lindsey looked up from her phone where she was about to open the first of four text messages, to see Damien Lucey walking through the mesh gates towards the Centre.

'Damien! What are you doing back here?' she walked towards him and held out her hand, which he ignored and instead, gathered her in a hug. Lindsey was absolutely not a hugger. In fact, she wasn't fond of being touched, full stop, but she was happy to see him.

Damien Lucey was almost eighteen now, but he was one of the first kids that Lindsey had ever worked with and was without doubt the most memorable. She was only two weeks on the job when sixteen-year-old

23

Damien called the *on call* number at two in the morning and got Lindsey. To this day, she's never forgotten that phone call. Damien's childlike, panicked voice. The screaming and crying in the background. Lindsey, in a mild state of panic herself, did all she could to assure him that help was coming, as she ran from her house to go to his. On the way she called his social worker and the police, all of whom got there at the same time as she did, but Damien was beaten to a pulp by then. His mother's boyfriend at the time had started with her, until Damien, who was scrawny for his age, came to her defence by hitting him over the head with a glass bowl. He took the brunt from there.

Damien and his fifteen-year-old sister were taken into emergency care that night and then entered into the foster care system. Naturally, he blamed himself for everything. He hit a guy with a bowl and now he was separated from his sister and they were both separated from their mother. But aside from a short spell of anti-social behaviour, what followed was the exception to the rule, in the form of Damien's cast iron resolve that he was going to better his life, starting with getting his leaving certificate exams.

'Well, I wanted you to be the first to know.'

'Know what?'

'I'll give you a hint… where's the last place you could ever imagine me going?'

'Antarctica. The way you always complained about the cold…' she smiled.

'Guess again.'

'I give up. Where are you going?'

'College. University of South Wales to be precise. Looks like I have a grant and everything.'

'Holy shit!' She grabbed him by the shoulders and shook him in delight. Then she surprised herself by hugging him. 'Tell me everything! What are you doing? When are you going?' She led him towards the low wall running around the perimeter of the Centre, with the mesh fence on top and they both sat down.

'It's all your fault.'

'Ah, if only I could take the credit for that one,' she laughed.

'You shoved my nose in a school book every day I was here. You made me forget about everything else and you organised all those extra grinds and stuff, remember?'

'But you did all the work, Damien.'

'Do you remember that day when you took me fishing out by the Anglers Rest?'

She nodded. She remembered it well.

'I was living in that shitty group home at that stage. It was a week after my sister was sent to hospital by another one of Mam's so-called boyfriends. Remember, after she ran away from her foster home and went back to Mam's house?'

'I remember.'

'I'd never picked up a fishing rod in my life before that day.'

'Me neither,' Lindsey laughed quietly.

'What? But you caught a trout?'

'While you were taking a leak behind a tree.'

He tilted his head and looked suspiciously at her. 'Are you telling me...?'

'That I bought a fish from the English Market that morning and brought it with me? Yes.' They both laughed now. 'One of us had to catch something!'

'You sneaky git.'

She nodded, still smiling.

'I was so fucking mad at my mother,' his smile faded now and he shook his head. 'She kept bringing these assholes into our house. They were more important to her than having us there with her. Laura wasn't even supposed to be there, remember? She was with that family on the South Side, the O'Halloran's. They took money from the state to foster kids, but they didn't give a shit about the kids themselves. She hated it there.'

Lindsey had nothing but admiration for foster families. But she hated no one more than *those* foster families.

'Anyway...' he shook his head and a slight smile returned to his face. 'You started harping on about why people do the things they do. Christ, you went on and on, I thought you'd never shut up,' he was laughing quietly again now.

'And you exploded,' she laughed with him. 'You gave me so much grief, you were lucky you didn't get a slap of a trout across the head.'

'Lindsey, you went off on a fucking tangent about the Middle East. Here I was, just looking to hit something, and you were going on about what makes innocent children grow up to be radicals? What makes soldiers volunteer time and time again to go to these places? You mentioned everything *but* my mother, or what makes women like her seek out the same man over and over, but that's all I could think about on the way home. I wanted to know and she couldn't tell me.' He smiled, 'I'm going for a degree in psychology, in case you hadn't guessed.'

'This must be what a proud parent feels like,' Lindsey couldn't help feeling giddy. Most kids who left the Centre for the last time never returned. Some went on to become fully fledged criminals; others went on to give birth to the next generation of troubled youth, while others dropped off the radar completely. This felt like one of the most rewarding days in her career.

'I'm just worried about what'll happen to my sister when I'm gone.'

'Jamie, your sister will be fine. You need to think about yourself now. Get your degree and then you can choose a life for yourself *and* your sister.'

Suddenly there was a loud explosion. An all too familiar and deafening BOOM, followed by the even louder WHACK as the explosion echoed all around them. Lindsey ducked and covered her head with one arm, while pulling Damien off the wall and towards the ground with her other.

'What the...?'

'Stay down!' she shouted at him, as she ran towards the Centre... towards the explosion, but when she got inside, there was a bunch of kids laughing and joking as they picked a long bench up off the floor.

She stood in the middle of the court, breathing hard, trying to take in the scene, but it was Frank's barking that got the attention of the kids, as he came running to Lindsey's side.

'What?' One of the kids walked towards her, looking more nervous the closer he got.

'It's alright, buddy,' Damien came and assured the boy that all was right with the world, as he turned Lindsey and gestured towards the door again.

She walked with him, but kept looking back. It was an explosion. She was certain of it. She felt it vibrate through her... she smelled it.

'You OK?'

She pulled away from him and turned back towards the kids. 'What happened here?'

The same boy turned towards her again. He was relatively new, but she should have known his name. And she did, she just couldn't remember it now. 'Jeez, sorry!' he opened his arms and shrugged by way of asking what her problem was. 'It was an accident, woman,' he indicated the long gym bench on the floor. The benches were stacked three high and this one had obviously fallen off the top with a loud bang.

Lindsey's breathing was still erratic and Frank was stuck to her, nudging her leg with the side of his head. As she looked around now at the faces staring back at her in bewilderment, she started to feel sick. 'OK... just put it back when you're finished,' she mumbled to the kids and turned away from them, but Damien was still there. 'Damien... congratulations again. Keep in touch, OK?' she forced a smile and rubbed his arm before walking away towards the stairs and towards her office.

'Hey... you sure you're OK?' Damien called after her.

She waved without turning around.

She jogged up the stairs towards her office, hoping not to meet anyone along the way. When she got there, as always, there was too much clutter to close the door, so she grabbed the stacked chairs and flung them out into the hallway and then slammed it shut, before making her way around the desk and into her chair. Frank of course, got there before her. She lowered her head into her hands. Nightmares were one thing, but this was something else. This hadn't happened before. She was losing her damn mind.

'Hey, what happened?' Mike barged into the office. Of course she couldn't expect him to knock seeing as it was his office too, but she wished that she could tell him to fuck off for now.

'Nothing,' she straightened up.

'Are you OK?'

'I'm grand, Mike. Can I just get a bloody minute?' she snapped at him; another relatively new occurrence.

He held his hands up and backed out the door, closing it behind him.

Lindsey sat without moving for almost an hour. She'd never felt more confused and embarrassed in her life. She was so sure that it was an explosion. God knows she'd heard enough of them to know what one sounded like… but the way everyone looked at her. A falling fucking bench and suddenly she was a lunatic.

When the hour was up, there was a gentle knock, followed by Mike's head coming around the door again. 'Can I come in yet?'

Lindsey dropped her head back and blew a long breath up towards the ceiling. 'Yeah.'

He placed two cups of tea on the desk and dragged one of the other chairs in from the hallway. Then he just sat there, looking at her.

Mike Hastings was who Lindsey had spent most of her new career so far with. He was forty-two years old and had been working as a youth worker for eighteen years, which was a remarkable achievement. Most burned out well before eighteen years. He had a wife, Marie, but the Centre was without doubt a third wheel in their marriage. It was the reason why they fought constantly. The reason why he'd been kicked out of home at least three times since Lindsey had known him and it was the subject of most of the ultimatums that were issued on an almost monthly basis by his wife. But he was the backbone of this place and Lindsey liked working with him, though she didn't want to talk to him just now.

'What, Mike?'

He shrugged and she finally smiled. 'Nearly every question I've asked today has been answered like that.'

He grinned, but of course he knew that she was deflecting. 'Has this happened before?'

'Has what happ…?'

'You know what. You took cover. You pulled Damien to cover.'

'Don't exaggerate.' She forced a smile again, as she reached in her bag and pulled out Frank's favourite; a packet of poached salmon and ricotta dog treats that cost more than her own food did. She gave him one, which he ate out of her hand and returned to lick her fingers.

'You haven't been sleeping?'

'I'm sleeping fine.'

'Are you?'

'Let's not psychoanalyse, eh Mike?'

'You bottle things up, Lindsey…'

'Mike, no offence, but you don't know what the hell you're talking about.' In her case, he didn't. Mike knew that she'd served in the army and he also knew that she had some nasty injuries, but he didn't know for a fact that the two were related, though he'd probably guessed as much. Still she felt bad for pointing it out. She closed her eyes and rubbed the bridge of her nose. 'Look, you're right. I'm tired. I'm gonna head home early, OK? Do you have the list for this weekend?'

'You sure you're up to it?'

'I'm fine. Actually I'm looking forward to it. I haven't been camping in ages.'

'OK. Well then we have four happy campers. Greg Patterson, Leah Mendelson, Jamie Cussons and Jerry Gleeson. And of course us two.'

'Jerry Gleeson?'

'The lad who dropped the bench.'

'Oh… yeah, OK. Greg has a bit of a bee in his bonnet about Jamie, so we need to keep a close eye on that.'

'Yes, ma'am,' he grinned.

'Right, well in that case, I'm off.'

'Good. And I don't want to see you back here 'til Thursday.'

'I'll be in tomorrow.'

'No. You won't. You've been working for twelve days straight. You're on edge, you need a break. Plus, we have small numbers for the next couple of days. Ray Allen was a big hit this morning, so he's agreed to come back on Wednesday for the full day. We have Mary coming in to give Maths and English grinds as well and believe it or not, I just spoke to Damien and he's agreed to come and have a chat with the kids about his time here and how he turned it around. See if he can't inspire them straight,' he smiled. 'I think he could be a real good influence on some of them.'

'Yeah, me too,' she nodded.

'So go.'

'OK.' She got to her feet and Frank jumped to his.

'You want me to call over when I'm finished here? I could bring a take away?'

There was no denying that Mike was a very handsome man. He was over six feet tall, and still very fit. Unfortunately though, being married didn't stop him wanting to spend more time than he should with his female colleague outside of work. Another fact that wasn't lost on his wife, who was not a big fan of Lindsey's.

'The best thing you could do after work is go home, buddy.' She squeezed his shoulder as she practically climbed over him on the way out the door. 'I'll see you on Thursday. Don't forget to pack your thermals,' she smiled and left.

CHAPTER THREE

She didn't even bother to get into bed that night. What was the point? Instead, she stopped at the off licence on the way home and picked up two bottles of wine.

Lindsey's front door led into her modest living area where there was a small, two-seater fake leather couch and a matching armchair, behind which was the little dining table with the mismatched chairs against the wall by the kitchenette. That night she pulled the armchair directly in line with the front door and proceeded to drink one of the bottles of wine while sitting in it. The lights were off and the living room's hurley was in her hand the whole time, but no one came, which was typical, because tonight, like last night, she genuinely hoped that they would. Some asshole with a warped sense of humour, or injustice, or whatever the hell was motivating them, was the reason why her mind was giving in to irrationality. She wanted them to come with their little thumb tacks and chicken shit notes, so that she could see how brave they really were. But nothing happened and the more she drank, the more she became convinced that it was all in her head. She was losing her mind. She'd been called a bitch several times today alone, and today was no different from any other. It was probably some dumb, scared kid looking for attention and they were no more of a threat than a bench falling to the floor, or the dreams that assaulted her sleep. Yet her grip was as tight as ever on the hurley and her eyes never left the front door.

The following day was a day off whether she wanted it or not, so she decided to spend the first half hour or so raiding her tiny barna shed, to see what she had and what she could do with it. The house needed a paint, but she didn't have any. That would wait until tomorrow. Another day off, at least some of which would be spent at B&Q. The roof was leaking, but she had no idea what she needed to fix it, aside from some slates, of which there were four stacked in the back corner of the shed, which she inherited with the house. They looked at least second hand and were possibly as bad as the ones on the roof, but they'd probably do. *How* exactly she was going to fix it was another job for Google and for tomorrow. For now, she pulled out the strimmer and lawnmower. There was a can of black Hammerite that would do the garden gate. Weed and feed. A large net bag of bulbs that had roots growing out of them already. Her power washer, for the garden path and some white paint for the windows. Finally, a large but half empty can of brown wood stain for the shed itself and her day was set.

She started with the strimmer to lower the almost knee-high grass, stopping several times to throw up last night's wine binge. She finished it off with the mower until the grass looked properly dead. What was left hadn't seen much light in recent times and had turned yellow, but it'd be back, she told herself, as she sprinkled *Weed and Feed* all over it. She then returned to the shed for a spade and proceeded to dig up the sod against the wall of the house, right around the perimeter and about four feet in width. She planted the bulbs here. She had no idea what, if anything would grow, but she knew that no one would get near her windows without leaving a print. Those same prints might not show as well on the concrete path, but now that it had been power washed to look like new, it couldn't hurt.

The small, rusty gate took far longer than it should have and Lindsey swore that, not only would she never use Hammerite again, but that she'd be writing a strongly worded letter to their customer service department.

It was like painting with glue. The wood stain was much easier to use and by the time she was finished, the shed made her garden look like someone who knew what they were doing lived there. At least to the naked eye. If they looked beyond the yellow grass.

By then, the sun that had been hiding behind clouds all day, finally gave up the ghost and set and when she finally went inside, the chair was still where she'd left it, as was the hurley. But she couldn't bring herself to sit there again tonight and it seemed that Frank agreed, as he jumped onto the chair and curled up facing the door. He was offering to take this watch even though he was tired after his day in the garden.

'Come on you,' she rubbed his head with both hands and kissed him, before moving the chair with him on it, back to its original position. A few minutes later, he joined her in the tiny kitchen and they ate together, beans on toast for Lindsey and ground beef for Frank. She had planned on making a stew with that, but cooking was the last thing she felt like doing. Instead she had a beer with her meal and tried to still her mind and body. She was exhausted, but restless at the same time. She was bouncing on her toes under the table, wishing for sleep, but knowing that she wasn't ready for it. Instead she got to her feet and went for a shower. She pumped up the heat to ease the tension in her muscles, then dried quickly and went to study her wardrobe. She looked first at her workout clothes and thought briefly about a long run and as much time as she could get away with at Street's, but that's not what she needed tonight.

Instead she pulled out the one and only mini skirt that she owned, black denim and more than a few years old. She put it on over her good, black lace underwear, all matching for once and she wore it with a simple, long sleeved top, finished with a pair of black stilettos. It wasn't chic by any means, but her legs looked extra long and very toned in it. They more than made up for the fact that she was fully covered on top. It was enough to get her what she wanted tonight and that's all she cared about. She topped up Frank's water bowl and left.

Twenty minutes later she was getting out of a taxi at a bar on the outskirts of the city centre, north side of the River Lee. Despite being a Tuesday night, the city centre pubs would be crawling with students and Lindsey had no interest in students. She didn't have much interest in being in a bar either for that matter, but she didn't plan on staying long. The place she chose was dark, even by day, and had the same number of patrons on a week night as at the weekend. Not revellers. Just drinkers. She'd been there a couple of times before, but not often enough that she knew anyone there. Or vice versa. She ordered a beer and sat on a stool at the far end of the bar.

Lindsey Ryan was by no means a vain woman, but she knew that she could get the attention of men when she wanted to. And sometimes when she didn't. She was five foot eight in bare feet and extremely fit, as she'd always been. Her body was toned and hard, her legs long and lean. Her chest was small though, and more muscular than a lot of men went for, but it didn't seem to matter much. Although her father was as Irish as they come, she had inherited her Brazilian mother's skin tone, which made her blue eyes stand out more. It also made her scars stand out more, at least in her eyes, but she counteracted them in every way she could. One of which was to keep her dark brown hair long enough to at least camouflage her bare skin when needed.

'You look lonesome.'

'Do I?' She grinned at the twenty something, who had just left his group of friends to approach her. He was taller than her and very broad. He looked like a bit of a meat-head and was wearing a tracksuit, but would otherwise have been good looking enough.

'Don't tell me you were stood up?'

'Is that your best line?' she drank her beer.

'OK then, why don't I just buy you a drink?'

'I have one.'

He guffawed quietly, but not quietly enough. 'I can tell this is going to be hard work.'

'What is it that you're working on?'

'I didn't plan on working at all,' he smiled. 'My friends and I were just having a few beers and a nice discussion until you walked in on those fucking legs and I haven't been able to concentrate on anything else since.'

Lindsey looked around and she had the attention of four more meat-heads in tracksuits. 'They don't seem to be discussing much now.'

'I can introduce you if you like?'

'I don't think we need to do that.'

'OK. So what *do* you want to do?'

'Why don't we finish these and go find out?'

His hand froze with his bottle half way to his mouth and then he laughed. 'You don't waste much time, do ya?'

'Who has time to waste?'

He nodded with an approving grin. 'I live near here.'

'Let's go then.' She got to her feet and looked at him until he put his almost full bottle on the counter and gestured towards the door.

As they walked up Blarney Street, she managed to block out some of his small talk, most of which was about body building. He walked like he was carrying a football under each arm, but his bulk seemed to make it difficult for him to walk quickly uphill. She found herself wondering what mix of chemicals he was on and what points on his body she would go for if she needed to defend herself.

Finally, he stepped ahead of her and opened a dilapidated wooden gate between two three-storey buildings. This led to a small courtyard crammed with overflowing bins. The smell of decaying household waste was horrific as they made their way through the clutter, which was lit only by the almost full moon. They entered the building through a backdoor and up one flight of thread bare carpeted stairs and she quickly realised they'd reached an apartment with no front door. There was just the short landing they were on, with four internal plywood doors that a four-year-old with a temper could break through. He quickly explained one led to his kitchen, one to a sitting room, one to the bathroom and the fourth to his bedroom. The stairs continued through his landing and up to the next apartment, which he said had a similar layout. To live here meant that when you stepped out of any of your rooms, you could be greeted by just about anyone. It was horrific as far as living standards went, but she didn't plan on being there for long. This was helped by the fact that he didn't offer a drink. Not that she expected him to. Instead, he unlocked and opened the door to the bedroom, then closed and locked it again when she followed him inside. Under normal circumstances, having someone lock her into their bedroom would have been a problem. But here it seemed to make perfect sense.

After that, she wasted no time looking around. She turned off the light as soon as he turned it on. Then she took his clothes off.

He worked just as quickly on hers and when his hands finally slowed down after having explored her with enthusiasm, his fingers lingered on the raised skin of the scars running from her chest, across her shoulder and half way down her arm, and when he was about to speak, she kissed him so that he wouldn't. He couldn't see them and seconds later she made sure that they were gone from his mind.

Their whole encounter lasted forty minutes from when he locked the door, with Lindsey leading the whole time and as soon as she finished she got up to leave.

'Hey, hey, hey! Where are you going?' he leaned up on his elbow and caught her arm.

'Home,' she smiled and gently pulled away from him.

'Holy shit, you're...' his words trailed off and he laughed, incredulous, as he turned on the bedside lamp, which was just a bare bulb.

'I'm what?' she turned her back to him and put her bra and top back on.

'Nothing,' he held his hands up in surrender. 'You didn't even tell me your bloody name?'

'Mary.'

'That sounds like bullshit.'

She continued to get dressed.

'I feel like I've just been raped,' he lay back and put his hands behind his head.

'You look happy enough.'

'I am. That's why I'm thinking you should stay, *Mary*. I'm Devon by the way. And yes, that is my real name.'

'Thanks. But I think we both know that this has run its course,' she smiled again as she picked up her bag.

'Christ girl, you're straight to the fucking point, aren't ya? he got off the bed, making no effort to hide his nudity, and moved between her and the door. Everything about him was big enough to dwarf her. He reached for the neck of her top and slipped his fingers inside, gently pulling it away from her skin. 'Who'd you piss off to get scars like them?'

She moved his hand away and went around him to the door. 'Bye, Devon.' She unlocked it and let herself out and though she could hear him cursing to himself, he didn't come after her. Nor did she look back.

'Fuck,' she muttered under her breath as she pulled the slate ripper out from under the broken roof slate. The YouTube roofer with the annoying voice made it look dead easy to cut nails out of broken roof tiles using one of those things, but so far hers didn't seem to be working. Then again, that guy was standing nice and comfortably on a ladder, working a second or third row slate out of his roof. Lindsey was closer to the peak of hers, without a second ladder with a roof hook. Instead she had a grappling hook slung over the top and a rope with various loops spread along it, each one just big enough for her to slip the toe of her boot into. The rope itself was wrapped around her left arm, which also held the slate ripper, while she worked the hammer with her right. It was typical really, that the dope on YouTube would pick an easy one, rather than filming the fact that men can't multi-task for shit.

She slid the ripper in again and felt around until she found the nail, then hooked it. She then began tapping the handle, gently at first, with the hammer. When it didn't budge, she began hitting harder, until finally, with one last blow, the slate ripper flew out and the slate loosened on one side. She repeated the action with the second nail and finally was able to slide out the cracked slate. She held it in her hands and smiled at it for a minute before checking that the garden below was clear, then throwing it down onto the grass.

She pulled herself up along the rope until she could reach the new slate which she'd left resting on top of the chimney pot. She lowered herself back and slid the slate into place. It already had the nail holes in it since its last job, so it took no time for her to nail it into place. Not too tight, not too loose and if her leak dried up, then she was happy to count this as a success.

'What in the name of fuck are you doing up there?'

Lindsey looked down to see Mike standing at her gate. 'What are you doing here?'

'I asked you first, but I'm on a break, if that's alright with you? Ray is playing a blinder with the woodwork and anyone who's not at that is having grinds with Mary; she's slightly less popular as you know, but still an' all, I was redundant for a bit so I thought I'd pop over, see how the day off is going… but again I ask, what in the name of fuck are you doing?'

'What does it look like?' She held up the hammer and slate ripper before unwrapping her arm and climbing down along the rope, putting her weight in the loops so as not to break any more slates on her way.

'Well, I know that's a hammer, but I have no idea what that other thing is, and it looks a bit like you're carrying out roof repairs.'

'Good man, Mike. You got it in one.'

'I could have done that for you.'

'Says the man who doesn't know what a slate ripper is.'

'Now I'm just embarrassed.'

She laughed quietly as she got onto the ladder and made her way down. 'Why are you really here?'

When Mike turned up at her house with a file under his arm, then her house was his. Likewise on the rare occasion that he arrived with a six pack in his hand at the end of a particularly harrowing day, but when he turned up out of the blue for no apparent reason, at a time when his marital bliss was severely lacking, then he didn't get pass her front door. She strongly suspected that this was one of those times.

'I told you...'

'Yeah... you were redundant,' in a place where there's more work to get done than anyone will ever have time for. Her tone implied as much, though she didn't say it. She sat down on the front step and waited for him to speak. Mike was an exceptional youth worker and a good friend, but when it came to his marital problems, he was more predictable than anyone she knew. First came the outrage; the, *I don't know what her problem is* phase. Then the nonchalance. *Whatever, I'm over it.* Then inevitably came the, *She doesn't get me like you do, Lindsey* phase, before finally the moping around phase comes just before the apology and the move back home. She could tell by looking at him, that home was somewhere he hadn't been for a few days, meaning that he'd probably been sleeping at the Centre.

'OK, OK, I needed a break. And I genuinely wasn't needed there and won't be until at least three.'

'OK. And what did you have in mind for this break?'

'Nothing. Just a chat,' he sat alongside her.

'Shoot.'

He laughed quietly. 'You really don't believe in small talk, do you?'

'I'll have you know, I'm a big fan of small talk. But I like to save it all up for the elderly couple up the road and the postman. I feel they need it more,' she rolled her eyes dramatically. 'If you insist though... I suppose the weather isn't too bad.' She smiled and he laughed again.

'You know I find it quite sad that a pair of dinosaurs and a man bringing you bills are the only other people you seem to talk to.'

'Correction; the only people I *small talk* to.'

'Do you ever spend your spare time with actual people?'

'Did you come here to talk about me, or Marie?'

'Am I that predictable?'

'What happened this time?'

'Same thing that happens every time; our incompatible lives clashed again.'

Lindsey didn't answer. Personally, she couldn't understand why they were still together. They weren't bound by children, although that seemed to be another sore subject. They fought more than they didn't and from what Lindsey could see, they made each other miserable.

'Is it supposed to be this hard?'

'You're asking the wrong person, Mike.'

He leaned back and studied her. 'When was the last time you had a boyfriend, Linds?'

'Seriously, let's talk about *your* problems. If we start on mine we'll be here all day and you only have half an hour left,' she smiled.

'I wish you believed in boyfriends. I'd be first in line if you did.'

'Because that'd solve all your problems.' She shook her head, not worried about the annoyance in her voice, as she stood up and headed for the gate.

'Sorry!' he announced, as he got up and followed her. But she knew him well enough to know that he wasn't. 'So… you all set for tomorrow?'

'I will be,' she held open the gate for him, but it still caught his eye as he walked through it.

'What the fuck happened to your gate?' he stuck his finger in one of the blobs of Hammerite on the gate's lower half.

'Two pieces of advice; don't ever use Hammerite and don't get that on your clothes or it's never coming out. Now go back to work and then, for fuck sake, Mike, go home.'

'That was more than two pieces of advice.'

'Well take whichever ones you want. Either way, I'll see you tomorrow.'

He nodded and walked back to his car. He sat there for a while before starting the engine, by which time, Lindsey had already gone inside.

'See? I rest my case,' she announced to Frank, who was watching her as she pulled a small step ladder into the middle of her bedroom and climbed on up. 'Could you imagine, as fucked up as I am, if I had to deal with *that* shit on a daily basis too?' She used a screwdriver to open a small tin of stain blocker, which the guy at B&Q insisted she needed, in between telling her his life story and offering his painting services. She poured some into a painting tray and ran her roller through it. 'How long d'you think it would take for him to go running back to his wife?' she smiled sarcastically. Frank tilted his head the way he usually did when she got into a heated conversation with him. She looked at him as if waiting for an answer and then she laughed out loud as she rolled the damp patch on the ceiling. 'He wouldn't last five minutes.'

The rest of the afternoon was spent painting the entire bedroom ceiling, thanks to the fact that the new patch made the rest of the ceiling look horrendous. The shade of the stain blocker was a bit funky, but at least it all looked the same by the time she was done. She then got to spend her evening doing something that she loved; packing for a camping trip. In her old life, she would have been preparing to go on the ground. Same thing really, except now it was with tents and a leisurely atmosphere. But she still packed in the same way; only bringing what she really needed, cutting down on bulk and being prepared for any eventuality.

In some ways, she loved remembering her past. Especially with things like this; getting ready for an exercise. The anxiety and nervousness that she always felt, as she focused on what lay ahead. Days, nights, sometimes weeks spent running on empty with only the piss taking and banter from the lads to get you through it. But the fond memories always led to pain. She'd spent thirteen years in the army and almost every single much-loved minute of it had been cast into a dark shadow. One that she could no longer see through.

Before her thoughts had a chance to drag her down, Frank, who was curled on the floor chewing on his favourite rubber chicken, started and ran barking from the room. By the time Lindsey caught up with him, his spit was hitting the front door he was that close to it, barking with everything he had. Lindsey grabbed the hurley and ran outside, but there was no one there. She ran to the gate and looked up and down the street, but saw no one. The street lights were on now and the place was deserted. Frank only stopped running when she shouted at him to do so, but he was still barking as they made their way back up the path and around the back of the house, ready to swing at the first thing she saw, but again, no one was there. She did a full lap, checking around the shed as well, but it was only when she got back to the front of the house that she saw the wreath leaning against the wall beside the front door. There was a mix of purple and white flowers, all wilted. This wreath wasn't new. There was no note this time, but there was a card skewered into the centre of the arrangement. It simply said:

'

CHAPTER FOUR

I'm tellin' ye lads, if it weren't for me, this place would fall down around ye all.' Lenny shook his head, feigning exasperation. The noise in the dining hall was constant, as it always was. It doubled as a bunker and everyone who was stationed with B-Coy in the tiny village of Haddatha, South Lebanon, was still sitting restlessly in there following a heavy night of shelling. Lenny, though, happily supped on his cup of tea and proceeded to tell them all how amazingly superb he was.

'You for one, would still be fucking snoring...' he pointed to Lindsey. 'You...' he was onto Street now, 'you'd be standing in front of a mirror admiring your chicken legs, and you Damo, my friend, would be scratching your balls wondering what the fuck was going on, if I didn't have the good sense to pull ye all out of the canteen last night before things really got going.' Lindsey was laughing as she remembered Lenny, standing on a table singing The Fields of Athenry, fucking up the lyrics the whole way until he fell off the table and was advised to go to bed, somewhere close to midnight, breaking up the party roughly two hours before the shelling started.

'You took another one for the team, Len,' Lindsey smiled at him and raised her cup in a toast.

'Lindsey?' a child's meek little voice called out from behind her.

When she looked back, she smiled and gave a small wave to Alya, the nine-year-old girl who lived just outside their camp and spoke with a perfect Irish accent due to the fact that she'd grown up here, surrounded by Irish soldiers. She never came into their building, but nothing seemed unusual about the fact that she was in it now.

Alya didn't speak again. She just pointed to something behind Lindsey.

When Lindsey turned back around, Lenny's chair was empty. The noise in the dining hall had died completely and everyone was looking directly at her.

'What?'

No answer. Not from anyone.

She looked down at herself, to see what they were all looking at. It was her hands, surely. They were covered in so much blood that she was sure no amount of soap and water would ever wash it away. It was dripping everywhere. A pool of blood was gathering on the plastic tablecloth, still, no one moved. No one spoke. They all just looked.

'Where's Lenny?' she asked, as she got to her feet with all eyes silently following her movements.

More questions wanted to come out, but something solid was lodged in her throat and somehow she knew that no air would pass through her body again until she got the blood off.

She walked quickly towards the service hatch, where even the cooks had put down their tools and were silently watching as she climbed through the hatch. She looked towards the sink and the block of harsh, industrial soap that sat near the tap, but she knew that wouldn't work. Her lungs were burning now and she was choking on the thing in her throat, but still no one moved. She walked towards the deep fat fryer and held her hands over the softly bubbling oil for a second and watched as it turned red from the blood that was dripping from her. Slowly, Lindsey lowered her hands into the scalding liquid and as the skin bubbled from her finger tips, right up along her arms, and a scalding pain spread through her body, she screamed…

Lindsey bolted up and out of the bed to a chorus of Frank's barking, which finally stopped when she was on her feet. Just the sound of his panting remained as he pressed his face against her bare legs, like he did on so many other nights. Only it wasn't night any more. Not quite. It was after half four on Thursday morning, meaning that she could finally go back to work.

'Seriously, Lindsey, how hard is it to make a bloody ham sandwich?'

Lindsey stopped what she was doing and looked at Sheila, waiting for the rest of her chastising, which she was sure was coming. Her eyebrows were raised and she had an incredulous look on her face, as she whipped two slices of bread apart and forcibly displayed their hamless insides.

'Would you be insulted if I begged you to please stop *helping* me?'

'Not at all,' Lindsey put down her butter knife and went to put the kettle on. She watched it for what seemed like an eternity before it finally boiled and she made a full pot of tea and poured a cup for Sheila, who was arranging a ton of food for their camping trip, not least of which was a hefty pile of trusted ham sandwiches.

As always, the sun was just coming up when Lindsey arrived at the Centre following a two-hour workout, through the city and ending up once again at Street's. Once she did get to the Centre, it took no time at all to catch up on what she'd missed during her time off, because Mike, true to his word, had everything under control. Sheila arrived not long after Lindsey and the pair set about making sandwiches. Or at least Sheila did. Lindsey simply created more work for Sheila to do, while her own mind was somewhere else entirely.

'Will you do me a favour and sit down for a minute?' Sheila took the cup from Lindsey and gestured towards one of the tables, before going to sit down herself.

Lindsey did as she asked, but she had a feeling that she wouldn't be staying long.

'Look love, you're a bit like myself; not one to air your laundry in public. I know that. But this isn't public, it's me. Please, tell me what's going on with you?'

Lindsey smiled and shook her head. 'There's nothing going on with me, Sheila.'

Sheila lit a cigarette and inhaled deeply before allowing the smoke to pour out of her nose, not once taking her eyes off Lindsey. She was clearly deciding which path to take in this conversation. 'You haven't been sleeping. No point in telling me you have, and something happened here on Monday. I don't pretend to know what, but something did,' she was wagging her tobacco stained finger now. 'You're pale, distracted, clearly exhausted… Frank has been clung to you since you got here. I was waving a rasher at him for ten fucking minutes earlier and he didn't budge. What gives?'

Lindsey looked at Frank who was curled at her feet. She went and got the rasher that was still sitting in the now cold frying pan and brought it back to him. He lifted his head, sniffed it and wolfed it down.

'I thought you didn't feed him that shit?' Sheila said with a small smile.

'I don't. But he likes to think he's getting one over on me every now and then,' she smiled back. 'He's just tired,' she mumbled.

'I can see that, but why Linds? Talk to me, girl, I'm worried about you.'

'Hello! Anyone here?' a woman's voice echoed up the stairs towards them.

Lindsey looked at her watch. It was only eight o'clock. Still too early for anyone to be here, but she got to her feet, glad of the interruption and headed for the stairs with Frank close behind her.

'Whoa… he's a big boy,' smiled the Garda standing at the end of the stairs with her cap in her hand.

'Don't worry, he's harmless.' Lindsey smiled. She knew a lot of the guards in the area, but she hadn't met this one before. She looked to be in her late twenties with a neat blonde bun tied low enough to make room for her hat. She wore no make-up and was extremely pretty. 'I'm Lindsey,' she held out her hand.

'Sinéad,' the woman shook it. 'Murray. Actually, it's you that I'm here to see, I think. Lindsey Ryan, right?'

'That's right. Can I get you a tea or something?' she thumbed in the direction of the stairs.

'Perfect.' Sinéad headed up behind her, reaching out tentatively to pet Frank on the way. She was clearly nervous around dogs, but was trying not to be.

'Sheila, this is Garda Murray,' Lindsey introduced them as they went into the dining area.

'Sinéad, please,' she held out her hand and Sheila shook it.

'Nice to meet you, love. There's a fresh pot of coffee just brewed or there's tea in that pot there. I'll leave you two to chat.' Sheila placed two clean cups on the table and went into the kitchen, closing the door behind her. Sheila was big on confidentiality, which was one of the reasons why she worked so well here.

'What can I do for you, Sinéad?' Lindsey filled the two cups and sat down opposite the woman.

'I wanted to talk to you about Jamie Cussons. You know him, don't you?'

'Yes, I know him. What happened? Is he alright?'

Sinéad smiled. 'That's why I wanted to talk to you. You actually give a shit.'

'Oh...'

'You know his story yeah? Mother died three years ago and this kid's life is thrown into total disarray.'

Lindsey nodded, still not sure where this was going.

'I've only been in Cork for six months. I transferred from Leitrim of all places, so as you can imagine, I love it here,' she smiled again.

'Welcome to Cork,' Lindsey offered.

'Thanks. Anyway, I know this kid, Jamie. He's been picked up a few times for shop lifting, but each time it's like he's *trying* to get caught. He takes completely random things that he certainly doesn't need, and he sticks them up his jumper, or loiters around outside the shop afterwards, or some other stupid move, so he's never surprised when we show up. Anyway, I was on foot patrol around Oliver Plunkett Street the night before last and who do I see heading into Maher's Sports Shop, only Jamie. First of all, it's getting dark. He shouldn't be in the city by himself, but that's neither here nor there, so I follow him in. I'm sure he sees me, but he pretends not to. He spends nearly twenty minutes browsing through the racks until he comes to the runners. Then he takes off his shoes, puts on a pair that were left sitting in a box and he gets up to leave.'

'What happened?'

She shrugged. 'I just reminded him that he brought his own shoes with him.'

Lindsey nodded and instantly liked Sinéad.

'I called one of my colleagues and we drove him home,' she looked into her cup and studied its contents.

'So what can I do?'

'Thing is, I'm off duty now. My shift ended at six, so this isn't an official conversation or anything...'

'OK.'

'You know his father is a businessman in town? An auctioneer. He has a wife and twin daughters aged six. The perfect family an' all that,' she looked up from her cup. 'Then one day Social Services arrived at his door, telling him that he has another son by a woman he can't even remember meeting, who by the way is now dead... here you go! He's all yours.'

Lindsey nodded again, but didn't interrupt. She could tell that Sinéad felt strongly about whatever it was that she wanted to ask.

'Needless to say, it caused hell in his marriage. No one wanted Jamie in that house. They still don't. Two cops show up at the house at nine o'clock at night with Jamie and not one single fuck was given. The father caught him by the arm and dragged him in the door, more concerned with making us believe that they were *not that kind of family*, than he was about Jamie. The wife meanwhile, stood at the kitchen door, rolled her eyes and walked away, ignoring Jamie altogether. The kid lives in a beautiful home with a *respectable* family... but he has nothing, Lindsey. He's bright, he's kind, he's sweet... he's gonna get in trouble and no one in his life will really care. And I mean real trouble. It's only a matter of time.'

'OK, I hear what you're saying.'

She nodded.

'How did you get my name?'

'Actually it was Frank's name that I had initially. From Jamie. He talked about him so much while we were driving him home that I started to wonder who this Frank character was. Your name I got when I called here yesterday. I spoke to Mike.'

Lindsey smiled. 'Ah! Well this chap under the table is Frank, and yeah… he and Jamie do get along well,' her smile faded. 'But I hear what you're saying and I agree.'

'I hear you're going camping today?'

'We sure are.'

'It's good to know that he at least has people like you lot in his life.'

'Likewise, Sinéad. And I appreciate you coming in.'

Sinéad pulled a notebook and pen out of her pocket and scribbled her name and number on it. 'Give me a call if you ever need anything, or if… I don't know… if you need volunteers or anything.'

'Hey, we always need volunteers,' Lindsey smiled and took the paper.

Sinéad was serious again now. 'Call me if Jamie needs anything.'

Lindsey nodded and followed Sinéad in getting to her feet. The women shook hands and Sinéad left.

The bus to take them camping wasn't due until eleven and the kids were told to be at the Centre by half ten, but Lindsey stood outside from eight-thirty onwards. No matter what time his day started, Jamie's father always dropped him off on his way to work. If that meant Jamie had to sit outside in the rain for two hours, waiting by himself, then that was just too bad. Of course, no one was ever left waiting outside, because one of them was always there at a time when they didn't have to be, but Jamie's dad didn't know that and just as she thought about what she'd like to say to him, his six-year-old Mercedes pulled up across the road.

Lindsey jogged over to catch the man before he pulled away. 'Hey Jamie, go on inside and say hi to Sheila,' she tousled his hair as he climbed out of the backseat. She then knocked on the driver's window.

The man looked at her with a hint of distain before finally pushing the button and lowering the window half way. He continued to look at her without speaking.

'Mr Higgins, we haven't met. I'm Lindsey Ryan. I'll be going camping with Jamie today.'

'And I'm late for work.'

She ignored his comment, knowing that he was nowhere near late and that as his own boss, a few minutes wouldn't hurt anyway. 'I'm sure Mike would have run through things with you, but is there anything you'd like to talk about with regard to how Jamie's getting on here?'

'Look, it's your job to deal with him while he's here. There's no need for you to come running to me if...'

'There's nothing to deal with, Mr Higgins, Jamie's a great kid. You know we're heading for the Galtees today, but in case you're worried, he'll be perfectly safe.'

He snorted out a laugh. 'A bit of hardship might do him good. Make him see how lucky he is. It's about time he started to appreciate everything we've done for him.'

The window buzzed up and the car pulled away from the kerb leaving Lindsey filled with the urge to pick up a rock and throw it through his back window.

It was the middle of the afternoon when they arrived at The Kings Yard, which was at the foot of the Galtee Mountains. Far enough from civilisation to give the kids a feel for the outdoors, but close enough that they could get back if needed. Mike drove his car so that they'd have it in case of an emergency, but Lindsey, Greg, Jamie, Leah Mendelson, Jerry Gleeson and of course, Frank, were dropped off by mini-bus, which would return to collect them at lunchtime on Saturday. There was a lot of cloud cover on the mountain, so hiking up wouldn't be an option for today, but it was after four o'clock anyway by the time they'd all pitched their own tents, which turned out to be an unmerciful ordeal and by then, the level of bickering was at an all-time high.

The campsite was very basic and completely empty aside from them, so building a fire and settling in at this stage would only guarantee boredom and a full blown fight before the night was out. But there was a wooded loop walk that started and finished near where they were. It went full circle for about three miles and Lindsey knew it well. It was the perfect way to burn off some of their energy for the evening, so she issued each of them with a printed map and a torch and stood them all together for a brief safety talk about the terrain, a general outline of the area and details of the arrows they needed to follow if any of them got lost. They were also instructed to reach the end with a sizable bundle of firewood per person. After that they all set off, with Greg and Jerry loudly protesting for the first ten minutes. But whether or not it was due to the fresh mountain air, even they got into it after a while.

Leah Mendelson was a bit of a surprise to Lindsey, though. She was a sixteen-year-old with very little respect or love for herself. Her peroxide blonde hair with black roots always looked greasy, as did her skin, which was always caked with a cheap pan stick, tons of eye make-up and the loudest lipstick colour she could find. Her wardrobe consisted of jeans, strategically torn around the bum and thighs, very short tight skirts with patterned tights and tops that were at least two sizes too small. She took any drug that was offered to her and any attention she could get, but today, dressed in her shortest and tightest, she powered ahead of the boys, using a stick to help with the terrain and seemed for the first time since Lindsey had known her, to be almost comfortable.

Lindsey jogged ahead to catch up with her. 'Hey, bet you're glad you wore the Doc Martin boots?' she smiled. They were knee high, but at least they were flat with some grip.

'How did you even know this place was here?' she asked, looking around.

'I've always loved places like this. Looks like I'm not the only one.'

She shrugged her shoulders. 'It's alright.'

'Have you been camping before?'

'My old man tried to get me to go once, but I'd rather tear my fingernails out one by one than be stuck in a tent with him and my mother.'

Leah was an only child to what seemed like a really nice couple, though Lindsey was always slow to presume to know people going only by their appearance. Her father was a primary school teacher, her mother a housewife and Leah rebelled against everything they both stood for. Her mother called the Centre at least once a week to see how she was getting on and if there was anything they could do, but she was all too aware that, for whatever reason, she was losing her little girl.

'Don't forget the firewood,' Lindsey pointed to a nice piece, which surprisingly, Leah went and got without question.

The walk took about an hour and a half, with a bit of off-track exploration, by which time it was getting dark, and when they got back to the camp site they busied themselves building a fire while Greg zipped himself into his tent and refused to contribute. Until of course, they started cooking. Sausages frying on an open fire were enough to stir his senses and finally bring him begrudgingly back to the group.

Wrapped in their warm clothes, the six of them sat around the sparking fire, telling ghost stories and tall tales until after eleven. There was no mention of family problems, or legal problems. Or any problems at all. Just story after story and before the night was out, even Greg was laughing. Whatever else happened over the coming days, that night at least was a success.

Not so much for Frank though. He was of course sharing Lindsey's tent, but for once, he was the one who couldn't settle. He kept whining and nudging at the door to get out, so finally she gave in and got up with him at around one.

'OK, Frank, go do your business and let's get some sleep, eh?' she whispered, as they got outside, but Frank wasn't going anywhere. Instead he stood still, sniffing the ground and staring off into the woods. When she following his gaze, she saw the flicker of torch light just inside the tree line.

Without making a sound, she picked up the strongest looking stick from the pile of firewood and made her way quietly towards where the light had been. It had gone out now. Frank was a few steps ahead of her all the way and by the time she reached the tree line, her night vision was good enough that she could make out Jerry Gleeson. He had one hand up Leah's top and his tongue was lost somewhere in her throat.

Lindsey turned on her torch and shone it directly at them, startling them enough that Leah left out a yelp, but Jerry just turned and smiled. Only when he was good and ready did he remove his hand from Leah's breast and take a small step back from her.

Lindsey didn't say anything. In her experience, there were times when an awkward silence was the best way to get someone talking. Finally, it was Jerry who spoke with a grin.

'What are you going to do, freak out again? Hey, maybe I have dynamite in my pants and I'm going to blow this place up,' he started laughing and Leah laughed with him, though she clearly had no idea what he was talking about. His laughed died away when Frank growled at him.

Lindsey still didn't speak. Instead she looked at Leah and waited. Finally she gave in.

'Look, he's my boyfriend OK...'

'Whoa, ease up girl; I'm no one's boyfriend,' Jerry held his hands in the air and laughed again. 'Especially not a skank like you.'

Leah's face visibly dropped before she forced a smile and pretended as always that she didn't care. 'Hey, I wouldn't go out with you anyway. I was only trying to keep us out of trouble.'

'Go back to your tent, Jerry. We'll talk in the morning.'

'Whatever.'

'You OK?' Lindsey asked Leah once he was gone.

She guffawed quietly. 'Course I am.'

'You and Jerry... really?'

'Look it's nothing, OK. I just wanted to see what he'd be like 'cause

53

he's nice looking.'

'So this was your idea?'

She shrugged.

'Do you like him?'

'He's nice looking.'

'Aside from that, what else do you like about him?'

She rolled her eyes and started walking back towards the tents. 'Look, it's really not a big deal, OK. I liked him, so I kissed him, simple as that.'

Lindsey walked with her. 'Does it bother you what he just said?'

She guffawed again. 'Course not. I don't want a boyfriend anyway.'

'You know you're too good to be used, Leah, don't you?'

'He didn't use me.'

'No?'

'I used him.'

Lindsey nodded, not believing her for a minute. 'OK...'

'Fuck you. I'll bet you're just an old maid, getting all dried up waiting for Prince Charming to come along.'

Lindsey couldn't help but laugh.

'What's so funny?'

'Nothing, just... Prince Charming?'

'Or whoever.'

'Actually, Leah, I'm not sure I believe in all that Prince Charming stuff.'

'So what are you giving me shit for then?'

'I'm not giving you shit. I just wish that you could see what other people see in you. That's all.'

'What, that I'm a skank?'

'Is that what you want them to think?'

'They think it anyway.'

'Personally, I couldn't give a damn what anyone thinks of me,' Lindsey shrugged. 'But whatever I decide to do and whoever I decide to do it with... it's always going to be because *I* want to. No one should touch you because *they* want to, Leah... OK?'

'I wanted him to.'

'Did you?'

She shrugged. 'Yeah… I wanted him to like me.'

It was the age-old problem of teenage girls everywhere and Lindsey didn't have much of an answer for her. She threw herself on the fire too from time to time, but not because she wanted anyone to like her. Also, she was an adult. She knew what she was doing, most of the time. 'Girl, if someone doesn't like you before you take off your clothes, then they're not going to think much more of you after, so please; like yourself more than you like eejits like him, eh?'

Her bottom lip quivered and a tear broke free from her eye. Lindsey threw an arm around her shoulder and smiled. 'Forget about him.'

'I'm so thick.'

'You're not thick. In fact you're far from it and underneath all that flash, you're a great girl, Leah. What's more, I think you might be the best hiker among us, the way you tore into that track today.'

She finally smiled and wiped her face.

'I brought spare hiking boots. Are you about a size five?'

She nodded, but of course Lindsey knew this already and knew that she wouldn't have brought proper footwear.

'Perfect. Let's see you tear up that mountain tomorrow in the right gear. Leave those boys for dust, eh?'

They stopped and looked up at the mountain for a minute and then Leah grinned and nodded. There was a definite spring in her step then as they walked on towards the tents and it was only when they got there, that Lindsey noticed that Frank wasn't with them. She turned around and shone the torch back towards the trees. He was standing on the edge of the woods, staring in.

'Go get some sleep, Leah. I'll see you in the morning.'

'Do you want me to go back with you?' Leah looked towards Frank. 'It's kinda creepy over there.'

'That's alright. He probably just spotted a rabbit that he fancies.'

Leah hesitated before going into her tent and only when her zip was all the way down, did Lindsey turn back towards Frank. She thought brief-ly about calling him, but didn't want to wake everyone else, so she walked back to where he was standing perfectly still, looking in amongst the trees.

'Hey boy, what's up?' She spoke softly when she reached him and shone the torch into the darkness of the woods.

He took a couple of steps in and Lindsey followed him. Then he stopped again. Her stomach was clenched in a tight knot and goose bumps made her skin prickle. She hoped to see one of the kids, just taking a leak, but was even more relieved when a badger strolled out from behind a tree, sending Frank into a fit of barking.

'Come on you nutter,' she caught him by the collar and pulled him back towards the camp site. If everyone wasn't awake before they probably were now, but Lindsey didn't care. From the minute she looked behind her and saw Frank standing stock still, staring into the darkness, she was overcome by the feeling of being watched again. It was a feeling that was becoming all too familiar to her now and badger or no badger, it didn't go away.

The next day was perfect, weather wise, and they spent almost six hours hiking on the Galtee Mountains, sticking to routes that were safe for kids with no climbing experience. Or no interest, as was the case with Jerry and Greg, who both woke up complaining and failed to stop all day. At some points they sat down on the mountain and refused to move, so progress was slow, but that was fine. It didn't matter how much of the mountain they actually conquered. What mattered was that they were doing something that was so far outside their comfort zone that they wouldn't be likely to forget it in a hurry. If what they were doing built a little more character into even one of these kids, then it would have been a success, and it was clear to see that had already happened with Leah. Within minutes of their tents being pitched the day before, Leah began to fall in love with her sur-roundings, just like Lindsey had the first time she did something like this.

Granted, her first time had been much more intense and high pressured during her army recruit training. But it was still the Galtee Mountains and she still fell in love. When they were moving, Leah powered ahead, asking questions and pointing out everything that looked good to her. When they were sitting out the boys' protests, she just stared at the breathtaking scenery all around her, oblivious to their complaining; oblivious to their obnoxious comments. Oblivious to all negativity which made it easy for Lindsey to block out the whingeing too and just take it in. Jamie hadn't said much at all since arriving, but he also had a contented look on his flushed face. He never once looked in Greg's direction either, Lindsey noticed. He didn't seem afraid of him, nor did he seem to hold a grudge, but he was quick to learn from his mistakes and Lindsey couldn't help thinking there was more to Jamie Cussons than met the eye.

By the time they got back to the campsite the sun was beginning to set and it was suddenly freezing cold at the foot of the mountain. Lindsey pulled all the extra clothing that she'd packed, knowing that they wouldn't, out of the extra backpack she ended up bringing and she handed out hoodies and jumpers to everyone. After supper, which consisted of bread rolls, beans and more sausages, Lindsey and Mike left the kids to have some time by themselves around the fire, while they caught up with each other in Mike's car.

Mike had spoken to Jerry about last night with Leah, but of course he got nowhere with him. He and Lindsey both agreed that nothing had happened by force, but of course it still had to go in their report. They kept a record of all *acting out* type behaviour in whatever form that might take. On the one hand, they were covering themselves. But Social Services, the courts, management – they all wanted records of everything to make sure that nothing came back to bite them. Of course they kept records of all the positive changes too, which was why more would be written about Leah than just her poor judgement. Likewise Jamie, as quiet as he was, was doing great. After struggling with his own tent, he still went on to help Leah and Jerry with theirs. He took charge of cooking supper on both nights and every now and then, without being asked, he wandered down to the edge of the woods and brought back more firewood. All pretty much without speaking, unless spoken to.

'I'm fucking freezing,' Mike complained, now that the kids couldn't hear him. He'd spent half the day telling them to stop complaining. Now it was his turn. 'Tell me again, what can you possibly love about this?'

Lindsey opened the car door and inhaled deeply. 'Smell that?'

'Camp fire?' he asked.

'And pine. And mountain dew. Actual fresh air,' she smiled. 'What's not to love?'

'The cold and misery.'

'Look at that lot,' she gestured towards the kids, their faces glowing in the firelight. Caps pulled down over their ears and whatever warm item they had, pulled up around their chins. They were bickering as always, but no one was making a move to fight, or to storm off. Instead they were laughing in between their goading. Jerry and Greg both claimed to be miserable, but now even they were accidentally enjoying themselves.

'Works every time, doesn't it?' Mike smiled.

Lindsey had introduced the camping trips not long after starting at the Centre and she aimed to take a group of kids several times a year where possible. With all the regulations though, there had to be at least one adult to every two kids, so groups were always small and as much as Mike complained in private, he was always outwardly enthusiastic to go. After all, no one could argue the benefits of time away from the troubled, urban, technology-filled lives of these kids.

He turned in his seat to look at her, 'Listen, I'm really sorry about the other day.'

'Forget about it.'

'No, look I always do it. My home life goes to shit and I bring it all to your doorstep.'

'Seriously, Mike, its fine.'

He straightened up again and looked in his lap. 'I've been thinking about you a lot actually...'

Lindsey rolled her eyes. 'Mike, don't...'

'Not like that. Lindsey, I know you haven't been honest with me about your injuries. You're ex-army and you served overseas. I'm putting two and two together and if I'm not mistaken, you're showing signs of PTSD, but I'd imagine you know that, right?'

'Fuck off, Mike,' she smiled.

Of course she knew that. It was the reason why she didn't trust her instincts any more. The reason why she was acting like a crazy person and maybe the reason why she was paranoid about being watched. Or maybe it wasn't. Either way, the last thing she wanted to do was talk about it, or to confirm the fact that she'd lied to him and in doing so, open up another can of worms. How could she possibly explain what was going on in her head, especially to someone who, even with all his experience and qualifications, couldn't possibly understand?

'You don't want to talk about it fine, it's your business. But did you ever think that talking about it might actually help.'

'Mike I was tired and a loud noise jolted me. That's it. I don't know what you're getting so worked up about.'

'Well like I said, Lindsey, I don't think you were honest with me about...' he made a circular motion around his own shoulder, 'that, and everything else makes me worry about you.'

She rubbed her eyes and shook her head in frustration. A couple of months after she started working at the Centre, Lindsey made the mistake of going drinking for a night with Mike. It was the night they got back from the first of these camping trips, which was a major success. That night though, was the complete opposite. Fuelled by Jack Daniels, Lindsey admitted that she'd tried therapy once. She told him about getting her first prescription for benzodiazepine and how she could barely remember her last two years in the army because of them. Of course she didn't talk much about her army career and she certainly didn't tell him about *that day*. There was no point. People who weren't soldiers didn't tend to *get* soldiers, so she avoided that part of the conversation by sleeping with him, which meant that he inadvertently got to see her scars. She lied them away by saying that she was in a car accident. She would have come up with something better had she been sober. Better yet, she wouldn't have let him see them in the first place, but she did. It happened once and Lindsey was happy to move on. Mike on the other hand, never quite did, making Lindsey realise that, like it or not, she'd finally shit on her own doorstep.

'Mike…' she rubbed her temples, exasperated.

'I'm leaving Marie.'

She looked at him, surprised and suspicious. 'Why?'

'It's time. This is no way to live.'

She didn't answer. She just kept looking at him, hoping that he wouldn't say something stupid.

'Don't worry. I'm not planning on making you a part of it.'

'Good. Because I'm not a part of it.'

He twisted to face her again. 'Would it be that bad to be with me?'

'Mike, you don't want me. You just think you do, and what's more, I don't want a relationship.'

'How do you know what I want?'

'Fine, then we'll stick to what I want. I want to come to work every day and have a friend there.'

'I'd still be that.'

'Like hell you would. Listen to me, Mike; you and I do not want the same things. Therefore, it would not work.' She was aware that she sounded like she was explaining something to a child, but she wanted to be as clear as she possibly could.

He got out of the car and slammed the door. Lindsey looked to the heavens and let out a frustrated groan before following him out. She leaned against the car for a second and stared up at the beautiful, clear sky black with the millions of stars shining down on them. Then she looked in the direction of the trees, again sensing that someone was there, but thinking better of it when she thought rationally about where they actually were. She shook her head and walked back to the camp fire, where she sat on a log between Jamie and Leah. Mike sat opposite her, between Greg and Jerry.

Mike might have been a walking disaster in his personal life, but his love for his job and for helping these kids, meant that he never brought his woes to their attention. He was a professional, which was why she wasn't surprised when he launched into the enthusiastic telling of another really good ghost story as soon as he sat down.

Frank was sleeping soundly beside the fire, which after his restless night last night, was reassuring. So for the rest of the evening, Lindsey tuned back into the kids and their witty one liners and did her best to forget about Mike's schoolboy crush and to forget about the imaginary eyes that were boring holes through her. Instead she focused her energy on enjoying their last night in one of her favourite places in Ireland, with this small group of people who at the very least, deserved her full attention.

But those hours passed quickly and once the kids drifted off to bed and the fire had died, Lindsey couldn't close her eyes without having visions of someone creeping around the tents outside. She startled to every sound and got up regularly to check on the kids. She was fairly sure that whoever was lurking in the background of her life had no interest in any of the people around her. But *fairly sure* wasn't good enough, so she checked on them anyway and carried a strong chunk of wood with her while she did. It was becoming more and more clear to her that the instincts she once relied so heavily upon were useless to her now. She had no choice but to stay on her guard and hope that she still had it in her to handle whatever the hell this was. And for however long it would last.

CHAPTER FIVE

It was mid afternoon on Saturday when they got back to the Centre, by which time it was just Lindsey, Jamie and Leah left on the bus. Greg was dropped at his mother's house *as it was on the way*, which it wasn't really, but Lindsey knew that no one would come to pick him up otherwise. Jerry was living in a group home in Glanmire, so he was dropped there.

'How did it go?' Leah's mother, Eileen, had been waiting for over an hour at the Centre by the time they pulled in.

Leah rolled her eyes and walked past her towards their car, lugging her small backpack on one shoulder.

'Hi Eileen,' Lindsey greeted her with a smile.

'How was she?' she asked hopefully.

'The best I've seen her in a long time,' Lindsey answered honestly and Eileen's face lit up. 'She was in her element.'

'Really? In the wilderness, like?' she looked more confused now. 'But she loves her bed. We always have murder trying to get her out of it.'

Lindsey shrugged. 'It's pretty breathtaking up there. Maybe that was enough to make up for the lack of luxuries.'

'Should we take her camping more often do you think?'

'I'd say yes,' Lindsey nodded. 'Or, if camping's not your thing, then I wouldn't force it, in which case, there's a great hill walking club in Cork. That wouldn't be a bad starting point.'

'Oh, I don't know about that...'

'There's some good people involved with them. I'd be happy to give them a call if you like. It might be a way for her to find her own space. She really did seem to enjoy it.'

'OK...' she nodded. 'Let me talk to her father about it and I'll get back to you. Is that OK?'

'Sure. You know where to find me.'

Eileen forced a quivery smile and nodded again. Then she left.

Whenever she spent time talking to Eileen Mendelson, Lindsey was left with the feeling that there was more going on in her life than just her daughter's rebellion. That maybe all wasn't as it seemed in the Mendelson household. This time she vowed to make more of an effort to find out.

'Hey Jamie, what are your plans for the rest of the day?'

The boy seemed confused by the question. He was sitting quietly on the wall, stroking Frank's head. 'My plans?'

'Yeah, you know – those things you make regarding all you're going to do to pass your time?' She smiled, and sat alongside him.

He shrugged.

Lindsey had been thinking a lot about her conversation with Sinéad. With some guidance and focus, Jamie had huge potential, but at the moment, he wasn't getting that from anyone. One idea that Lindsey had, was the last thing in the world she wanted to do herself, but looking at this clever, caring kid, she had no choice but to get over herself.

'OK. I'm gonna ring your dad and ask if we can do something. Is that OK?'

'Something like what?'

'It's a surprise.'

A small smile played on his lips and he nodded.

She left Jamie with Frank, while she went to her office to make the phone call. She took the stairs two at a time and called out a loud, 'Hey Sheila!' before making her way around her desk.

As she picked up the receiver with one hand, she picked up an A4 manila envelope, which was resting on the desk, with the other. She cradled the phone between her ear and shoulder and tore open the unmarked package, but when she tipped out its contents, she put the receiver back.

Four photos scattered onto the desk. One was a close up of Lindsey pitching her tent. One was of her laughing, while Jerry was getting tangled up in his. One of her talking to Jamie on the camp site and one where her arm was around Leah's shoulder. On the back of each photo was a single

'Sheila!'

'What?' Sheila shouted back from the kitchen.

Lindsey packed the photos back into the envelope. 'Who was in here today?' She came out of the office and stood by the door.

'What'd you mean?'

'I *mean*, who was in this office today.'

'No one was,' she came out of the kitchen now and was looking at Lindsey in bewilderment. 'It was locked all day until Mike came back about an hour ago. He only stayed a few minutes though.'

'Were you here all day?'

'Pretty much.'

'Pretty much?'

'I went out for a fag… or two.'

'And you didn't see anyone else coming in?'

'What's wrong? Is something missing?'

'Forget about it.'

Sheila rolled her eyes. 'It's like talking to the fucking wall. Tell me, what's missing?'

'Nothing's missing. Forget it… it's fine.'

'You know, you worry me, Lindsey. You really do.'

'Yeah,' Lindsey answered, though she didn't hear what Sheila had said. She shoved the envelope in her bag and picked up the phone to call Jamie's dad, who of course didn't care what she did with him for the day, so long as *he* didn't have to do anything.

'OK, come on,' she walked past Jamie and Frank, heading for the car and they both followed her.

'Where we going?'

She didn't answer him. She was still thinking about the photos and the fact that someone was watching her the night before. Frank knew it. She knew it too, but now she also knew that it wasn't paranoia this time.

'Where are we?' Jamie looked around the laneway with no shop fronts, which was pretty much deserted, even at four in the afternoon.

'This is my friend, Street's place. Come on.' She pushed open the door, not needing to use her key this time. It was the first time she'd been there during opening hours.

Inside it was busy. Two wiry looking young lads were sparring in the ring, with an audience of six leaning on the ropes. Both speed bags and one heavy bag were in use, as were the weight plates and two skipping ropes. Jamie stood for a minute, staring at the guys in the ring, but then they did look impressive.

She could feel eyes on her before she looked towards Street's office and only when she felt the slight ache in her rip cage did she realise that she was shaking from the inside, out. She closed her eyes for a second and took a breath, before turning to face him.

'Adam,' she smiled and pulled Jamie towards him. 'Jamie, this is my friend, Adam Street. Adam, this is Jamie Cussons.'

Adam kept his eyes on her for a second, before turning his attention to Jamie. He smiled and held out his hand, which Jamie shook.

Adam Street was a foot taller than Lindsey, built of pure muscle and Lindsey knew absolutely everything about him. His thirty-ninth birthday was three days ago. He grew up in Douglas with a nurse for a mother, a soldier for a father, two older brothers and a twin sister called Emma. He was a Munster rugby fanatic and had a thing for engines. He spent the latter half of his twenties restoring a 1977 Harley Davidson Low Rider, which was left to him by his grandfather and has since travelled almost everywhere on it. Over the years he'd been offered ridiculous amounts of money to sell it, but Lindsey knew that he'd probably be buried with it. His favourite crap food was Taco fries; his favourite nice food was *duck à l'orange*. Tea with milk and three sugars, but don't ask him to drink it without a chocolate accompaniment. His sense of humour was nicely warped, but he got the major hump if anyone said anything disrespectful about someone who was having a hard time. In fact he was a sucker for an underdog. He was also a sucker for a blonde with a nice bum and had more ex-girlfriend's fitting that description than Hugh Heffner did. Adam Street was one of the best friends she'd ever had and she hadn't spoken to him in three years.

'Do you own this place?' Jamie asked, after he'd eyed all the trophies and memorabilia on display in Street's office. He was already in awe of Adam, who was towering over him, but looking him straight in the eye while they spoke, man to man.

'I do. What do you think?'

Jamie shrugged, but was smiling. He liked it.

'Hey, Owen?' Adam called to a man in his mid-twenties with a shiny bald head, who had been in the ring with the sparring lads when they arrived.

He nodded and made his way over.

Adam pulled a pair of gloves out of the locker. 'Owen here is going to show you around, Jamie. Here, try these on…' he handed him the gloves.

Owen held out his hand to shake Jamie's. He then offered his hand to Lindsey.

'Sorry… I'm Lindsey,' she shook his hand firmly.

'Lindsey?' he raised his eyebrows and looked at Adam. 'Ryan, am I right?'

'Eh… yeah.'

After a few seconds of silence, he finally smiled at Jamie. 'How about that look around?'

As they walked away, Lindsey could hear Jamie talking enthusiastically about the gloves he'd just been given. He was full of questions and she hadn't heard so many syllables leaving the boys mouth, ever.

'Bit early in the day for you, isn't it?' Adam spoke with a slight smile as he gestured towards his office, which almost made Lindsey's look spacious.

'I wanted to bring Jamie in. I thought maybe you could...'

'No problem, Linds,' he sat down, resting his elbows on his parted knees and just looked at her. He didn't want to talk about Jamie just yet.

'Look... sorry I haven't been in touch. I've had a lot on.'

'I know. You've been kicking the shit out of my bags for some time now.'

She took a seat, just to do something other than respond.

'It gets pretty personal down here some nights.'

She leaned back and let out a long breath, while she looked at the many photos scattered around his office, of different boxers, different competitions, different belts and trophies. She still didn't respond, but her discomfort was probably apparent.

'I don't have to wonder what you're thinking about when you're going all out.'

'Just blowing off steam, Street, that's all,' she finally answered.

He nodded.

'I should say thanks for always leaving the ice out.'

He smiled and caught her by the hand and examined her wrist. 'You know you'll be as arthritic as fuck if you don't start wrapping those hands.'

'How do you...?'

He pointed towards the CCTV camera outside his office.

'Oh... Listen, can we talk about Jamie for a second?'

'Shoot,' he let go of her wrist and sat back.

'He's a great kid, Adam. He just badly needs something productive to pass his time with and someone to look up to. Dad doesn't give a shit and his mother is gone. No brothers, no friends really... he's going to get himself in trouble and he deserves so much more. I just thought...' she gestured to their surroundings, 'best place in Cork to vent your frustrations.' she smiled, but was becoming more uncomfortable by the second and this bothered her immensely. Adam Street was once the person she was most comfortable around. Him and others like him. Now she wanted to get as far away from him as she possibly could and she wanted to go now.

She got to her feet and left the office, heading towards Jamie. Towards a distraction. A moment later Adam followed her.

'Linds, can we please talk for a minute? Properly?' he put his hand on her shoulder and spoke quietly.

'I can't. Not just now, OK?' For the first time in three years, they finally made eye contact, but instead of seeing his familiar green, smiling eyes, or all the things they'd been through together, all she felt was fear. An irrational and all-consuming fear.

She turned and walked outside, leaving Jamie there with them. She was breathing erratically and a tightness was spreading across her chest making her feel like she was having a heart attack. She clutched her chest and headed for the next doorway, just to be slightly more out of sight. She was hyperventilating and as she threw up against the door to an abandoned building, she almost choked.

'Get it all up, girl,' came a voice from the doorway directly across from where she was hunched over.

Lindsey started and looked across at the man she'd seen on so many nights when she came here. This was the first time she'd seen him during the day and looking almost sober. She turned her back on him. This was her day time life and he belonged in the other one. She'd been doing her best to keep the two separate, but now they were clashing and she was hating every second of it.

'Hey, you're her, aren't you?'

Lindsey half turned to look at him again.

'The beautiful girl with the ugly scars.'

'Lindsey?' Jamie stepped out of the gym.

She tore her eyes away from the man in the doorway, but he didn't take his eyes off her.

She cleared her throat and roughly wiped her face. 'Yeah?'

'You're not going without me, are ya?'

'Course not. I just needed some air,' she headed back towards Street's and nudged Jamie in ahead of her.

'No need to be afraid of me, Lindsey,' the man had a grin on his face as he spoke to her one last time.

She stopped and returned his stare for a minute. It didn't occur to her to believe him or not believe him; just to study him, slightly annoyed that he now knew her name.

Finally, she followed Jamie inside and as he went back to the group, she went to sit on a bench farthest away from Street, who was going through some moves with Jamie and some other kids. She rested her elbows on her restless knees and did her best to give a thumbs up to Jamie every time he looked her way, with an all too rare smile on his face, which she tried to remind herself, was the reason why she was here. But her mind was taking her somewhere she didn't want to go. Someone would drop a weight on the concrete floor and an explosion went off in Lindsey's head. Someone grunted with the effort of hitting a bag and it became an agonised scream to her ears. The walls were closing in on her and her lungs were struggling for air. And nothing was making sense.

'Hey...' the word came out louder than she intended and she now had the attention of everyone in the gym, instead of just Jamie and Street. She got to her feet with a forced smile and walked closer to them. 'Listen, will you two be OK by yourselves for half an hour? I have a few things I need to do?'

'No problem,' Street looked at her in a way that made her feel like he was reading her mind, a skill that he'd acquired years ago. But now hers was a mind that no one should be subjected to. Jamie on the other hand, was just waiting for her to go now so that they could get back to what they were doing.

'See you in a while,' she squeezed Jamie's shoulder and left.

Once outside, she walked quickly away from Street's, around by the bus station, not quite sure where she was headed until she eventually found herself at the docks, walking along the quay wall. She walked as far as she could, away from the noise and the bustle of the city streets, before sitting on the edge, with her feet dangling towards the murky River Lee. She wished Frank was with her, but she left him at the Centre to rest after his camping trip. She knew what was happening. It had happened before, but not for years. Not since just after. But knowing what was happening wasn't enough to stop it from happening. Being aware that none of it was real, not the explosions, not the screaming, none of it, didn't mean that it didn't still scare the shit out of her every time. Therapy didn't work for her, but then how could it when she didn't believe in it? Pills though… they worked for a bit.

She thought briefly about her new friend in the doorway and what he might be able to offer her. Then she thought about the zombie that she became while on meds. Even the legal ones. The friends she'd disregarded; the degree she almost didn't get. But what did she have to lose this time? Her family? Not really. Her parents had been living in Brazil for over ten years now. She hardly saw them anyway. She'd lost touch with the friends that mattered. In fact she could die right now and the only one who'd miss her would be Frank. Eventually Sheila and Mike would notice and Liam, the Centre manager, would complain about the extra paperwork that would befall him, but that was it really. Nothing that they wouldn't get over with a shake of the head and a few tuts.

She stared into the river, unable to see much of a reflection on the choppy brown surface. No one was around to see her if she wanted to go in…

'What the fuck is wrong with you?' she chastised herself and quickly got to her feet. She angrily wiped the back of her jeans and walked briskly away from the docks. She was seething with herself for being so weak. For melting down when she should have been strong enough not to and as she took the longer route back to Street's, she talked sense to herself the whole way, so that by the time she got there, she felt calmer, but even less sociable. She wanted to grab Jamie, drop him at home without further conversation and then go home herself with someone who could relate to her without speaking, and the only one who could possibly do that, was Frank.

All the way back to the Centre, Jamie talked on and on about Adam Street and Lindsey knew that the boy had found a new hero. All-Army boxing champion, All-Ireland boxing champion, coach to three Olympic boxers and they were just his sporting achievements. The rest Jamie would know nothing about. At least not from Street. But it was still enough.

Once they picked Frank up on the way, he too got the whole story. All the new moves he'd learned and the fact that Street said that Jamie reminded him of a young Conor McGregor, only less mouthy. It was Street this and Street that all the way home. Once they got there, Lindsey explained to Jamie's stepmother about the boxing club that Jamie was now a member of. She'd sort out the details of that later with Street.

'Boxing? You don't think he's enough trouble as it is without being taught how to be more violent?' she asked bitterly.

'Actually Mrs Higgins, Jamie's never exhibited any violent tendencies, whatsoever.' She spoke in her best professional tone, once again putting her *compartmentalising* tactic into use. It was the one and only thing that she found useful on days like this. 'In my professional opinion, what Jamie needs is something to focus his energy on. There's an amazing group of people working there, who've mentored more kids than I can count...'

'Look, if it doesn't bring more trouble to my door, I honestly don't care.'

Of course you don't, Lindsey thought, but didn't say. Instead she painted on a smile. 'Perfect. So he'll still be attending the Centre for eight hours a week, but he'll have training on Monday, Wednesday and Friday's for the summer months too. If there's any problem getting him there, I can arrange transport if needed.' In other words, either she, Street or one of his guys would have to step in where Jamie's so-called parents wouldn't and needless to say, Mrs Higgins was happy with that.

It was getting dark when she finally pulled up outside her house and was more than a little bit surprised to find Garda Sinéad Murray sitting on her front step. She was in civvies; blue jeans and a plain white T-shirt, with her blonde hair lose around her shoulders. She didn't look very happy.

'Sinéad... hi.'

She stood up as Lindsey approached. 'Lindsey, I'm sorry to drop by like this. I actually wanted to see how Jamie got on, but... there's something else I need to talk to you about. Would you mind opening the door and letting me go in ahead of you?'

Lindsey furrowed her brow and couldn't help smiling at Sinéad's *official Garda* tone. 'And why would you want to do that?'

She took a breath before she spoke. It looked rehearsed, like she was preparing herself to deliver some bad news. 'I don't want you to panic...'

'I won't. What is it?' Lindsey unlocked the door and stepped inside, to Sinéad's clear dismay, but she followed her in immediately. Frank trotted past them both, headed for the kitchen and for his empty bowl, where he would wait impatiently for it to be filled.

'Do you mind if I look around?' she was on her guard, her eyes taking in everything in the room.

'Sinéad, spit it out girl. What is it?' Lindsey went to the kitchen and began crushing Frank's supplements and mixing them with his food.

Sinéad placed a photograph on the kitchen table. Lindsey couldn't yet see what it was, but she had a good idea. She continued what she was doing refusing to let whoever this asshole was, get another reaction from her.

'It was stuck to your front door.'

'Right.' Another God damn thumb tack hole.

'I take it by your lack of concern that this isn't the first?'

'Show me?' Lindsey picked up the photo. This time it was of her, by herself on the campsite. She was leaning against Mike's car with a sad expression on her face and she made a mental note to watch that in future. She remembered leaning against the car, but didn't realise that she'd been moping while she was with the kids and Mike. Yet here was photographic evidence to the contrary. But that wasn't the problem as far as Sinéad was concerned. She was more bothered by the block capital letters sprawled above the image, stating: *I'm gonna destroy you, bitch.*

She dropped the photo back on the table and returned her attention to Frank. She placed his dinner on the floor and replenished his water bowl. Surprisingly, what started out as pretend nonchalance was now *actual* nonchalance. In fact, she felt numb. The idea of throwing herself in the Lee had crossed her mind today. What could this person, who was probably a kid, possibly do to hurt her?

'Lindsey, what's going on? Who is this?'

'It's nobody.' Lindsey opened the fridge and took out a bottle of white wine. She wasn't used to having company here, so it took her a while to find two wine glasses, but eventually she did and she filled them to capacity. 'Here, drink that.' She sat down on the couch and eventually Sinéad followed her.

'Clearly it's somebody, Linds.'

'Not as far as I'm concerned.'

'What else have they done?'

'Just a few notes stuck to the door over the past few weeks. It's nothing.'

'Do you still have them?'

'No,' she lied.

'Anything else?'

Lindsey shrugged. 'They stole a wreath off someone's grave and left it here for me. And then there's these,' she reached into her bag on the floor and pulled out the manila envelope and dropped it in Sinéad's lap.

Sinéad pulled out the photos and glanced at them, turning each one over to see the writing on the back.

'You know who's doing it, or why?'

She took a long drink of wine and then smiled and shook her head.

73

'I work with a lot of troubled young people, Sinéad. The vast majority are actually good kids once you get past the tough exterior. Of course, I would have bugged or bothered or pissed off some of them along the way. This is just their way of letting me know that.'

'You a hurler?' Sinéad nodded towards the hurley in the corner of the room.

'Sometimes.'

'Or is it for protection?'

Lindsey smiled again. 'Sinéad, you needn't worry about me, OK? I have Frank here. He's like an early warning system. Anyone comes near this place while I'm here, I know about it. And some little runt with a Smartphone and a small imagination wouldn't have the balls to stick around once he kicks off.'

'Lindsey do me a favour; keep everything from now on, and keep a log. Anything that gets left here, any communication at all, any odd feelings that you get… write it all down. Ring me, any time. ALL the time and if anyone approaches you or does anything to make you nervous, please, girl, ring 999.'

'I appreciate that, Sinéad.' Lindsey smiled reassuringly at her. She liked Sinéad and was surprisingly happy that she was here. But she no longer wanted to talk about herself. 'So… you wanted to know how Jamie got on.'

'OK then… moving on,' she replied, begrudgingly.

'You know what I've noticed? He actually enjoys everything that he does with us. He was quiet as always on the trip, but he clearly enjoyed it. Here's what's new; I took him to my friend, Adam's boxing gym today.'

'Boxing?' she nodded approvingly.

'Yip. And he loved that too. Or at least the environment that he was in. The lads there are great and when we were there, the place was half full of kids Jamie's age. Honestly, Sinéad, if anyone can make him feel like he belongs somewhere, it's Street. He's a tough nut, but I could almost guarantee that he'll root out Jamie's potential in no time. And all going well, it'll take up at least three of his evenings each week. But knowing Adam

Street, it'll be a lot more than that,' she was smiling while she spoke. Partly because of Jamie's reaction to the whole weekend and partly because of the wine.

'So...' Sinéad leaned her head against her closed fist and grinned broadly at her. 'Who's this Adam Street guy?'

Lindsey laughed and got up to find another bottle of wine. 'You can forget about that one, straight off.'

'Come on; you were lit up like a Christmas tree talking about him and you don't strike me as someone who lights up like that very often at all.'

'It's called wine,' she held up a new bottle with a smile and Sinéad held out her glass. 'Actually...' Lindsey stood back and looked at Sinéad, laughing again now. 'You are exactly Street's type, but you know what? I like you, so I won't introduce you unless you ask me to.'

She raised her eyebrows. 'What does he look like?'

'Oh there's no problem with what he looks like. Most women tend to drop their drawers on sight.'

Sinéad laughed. 'And what makes you immune to his charms?'

'Well... it's like someone telling you that your brother is gorgeous. Maybe he is, but that's nothing to do with you.'

'Yeah, yeah. You keep telling yourself that.'

Lindsey just laughed and shook her head. There was no point in trying to explain it. She'd never get it, but that was OK. She didn't need to.

Lindsey had almost forgotten what it was like to sit with another woman and drink, and laugh like normal women in their thirties did, and by the time Sinéad finally left, Lindsey felt more drunk and therefore more relaxed than she had in weeks, despite the day she'd had. So much so that she almost let herself imagine that a deep and dreamless sleep would come her way that night. But of course she knew better.

CHAPTER SIX

'... and before I knew what was happening, her hulk of a fucking boyfriend was outside the car window, looking in at my snowy white arse and his girlfriend's ankles dangling around my ears and that's how my bastarding nose got broken for the second time.'

The heat was stifling as they patrolled the badly maintained, dusty road just outside Al Qunaytirah, near the Syrian border. But it wasn't enough to stop them from laughing at another one of Lenny Jones's one night stand horror stories, of which he had enough to write a How not to guide, that all adolescent boys should have to read before being released upon society.

Lindsey could feel a trickle of sweat rolling down her chest. All eyes were scanning their surroundings and no one let their guard down, even for a second. Such a thing could prove fatal in the Golan Heights, but the nervous tension had to be broken every now and then and most of the time it was Lenny who broke it. A short, loud mouthed North-sider, who would have had very ginger hair if he didn't shave his head daily.

She could hear kids laughing, but couldn't see any. Not until they went further up the road and the armoured personnel carrier in front of their patrol had passed them. Some boys were playing football and a little girl in a faded and dirty yellow dress was wandering around by herself. The boys didn't want her near them. Even with the language barrier, Lindsey could tell that they were telling her where to go. The little girl watched their patrol for a bit and was smiling at them all the time. Then something else caught her eye and she moved off in another direction. Lindsey followed the direction of her stare, to see what she was looking at and her eyes came to rest half way between them and the girl. Just off the side of the road, was a semi-inflated football.

The little girl was making her way quickly towards it and the tension in Lindsey's stomach began to make its presence felt. 'Lads…' she spoke but didn't quite trust herself.

'What is it?' Street was directly across from her, on the other side of the road.

Her ringing phone startled her awake. She was still on the couch where she'd stayed to finish the second bottle of wine after Sinéad left and she was lying at a funny angle. She sat up and stretched her aching neck before looking around, with no idea where her phone was. Frank was standing a few feet away, watching her intently. He made no attempt to help her find the source of the ringing, as he finally curled up on the floor beside the couch and closed his eyes, possibly for the first time in hours.

She pulled the phone out from under a cushion, just as it stopped ringing, but only for a second before it started again.

'Hello?'

'I'm outside with coffee,' it was Street.

'Wh…' *fuck.* 'Give me a minute, I was asleep.'

She hung up the phone and stood up, straightening the same clothes that she had on yesterday, before deciding that he wouldn't get to see her like this. She went to the bathroom and stripped quickly, then stepped under a cold shower for no more than two minutes. Just enough time to run a soapy loofah over her body and brush her teeth. Then she quickly dressed again in clean jeans and a black T-shirt and five minutes after the phone first rang, Street was in her living room with two cups of coffee from Costa in Blackpool.

'I waited up for you last night, but either you never came, or you snuck in when I fell asleep.'

'I do have a life you know,' she took a cup from him, removed the lid and busied herself blowing on the hot liquid inside.

He didn't wait for an invitation to sit down. 'Good to know. So, what's going on with you?'

'Not much,' she went to the kitchen to once again prepare a meal for Frank. Even though he was asleep, he was becoming the perfect distraction for her now that uninvited guests kept dropping by.

'OK, fuck this.' Street sat forward in the armchair, elbows on his knees again. 'You walk in my door yesterday after nearly three years and you still can't bloody look at me?'

She turned around and looked pointedly at him.

'That's better,' he smiled, and sat back again.

Adam Street could look relaxed just about anywhere, under any circumstance and Lindsey envied him that. It was a look that she strived for most days.

'Look, we don't have to talk about anything. I just want to know that you're doing OK.'

'I am.'

'So why all the late-night shit kickings over the past few months?'

'Because I don't take pills any more.' The last time she'd seen him, she was in her zombie state of not giving a fuck.

'You don't think I know that?'

'How would you?'

'Lindsey, I lost one person that day. I wasn't about to lose another. You told me to leave you alone and I did. As far as you were aware. You did well to straighten yourself out the way you have and I'm proud of you, girl. The lone wolf, eh?' he smiled wryly.

His confession didn't surprise her as much as it should have, but she couldn't think of a response. Seems she didn't need one.

'I know. You can't look at me without seeing him. I get it. I feel the same way sometimes.'

'So... let me know how much I owe you for Jamie's membership. I'll cover it OK?'

'Sure,' he was smiling at her again now. 'So you had company here last night?' he stuck his thumb in the direction of the two wine glasses still sitting on the coffee table. 'He's not still here, is he?' he whispered dramatically.

Lindsey finally smiled. 'My *company* was more your type than mine.'

He shook his head and wagged his finger at her. 'I'm a changed man.'

'Yeah, right.'

'So listen; myself and the lads from the gym are having a bit of a night out at the weekend. No pressure; no trips down memory lane; just a few drinks and a bit of craic. Say yes and I'll leave this minute, like I know you're praying I will. Say no and I'm here for the day.' It was the grin that was plastered across his face now that made her genuinely laugh for the first time since seeing him again.

'Christ, fine! I'll come.'

'Good.' He got to his feet. 'Saturday. Be in the Old Oak for six.'

Before leaving he hunched down on the floor next to Frank to give him some much appreciated attention. They scratched, nudged and conversed with each other for a few minutes, before he finally headed for the door taking his empty cup with him. 'Good to see you, Linds.'

By the time Saturday came around, Lindsey was beyond allergic to her night out with Street and his gym buddies. There was a time when a boy's night out was completely normal to her. She was never the odd one out and was perfectly at home in that environment. But she didn't know any of these guys, apart from Street, and she had no interest in being a curiosity for anyone. If she didn't turn up, then Street would be back on her case. Now that he was back in her life it would come naturally to him, so she did the only other thing she could think of; 'Sinéad?'

'Hey, Lindsey,' Sinéad answered after three rings and sounded immediately suspicious upon hearing her voice. 'What happened? Is everything alright?'

'Well, that depends; what are you doing tonight?'

'Same thing I do on all my nights off. Fuck all. Why?'

'Well I got roped into a bit of a boy's night out tonight and I could do with a wing woman.'

'Yes! Tell me where and when.' She sounded excited now and Lindsey was glad that she'd called her. She suspected that Sinéad was a little bit on the lonely side, having moved to a new county only six months ago.

'Old Oak at seven.'

'I'll be there.'

And she was. Waiting outside the door when Lindsey arrived in fact, looking nothing like a member of *An Garda Siochána*. She was wearing a mid thigh length black skirt with opaque tights and a black and silver sequence vest. She looked stunning and Lindsey feel slightly under dressed in her black skinny jeans and full coverage top. In fact, she probably looked like a Mormon next to Sinéad, but she didn't care. Although she was suddenly nervous. It'd been so long since she was on an actual night out, that she didn't quite know if she could be sociable enough by normal standards. When the hell had she become this person?

'Wow, look at you!'

Sinéad rolled her eyes. 'Yeah, bet you didn't recognise me without my beaner's arse.'

Lindsey laughed. 'Your what?'

'Let's just say that *An Garda Siochána* have yet to create a uniform that suits the female posterior. So who are we meeting on this boy's night out?' she held the door open for Lindsey and followed her inside.

'Not sure. I only know one of them.'

'What bloody time do you call this?' Street was standing by the bar closest to the door when they went in.

'Holy Mother of God. That must be Adam Street.' Sinéad mumbled in her ear while maintaining her pleasant smile, making Lindsey laugh. She could envisage where this night would end; with Garda Murray in Adam Street's bed.

'Adam, this is Sinéad,' Lindsey introduced her old friend to her new.

He gave her his killer smile before taking their drinks order and adding them to the round that he was buying. It consisted of four drinks in total. 'We're up the back,' he handed Sinéad her glass of Merlot and Lindsey her bottle of beer and led the way.

Standing on his own, leaning against a poll was Owen. His full attention was on a hen party, who were making a big display of their dancing/gyrating skills not too far away from him.

'This is your big gym night out?' Lindsey asked with a smile.

'Well all the staff are here,' he smiled broadly before taking a mouthful of Jack and Coke. 'Most of the lads are gone to a cross fit competition in Limerick today. They're stopping in on their way back. Shouldn't be much longer.'

'Boxer's doing cross fit? What's the world coming to?' Lindsey smiled and both Owen and Street made strange faces in agreement.

The first hour was spent discussing the hen party, Sinéad's move from Leitrim to Cork, about three minutes of which was spent talking about her job, after which time she changed the subject to Lindsey's job and Jamie Cussons, who apparently was at the gym four days that week, including most of that day. He was loving it by all accounts and Street clearly had a new soft spot for him, which Lindsey knew he would. Jamie was an underdog after all.

Lindsey made her way to the bar to get another round and when she got back, they'd been joined by a large group of athletic looking lads, all wearing jeans and T-shirts, the minimum dress code for city centre pubs, and all had gear bags at their feet. Sinéad was being enthusiastically chatted up by four of them by the time Lindsey got to hand over her drink and she seemed happy enough that Lindsey didn't feel the need to rescue her. Instead she placed a drink in her hand and headed for Street, just as Owen left to mingle.

'So, was I right?' she asked.

'I doubt it,' he brought his drink to his lips and took a sup. 'About what though?'

'She's more your type than mine,' she gestured towards Sinéad.

He shrugged his shoulders. 'She seems more intelligent than the ones I would have gone for.'

'True,' Lindsey smiled.

'Mary?'

Lindsey turned to see Devon closing in on her.

'Mary?' Street mumbled with his eyebrows raised.

'Devon... hey.' She was hoping that her face didn't fall as much as it tried to.

'Hey, man.' Devon nodded at Street, who smiled and nodded in response.

'So... how are things?' he asked Lindsey.

'Good... you?'

'Hey, Lindsey?' one of the unknown boxers came and stood beside them. 'That young lad you sent over last week is a little whippet.'

'Lindsey?' Devon smiled and shook his head.

Lindsey moved away from Street and the boxer, to the other side of Devon and lowered her voice. 'Sorry, Devon. I just wasn't looking for a... *thing*.'

'I knew that five seconds after meeting you. Devon Forrest, nice to meet you,' he held out his hand with more than a hint of sarcasm in his smile.

'Lindsey Ryan,' she half smiled back and shook it. 'So we don't need to get into anything here then.'

'Fine.' He guffawed and walked away.

Lindsey rolled her eyes and blew out a breath before returning to Street who had been watching their exchange.

He looked at her with his usual grin.

'What?' she picked up her bottle and took a drink.

'Nothing...' he shrugged '... Mary.' he laughed quietly.

'Fuck off,' she smiled finally.

'So…' he turned towards her, 'I presume that little exchange means that you're not seeing anyone?'

'Good guess. You?'

'Nope. I gave up on women a while back.'

'You're sticking with that story huh? How's that suiting you?' she laughed. Street was a notorious ladies' man and she had trouble believing that he'd changed that drastically.

He shrugged, but was only half smiling. 'Ah Jaysus, he's coming back.'

'Who?' Lindsey looked behind her to see Devon making his way towards her again with his phone in his hand.

'When was the last time you looked at your Facebook page?' Devon was holding his phone up.

'I don't use Facebook.'

'But you have a page,' he was smiling now.

'I doubt it's still active though… why?'

'Because someone really doesn't like you.' He handed his phone to her, which had Lindsey's Facebook page open on the screen.

She'd stopped using Facebook a long time ago. In fact, she'd stopped using most methods of communication, except for her phone which she mostly used for work. But while she wasn't using her Facebook page, it seemed that someone by the name of *Phoenix* was. There was post after post on her wall, describing Lindsey as everything from a bitch, to a whore, to a nasty piece of shit, along with threats to destroy her. She was even labelled a home wrecker in one post. It went on and on. There were photographs posted of her at the Centre, with various kids with captions like *liar* and *bitch*.

Lindsey closed Facebook and made a mental note to delete the page the next day.

'You need to be more careful, Lindsey. I can see how you could piss someone off.' Devon still had a slight smile on his face, but it seemed more bitter than friendly.

'What the fuck did you say?' Street shoved himself in front of Lindsey and squared up to Devon.

Devon shrugged. 'Just saying,' then he turned to leave. 'You need to check your woman.'

Street made to go after him, but Lindsey stopped him. 'Forget it.'

'What the fuck was that about?'

'It's nothing.'

'Lindsey...'

'It's nothing, Adam. Just some kid with a grudge.'

'You knew all that shit was on your wall?'

'Course not. Like I said, I don't use Facebook.

'But?'

'But nothing. They've obviously realised that I don't use it. The last post was six weeks ago,' right about the time that they started leaving notes at her house. But Street didn't need to know that.

'You're coming to stay with me for a while.'

She laughed. 'I am in my arse.'

'Lindsey...'

'Adam, stop.'

'What about him? Where the hell did you pick him up?'

'How's that your business?'

'I don't like him.' Street was craning his neck to see Devon in the crowd, but he was gone. Lindsey saw him leave.

'You don't have to like him.'

'Does he know where you live?'

'Of course not,' she rolled her eyes.

He turned towards her again. 'Hey, next time you need a booty call, let me give you a list of some sane individuals, with more than a lump of ham between their ears.'

'You're one to talk,' she smiled, hoping to lighten the conversation again.

'*Touché*,' he raised his glass in a toast, before taking a drink.

That night Lindsey lay wide awake, staring at the ceiling, while Frank snored gently beside her. Her mind was in overdrive. She'd decided not to wait until morning to sort out her Facebook page, but before deleting anything, she clicked on *Phoenix* to see who was picking a fight with her. Of course there were no details of the human behind the character assassination, but that didn't stop her from clicking on every icon. The page was created just over a year ago; the profile picture was of a phoenix – naturally. There were no posts, other than those that were posted directly to Lindsey's page. Photos of her were also the only ones associated with the page. There was nothing there to go on, so she then made the mistake of reading through the messages that were posted by Phoenix to the Lindsey Ryan page. It was pretty repetitive stuff, the name calling, the threats – never to physically hurt or kill her; just to destroy her. Whoever it was, was careful enough to know that without being very specific in their threats, there was virtually nothing that the law could do.

On the one hand though, she found the photographs mildly reassuring. They meant that she wasn't losing her mind to paranoia or to PTSD when she constantly felt like she was being watched. She actually was. But her relief quickly turned to anger at the fact that someone was invading her life like this.

She rolled onto her side facing the window, stretched out her hand and pulled back one of the curtains as far as she could reach, just enough for her to see a sliver of her garden and the street outside. She wondered if there was someone out there now, looking back at her. It was almost five o'clock on Sunday morning. There was no way she was going to sleep now, so she got up and dressed for a run. If someone was out there, then let them come at her. At this point in time, she honestly didn't care.

She quietly left the room so that Frank could rest and as she walked through the living room, towards the door, she was startled out of her thoughts once more.

'Can I come?'

'Jesus!' she turned towards the couch with her hand on her chest, the other instinctively reached for the hurley leaning against the wall beside her.

Street sat up and leaned his head on the back of the couch, looking at her first, then at the hurley. 'Jaysus, I'm lucky I stuck my head up when I did,' he smiled.

'Go back to sleep,' she turned and headed back towards her bedroom. How could she forget that he was there after he so strongly insisted upon it?

'Were you headed for my place? This is about your time.'

'I couldn't sleep.'

'Me neither,' he got to his feet and stretched, before reaching to put on his boots. 'So I'll come with you.'

'For a run? In those things?' she gestured towards his chunky brown boots.

'No problem.'

'Forget it. Put the kettle on instead, seeing as we're all awake.'

He kicked off his boots again and headed for the kitchen, where he quietly made a *cafétière* of coffee.

Lindsey watched him in silence. She'd cut Street from her life thinking that it would help. It was too hard to look at him, so it was probably what she needed to do at the time, to get off the pills. Plus, he was trying too hard to help her, which only made her *want* the pills just to spite him. Lindsey was stubborn like that. She hadn't taken so much as an aspirin in almost two years, but she still couldn't bring herself to go and see him. It hurt too much.

During one of the three therapy sessions that she'd turned up for, she'd been told that the people associated with the event could trigger PTSD symptoms. So could smells apparently; and stress, and sounds... it seemed just about anything could trigger it. At least according to the people who write the books on these things and they were probably right.

But it wasn't Street who triggered anything. Not this time at least.

'Did I wake you?' she asked, when he handed her a cup and sat beside her on the couch.

'Nah, I don't sleep much.'

'Since when do you drink coffee?' she looked into his cup. 'Without milk, sugar and chocolate.'

'I've changed a lot of things since I saw you last.'

She was starting to see that too. 'What do you do to help you sleep?' she didn't ask *why* he didn't sleep. She didn't need to.

He shrugged. 'I wait for you to come.'

She raised her eyebrows. 'To the gym?'

He nodded with a slight smile.

'OK, so that accounts for the past couple of months. What about before that?'

'I slept fine before that,' he took another drink and sat back, bringing his feet up onto the coffee table, looking perfectly relaxed as always.

Lindsey on the other hand, felt like she'd been slapped in the face. Here she was, so caught up in her own shit that it never even crossed her mind that sneaking back into Street's life could possibly be a trigger for him.

'Stop feeling sorry for yourself, Linds,' he dropped his head against the soft back of the couch and turned towards her.

'I'm not. I'm feeling shit sorry for you now though,' she forced a smile again.

'Don't.'

'Nightmares?'

'Well, I see your bloody mug every time I close my eyes, so I'd say, yeah; nightmares.'

She closed her fist and punched him on the arm and they both laughed quietly for a bit, though nothing about this was funny.

'Sorry, Adam.'

'Shut the fuck up. But you do owe me a proper conversation, so what happened?'

That question from a therapist, or anyone else for that matter, would leave her scrambling for an answer. More like an excuse. Even if Street had asked her in the past, he wouldn't have gotten anything close to an explanation. But it was suddenly clear that, if anyone could understand what was going on in her head, even if she didn't, then it was him.

She could pinpoint the exact day when all this started again. 'I was perfect, up until a few months ago.'

'Perfect eh?' he smiled.

'Pretty damn close,' she smiled smugly.

'Then what?'

'I was at the Centre one night. There'd been a basketball match between a group of our kids and a team made up of guards from the station at Anglesea Street. It went on until after eight and by the time everyone left, it was dark and I was locking up.' She shook her head. 'I don't know how to describe it, but I got this feeling that someone was watching me. I checked out the whole place, inside and out with a torch, but there was no one there. I couldn't shake the feeling though and I had it again the next day, from the time I left my house, *all* day.

I didn't give it too much thought to be honest; I was so busy at work and all that. But then one night...' she shook her head, 'I was back in Golan. Everything was so real...' she glanced at him before deciding not to elaborate on that particular nightmare and make it real for him too. 'Frank was frantic trying to wake me. I had scratches on my face that I'd given myself in my sleep. Let's just say, it was a bad night. The feeling that I was being watched came and went, but I couldn't sleep any more after that. I either dreamed too much, or my body refused to take the chance. That's when my training sessions moved to the early hours and I started to use your place again. I didn't think about the fact that you knew I was there, even though I know you left ice out for me. I certainly didn't think that my going there would shake things up for you.'

'Don't flatter yourself, girl,' he smiled again, but was looking straight up at the ceiling with his head back. 'And the whole being watched thing?'

She shrugged and chose to lie. 'All in my mind.'

'You're sticking with that story, even after seeing your Facebook page?'

'Some keyboard warrior with nothing better to do.'

'You have an answer for everything,' he turned towards her again with a soft smile.

'So I'm a bit of a pain in your ass at the moment,' again, she tried to lighten the conversation.

'Woman, you've always been a pain in my ass,' he topped up their coffees.

'So tell me about this whole, swearing off women, thing.'

'Hey, it's not as if I was that bad.'

She raised her eyebrows. 'I never said you were bad. Casanova wasn't bad either.'

He laughed and shook his head. 'I was a young pup with a six pack then. I had to make use of it while I could.'

'So what are you now?'

'An old dog.'

'With a six pack,' she slapped his bare stomach. Thankfully he'd left his jeans on, but for a guy pushing forty, he looked good. Very good.

'Older and wiser then?'

'You're asking me?' she laughed.

He got up and went to the kitchen to put the kettle back on for more coffee and she realised that he was no longer the man that she knew everything about.

'OK, so I told you. Now it's your turn. What happened?'

'You don't wanna know.'

She didn't push him, knowing how that felt. She just kept quiet and waited until he finally came back and filled their cups for a third time.

'I lost the fucking plot,' he didn't look at her while he spoke. 'You were at college...'

'Stoned most of the time.'

He nodded. 'Damo threw himself into training for an iron man challenge, so he went off the map. Wesley moved to Australia to work in private security, while myself, Gordon and Murph hit the town like a bunch of seventeen-year olds. Tearing the arse out of the drinking, clubbing in places where the average age was nineteen and one of us was guaranteed to be in a punch up before each night ended. I was arrested twice by the guards and three times by the MPs before being asked nicely to leave the army the minute my contract was up. That way they didn't have to be seen throwing out someone with my *experience*. They actually said as much,' he guffawed. He still hadn't looked at her and she knew that there was more.

'One night we were out and I met this…' he smiled, but there was a hint of bitterness in it, 'I wouldn't even say *my usual type*. At that stage if you put a girl's wig on a broom handle I would have tried to climb it. Turns out, her name was Jenny and she was twenty-one years old. We went back to her place; she was a student at UCC with rented digs on the college road. Anyway, I fell asleep afterwards and when I woke up, there were three girls screaming their heads off in the bedroom,' he put his cup down and brought his hands to his head. Lindsey still didn't speak. 'I was dreaming or whatever… the poor girl woke up with me on top of her, shaking her by the shoulders, roaring in her face. She screamed and her friends all barged in…' he forced a laugh. 'As far as they were concerned, I was some nut-job she'd picked up in the club who was strangling her in her sleep. She had me arrested for assault, and rightly so,' he looked at her finally. 'Thing is, one of the guards who arrested me, Jim Duggan is his name, was ex-army. He knew of me. He knew of *us*. He spoke to her and her family and they dropped the charges. He got some veterans on my case and actually helped me get the loan for the gym. I moved in there and well… you know the rest.'

That was well over a year ago. She remembered because she'd just started working at the Centre, when an envelope arrived in the post for her. It contained a key and the address of Street's gym.

'Christ, turn my back on you for a minute…' she smiled and finally he did too. A more natural smile anyway. 'So that explains your oath of celibacy.'

'Well… I wouldn't say celibacy,' he smiled broadly. 'I'm just much pickier these days and I definitely stick within my own age bracket. Meanwhile, here you are out picking up nut-jobs like me.'

'That's not a habit. Just… every now and then, when a run, or a punching bag just won't do it,' she didn't want to admit that what she liked more than the running, or the boxing, or the sex with strangers, was the risk associated with everything she did while she should have been asleep. It boosted her adrenaline and made her feel like she was living in the present and not the past.

'Linds, I'm sure you're not short on offers from decent blokes.'

'What would I do with one of them?' she smiled. 'They too would wake up while being strangled and I wouldn't even be dreaming at the time.'

He laughed out loud now.

CHAPTER SEVEN

'Mike? A word when you have a minute.' Lindsey tapped him on the shoulder as she passed him, while he was talking to Greg about a football league that he was starting.

He nodded and continued with his conversation, while Lindsey carried on towards the stairs and their office. She didn't quite know how to start the conversation that she wanted to have, but by going head first in, she knew she'd come up with something.

Of all the names she'd been called by her new chicken shit friend, *home wrecker* was the one that bothered her the most. The only person that it could possibly point to was Mike. But she'd spent hours looking at the photos and trying to remember where everyone was when each of them was taken. She couldn't pin point where he was for almost any of them; except one. The one where she was moping against his car. That was just after Mike told her that he was leaving Marie. He stormed off and at the only time the photo could have been taken Mike was sitting at the camp fire with the kids. So it couldn't have been him, and as soon as she realised that, she almost felt bad for thinking that it might have been. Almost. Because if it wasn't him, then that left just one other person.

'Hey. What's up?' he came through the door with a bundle of paperwork and added it to the pile that was already on the desk.

'How did you get on with Marie?' Launch straight in. It was the only way.

He tilted his head with a curious expression on his face and finally he sat down and answered her. 'I left.'

'How did she take it?'

'How do you think?'

Lindsey shrugged.

'Look, Lindsey I wanted to…'

'Mike… it's nothing to do with me,' she held her hand up.

'So why ask?'

'What did Marie do for the weekend while we were camping?'

'How do you mean?'

'I mean, did she know where we were?'

'Of course she did.'

'And where was she?'

'Lindsey, what's this about?'

'Mike, does Marie know that we slept together?'

'No.'

'Why are you so sure?'

'Because I didn't tell her.'

Lindsey shook her head in disbelief at his naivety. 'And you think that because you didn't tell her, that she couldn't possibly figure it out? Did you talk about me at home?'

'Sometimes,' he was becoming more defensive in his answers now.

'How often?'

He shrugged, but she could see that he was thinking and that maybe his *sometimes* was enough for a woman with half a brain to put two and two together. After all most men, as far as Lindsey knew, weren't nearly as subtle as they thought they were.

'Where was she while we were camping?'

'London.'

'Why London?'

'Her sister lives there.'

'How do you know that she actually went?'

He pulled his phone out of his pocket and started scrolling through it. He then dropped it in front of her with Marie's Facebook page open to where she'd added eleven new photos, time, date, and location stamped.

She handed the phone back to him. 'OK, thanks,' there went her the-

93

ory.

'Now would you mind telling me what this is all about?'

She did mind. But she had to come up with something, so she said the next best thing, which was also true. 'Sorry, Mike. Look, I just don't want there to be any confusion, that's all.'

'Don't worry; you've made yourself perfectly clear. Unless of course you changed your mind, now that I'm separated instead of married.'

She shook her head. 'I haven't.'

'So why sleep with me?'

'Same reason you slept with me, Mike. Curiosity,' she smiled. She didn't want to come straight out and say what it really was: a mistake.

'You're very blasé about sex, aren't you?'

'You're the one who was married.'

'Can I ask you…? Never mind.'

'Ask,' the least she could do was answer a question after the grilling she just gave him.

'How many married men have you slept with?'

'One, as far as I know.'

That was true. But then she never asked. If they weren't wearing a ring, then they were fair game as far as she was concerned.

'Is it wrong of me to say that I wish we hadn't?'

'Not if that's what you think. Plus, I agree.'

'Yeah, but I think we have different reasons for feeling like that.'

'But at least we agree,' she tried again, feeling like a bitch for rehashing this conversation, but it was better than the old, *I think your wife's a stalker* conversation.

'OK, you've had your say, now it's my turn and I'm only going to say this once. Then I won't bring it up again.'

'Fair enough.'

'Sleeping with you while I was married to Marie… that's not me.'

'It was a slip on both our parts.'

'Let me finish. I'm not a man who cheats on women. Even before I met Marie, I was always in a relationship. I was never a one night stand kind of guy. They never interested me and if I met someone else while I had a girlfriend, then I weighed it all up and either broke up with my girlfriend before pursuing the new girl, or I walked away.'

'Mike...'

He held up his hand. 'Please, Linds. When you walked in here for the first time, I remember thinking, thank God! Another pair of hands.'

She smiled.

'You came with all your new ideas and experience from the army and you freshened this place up like you wouldn't believe. Then you got that call from young Damien and I'll never forget how cool under pressure you were and I remember thinking...' he wagged his finger, 'this is not your average newbie. Your first week on the job and you knew exactly what to do. I'd almost say you were the calmest person on the scene. That's when I really *noticed* you.'

He lowered his head and wiped his hand slowly across his face, looking like he didn't quite believe that he was saying all this, but Lindsey stayed quiet.

'I've told you that I like you... that I really like you and I know I shouldn't have done that while I was with Marie. I shouldn't have done that to either of you. If I were you, I wouldn't trust me either. But I wouldn't treat you like that, Linds. I wouldn't treat anyone like that ever again. Give me a shot and I promise, I'll be good to you.'

Now she really felt like shit and she wished that she'd just come straight out and asked if his wife was a stalker. The truth was, she did like Mike. Very much. He was handsome and funny and for the most part, he had a heart of gold. She also believed him when he said that he wasn't a natural cheater. *She* seduced *him* that night. She remembered it well and she was sorry for the obvious pain it had caused him. But she knew in her heart and soul that she and Mike would be incompatible as a couple. He'd never understand the *real* Lindsey Ryan and she could never be the type of woman he wanted. And as far as trust went; she was the one who couldn't be trusted. In fact, she would have had sex with him right there and then if he wasn't so emotionally involved, so what did that say about her?

'I know you would, Mike. I know it sounds like the ultimate cliché, but it's genuinely not you. It's me. I'm not up for a relationship of any kind just now.'

'I know you're going through something that you don't want to tell me about.'

'I have some things on my mind, yeah,' she wanted to be as honest as she could with him. 'I'd like to say that I just need to sort myself out…' she smiled, 'but I've been saying that for years. I could be saying it for years more and in the meantime, I've lost enough friends. I don't want to lose another one.'

'OK. Well…' he got to his feet, 'I promised that I wouldn't bring it up again, so I won't. But if you ever change your mind…'

She nodded as he turned to leave. 'Hey and Mike?'

'Yeah?'

'Don't ever think that I don't trust you.'

He gave a lopsided grin as he left the office, leaving Lindsey to blow out the breath that she didn't realise she was holding.

That night as she lay awake staring at the ceiling again, all her instincts screamed at her to go out and find a new Devon. But instead she dressed in shorts and a vest and ran for eight miles around the city, ending at Street's front door. As she stooped to catch her breath, she noticed that the familiar face from the doorway was missing.

She straightened up and walked the length of the alley, checking each doorway, but he wasn't there. No one was. She stood for a minute outside his usual spot, debating with herself, until her irrational side won over and she pushed open the door to the abandoned building next to Street's. Inside was a dark, empty shell that smelled of urine, rubbish and something else that she couldn't quite put a finger on. There were people lying asleep or passed out on the floor here and there. Some were covered with cardboard or old sleeping bags, while others made no effort to shield themselves from the elements. Maybe because they were unaware of them.

She lifted back the covers off one or two people to see who they were.

Some groaned, others made no acknowledgment that she was there and the further she went into the building, the more her stomach twisted, while her fists began to clench and unclench.

'You,' came the familiar, but now croaky voice from the darkest corner.

She walked over to him but said nothing.

'You're looking for something.'

'What's your name?'

'I don't know who the fuck I am any more. I know you though,' he grinned.

'You don't. And I just wanted to make sure you were still alive, that's all. Clearly you are, so I'll go now.'

'Oh but I do know you. You're here telling yourself that you don't want anything... you might even believe it. But you want something. Trust me,' he laughed now.

'What do I want?'

'A way out,' he tapped the side of his head. 'To forget.'

She didn't answer. Maybe he was right.

'I can get you something for the pain, if you have the money?'

'What makes you think I have pain?'

He laughed again. 'Shit girl, someone without pain would never find themselves in a shithole like this. You're all torn up on the outside...' he was looking at her scars, 'I'm all torn up on the inside. Every fucker in here is torn up. Come and sit with me,' he moved over and patted the ground next to him.

'Who's your friend, Stabber?' the voice came from behind her and she turned quickly to see another man standing no more than three feet from her. He was skinny with a pockmarked face and brown teeth showing through his leering grin.

'That's Lindsey,' Stabber replied, smiling. The fact that she now knew his nickname did nothing to reassure her, nor did the fact that he himself

97

seemed more menacing now that his buddy was there.

'Maybe she can be my friend too?' the new arrival grabbed his crotch and pulled a flick-knife out of the pocket of his filthy jeans.

Stabber was laughing quietly, while his friend made the mistake of holding his knife limply by his side, which he clearly expected to be enough of a threat. Without thinking, Lindsey quickly closed the gap between them and jabbed her closed fist into his windpipe with as much force as she possibly could, before he had a chance to do whatever he planned to do with her and his knife. As she had hoped, his drug riddled body wasn't strong enough to withhold and he crumpled to the ground, clutching his throat and gasping for air.

Stabber laughed a little harder now, but she didn't stick around any longer. She walked as quickly as she could to the front door and slammed it shut behind her.

That was by far the most stupid thing she'd ever done. And yet she felt more elated than she had in years.

She quickly let herself into Street's and pictured Stabber and his scabby friend, as she went to town on the bag and by the time she was done in, fifty minutes later, she was shaking all over. What the hell was she thinking?

She paced the floor of the gym for ten minutes. Her limbs were tight and achy and her hands were shaking. It was adrenaline, she knew, but she wanted it to stop. One side of her brain was reminding her that she could have been killed, while the other side was telling her to go back and look for them; give them more to think about, especially Stabber, who laughed through it all.

She was mumbling to herself now and didn't trust herself to go back outside, so she slowed herself down – her movements, her breathing, her thoughts. This took another half hour, before she finally felt like she could keep her mouth shut and her body still, at which point she walked as quietly as she could towards the stairs.

The second floor, over the gym, was pretty much a mirror image of downstairs, only Street had put up some partition walls. The door at the top of the stairs was unlocked, so she opened it quietly and went into his small, but neat sitting room. One black leather three-seater couch, a coffee table and a television. Through an opening in the partition was a small kitchenette, again spotlessly clean and tidy, and beyond that was Street's bedroom. She stood in his doorway for a minute looking at him. With the light of the moon coming through the net curtain on his window, she could see the outline of him. He was breathing quietly and rhythmically and she thought briefly about getting into bed with him. But even in her state, she knew the effects of adrenaline and this was one of them. The last thing she needed was to add another mistake to her glowing resumé, so she turned and headed quietly back to the sitting room and lay down on the couch. Within minutes, she could feel her body shutting down. The cut-out switch had been flipped and she finally landed in a deep, dream-less, coma like sleep.

It was almost lunchtime the next day when she came round and at first she had no idea where she was. Not until Street landed a cup of coffee on the table in front of her.

'What time is it?' She rubbed her eyes and pulled herself into a sitting position, feeling like she'd been hit by a bus. It was the second time in her life she'd experienced an adrenaline dump like it and she hoped it would be the last. She could have gotten herself killed last night and that was just the heart palpitations. Never mind the junky with the knife she all but went looking for.

'Half twelve.'

She stopped rubbing her eyes and forced them to adjust. 'In the day? Fuck.' She got to her feet.

'Sit down woman, will ya?'

'Shit, I don't have my phone. I'm supposed to be at work.'

'I called them. Said you were sick.'

'What are you, my mam? I have to call them. Can I use your phone?'

He handed it to her. 'Relax. I talked to yer man, Mike. He said not to worry about it, the day was covered.'

She closed her eyes and tried to think about what was on there today. *An Garda Siochána.* They were popping in for a chat; Sinéad's idea. The kids would hate it, but it would keep them busy. They agreed to a basketball match afterwards, which would end as always with every Garda on the team going home with bruised shins.

'Mike?' he picked up on the seventh ring.

'Hey, how you feeling?'

'Like shit actually,' she smiled, though it was true. 'You need me to come in?'

'Nah, we're covered here. No point in spreading whatever it is that you have.'

No chance it was catching, but she wasn't about to argue. 'OK. I'll see you in the morning then?'

'Mind yourself.'

She hung up on Mike and then dialled one of the other numbers that she knew by heart. 'Mr Hennessey, it's Lindsey.'

'Hello love, how are you?'

'I'm good thanks. How are you? How's Irene?'

'Ah she's grand. You know yourself.' Irene was in the clutches of Alzheimer's and was far from grand, but *grand* was his standard response. 'Everything OK?'

'I'm just wondering if you'd have time to pop into my place and let Frank out for a bit and put out some food for him. Something came up and I had to leave very early this morning and he was still asleep.'

'No problem at all. Shur I haven't seen the bold pup in ages.'

She could hear the smile in his voice. There was a lot to be said for having elderly neighbours who were always home. He also had a spare key to her house for reasons exactly like this. 'Thanks, Mr Hennessey. I owe you one.'

'Bye love.'

'All set?' asked Street as he refilled his coffee cup.

'You drink a lot of coffee, Street.'

'It's better than some of my other vices.'

'True that,' she raised her own cup and took a sip, though she needed something to bring her blood sugar back to normal. She still felt washed out. 'You have any food here?'

He went and put four slices of bread in the toaster.

'Hey, sorry for crashing in on you.'

'No problem. It must have been an all-nighter. What was it, half four when you got here and you'd already had over an hour downstairs before that?'

'Were you awake? Why didn't you say something?'

He smiled. 'I was too busy enjoying myself. It's been a while since I've been eyed up in my sleep by a beautiful woman.'

She threw a cushion at him. 'You're an ass. And actually, I was just debating whether or not I could kick you out of your own bed, but as you can see, I'm too nice a person to do that.'

'Tell the truth; you were thinking about jumping me,' he was laughing now. 'You'd just finished kicking the shit out of whoever you were picturing downstairs; the adrenaline was pumping and you thought... hmmm.'

'Don't flatter yourself... but OK, you're right,' she laughed a little harder and so did he. 'Christ, three years of nothing and now all this. I'd have to worry about what kind of impression I'm giving you.'

'Yeah, I'd say you're really worried about that. Anyway it's too late for impressions. You made yours years ago.'

She nodded with a smile, thinking about how long they'd known each other and Street laughed again.

'What?'

'I remember the first impression you made on me. You were dressed like a firs bush, standing in a squat position holding a GPMG over your head, as punishment for *correcting* an NCO during an exercise in the Glen of Imaal. You were a fucking red arse recruit! Five weeks into your career and you knew it all.'

'I still do. And that wasn't just any NCO. I believe it was you, Corporal Street, so really, you should be the one worried about first impressions,' she laughed. 'Because that one wasn't great.'

His smile faded then and his eyes went to her left shoulder. 'You made a much bigger impression than that over the years, Linds.'

She didn't like the fact that her scars were still on display in last night's vest, even to Street, who'd seen those same scars in the making. She got up and went to get the toast. She buttered four slices and put them on one plate for them to share.

He clearly noticed her sudden discomfort, so he continued in a lighter tone again. 'So to put your mind at ease, you could work your way through a whole ship of sailors and it wouldn't tarnish your sterling reputation.'

She sat down and put the plate on the coffee table. 'Sailors... really?'

He shrugged. 'I was trying to think of the worse possible scenario,' his smile melted away as he traced his finger along the raised skin. 'I haven't seen these for a while.'

'They only come out at night. Along with my dark side,' she grinned, finally relaxing more than she thought was possible while someone was looking at, touching, or even mentioning her scars.

'I think I like your dark side.'

It was early in the evening when Lindsey finally left the sanctuary of Street's place, wearing one of his hoodies and a fleece lined jacket to keep out the cold as he drove her through the city on the back of his Harley. It was exhilarating and by the time she got home, she was calm, tired and almost felt like she could sleep again, even though Stabber and his friend were still in the back of her mind.

She was willing to acknowledge the fact that she'd been ridiculously stupid and as she lay on her bed later that night with heavy eyes, she actually believed herself when she said that it was the last time.

CHAPTER EIGHT

But of course that wasn't the last time. As midnight rolled around, her heavy eyes had become light as feathers and Stabber had manifested himself in her mind as her stalker and the reason why she'd almost been robbed, raped, killed, or whatever his friend's intentions for her were the night before. Suddenly, it was all down to him.

She swung her legs out of bed and sat there in the dark for a minute, trying to think. But it didn't work. It seemed the time for thinking was over, so she got dressed in jeans and Street's hoody and seeing as Frank was wide awake too, standing by the bedroom door, she gave in to his silent demands and took him with her.

She parked her car near Penrose Wharf and walked to where she knew she'd find him. There were sirens in the distance and a few stragglers, perhaps on their way home after a few drinks, but otherwise this part of the city was relatively quiet and as always, so was Street's laneway.

In Stabber's usual doorway was another man. He was much older than Stabber, with a greying black beard. She was about to go back inside the abandoned building, but before she did, she thought to ask the new guy instead, so she pulled a fiver out of her pocket and held it towards him.

'Do you know where Stabber is?' she asked, not yet releasing her grip on the note.

'Who's asking?'

'I am.'

103

He considered her for a minute before deciding that she was no threat. 'He got a bed in Simon for the night.'

Lindsey let go of the money and walked away. The Simon Community shelter was only a few minutes' walk from there and that was where she headed next. When she arrived, she rang the buzzer on the security door and waited for the voice over the intercom.

'We're full for the night,' the slightly haggard sounding woman announced with no further pleasantries.

'I'm not looking for a bed,' Lindsey responded, again using her most professional tone. 'My name is Lindsey Ryan. I work at the Tús Núa Centre. I need to find someone who I think might be staying with you tonight.'

There was a moment's pause before the buzzer sounded and the door clicked. Lindsey pushed it open and went inside, letting Frank in ahead of her but holding tight to his collar. What she noticed first was the smell. It was like damp clothes and unwashed bodies and as she paused in the hallway she could hear a lot of noise and the type of commotion that was probably constant and completely normal in a place like this. She couldn't see many people from where she stood just inside the door, but she knew that the place was filled to capacity with people who had nothing more than the clothes they wore and the emotional baggage they carried. The looks on some of the faces she could see were menacing, while others looked utterly defeated. It was a depressing place to be.

'Who is it you're looking for?' A woman in her late forties with wild black hair stepped into the hall in front of her and that was when Lindsey realised that she didn't know Stabber's real name. 'Christ, he won't bite will he? I fucking hate dogs.'

She rubbed her forehead suddenly feeling like an idiot. 'No, he won't bite. I'm sorry; I only have a nickname... Stabber?'

The woman looked at her like she was just another person sent there to try her nerves.

'He's taller than me, maybe late twenties, dark hair...'

'Girl, look around you. You've just described half of Cork...' with that a fight broke out somewhere. The shouts echoed around the building and people went running, either to join in or break it up. Or maybe just to watch. 'I have to go. Find out who you're looking for and come back. I can't let you in any further I'm afraid,' she was already backing away from Lindsey.

'OK... I'll leave my information here if anyone by that name turns up,' she called after her, as the woman turned and broke into a run to attend to the ensuing mayhem.

Lindsey could see exactly why the woman seemed so jaded. Two minutes in the hallway of the Simon community left her never wanting to be there again. It also left her with a renewed admiration for the people who worked there. Without doubt it took a special kind of person.

By the time she stepped back out into the fresh air, the urge to find Stabber wasn't so overwhelming any more. But she was still convinced it was him, or someone he knew who was bothering her. So she'd written down her name and the name of the Centre where he could find her and she left it for the Simon staff. Now she just wondered if he'd have the balls to come and see her face to face.

'Ehm, can I talk to you about something?' Leah Mendelson brought her out of her daydream, if that's what you'd call being asleep with your eyes open, staring into a cup of coffee.

Lindsey went straight to the Centre after she left Simon the night before, conscious that she'd taken more days off in the past week than she had since starting there, but even Sheila gave up on talking to her that morning. Conversationally, she was the very definition of useless, but it was time to switch on now and Leah was attempting to help her with that.

'Yeah, Leah. Come and sit down,' she indicated the long bench on the other side of the table facing her. She didn't feel the need to take it into the office, seeing as there wasn't much more privacy in there than in the still empty dining area.

'Jamie said that the fella at the boxing club told him that you were a soldier. Is that right?'

'Eh… yeah. Once.' She sat up straight now in an attempt to pay attention. She didn't want to talk about this, but was curious to know where it was headed.

'That's what I want.' Leah looked excited suddenly, like she'd just had an epiphany.

'What's what you want?'

'To be a soldier. In the army. Can you help me?'

'No.'

Lindsey stood up and took her cup to the kitchen, where Sheila was looking at her like she'd just told a five-year-old that the Easter Bunny had been brutally murdered by Santa Claus. Lindsey ignored her and passed Leah again on her way to the office. She pushed the door closed, took a seat behind her desk and sat there for a minute, staring straight ahead. 'Fuck.' She stood up again and went outside in time to see Leah making her way down the stairs.

'Leah?'

She turned around but said nothing. She looked dejected.

Lindsey motioned to her with her head, to follow her back to the office.

'Have a seat.'

Leah still hadn't spoken, but she did sit down.

'What makes you think you want to join the army?'

She shrugged.

'I'm gonna need more than that if you want me to help you.'

'I didn't until the other day.'

'What happened the other day?'

'Me and Jamie were talking about being up the Galtees and he was on about some boxer fella, sayin that he was teachin' him all sorts… then he started goin' on about what we were going to do when we're older an' all that. He wants to be a Garda, so he said yer man is going to teach him self defence an' all that, so he'll have a better chance of getting in.'

Lindsey nodded and despite her semi-awake state, a small smile made its way across her lips. To know that Jamie was planning a career made her day. 'OK.'

'Well, I never *really* thought about what I wanted to be.'

'Never? Didn't your parents ever talk to you about it?'

'My mother goes on sometimes. She likes to tell me about all the so-called opportunities I'm throwing away. She started off telling me I should be a doctor. Then when she realised that would never happen, she down-graded me to a nurse, then a Montessori teacher. The last one she came up with was an Avon lady.'

Lindsey lost her smile. 'Did she ever ask you what you'd like to do?'

'They don't know the first thing about me.'

This was when Lindsey remembered her aim to find out more about what Leah's home life was really like.

'What about your dad? Did he have suggestions?'

She snorted out a laugh.

'Why's that funny?'

'Because you don't know my dad.'

'Fair enough. Tell me about him.'

Leah looked at her and seemed suddenly mistrusting. 'I didn't come here to talk about him.'

'OK. I'm just trying to understand how you go from doctor to soldier without ever having thought about it.'

'Well first of all, I was never going to be a doctor. That was my mother's notion, but if she took a second to realise that I hate school, I hate studying and I hate everything to do with hospitals, then she'd know what a stupid fucking idea that was.'

Lindsey nodded, but waited quietly for her to continue.

'And if my dad *did* decide to make a suggestion for me, it would probably be along the lines of, cook, cleaner and child-bearing wife with unseeing eyes and a quiet mouth.'

Lindsey was momentarily caught off guard by her choice of words. They didn't come off the top of her head. They'd been playing on her mind for a while, she could tell.

'Like your mam?'

Leah looked at her again and her eyes confirmed her answer.

Lindsey let the silence hang in the air for another few seconds, sure that Leah would want to fill it. And she was right.

'Look, he's a womanising scumbag who likes to connect the back of his hand with my stupid mother's face. And these are the people who think they know what's best for me!' She jumped to her feet and struggled to get round her chair to the door.

'Leah, stay.'

'I said I don't want to talk about this.'

'Then we won't.'

She hesitated for a second, before finally sitting back down.

'So… the army?'

'Lindsey, I've never pictured myself doing anything. The more my mother threw these things at me, the less I thought about what I would actually do. Then me and Jamie were talking, like I said, and we were on about the Galtees. He said that he was telling yer man…'

'Adam. His name is Adam Street.'

'Yeah, him. Jamie was telling him about going up the mountain and Adam told him that you were a bad-ass when it came to mountains because you were a soldier.'

'Right…'

'I loved it Lindsey. It was the first time I ever actually thought… I could do that.'

Lindsey leaned forward on her desk with her hands together. She could see genuine excitement in Leah's eyes and she wanted her to know that she had her full attention. But how could she send this girl in the directions she herself had gone? 'I hear you. But Leah there's so much more to the army than a great camping trip on the Galtees. That was easy. It was to be enjoyed and we all did. And you by the way impressed me no end.'

She smiled one of her rare, genuine smiles.

'Army training is not to be enjoyed. You hate your parents telling you what to do? In the army you have people screaming orders in your face, day in, day out...'

'I know that!' she shook her head. 'You think I don't know that? Lindsey, the difference is that they'd be soldiers... like you. They know what the fuck they're talking about. My mother wants to live the life she really wanted, through me. My father hasn't a bloody clue, because he doesn't believe that women can be of any use to anyone.' She too leaned forward on the desk now, letting Lindsey know that she too was serious. 'I'm never going to college, Lindsay. I'll never work in an office, or a bank or a fucking hospital...'

'OK, OK.' Lindsey lowered her head into her hands. 'Let me think.' She took a few breaths, trying her best to think about the twelve years before her career ended, when the army was her life and her passion. A passion that she hadn't felt since. She raised her head and looked at the sixteen-year-old opposite her, with too much make-up on and torn fishnet tights under her raggedy edged denim mini skirt. 'Right... well if the army is what you really want, then you're in the perfect position to get it.'

Leah sat up straighter now, slightly surprised by Lindsey's answer. 'You'll help me?'

'I can't get you in there, Leah. But I'll help you.'

'OK,' she smiled.

'So you know you need to be eighteen?'

Disappointment returned to her face.

'Leah, that's a good thing. That means you have time to get to where you need to be. Here's what you need to do. The Irish army doesn't take just anyone. They want to know that you're driven. That you're hungry enough to do what needs to be done.'

'I am.'

'Then you'll need your leaving cert.'

Her smile dropped again.

'That's not debatable, Leah. What's the alternative? You turn up for your interview and tell them that you couldn't be bothered?' she looked pointedly at her for a second. 'You'll have to compete for your place, so you'll need as many positives in your favour as possible.'

She rolled her eyes. 'Fine. What else.'

'Ease up on the make-up and be yourself. You're going to be a minority in any branch of the defence forces, you understand that? But that's not to say that you don't want to stand out. You absolutely do. But for the right reasons.'

She nodded.

'Fitness is another thing that'll work in your favour. Plus, it'll make your recruit training a little less painful. What sports are you interested in?'

She shrugged her shoulders, then looked sceptically at Lindsey. 'Not boxing, if that's what you're getting at.'

Lindsey smiled. She could imagine Eileen Mendelson's reaction if she was told that her daughter was taking up boxing. 'Running?'

'I never really tried it.'

'Why don't we try it together then? Leah, it's only a year and a half. If you knuckle down now, then by the time your turn comes around, you'll be more than ready. Make it impossible for them to say no to you, you hear me? So how about you bring some gear tomorrow and we'll head out while the soccer league is on?'

She nodded enthusiastically. 'OK, I hate soccer anyway.'

'I know.' Lindsey smiled and went rooting in her drawer for one of her cards. When she finally found one, she handed it to Leah. 'Take this. You ring me if things kick off at home, or if you need anything. Doesn't matter what time it is.'

Leah reached out hesitantly and took it with a quivery smile, before leaving the office, and despite her sheer exhaustion, Lindsey felt slightly more refreshed.

She leaned back and stretched her arms over her head. She had a pain in the back of her eyes, which she knew were bloodshot from lack of sleep. She got to her feet and went outside for some air, but within minutes, she wished she hadn't. Standing outside the mesh gates, leaning against the wall, was the man she knew only as Stabber.

She paused for a minute, looking at the back of his head, not quite

sure what to do. Once again, she'd been ridiculously stupid in going looking for him and this was the result. She found him. Or rather, he found
her.

'You came,' she finally walked out the gate and stood facing him.

'Why were you looking for me?'

'Why do you think?'

He shrugged.

'Well, let's start with you and your scummy friend pulling a knife on
me the other night and we can move onto why you're following me.'

He looked at her with a blank expression. His hands were shoved
deep into his pockets and he was strung out and jittery enough for Lindsey to realise that he badly needed a fix.

'What the fuck…? Are you giving me money?'

'Why would I do that?'

He kicked the wall. 'Why the fuck did you look for me and why did
you tell me to come here? You want something or not?'

'I want to know why you're following me.'

An anguished laugh escaped his lips. 'Are you fucking mad woman?'
he tapped the side of his head angrily. 'Unless someone's leaving a trail of
H behind them, I'm not following anyone.'

'Fine. What about the other night?'

He shook his head with the same jittery laugh. 'Did I invite you in
there? No, I didn't. You went in there looking for trouble and you found
it. Now you wanna blame me? You're one twisted fucking bitch, you know
that?'

She turned and walked away from him, back towards the Centre,
knowing now that he wasn't capable of getting himself together for long
enough to follow anyone. He certainly couldn't have gotten himself to the
Kings Yard, with or without a Smartphone camera.

Hey, gi'me something?' his hand was out and he had a pathetic look
on his face.

'Go ask your friend with the knife.'

CHAPTER NINE

For the next few weeks, Lindsey threw herself into Leah's life. She took her running every chance she got on each of her days at the Centre, and also met her other times when she could. For Leah's part, half a kilometre into her first run, she wanted to throw in the towel and never run again. Two weeks later she was almost up to 3k. She may as well have won the Olympics when Lindsey told her what distance she'd covered that day and her reaction was enough to prompt Lindsey to continue training her.

She'd also gotten in touch with the Cork City Hill Walking Club and gotten a full list of their upcoming beginner's walks. So far Leah's father wasn't allowing her to go, but that was something Lindsey would have to work on.

'Damien, you're back,' she greeted him with a smile as he walked into the Centre, just as Lindsey was closing up for the day.

'Yeah… is Mike around?'

'You just missed him. What's up? Is everything OK?' he seemed nowhere near as excited as he was the last time she'd seen him. In fact he seemed quite on edge.

'I need him to help me with this college thing… I need to put it off for a year or two.'

'What? Why?'

'I'm needed here for now. Hopefully next year, I'll…'

'Damien, no. This is an amazing opportunity for you. You cannot pass it up.'

'Look, my mother and my sister need me here.'

'OK, sit down,' she sat on one of the courtside benches and waited for him to sit alongside her. 'What are you planning to do for them if you stay here?'

'They need me to be here. Plus, they need money, Lindsey. I'll get a job…'

'Doing what?'

'I don't know,' he replied more forcefully now and she could see how frustrated he was.

'Damien, listen to me; I know you think you're doing the only thing that you can for your family by staying. But the reality of that decision is you'll get a job that won't pay well enough to support three people. This means you'll be working day in day out, in a job that you'll hate before long and you'll be getting nowhere. The money will be gone as soon as you get it, so this time next year, you won't be any better off financially than you are now and neither will your family. So, if you're in the same position next year as you are now, are you telling me that you'll quit that job and go to Wales? You'll leave your family then in the same situation they're in now?'

He brought his hands to his head.

'Damien, the best thing that you can do for yourself and for your family in the long run, is to go! Get your degree. Or I promise you, you'll look back years from now and sincerely regret throwing away this opportunity.'

His cheeks were wet when he took his hands away and she put her arm around his shoulder. He was a good kid with the potential to be a very good man. But he needed to go and make a life for himself.

'What about them?'

'Tell me what's happening with them?'

'Mam's by herself now.'

'What does she say about this?'

He looked at her for the first time. 'That I'm a selfish bollix if I go.'

Lindsey tried to keep her face neutral, though she wanted to see the lovely Ms Lucey so that she could slap her in the head. 'Where's your sister?'

'She has another year before she's officially out of the foster system.'

'Does she see your mother much?'

He shook his head. 'She hasn't spoken to my mother in over a year. She's not doing too good though.'

'In what way?'

'Her last two foster families kicked her out, so she's in a group home now. She's getting in fights all the time. I think she's taking drugs, I don't know what though. The guys she hangs around with…' he shook his head again. 'She barely talks to me. She seems to hate me.'

'I doubt that…'

'She does. I can see it in her face.'

'I'm sorry, Damien. But look, that was pretty much you this time last year. Not the drugs, but the fighting, remember? You were in her exact same place and you pulled yourself out of it. She has to do the same for herself. You can't do it for her.'

'But I had you and Mike helping me.'

'And she has the staff at the home.' Lindsey had no idea how much time those people had for individual attention to those kids, but she had to make Damien go. He'd never get or take the chance again. 'They're your family, I get it. But throwing away the best opportunity you've had in your life isn't going to be what helps them, you hear me?'

His face was buried in his hands again, but he nodded. 'Do you want help locking up?' he mumbled.

'Nah, I have it covered.' She got to her feet and so did Damien. 'Think seriously about what I said, Damien and ring me if you need to, OK? You still have my number?'

'Yeah, I have it,' he half smiled, visibly pulling himself together. 'Thanks. And hey, be careful. You shouldn't be hanging around here by yourself after dark.'

She nodded and smiled as he walked away, somehow looking as confident as ever and Lindsey was left wondering how some families could work so hard to make life next to impossible for each other.

It seemed like the whole world had slowed down, but Lindsey's heart was hammering in her chest. Aside from her heart though, the little girl in the faded yellow dress was the only other thing that was moving too fast. Her eyes were glued to the abandoned football and her hands were almost on it by the time Lindsey broke formation and ran towards her.

She was almost sure it was Lenny's voice she heard, screaming the three little letters that were spinning around in her head, but never quite made it past her own lips – IED.

She didn't reach the girl on time and as she looked down on herself, lying on the ground, she could still hear the high-pitched squeal that some people call a ringing in your ears.

She could hear Street's voice, calling for the APC to come back and she could hear its engines roaring as it tore into reverse.

'Lindsey?'

She wasn't looking down on herself any more. She was lying down now with Lenny leaning over her, calling her name.

'Lindsey?' he shouted in her face. 'Get that fucking APC back here now!' he shouted to anyone who could hear him.

She turned her head. The little arm was limp on the ground, the sleeve of the faded yellow dress was no longer yellow and neither the arm nor the dress was still attached to the curious little girl. The man who was hunched over, with one hand resting against the remains of a car, turned his head now to look at Lindsey. The man was Street, and as he moved she caught a glimpse of the ruin beneath him, which was once a child.

It felt as though her lungs would burst into flames as she screamed, while Lenny held her face in his hands and turned her head to look at him, just as his head jerked violently and the life immediately left his eyes...

She woke to the sound of her own piercing scream amidst Frank's barking. His paws were on her chest and as her screaming finally subsided, Frank too became more still, but because of his position, she couldn't help covering him with her vomit as she threw up violently, just about managing to roll onto her side before choking.

She was destroyed. Her bed was destroyed and Frank was destroyed, though he never let on if he was bothered by this. Instead he kept his head against her until such time as she was able to move. Fifteen minutes or there abouts. Then he walked to the bedroom door and waited for her to open it and leave the house, like she always did.

But she didn't this time. She barely had enough strength in her legs to carry her to the bathroom, where she turned on the shower and crawled into the bath. She sat with her knees pulled tight into her chest and as the hot water washed over her, she cried hard enough to make her throw up again.

It wasn't until the water turned lukewarm that she lifted her head to look into the eyes that never left her. His muzzle was leaning on the rim of the bath and he too was whimpering softly.

She pulled herself to her feet and stepped out of the bath, where she stooped and lifted Frank in. Then she climbed in with him.

'Sorry, Frankie.'

He whined loudly, but for his own sake this time. Frank hated nothing more than being washed. She turned the nozzle on him and poured some shampoo over his coat and scrubbed as quickly as she could, while he did his best to go through the side of the bath. The poor dog had had enough torture for one night. And so had she.

By the time she'd dried off and stripped the bed, the sun was up. It was almost seven in the morning and for the first time, she was thankful for the fact that she didn't have to go to work today. Or tomorrow for that matter. The last thing she wanted was to be around people now. She still felt sick and she could see Lenny's face as clearly as if he was standing right in front of her. The girl too. But she also saw the horror on Street's face as he leaned over what was left of a child, who just moments earlier had been smiling and skipping towards them.

A text message beeped through on her phone and she picked it up to distract herself.

'Breakfast?'

It was Street and his invitation meant that he was probably on his way over. It was all she needed to get her moving.

She pulled her backpack out of the back of the wardrobe and began stuffing layers of warm clothing into it. She then moved quickly into the kitchen and pulled her outdoor cooking equipment out of the cupboard, along with some non-perishable food, and packed them hastily. So hastily in fact, that she was almost sure she'd leave without something vital, but at that point in time, she didn't care. She loved the man dearly, but she had to be gone before he, or anyone else, turned up. She grabbed some stuff for Frank and her tent from under the bed and she left.

She drove without giving any thought as to where she was going, but in just over an hour she was passing through Dungarvan in County Waterford. Her phone rang four more times during the journey and each call was followed by a message, all of which she ignored, and as she took the turn for Mahon Bridge, headed for the Comeragh Mountains, it rang one last time before she reached over and switched it off. Finally, once she'd parked the car at Kilclooney woods, she sat there for almost an hour, staring at the beautifully deserted landscape ahead of her. She was so tired and distracted that by the time she could finally bring herself to move, she had no idea what specifically had been going through her mind since the time she closed and locked her front door behind her. She grabbed her gear, opened the door for Frank and the pair started walking.

Frank trotted ahead of her through the woods until they reached the foot of the mountain, at which point he waited and then walked with her. They headed upwards at a pace which was brisker than necessary, following one of several worn paths, until they eventually came to a pond; at which point Frank went nuts. The pond was full of frogs and tadpoles and it took everything she had to drag him away before he had a chance to do any damage. When she chose this route, she did take the pond and its inhabitants into consideration, but this route was the lesser of two evils as far as Frank was concerned. If they had taken a right back along, instead of a left, he'd be chasing sheep and their lambs all over the mountain by now, and that certainly wouldn't do.

It took some stern persuasion but she finally got him to walk on, past a field of bog cotton that didn't interest him in the slightest. But then his mind was probably still on the tadpoles. They continued up and over the next crest where they stopped to take in the breathtaking view of the glacial lake below, the highlight of the Comeragh Mountains for sure. Lindsey sat down on the wet ground and slipped on Frank's leash, as a few sheep moved along the ridge to their left.

'This is much better, isn't it boy?' she looked around and all she could see for miles was mountain. It was like they had the whole world to themselves, which was exactly what she needed if she was going to lose the plot; something that could happen at any minute.

She pulled out a pouch of food for Frank, tore it apart and laid it on the ground for him, while she pulled back the ring pull on a tin of beans for herself and the pair ate in companionable silence. By the time they moved off again a mist had started in on them, but they carried on upwards along a ridge path, scrambling in places with Frank showing that he was still a fit dog, despite his age.

They walked for nearly five hours in total, stopping at intervals for water and all the time surrounded by breath taking scenery, very little of which Lindsey actually noticed. She was too busy focusing her mind on the wet and sometimes difficult ground beneath her and making sure that Frank was OK. On the odd occasions she did look up and see a glimpse of the majestic view, the images still fresh in her mind from last night moved front and centre once again to ruin it.

It was close to five o'clock when they reached the highest point of the mountain and the weather was just about holding out. The cloud was low overhead and it was getting much colder. The mist had cleared, but it was getting dark early and while Lindsey didn't particularly care whether or how she got back down, she did care that Frank was with her.

They began their descent along a spur, with Lindsey going ahead of Frank when it got steep in places, but before long they were back at the lake, which was where she planned to set up camp for the night. But it seemed they weren't the only ones, as there were three one-man tents set up beside the lake. She couldn't see anyone yet, but she could hear their laughter as it echoed towards them.

'Fuck,' she mumbled. It was almost dark now and she didn't want to continue with Frank. He was tired and hungry and she didn't want to risk him getting injured in this terrain in the dark. But she didn't want to mingle with strangers and make small talk for the night either.

Their tents were pitched right by the lake, so she stayed well back and pitched behind a large boulder, hoping they wouldn't notice her. Of course that hope was short lived, as Frank made a dash for the lake as soon as she dropped her gear.

'Holy fuck, where'd he come from?' said one of the three men, who were cooking around a small fire as Frank dashed past and splashed them all in his enthusiasm.

Two of them looked to be in their thirties, while one looked closer to his early twenties and actually, they all had a military look about them. But then so did a lot of guys who lived the kind of lifestyle that saw them camped out on the side of a mountain this far from civilisation.

'Sorry… he's with me.' Lindsey stepped begrudgingly out from behind her boulder.

There was a moment's pause as they all turned to look at her, before the younger looking one finally spoke.

'Well that answers that. So my next question is, where'd you come from?'

Lindsey smiled half-heartedly and pointed upwards.

'Are you by yourself?' The one doing all the talking had a bushy goatee and a cocky smile and Lindsey already had him pegged as a pain in the ass.

'Nope,' she pointed towards Frank.

'Well in that case, you'd better sit down,' one of the others finally spoke.

This one had a black wool hat pulled down over his ears. He had stubble around his face, which made Lindsey think they'd been on the go for a few days at least.

'Pebbles, Dirty and Shakes,' the man with the cap said, as he pointed at each of them in turn, by way of introductions. It seemed he was Pebbles, the youngest one with the goatee was Dirty, that figured, and the one who had yet to speak was Shakes and the nicknames made Lindsey even more convinced they were military. Army probably.

'Lindsey,' she replied, doing her best to sound polite, but she wished that Frank would get his ass out of the lake so that she could part company with her fellow campers.

'Sit yourself down, Lindsay.' Shakes finally spoke. Like the others, he had a few days growth on his face, but was the better looking one by far.

'Maybe later.' She turned and headed back towards where her gear was. 'Frank!' she called and he immediately floundered his way out of the water, splashing the three men again as he dashed past them.

She wasted no time getting her tent up and putting on some extra layers of clothes, using a spare fleece to dry Frank off, before building a small fire of her own and cooking up a cuppa soup, mixed with instant noodles. She opened two pouches of food for Frank. He needed the extra calories after the tough day he'd endured like a champion and not long after they'd finished eating they climbed into Lindsey's tent with the intention that at least one of them would get some sleep. That was when Lindsey realised that she had in fact left home without something vital; her sleeping bag. And it was freezing now.

'Fuck,' she muttered again, as she dragged her backpack into the tent with her. She pulled out all the clothes that were in it and put on a few more layers. She also tied a warm fleece around Frank, who fell asleep almost as soon as he lay down. Lindsey lay down beside him and tucked herself in close to feel his warmth, though sleep for her was a long way off. Plus it was the last thing she wanted to do under the circumstances. She wasn't alone up here, like she planned to be. Instead the three amigos were within feet of her and even though she didn't know them, she still didn't want them waking up on the side of a lonely mountain, to the sound of a screaming lunatic. It'd be like a real life horror movie for everyone involved and she didn't fancy it.

Never the less she closed her eyes.

'Hey, Lindsey? We have Jameson.'

She opened her eyes again. The voice came from over the boulder, where the three tents were pitched.

'Come on girl, we're better company than any dog.' it was Dirty's voice.

'I doubt that,' she mumbled.

She lifted her head slightly and looked at Frank. He was fast asleep. She got up as slowly and quietly as she could and crept out of the tent, leaving the zip open just enough that he could get out if he wanted to. She stood for a second on her own side of the boulder and blew into her gloved hands. She was in the middle of nowhere with three strange men and a bottle of whiskey. 'What could possibly go wrong?' she mumbled, before stepping around the rock and heading towards their fire.

'Yeaaaay, you came!' Dirty had clearly started into the whiskey well before now.

She went and sat on the ground between Shakes and Pebbles.

'Glad you could make it.' Pebbles handed her a small plastic cup from the top of a flask and half filled it with neat whiskey.

'Cheers,' she raised the cup to them and downed the potent liquid, making her shudder before she was able to appreciate the warmth that began to spread throughout her body.

'So, Lindsey... what brings a woman like you to a place like this, all by herself?'

'I'm not by myself,' she smiled. 'But we won't split hairs. I'm probably here for the same reason you lot are; to take it all in.' She gestured to their surroundings and congratulated herself for managing to sound plausible.

'Well technically, me and Pebbles are training,' said Dirty with a grin. 'We've an NCO course starting in a few weeks, so we're getting acclimatised to the elements.'

She nodded.

'Do you know what an NCO course is?' Dirty asked her. He still had a grin on his face that was becoming a bit ridiculous looking. Though he didn't wait for her to answer. 'Well… obviously, we're soldiers,' he opened his arms out by way of asking what else could they possibly be. 'Me and him are about to be promoted, but first we have to go through nineteen weeks of pure hell. 'To give you an idea…'

'Give it a rest, Dirty,' Shakes interrupted. 'She didn't come all the way up here so she could listen to you blowing your hole.'

Lindsey laughed quietly as Pebbles topped up her cup. 'What about you, Shakes? You on that course too?'

He shook his head.

'Shakes is off to Golan in a few weeks,' Pebbles replied when Shakes didn't.

'That's in Syria.' Dirty pointed out and Lindsey realised that he somehow thought she was thick. Which was fine, so she nodded her understanding.

'Jeez, you lot like to talk about work, don't you?'

'She's right. Move on,' said Shakes. 'I'll have plenty of time to think about the Golan fucking Heights when I get there.'

And then some, Lindsey thought.

Considering where she was and why she was there, it was Murphy's bloody law that she'd run into a bunch of soldiers talking about the Golan Heights; the last place in the world she ever wanted to talk about, least of all now.

'So what do you do, Lindsey?' Shakes asked.

She liked Shakes. He seemed like the strong silent type, who so far only spoke to shut the other two up. 'I'm a waitress,' she replied.

'A waitress who spends her spare time rambling around on mountains with a big ass dog? Haven't met one of those before.'

'You have now, Pebbles,' she half smiled, as she took the bottle that was being passed around again.

'Correction; a waitress who rambles around on mountains with a big ass dog, who also knows how to drink,' Pebbles raised his plastic cup and she returned the gesture.

She wasn't counting how many times her cup was refilled, because she didn't particularly care. But she was a lot warmer now than she had been and she and her new temporary friends spent the next hour or so talking about this particular mountain and others like it; what routes they'd taken and what routes they'd never take again. Then the conversation turned to football, which Lindsey knew nothing about; then rugby, which she could make passable conversation about, particularly the last world cup and then disappointingly, it went back to football again, in particular the French and German game in Le Stade de France, Paris, in November 2015. Naturally this raised the subject of the terrorist attack there, then terrorism in general, then the migrant crisis and the overall state of the Middle East and Lindsey could feel her time around this campfire coming to an end.

'Do you know anyone who ever went to the Middle East?' Dirty asked, but Lindsey didn't move her eyes away from the fire. It was inevitable that a group of soldiers would eventually start telling war stories, especially over a drink and she had a strong feeling that that was just about to happen. When she didn't answer, Dirty continued. 'You know some people think that Irish soldiers just fanny about the place. All the years we've been going to places like The Leb… what do you think happens there, Lindsey?'

She shrugged. 'You get a nice tan and pick up some cheap gold?'

She'd done two tours in The Leb, one in Chad and one in Syria. She knew exactly what happened there, but he didn't need to know that. She also knew the answer that he expected to hear from a civilian.

'See?' he pointed dramatically at her and looked at the other two. 'This is what I'm talking about.'

Shakes was saying nothing, while Pebbles was smiling and shaking his head.

Dirty leaned in closer to the fire, looking intently at Lindsey. He was about to *make her understand* something.

'You know how many Peacekeepers have been killed in the Leb, Lindsey? And as for Syria!' he straightened up and rubbed the palms of his hands up and down his thighs. 'Four years ago, a group of Irish soldiers were on foot patrol in the Golan Heights. Just an average day out there...' he shook his head and was wide eyed as he told the last story in the world that she wanted to hear. Still, she was curious to hear his version, so she stayed quiet and let him continue. 'Next thing you know, they come across an IED. That's an improvised explosive device...' he paused again, to make sure that she was following. At this point she had to stop herself from diving across the flames and punching him in the face until he shut up. 'One of them, a woman actually...' he gestured dramatically towards her, like as a fellow member of womankind, she should instantly be more concerned, '... she was blown to shit and ribbons, girl. But anyway she somehow managed to survive with half her fucking face blown off and now she's out there, living like some kind of a recluse or something, maimed for life because she did this job. But that's not the worst of it. While they were trying to patch her up, one of them was shot in the head by a fucking sniper...'

Lindsey got to her feet and knocked back what was left of her whiskey, as Frank came trotting out of the tent towards her.

'Hey, hey, Lindsey... stay.' Shakes got up and put his hand on her shoulder and then he turned to the youngest, mouthiest member of their party. 'Dirty if you don't shut the fuck up about shit you know nothing about, I swear to Christ, I'll shut your mouth for you.'

Pebbles was laughing into his cup now, but then soldiers did like a bit of drama.

'I don't know what I'm talking about?' Dirty asked, incredulous.

'You knew Lenny did ya?' Shakes asked forcibly and Lindsey startled at the mention of his name. And the fact that Shakes seemed to have known him.

'I'm gonna leave ye to it lads.' Lindsey turned back towards her tent, with Frank by her side.

'I'll shut up,' Dirty called after her.

'No need,' she called back.

'Fuck this, I'm gonna hit the hay too.' Pebbles got to his feet.

'Ah for fuck sake,' Dirty protested, as Shakes too headed silently towards his tent.

For another hour, Lindsey lay curled up against Frank staring at the wall of her tent. So that was the story? *She*, whoever she was, was blown to shit and ribbons, maimed for life and now lived somewhere as a recluse with half a face. That was how she was imagined by the soldiers who'd never met her. No doubt, knowing how an army barracks works, there'd be multiple versions of that story and as sure as day turned to night, she would have been to blame for the whole thing in at least some of them. The more accurate ones perhaps.

She sat up again and pulled off her wool hat, to rub the pins and needles out of her head. Then she replaced the hat and crawled out of the tent again. She stood leaning against the boulder for a few minutes, trying to decide if she could talk herself out of what she was about to do. But the truth was, she didn't want to talk herself out of it, so she moved quietly towards the tent on the far left of the three. She quietly raised the zip and crawled inside.

Shakes started awake. She brought her finger to her lips, asking him to be quiet and then she kissed him. It didn't take long for him to take the lead from her, after he opened his sleeping bag and covered them both. Then he made love to her in the confines of a one-man tent, without either of them making a sound, the result of which was one of the most intense orgasms she'd ever had.

Falling asleep beside him was nowhere in her plan, but against all odds, she did it anyway. She had no idea how long she'd been out for, but even before opening her eyes, she could tell that it was getting bright out and that there was a finger tracing its way down the side of her face.

When she opened her eyes, Shakes' face was a couple of inches from hers. He was leaning up on one elbow with his head resting in his hand. It took her a few seconds to realise that her hat was off and his finger was actually tracing its way from her forehead, down along her temple, the full length of her scar. She rolled away and sat up as much as she could in the tiny enclosure.

'Hey, stay.' His voice was low enough that only she could hear it, and it was the kind of voice that under normal circumstances she would have liked to listen to forever.

'I have to go,' she found her hat and pulled it back on.

'Do you want to tell me how you got that… and the others?'

'Car accident.'

'Those stories from last night…'

'Leave it, Shakes.'

'You know that woman? Her name was Lindsey.' He paused as she struggled out from under his sleeping bag, while he studied her face. 'Tell me your surname.'

'Look, it was nice to meet you… good luck in Golan.' She opened the zip and shuffled outside and by the time she got back to her own tent, she could feel his eyes on her, but she didn't turn around.

'Come on Frankie,' she nudged him awake and while he went outside to do what he needed to do, Lindsey quickly packed everything as hastily as she had yesterday. She had her tent down in record time and she was ready to move out less than ten minutes after leaving Shakes' tent. Before leaving she glanced back and saw him sitting where he'd sat last night, watching her with the expression of someone who'd known her all her life.

CHAPTER TEN

'Lindsey, where the fuck have you been?' Street was sitting on her front step when she arrived back at lunchtime that day.

But he wasn't the first thing to catch her eye. Her house, which was still an old and grubby shade of red, was covered in badly painted graffiti. *Whore* was one of the messages. That was written in large, runny letters on the right side of the front door. On the left, in equally large and runny white paint was a full sentence; *Your fucking dead, bitch.*

'Shit.' Lindsey stood at her gate looking at her house, as anger bubbled up from the pit of her stomach.

'Shit? That's all you have to say?' Street was freaking out. 'Where the fuck were you?'

She finally looked at him. 'I went camping, Street, OK? I didn't think I needed permission.'

'Are you shitting me? We're dealing with someone who clearly wants to fuck with you here and you head off camping, BY YOURSELF!' he roared the last two words.

She walked past him and let herself in, leaving the door open for him to follow.

'Will you please tell me something that makes sense?'

'OK, first of all, *we're* not dealing with anything, *I* am. And I'm dealing with it. Secondly, this wasn't here when I left...' she left him in the sitting room while she went to the bedroom, but continued to talk to him while she changed into old work clothes. 'And another thing, if I want to go camping, then I'll go camping, Street. This is the work, if you could call it that, of an immature coward…' she returned to the sitting room and went looking in the kitchen drawer for the key to her shed.

'They might be a coward, Linds, but even cowards have been known to do damage.' He followed her to the shed, lecturing her all the way, but he still grabbed a roller and helped her carry stuff back towards the house.

'They've been dragging this out for months. If they were going to do something, surely they would have done it by now.'

'You know what actually worries me?'

She didn't answer, as she poured paint onto a tray and started with the front wall.

'You actually don't give a shit.'

She guffawed. 'I don't give a shit? Street, I want nothing more than to catch this little shit and give him something to really dislike me for.'

'That's what I mean. You're not taking this seriously.'

She rolled her eyes. 'How would you know?'

'Did you call the guards?'

'I spoke to Sinéad.'

'Officially?'

'Will you please stop? Look, even she said there was nothing that could be done. Technically, they haven't done anything. This…' she gestured to the house, 'is nothing more than vandalism. At best it'd be worth a slap on the wrist to them.'

'So you're telling me the cops won't get off their arses for anything less than physical harm? he was outraged.

'Pretty much.'

'But it's too fucking late by then!' he roared at her, and when she didn't answer, he was quiet for a minute before speaking again. 'Well then, I'm moving in.'

She laughed. 'You're not.'

'I am.'

'Just paint man, will ya?'

'What the f…' Sinéad's voice trailed off as she stood outside the gate looking at the house. There was another Garda with her and both were in uniform. 'I don't suppose either of you saw who did this?'

'Sinéad… what brings you here?' Lindsey glanced at Street.

He shrugged dramatically. 'Yes, I called her.'

'Sorry I'm only getting here now, we were in the middle of something else. Although I see the missing person is no longer a missing person.' She had a small smile, but there was no humour behind it.

Lindsey rolled her eyes. 'I wasn't missing for a minute, girl. I went camping and forgot to ask Mammy,' she thumbed in Street's direction and he too rolled his eyes.

Sinéad blew out a long breath. 'I don't suppose anyone took photos before you started painting over the evidence?'

Street pulled his phone out of his back pocket and scrolled through it before handing it over to her. He had a total of forty-five images, covering every angle of the house from varying distances.

Lindsey looked at him deadpan. 'Well aren't you the new Colombo.'

He shook his head and went back to painting the house.

'Look, Sinéad there's nothing you can do, I know.'

'Linds, I think you need to come down to the station sometime soon. It's time to start going through the list of people who might hold some sort of grudge against you.'

'Could be a long list,' Lindsey injected some humour into her tone, but no one responded accordingly. 'OK, I'll do that. Now I don't suppose you two want to pick up a roller?' she smiled, wanting the conversation to move on.

The Garda with Sinéad smiled and spoke for the first time. 'Believe me, if I thought it would get us out of going on our next call, I'd paint the place myself, no problem.'

'Sorry, Lindsey, this is Shane Collins. Shane, Lindsey Ryan and Adam Street.'

Shane shook hands with both of them and then the pair turned to leave.

'And Lindsey, couldn't you ease up on the lone camping trips for a while, just 'til this all blows over?'

'No problem,' Lindsey smiled, but if anything, all the concerned advice against going camping only made her want to pack up the car again and take off, somewhere even more remote this time. But she held her tongue and her annoyance in check until they'd both gone, then she moaned loudly as she returned her attention to the job at hand.

The house took three coats of paint and the end result was actually nice. It was no longer the faded red, almost pink, grubby looking cottage. Now it was a fresh blue/grey with a white trim and she was happy with the job they'd done, even if most of it was done in stubborn silence. Although she'd bought the paint weeks ago with the intention of freshening the place up, it bugged her that someone forced her into finally doing it.

'Dinner's on you,' Street grumbled, as he dropped into the armchair with a beer in his hand, which he'd helped himself to. He'd also opened one for Lindsey.

She picked up the phone and dialled the Great Wall Chinese restaurant in Blackpool, who promised to feed them both within a half hour. Street already had his shoes off and his feet on the coffee table and Lindsey knew that he wasn't planning on leaving tonight. Which was fine. She was tired, but didn't particularly feel like being by herself. Not when she had the option of being with someone she didn't have to entertain.

'OK, can we move on from all the bullshit for a while? I've hit my quota for the day,' she asked, putting the phone down and picking up her beer.

'Let me just call you an idiot one more time and them I'm done. You're an idiot.'

'Done?'

He nodded with a slight grin.

'Good, then wait 'til I tell you about the crowd I ran into last night.'

'Where?'

'On the Comeraghs, by the lake. Three lads huddled around a camp fire...'

'And you by yourself, but of course you stayed,' he rolled his eyes, but Lindsey ignored him and continued with her story.

'Turns out two of them are getting ready for an NCO course and one is headed for Golan,' then she started laughing.

'It's typical that you'd manage to find them. What's funny?' he smiled, bringing his beer to his lips.

'This young fella was trying to explain to me, a simple waitress...'

He laughed quietly.

'... that the Irish army do more than just fanny about. When the waitress didn't believe him, he launched into a horror story about a foot patrol in the Golan, where a soldier... a woman, mind you...' she pointed dramatically at Street, 'was blown to shit and ribbons, maimed for life and now lives out what's left of her life as a recluse with half a face.'

'You are shitting me?' he looked at her deadpan.

'I shit you not. What are the bloody chances? I head off into the middle of nowhere and run into the exact thing that I was trying to get away from.'

'That's exactly your luck.'

'One of them knew Lenny.'

His smile faded. 'What was his name?'

She shrugged. 'Shakes. That's all I know.'

'Shakes Maloney,' he nodded. 'Himself and Lenny joined up together.'

'You know him?' she failed to keep the surprise out of her voice.

'Not really. Just to see. Why the face?'

'What face? I'm just surprised that you know him?'

'Why would you be surprised? It's the army; everyone knows everyone. By name at least. If you gave them your real name, I guarantee they would have known you too.'

She nodded.

'Did you?'

'What?'

'Give your real name. Did they know who they were talking shite to?'

She shrugged. 'The idiot didn't. Not sure about the second one... but I think Shakes did by the time I left.'

He studied her face. 'By the time you left?'

She nodded. 'Hmm.'

'If Shakes knew by the time you left, then why wouldn't the other two?' A grin was making its way across his face.

She shrugged again. 'Maybe he was more switched on than the other two.'

'Linds, you didn't?' he grinned broadly and she had no idea how the hell he could possibly know by her stony face.

'What are you on about?'

'On a fucking mountain?' he laughed out loud. 'Jesus girl, you're worse than I ever was.'

'It was cold and I forgot my sleeping bag,' she finally conceded, and laughed with him. There was absolutely no point in denying it to Street. He saw through her every single time and always had.

Their food arrived soon after and for the rest of the night they talked, laughed, and watched brain dead TV until Adam dozed off. Lindsey threw a blanket over him and went to bed, where she actually slept for four hours straight. She woke naturally at half six, feeling something close to normal, but when she went out to the living room, despite the early hour, Street was gone.

Later that morning Lindsey and Mike met up at the Centre ahead of the kids arriving. They were separating for the day and had a few things to run through before they all left. Mike was taking seven kids to Anglesea Street Garda station, where Sinéad had arranged for herself and some of her colleagues to let them shadow them for the day. This would include some quality time in the cells, some ride alongs and front row seats to a training exercise involving a road traffic accident caused by a drunk driver. According to Sinéad, it would be horrific. Even more so, as the kids wouldn't know that it was a training exercise until much later. Unfortunately, seven was their cut off number, which left three who wouldn't be able to go, but Sinéad did promise that those who'd missed out could spend a day with them the following week.

Naturally enough, Jamie was on the list of kids who'd get to spend the day with the guards. Now that he'd expressed an interest in a career as a Garda, Lindsey and Mike would do whatever they could to encourage him in that direction. Lindsey had let Sinéad know this too, so she planned to show him the best of everything.

This left Lindsey at a loose end with three kids, one of whom would be Leah, which made it easy enough for her to find something for them to do. It began with a phone call to Tim Minihan, the secretary of the Cork City Hill Walking Club. Leah's dad might not have allowed her to join the hill walking club, but while she was court ordered to attend their Centre and their activities, Lindsey knew that he wouldn't say no to her going along with them for a day and she was right.

Most clubs and organisations were happy to help out when it came to providing activities for the kids at the Centre and Tim was no different. He arranged a mid-level loop walk around the Claragh Mountains in Millstreet, County Cork. More members of the club would also be going, so that there would be far more adults than kids, which was perfect. Plus, according to Tim's Garda vetting form, he was once a social worker, which swayed Liam in her favour when it came to convincing him to let her take them without Mike. Of course Tim was in his sixties now and didn't realise that his previous occupation was a factor in his day out, but Lindsey used what details she could to get this organised. When her three kids became two due to illness, the day promised to run even more smoothly. It left her with Leah and Greg for what she hoped would be an enjoyable day.

The minibus picked them all up at nine and dropped them at Anglesea Street, with most going inside the Garda station there. Lindsey, Greg and Leah walked the rest of the way to City Hall, where they were meeting the hill walkers and their minibus, before hitting the road for the hour-long journey to Millstreet.

'Hello?' Lindsey finally rooted her phone out of her small backpack, as the old bus ambled its way along the country roads somewhere near Macroom. It had been ringing for some time before she managed to find it.

'Hey,' it was Street.

'Where'd you go?'

'I couldn't sleep.'

'Could've fooled me. Your snoring was cracking the foundations when I went to bed.'

'You can talk. I thought there was a tractor rolling around inside your room when I was leaving.'

'Leaving for where?'

'I thought I'd try your routine; a run and some boxing – if that's what you'd call what you do.'

'And how'd that go for you?'

'Nearly killed me,' she could hear the smile in his voice. 'So what are you up to?'

'Well, some of us work for a living, so I'm on my way to Millstreet.'

'What's down there?'

'The Claragh Mountain loop walk.'

'And you're coming back tonight.'

'Are you checking up on me?'

'Someone has to.'

'Shag off.'

'OK, but I'll see you later.'

'Street, you're not sleeping on my couch again tonight.'

'Is that an invitation to sleep in your room?'

'I'll rephrase. You're not sleeping at my house tonight.'

'Look, it's just until…'

'I don't need a babysitter, Street,' she kept her voice down, but she wasn't being overheard anyway. Not with Tim on the PA system issuing the safety briefing and details of the terrain.

'I'm not worried about you. I'm worried about the poor bastard who thought it'd be funny to fuck up your house,' she could tell that he was smiling.

'I have to go.'

'Hey...'

'Yeah?'

'If you start to feel cold up on that mountain, put on a fucking jumper, will ya.'

She rolled her eyes and hung up.

During her time in the army, Lindsey had always managed to keep her private life pretty much private. This was mainly due to the fact that she never got involved with soldiers and rarely with their friends. Plus, she was quite fussy about who she took her clothes off with. But even then, Street could read her like a book. Now the less she knew about a person, the more attracted to them she was. The less chance she had of ever seeing them again the better, and she didn't care what opinions they formed of her during their time together. In fact, the more she knew that she *shouldn't*, the more she wanted to, and the more actively she went for it. Everything about her and her life had changed, but Street could still read her and that old familiarity brought her comfort during the times when it wasn't filling her with an all-consuming and irrational, fear.

She packed her phone away and looked towards the back of the bus. Leah was half talking to/half ignoring a girl who looked not far off her own age and a little bit out of place considering the rest of their group, while Greg had his forehead stuck to the window and was staring out at the passing landscape, actively avoiding conversation with anyone. Of course he didn't want to be there, but he wanted to be at Anglesea Street even less. Everyone else on the bus ranged in age from early fifties to late sixties, mostly retired professionals and at least one who Lindsey guessed was a housewife. But all looked like seasoned hill walkers. At least judging by the amount of gear that each of them had; gaiters around their well used, but well cleaned hiking boots, walking poles, whistles and compasses around their necks, power bars hanging off belts around their waists and she could only imagine what was in each of their backpacks for a pleasant day's hiking.

Tim was still on the PA, which really wasn't necessary considering the fact that it was a *mini* bus, but he seemed to be enjoying his role as the official leader of the group. This time he was letting everyone know that they had some *new faces* in the crowd today and that if anyone ran into any problems, they could approach any of the club members, who'd be more than happy to help.

They'd been walking for a while on a nice hilly loop around the shoulder of the Claragh Mountains, when they came to a small metal gate and Tim halted the group. As nice as the place was, Lindsey was a little bored. The pace was slow and the conversation was dominated by graphic bunion descriptions, knee replacements and free travel passes. Leah was engrossed in conversation with her new friend the whole way, while Greg moped his way along the path completely by himself, leaving Lindsey with no choice but to accept a lot of advice on how to live a long and happy life.

'OK, so who's up for a little detour?' Tim asked, with a large smile on his face, clearly knowing that his group of regulars would of course say yes.

'Sure,' Lindsey smiled.

'To the top!' Tim announced, jabbing his finger in the air.

'Fuck, do we have to?' Leah was beside her suddenly and had the good grace to keep her complaint low enough that only Lindsey heard her. Greg on the other hand, groaned as loudly as he could.

Lindsey had researched their route well enough to know that this detour took them to the summit and would add just about a half hour, at this pace, to their journey.

'It's not a long detour,' she replied quietly to Leah. 'Why? You looked like you were enjoying yourself.'

'I would be...' she looked around to see where her new friend was, 'but she's wrecking my head.'

'How so?'

'Well, she obviously knows that we're from the trouble maker centre, but for fuck sake, I feel like I just got off the special bus.'

Lindsey couldn't help smirking.

'It's non-stop questions; What did you do? How long do you have to keep going there for? Who's your one? Meaning you of course. She's doing my bloody nut.'

'OK well stick with me instead.' She smiled and pushed Leah up over a particularly steep little ledge.

'We're on a fucking mountain. There'll be no getting away from her.'

Lindsey groaned inwardly and picked up the pace, despite the steep incline.

As predicted, they reached the top in about twenty minutes, where they took some time to take in the view, eat the obligatory ham sandwich and drink some soup from a flask, before heading back down towards the metal gate again, where the loop continued to the right, pretty much descending the whole way.

'Aw fuckin' hell,' Leah groaned, as she glanced behind them and suddenly hurried away from Lindsey, making a beeline for Greg.

'You're Lindsey?'

The only other teenager in the group arrived by her side before Lindsey had a chance to wonder what caused Leah to flee. The girl was sixteen or seventeen at most and looked vaguely familiar. But then most of the teenage girls that crossed Lindsey's path bore striking similarities to each other, in the sense that they all strived to look older than they were. Most wore too much make-up with messy looking hairstyles, which probably took forever to arrange properly, and almost all had the kind of attitude that was clearly noticeable, even before they opened their mouths to speak. This girl was no different in her appearance. She wore very large hooped earrings for a day out on a mountain, but in contrast to these, she had a delicate silver chain around her neck, with a tiny silver crucifix hanging from it. The kind of thing a parent might give to a child when they make their first holy communion. Her hiking gear wasn't much more suitable than what Leah was wearing today, but at least it consisted of a tracksuit pants and runners. She also carried the same air of nonchalance, or boredom, or whatever sulky looking emotion it was that most teenagers tried their upmost to pull off.

'Hi.' Lindsey smiled. She was just a kid after all and would have been very pretty, had she not destroyed herself in heavy and over-stated make-up. Maybe that's what bugged Leah so much; the realisation that her own unique look wasn't all that unique.

'She was telling me that you love all this kinda thing,' the girl looked all around them and Lindsey could only presume that *she* was Leah.

'What's not to love?' Lindsey smiled. 'How about you, do you do much hill walking?'

She guffawed and shook her head, with a face that said, *as if!* 'Just thought I'd try it for a day, but I won't bother next time.'

'You don't like it?'

She laughed again, but it lacked humour.

'That's a shame. Although you and Leah did look like ye might be enjoying yourselves earlier. Just a bit,' she held her thumb and index finger an inch apart and grinned. Why could they never admit to enjoying something?

'*She* might be, but not me,' she lowered her voice then, but not enough by far, as she pointed towards the official club members who were walking together in a group, probably still talking about their bunions. 'Who the fuck would want to go on a day out with that lot?'

As nice as they were, they weren't really Lindsey's cup of tea either. But she appreciated the fact that they'd let their group come along for the day and so she didn't appreciate the way this kid had just disrespected them within earshot. They probably hadn't heard her, but that wasn't the point.

'So, you work with these guys, huh?'

'Sorry, I didn't get your name?'

'Oh, it's Laura.'

Lindsey nodded. 'You from Cork, Laura?'

'Maryborough, in Douglas,' she smiled.

Maryborough was one of the more affluent addresses in Cork. 'Nice area.'

Laura shrugged. 'I suppose. My parents work all the time though.'

They'd have to in order to pay for a house in Maryborough, she thought. 'Yeah? What do they do?'

'Mam's a teacher and Dad's a solicitor.'

'And where do you go to school?'

'It's holiday's now,' she smiled. 'They can be kinda long and boring though. Hey, maybe I could do some more things with you and them?' again she gestured towards Leah and Greg. 'Do any of them go to school?' she whispered.

'What do you mean?'

'I mean… they're all delinquents, aren't they? They're all in trouble with the law.'

'What makes you say that?'

'She told me,' again, she nodded towards Leah.

'You're very interested in other people, aren't you Laura?'

'Yeah, I'm gonna be a social worker,' she replied as a matter of fact. 'Are their families all trouble too?'

Lindsey stopped walking and looked at her. 'Laura, if you really want to be a social worker, then you'll need to learn that you can't assume to know people. Not when you really don't.'

'So you know all of their families?'

'Their families are no more my concern than they are yours. We should pick up the pace a bit.' She walked on ahead of Laura. On the one hand, she felt bad for being so irritated by a girl who clearly needed some attention. On the other hand, she could see exactly why she bugged Leah so much.

'Sorry,' Laura called after her, as she struggled to catch up. 'I'm just curious. So basically, you only get involved with people who've been arrested for something and never with their families?'

Lindsey rolled her eyes, which Leah saw and she smiled.

'You ask a lot of questions, Laura. Why not focus on your breathing and take in the beautiful scenery?' she gestured, even though now they were pretty much surrounded by woodland.

'I just find it interesting, that's all. Did I annoy you?'

Now she felt bad. 'You didn't annoy me. I just don't talk about other people's private business, that's all.'

Laura mumbled something that Lindsey couldn't make out and then she slowed down so that Lindsey would go ahead of her once again. There was something about the girl that made Lindsey worry. She seemed almost aggressive in her questioning, angry almost, but was clearly putting on a show of being merely inquisitive and Lindsey found herself wondering if her seemingly perfect family was really all that wonderful. And if so, then why did this girl seem like one of the loneliest people she'd ever met?

By the time they got back to the Centre, Lindsey was feeling tiredness in her bones. The past few weeks were catching up with her and she could feel herself becoming lethargic. The Anglesea Street group had just arrived back ahead of them and they were buzzing over the accident training scene.

'Hey, Jamie?' Lindsey called him as soon as she spotted him. They'd all been tasked with tidying up the downstairs section of the Centre before going home and despite how she felt physically, she'd been dying to find out how he got on.

When he turned around, she could tell by his face that he loved it. 'Well… how'd it go?'

'You should have seen it!' his eyes were wide with excitement. 'At first, no one knew what was happening, just that the Gardaí were called because there was a car crash. Then they put us all into the Paddy Wagon and when we got there, there was one car upside down and there was a man, covered in blood, staggering all over the place.' He had actions to go with his story now and Lindsey couldn't help smiling. 'Then there was another woman and she was dead in the middle of the road. She came right out through the windscreen. Then Garda Murray did...' he shook his head, trying to remember every detail, '... she stuck a machine in the fella who was covered in blood and it turned out that he was drunk! He was a drunk driver and he crashed into the other woman and she died. Then when the ambulance came and took her away and all that, they put the drunk fella into the Paddy Wagon with us! He was shouting and roaring and trying to beat everyone up, so Garda Murray had to restrain him, but he kept singing and shouting the whole way back to the station.' The delight was oozing from his pores. 'But then...' he held his finger in the air. 'It turned out that he was a Garda too. He was undercover, because it wasn't real at all! None of it was! It was all just training.'

Lindsey was smiling the whole way through his enthusiastic telling of the day's events. She was excited for him. 'And the scary thing is that kind of thing happens a lot,' Lindsey added, as she helped him to stack the benches. 'What would you do if you were a Garda who was called to something like that for real?'

'They said the first thing you do is check scene safety, so I'd do that first. See, you have to make sure that you're not going to get injured or anything and that other cars aren't going to crash into everything and make it even worse.'

Lindsey nodded. 'Good thinking. You know, you'd make a great Garda.'

He smiled shyly. 'Adam said that too.'

'He's cleverer than he looks, with his wonky old nose,' Lindsey nudged him with a smile.

'Is he your boyfriend or something?'

'He's my friend. We've known each other for years.'

'Since you were soldiers?'

She nodded.

'When I was small, my mam used to tell me that my dad was a soldier who had to go off to war. I used to think that he must've been kinda cool. Like Adam.'

'You know she would have said that because she wanted to protect you?'

'She said it because she knew that my real dad is nothing like that. She must've known that he wouldn't want me.'

They lifted a bench between them and stacked it on top of another. 'I think when your mam died, Jamie, it shocked everyone; your dad included.'

'She should have told him about me before she...' his voice trailed off.

'And I'm sure if she had her time again, she would have. But Jamie, she didn't know that she was going to get sick. How could she? She didn't tell either of you because as far as she was concerned, she'd always be there to look after you. Maybe she planned to tell you when you were older,' she shrugged. 'She adored you, you know that?' she gave him a small smile, even though he hadn't looked at her since bringing up this conversation. She never knew Jamie's mother, but apparently she was a hard working single mother to a son who she loved. Jamie's problems only started after she died.

He shrugged one shoulder and started throwing loose odds and ends into a storage box. 'She'd give *him* a toe in the hole if she saw him now,' he half smiled, talking of course about his dad.

'Maybe she would.'

'Oh no; she definitely would. She used always say that; Jamie, if you don't finish your homework, you'll get a toe in the hole, or, One more stale loaf off that bread man and his next payment will be a toe in the hole,' he laughed quietly. 'She always used to say, Toe in the hole.'

She'd never heard him talking about his mother before. 'She sounds like my kinda woman,' Lindsey smiled. 'You know she'd be extremely proud of you.'

'How do you know that?' he mumbled.

'Because you're one of the nicest bo... young men I've ever met.

142

You're intelligent and kind... but of course she would have known that already. And you're gonna be one hell of a Garda, if that's what you decide to do.'

'That is what I'm going to do.'

'See? That's what I mean. A lot of people in your position would let the negative things in their lives define who they are. You're the opposite. You're going to use them to make you stronger. So Jamie, you must know how proud your mother would be. I'm proud,' she smiled.

There were tears in his eyes, but he wiped them away.

'Hey, you're lucky you were at Anglesea Street today and not with us,' she whispered conspiratorially, to try to ease his sadness. 'We spent all day with a group of... kinda old people, walking very slowly up a mountain.'

Finally he laughed.

'Garda Murray said that I could go again next week with the other group, if it's OK with everyone here?'

'Course it is. Come on, you have done enough work here,' she threw her arm around his shoulder and for the first time, he didn't shrug her off. They headed for the door to wait for his dad.

'Where's Frank?'

'He's probably in a bacon induced coma upstairs. He spent the day with Sheila.'

Jamie laughed again.

By now, Lindsey felt like she was walking around under water but never the less, it was at times like this, seeing a kid getting so much out of their day, that Lindsey really loved her job.

CHAPTER ELEVEN

By the time she got home, Lindsey's mind and body were exhausted. Her limbs felt weak and when she sat down, her legs immediately started to tingle, before going into full blown pins and needles. Her head felt like it was in a fog and she had a pain starting at the back of her eyeballs. It had been weeks since she'd had a full night's sleep and she felt in desperate need of one tonight, in spite of what that much needed sleep might bring with it.

She went to the cupboard and rooted around until she found a box of herbal sleeping pills, which apparently were aimed at insomniacs. She bought them after coming off the benzodiazepines. They'd never worked for her in the past, but she was willing to try anything tonight. The box said to take two with water, so she poured six into her hand and took them with half a bottle of wine and went to bed.

As predicted, she lay there looking at the ceiling for at least an hour, before finally her eyes started to get heavy and her mind began to shut down.

It was the cold that eventually brought her round. Her legs were freezing and her feet… there were sharp things sticking into the soles of both of them. But it was the gust of wind and the noise, both coming from a fast moving vehicle that finally prompted her to open her eyes and her heart immediately started to pound in her chest.

Another car flew past just inches from where she stood on the hard shoulder, on the side of a main road. She dropped to the ground, certain that she was having a heart attack. Her chest felt like it was in a vice and she couldn't catch her breath. She couldn't catch her bearings either. It was pitch dark and she was wearing nothing but the black T-shirt and knickers she went to bed in. By the time the next car passed moments later, she was hyperventilating. The glow of red lights lit her up as the car slowed and eventually pulled in up the road from where she was crumpled in a heap. She didn't know whether anyone got out of the car or not, she was too busy trying to get any air at all to pass through her lungs. The red lights started to fade and the darkness that already surrounded her became pitch black.

The next time she opened her eyes, she threw up immediately. It was nothing more than green bile and the sight of it made her feel worse. There was a kidney shaped dish under her chin and a gloved hand turning her head. There was also something stuck to her forehead. She was strapped down but felt that if she wasn't, then she'd be on the floor instead of whatever it was that she was actually lying on, because they seemed to be moving fast. As soon as she stopped getting sick, an oxygen mask was moved from her forehead, back to her mouth, which she immediately tried to claw off. She didn't like the confinement of it, but the gloved hand struggled with her for a moment and then it won.

There was a harsh white light overhead and a paramedic was speaking to her; asking her name, where she lived, if she knew what happened. But at this moment in time, she couldn't answer any of his questions.

'Never mind the siren...' he continued in a relaxed, conversational tone, '... that's nothing to worry about. We just put that on so that you don't have to stay lying there for too long. I'd say you're feeling a bit of motion sickness, yeah? That's normal enough. Most people riding in the back of one of these things will feel the same, myself included sometimes.' He had a calm smile on his face, like he was talking to a friend. She'd never suffered from motion sickness before and yet she instinctively knew that if she could just get up and walk around, she'd feel better, because he was right; she was feeling horrendous. But she couldn't get up and it was almost ten more minutes before they veered sharply to the right, around a bend and then slowed down dramatically.

'You're gonna be alright, girl,' the paramedic, who'd been talking to her nonstop, assured her, as they came to a stop and the back door of the ambulance opened, letting in a cold but welcome gust of fresh air.

Another paramedic appeared and the pair of them slid her out on the gurney and proceeded to roll her through the emergency entrance of the Cork University Hospital.

'It could be mayhem in here now, love, but don't worry, we'll be with ya,' the second paramedic said with the same, friendly smile, though he didn't look like he expected a response. 'Good to see you're awake. You were out for the count there for a minute.' He chuckled a bit, but when he looked at his colleague, the kindness in his eyes was replaced with concern.

Once inside, the one who was with her in the back immediately started issuing statements of fact to someone else, presumably a doctor.

'We have a lady here, name unknown, found by a passing motorist along the Commons Road. No ID on her. She was in a state of undress when she was found and is non-communicative. The guy who found her said that she seemed to be hyperventilating and she was semi-conscious when we got there. Heart rate 120, BP 140 over 90. Severe scaring around the chest and right shoulder and one scar on the right temple, none look recent. No other visible injuries...'

He continued his handover of her, but the words, *lady, name unknown*, jolted her. 'Lindsey...' she pulled the mask off her face, 'My name is Lindsey,' she barely recognised her own voice. She sounded as panicked as she felt. Her chest was still tight, but breathing was coming a little easier now.

The two paramedics smiled at her. One, the driver, patted her shoulder with a smile, while the other one said, 'Well, Lindsey, it's lovely to meet you. I'm Jason and that's Jack.'

They signed some paperwork, while a nurse stuck a blood pressure machine on her arm and she was somehow transferred off the gurney and onto a hospital trolley. The paramedics' radio crackled to life and they looked like they were about to leave.

'Thank you,' Lindsey found her voice again. She had no idea what had happened to her but she did know that these men possibly saved her.

'Our pleasure,' Jason replied. 'You mind yourself, OK?'

'Lindsey, what can you tell me about all this?' asked a very tired looking doctor. Her name tag said Dr Elaine Cronin.

Lindsey shook her head, 'I don't know.'

'Has anything like this happened before?'

'No. I went to bed and woke up on the side of the road.'

Elaine Cronin rolled her trolley into a bay and pulled a curtain around her.

'Did you take anything before you went to bed?'

'Herbal sleeping pills and some wine.'

'Herbal?'

'From the health shop.'

'I don't suppose you brought the box with you?'

'I didn't bring my pants with me,' Lindsey answered, without a hint of humour in her sarcastic response and it seemed the doc was ready to move on from her stupid question.

'Was anyone with you?'

Lindsey sat up straight. 'My dog. Frank. I have to call someone. He would have come with me... did anyone find him?'

'OK, calm down Lindsey. Who can we call?'

'Adam Street... his number would be under Street's Boxing Gym.' Street was the last person she wanted to see her like this, but she had to know that Frank was alright. He would never have let her leave... whatever way she left.

Elaine wrote down the details and called an orderly. 'Can you find this number please? You're looking for Adam Street.'

'Just tell him he needs to check on Frank,' Lindsey called to the man, who was looking at her like he wanted to kill her. She was just another pain in the ass, adding to his workload, no doubt. 'He doesn't need to come here.'

The man disappeared and Elaine closed the curtain again.

'What's the last thing you remember?'

'Going to bed.'

'Where was that?'

'At my house. It's near the Commons Road.'

'How far is that from where you were found?'

'Where was I found?'

She checked the document in her hand. 'Just beyond the petrol station, on the opposite side of the road.'

'Not that far then. Maybe half a mile.'

'It is quite far when you don't know how you got there. Tell me about the scarring, Lindsey? May I?' She indicated Lindsey's T-shirt, which had been cut from the neck to her sternum, by scissors.

Lindsey nodded and Elaine pulled back the material. 'That's old. Nothing to do with... this.'

'It's quite severe. Did someone do that to you?' she was still examining the scars, but she glanced up to meet Lindsey's eyes.

'It was caused by an IED in Syria.'

She stood up straight and studied her for a second. 'And you still maintain that had nothing to do with this? Either way, my admiration for you just notched up quite a lot.'

Lindsey didn't reply.

'How do you sleep?'

'I don't.'

'PTSD?'

She nodded.

'What do you take?'

'Nothing, and I won't be starting. I tried all that, but it really didn't help. I've been fine... it's just resurfaced in the past few months.'

'I got a hold of Adam Street,' the orderly stuck his head around the curtain again. 'He said to tell you he'd sort the dog out and he'd be here as soon as he could.'

'He doesn't need to come here,' Lindsey reiterated her earlier request.

'And I'm not a secretary,' the man said and closed the curtain between them. A few seconds later, he popped his head around the curtain again. 'Sorry... I did mention that you had said that, but I don't think he was listening.'

Elaine gave the man a tired smile, as he left again. 'Long hours I'm afraid. They can get the better of people.'

Lindsey flopped her head back onto the hard, flat pillow.

'I'm gonna order a few tests, Lindsey, but if I had to hazard a guess; we might be talking about an episode of sleep walking.'

Lindsey shook her head. 'I don't sleep walk.'

'It happens. It can be a symptom of PTSD, along with panic attacks, which I believe may also have occurred tonight.'

'I know the symptoms. I've had most of them at some stage. But sleep walking? Out of my house and a half mile up the main road?'

'It's more common for sleep walkers to just wander around their immediate vicinity, but believe it or not, this does actually happen.'

'Not to me.'

Elaine nodded. 'And it might never happen again, Lindsey. Look, I'm gonna get these tests ordered and we'll have a better idea, OK? You might as well get comfy, you could be here for a while.' She smiled sympathetically but Lindsey officially reached her *sympathy* limit for the night.

She sat up and threw back the blanket that was covering her bare legs. 'Thanks Dr Cronin, you're right. That's exactly what happened. There's no need for tests and all that, I just need to go home.'

'Lindsey...' Elaine put her hand on Lindsey's arm. 'I get it. This is shitty and you do not want to be here. But please, give me a couple of hours of your time. I'll rush everything through as best I can. By then your friend will be here and we'll get you home as soon as we possibly can. Let's just do this, yeah? Plus...' she smiled, 'you can't very well go home in your drawers, can you?'

'Elaine, you might not get this, but I need to know that my dog's OK. If that means running home in my drawers, then that's what I'll do. That'd be nothing, considering the fact that he'd go through fire for me.'

'Is he a service dog?'

'The best there is.'

'I do get it. But you clearly trust Adam Street and he said he'd deal with it. Wait until he gets here and then if you still say you want to go, I can't stop you.'

Lindsey looked to the ceiling and blew out a breath.

'OK?'

'OK,' she conceded finally.

'What happened?' Street came barging into her cubicle half an hour later.

'Is he OK?' Lindsey bolted up straight.

'He's in foul humour, but he's fine. He was locked in the bathroom. Lindsey, what the fuck happened? They wouldn't tell me anything.'

'Nothing. I went sleep walking apparently.'

He looked at her sceptically. 'Sleep walking? Fuck off, what really happened? Are you alright?'

She nodded. 'Seriously; sleep walking.'

'And what, you walked into a wall? How'd you end up here?'

She rolled her eyes, mortified. 'Not quite. I was half way to Limerick before someone found me.'

He just sat there on the edge of her trolley, staring at her; clearly unsure whether she was serious and his face, along with the knowledge that Frank was safe, were enough to make her laugh quietly, despite what had happened.

'Are you being serious?'

'Unfortunately, yes.'

'You walked up the main road in your sleep?'

'And in my knickers.'

That was when he seemed to notice her cut up T-shirt. 'Holy fuck, Linds.'

'I know. But I'm fine. And I've had enough hanging around here. Can you find some sort of a gown or...' she pulled back her blanket, '...something. I'm going home.'

'Wait, just...'

'Street, I don't need to be here. I know what happened. I took something to help me sleep and had some wine, so that whatever went on in my head, and even Frank, wasn't enough to wake me. So I walked. It won't happen again, but I don't need to be here, getting poked and prodded. There's nothing wrong with me, aside from the obvious.'

'Fine,' he got up. 'Give me a minute.'

He was gone nearly ten minutes before he finally returned with a set of faded orange scrubs. 'Turns out, they don't just leave these things hanging around.'

She took them and put them on. 'Come on.'

They left the hospital with no one challenging them. But then the Cork University Hospital was mayhem, just as the paramedic said it would be. Like any other public hospital, there were too many patients and not enough staff. As far as Lindsey was concerned, she was doing them a favour.

It was mid morning by the time they got back to Lindsey's house, and riding on the back of a Harley in a pair of light scrubs almost left her frozen to death. Still, she was glad to be home and as soon as she opened the front door, she was almost floored again by Frank, who was beside himself. He pounced, so that his front paws were on her shoulders and he whined and licked every inch of her face.

'I'm sorry, buddy,' she lowered him down gently and kissed him. 'I can't believe I locked him in the bathroom,' she mumbled to Street. 'How can I not remember that?'

There was no answer. It seemed this was new to all of them.

'I need to call work.'

'I did that.'

'Thanks, but… I'm fucking up this new job, big time. I've been missing more than I'm there these days.'

'And before that, you never missed a day. In fact you've worked more free overtime than anyone I know.'

'How would you…'

'Please stop asking me how I know things. I know, OK,' he smiled.

'I'm gonna call Mike anyway,' she started to look for her phone but had no idea where it was. 'Shit.'

'What?'

'I don't know where my phone is. Can I use yours?'

He pulled out his phone and scrolled through his call log until he came to the number that he wanted, which he'd clearly gotten from somewhere other than Lindsey. He handed the phone to her.

'Why does it say *Mike the wanker*?' she looked from the phone to Street.

He shrugged.

She rolled her eyes and hit the call button. 'Mike, it's me.'

'Hey, you OK? I'm on my way to the hospital.'

'Why, what happened?'

'Eh… you're there.'

'Oh… no need, Mike. I left.'

'Lindsey, for fuck sake…'

'Don't you start. I have Street here acting like my mammy already. I don't need another one.'

'Street's there? He brought you home?'

'Yeah. Look, Mike, I'm really sorry about all this missed time.'

'Forget about that, Linds. Look, you're one of the best we've had here for a long time and we need you in one piece, so please, take whatever time you need. Can I come see you some time?'

'Sure… if you want, but I'll be back in a day or two, OK?'

'Like I said, there's no rush. Take care of yourself, alright?'

'Thanks. See ya, Mike.'

'He has a serious hard on for you.' Street shook his head as she hung up. He was headed for the kitchen to put on the kettle.

That's when Lindsey looked around for the first time. 'Street?'

'Yeah?'

'Did you move my hurley?' It was gone from its usual corner.

'Why would I do that?' he turned around while the kettle began to boil.

She got up and walked to the kitchen. Her second hurley was gone too. The iron bar was still in the bathroom, but then Frank was locked in there with it, but the baseball bat was gone from her bedroom and that wasn't all. Her room was a tip. Her clothes were all out of the wardrobe on the floor and some of them had been cut up.

Street caught up with her in the bedroom. 'What is it?'

'Were you in here earlier?'

'No. When I arrived Frank was going berserk in the bathroom. I just let him out, fed him and hauled ass to the hospital.' He looked around at the mess, and at first he didn't seem to think that there was anything un-usual about it. But then he hadn't spent enough time in Lindsey's bedroom to know how she normally kept it. It wasn't until he picked up one of her T-shirts and saw that it had been cut to ribbons that he thought to ask the question; 'Did you do this?'

Lindsey shook her head, but she honestly couldn't answer the question. 'I don't know. Why would I do this?'

Street was rummaging through the room now, checking clothes, checking the wardrobe, checking everything. Then he left and moved onto the other rooms.

'But I locked Frank in the bathroom. I left the house and walked up the main road and I don't remember any of that either. Maybe I did...' she sat on the edge of the bed feeling more confused than she ever had. Somewhere in her gut, she knew that she wouldn't have done this. But how could she possibly trust her gut at this stage?

CHAPTER TWELVE

'Street, watch Frank,' Lindsey headed for the door with her car keys in her hand.

'Where you going?'

'I'll be right back.'

She drove the short distance to Blackpool shopping centre and into the first of three sports shops in the area. But they had no bats and the only hurleys they sold were the new ones that were made for kids. They were softer to ensure that they wouldn't do damage if they connected with each other's heads. In other words, they were of no use to her. The second sports shop was similar. They had no hurleys, only bats made of foam. No good. She crossed the junction and jogged into one last sports shop. They had golf clubs. She picked up four drivers and made her way to the till. She didn't like the idea of golf clubs because they were too long and the only area that could do damage was too small. But they'd do until she could get her hands on something more suitable.

'Miss, you know you have four drivers here?' the sales assistant, who looked like a golfer and a dickhead, asked her with the most patronising smile she'd seen in a long time. 'Here, let me take three of these back and we can talk about what else you need,' he put his hand on three of her drivers with the aim of relieving her of them.

She grabbed him by the wrist with her free hand. 'If I wanted your advice, I would have asked for it. Now kindly take your God damn hand off my drivers,' she shook his hand away and had she been in a better mood, she would have laughed at his expression. But she wasn't in a better mood, so she turned her back on him and continued on her way to the till.

While she stood in the small queue, she considered ignoring the dickhead, as he surrounded himself with two more sales assistants, who joined him in throwing daggers in her direction. But she didn't ignore them. Instead, she turned and stared at all three of them until they became uncomfortable enough to break up their mother's meeting and wait for her to leave before continuing their conversation about her.

Ten minutes later, she was back home, placing the clubs where their predecessors once stood.

'Ah, you're taking up golf?' Street asked with a half smile.

'You can't get a bloody hurley for love nor money in this town.'

'Linds, forget the clubs. Forget the hurley. Come stay with me. I don't like this shit.'

'I'm not leaving my house.'

'Don't be stupid.'

'I'm stupid?' she stared at him, incredulous and could feel her temper finally getting the better of her. '*I'm* stupid?'

'Calm down, that's not what I meant. Look, I called Sinéad.'

'Jesus, Street,' she turned on him. 'This is the most humiliating thing that's ever happened to me and now you want to tell the whole fucking world about it?'

'No one's telling the world, woman, you're telling the bloody cops. Linds, you have someone who clearly wants to mess with you. You come home and your house is fucked up, outside first and now inside...'

'I probably did it myself,' she shouted at him.

'But you mightn't have,' he shouted back.

She let out a frustrated roar before turning on him again. 'Street you need to go.'

'Lindsey, I'm not...'

'Go home, Adam.'

'No. Someone was in your God damn house!' His loud and angry tone matched hers perfectly now.

'Get out.' She physically shoved him towards the door.

He looked at her for a long minute and then he turned and left without another word and she slammed the door shut behind him. When she was finally alone and the house fell silent, she roared as loud as she could for as long as she could and then she dropped to the floor and cried.

The knocking on the door was persistent and showed no signs of letting up, so she finally got up off the floor and opened it.

'Jesus…' Sinéad looked her up and down, and Lindsey immediately knew that she looked a state. It was written all over Sinéad's face. 'Are you alright?'

Lindsey stepped back and gestured for her to come in. She was followed immediately by another Garda who looked to be in his fifties.

'Lindsey, this is Jim Duggan.'

Jim Duggan. The one who helped Street get his gym up and running. She greeted him with a nod, which she had to force. She didn't want them in her house. She didn't want anyone in her house. She wanted them all to leave her the fuck alone. But she had to at least try to behave like a normal, rational human being. It was the only way that she stood a chance of getting rid of them.

'Street called us…' Sinéad was looking around. 'Is he still here?'

'No.'

'You mind if we have a look around?'

Lindsey gestured with her two hands and what was probably a bitchy look on her face, then she went and sat down.

Jim headed towards the bedroom while Sinéad sat on the couch, facing Lindsey.

Lindsey held her hand up before she had a chance to speak. 'Sinéad, if you want to look around, then do. Knock yourself out. But I'm not in the mood for a friendly chat just now, OK? So please… just do your job and then you can both go.'

Sinéad got to her feet and walked slowly to the kitchen, looking at everything. 'Your hurleys aren't here?'

'No.'

'Are these new?' she picked up the driver from the kitchen.

'Yip.'

'What do you intend to do with them?'

'Same thing I intended to do with the hurleys; play sport.'

Sinéad put down the club and continued to look around. 'So you don't remember anything from last night?'

'If you spoke to Street, then you know as much as I do.'

'Do you think there was someone in your house?'

'Like I said, you know as much as I do.'

Jim came back out of the bedroom. 'Is this your knife?' using something that looked like a large pair of pliers, but probably had a more technical name, he held up a jagged kitchen knife.

Lindsey looked carefully at it. 'Yes, it's mine.'

'Did you bring it into your room?'

She rolled her eyes and got to her feet. 'Look, I don't know, OK? You're completely wasting your time here, because there's every chance that, yes, I did bring that knife into my room and cut up my clothes. I don't know what the fuck I did last night, but clearly I did quite a lot,' she brought her hands to her head. 'Can you please leave?'

'Lindsey, you need to make a statement.'

'And say what? I went to sleep last night and woke up on the side of the Commons Road. For some reason I locked my dog in the bathroom, my house is trashed and some of my things are missing. Yes, that would be an informative statement, wouldn't it? Look, I didn't ask you to come and I don't want to make a statement. Would you mind leaving... please?'

'I'm gonna take this, if that's alright?' Jim placed the knife in a zip lock plastic bag that he seemed to have brought with him. He then sealed the top. 'I photographed the room,' he said quietly to Sinéad, and she nodded in response.

'Fine, take what you want, but I really want you to go... please?' She opened the front door and held it there for them.

Sinéad stood looking at her for a minute, as did Jim. He looked like he wanted to say something, but decided against it.

'OK, Lindsey. But we're on for the night, so call us any time. Please,' she squeezed Lindsey's arm before they both finally left.

Once they stepped outside, she shoved the door closed and returned to her armchair, where she sat for the next four hours, staring at the window. People walked past outside, but she didn't notice any of them. She was too caught up in the fact that her once strong mind was letting her down badly. It was failing her on a level that she couldn't understand. She wasn't the kind of person who had no control over her own actions. She was the complete opposite and she knew for a fact that she could cope with just about anything; the vivid memories, the scars, the nightmares, the seclusion that they'd all led her to. That was her life now and that was fine. But this; this was something that she couldn't take. If she couldn't trust herself, then what was the point?

As the street lights came on outside, she realised she'd been sitting in the dark for some time. Not that she cared, but she was tired of it. She was tired of the internal battle that she'd been having with herself all day and most of last night. She'd had enough. She'd had enough of all of it.

She got to her feet and went to her room, where she pulled a small backpack out from under the bed. She brought it back to the kitchen and began filling it with enough of Frank's food, joint health supplements and treats to last at least a week. She then fitted his brace and his leash and led him out of the house. He could sense that something wasn't right, or maybe that he was about to go somewhere he wouldn't be happy with, because he strained against her. Usually, he was the one pulling her out the door, but tonight it was the other way around.

They walked to the next house and only when she opened the front gate did Frank perk up. He trotted up the path ahead of her and when they got to the front door, Lindsey paused before knocking. She got down on one knee and caught Frank's head in her hands.

'You be a good boy, you hear me?' She kissed him numerous times and hugged him tightly. 'I love you, OK.'

After a long moment, she eased her grip and smiled at him, and as she got to her feet again, Frank started to cry. She did her best to ignore the sound, as she finally brought herself to knock on the door. It took a while to get an answer, like it always did, but she waited patiently. Eventually, shuffling footsteps made their way towards the door and it opened. Mr Hennessey was already in his pyjamas and dressing gown and looked concerned by the fact that someone was calling after dark.

'Lindsey? Is everything alright?' asked the kindly old man.

'Mr Hennessey, I have to go away for the night... it might stretch to a couple of days. Would you mind taking Frank for me?'

'He's not going with you?'

'Not this time. I won't have a chance to take care of him.'

He paused for a minute with a sudden look of sadness in his eyes. 'And who'll take care of you?'

She held the leash towards him and Mr Hennessey took it. 'There's enough food in here to last a while and I normally crush up the supplements and mix them in. He won't take them otherwise.'

'I know that, love. Frank'll be fine.'

'I appreciate this, Mr Hennessey,' she smiled at him and did her best to block out Frank's whining, as she turned to leave.

'Lindsey?'

She stopped and looked back.

He led Frank into the hall and then stepped back out and closed the door, before walking down the path towards her. 'I might be an old man, love, but I've been around the block more than a few times.' He smiled, with the same sadness in his eyes. 'Don't you ever feel like you have nowhere to turn, you hear me?'

She smiled and his kindness brought a tear to her eyes. 'Thank you. How's Mrs Hennessey?' she finally asked, out of genuine concern and to change the subject. Irene Hennessey was in the clutches of Alzheimer's and this lovely man, Terry, was taking care of her like a true hero.

He shrugged. 'We had a long night last night. She took off out the front door while I was asleep. By the time I realised she was gone, she'd walked all the way to her home place in Blackpool. She was looking for her mother again. Luckily I know that's where she always heads for, but it worried me that I didn't wake up this time.'

It was like another version of her own night and she felt in her heart for both of them. 'You can't be on your guard twenty-four hours a day, Mr Hennessey,' she rubbed his arm. 'She's very lucky to have you.'

He caught her hand in both of his. 'Having the pup here will do her good,' he smiled. 'It'll do us both good,' his smile faded and he wasn't letting go of her hand, until he finally said what he wanted to say. 'Lindsey, even a tired old fart like me can see that you're struggling with something too. Now I'm not going to try to stop you from going wherever it is that you need to go, but I want you to remember that a lot of people rely on you.'

She smiled again. 'Not so much these days.'

'Nonsense,' he said, with the firm edge of the school principal he once was. 'You might think that you live in your own little world sometimes, but I know what you do. You take kids that no one else gives a damn about and you give a damn,' he jabbed his finger adamantly at her. 'Adam's told me all about young Jamie and how he's like a whole new boy because of you. And he's not the only one.'

'How do you know Adam?' she shook her head, confused.

'Oh, he came around here looking for you once… it must be two, three years ago. You weren't there and to be honest, I'd only clapped eyes on you once or twice myself at that stage,' he chuckled quietly. 'I used to think you were a bit of an oddball. You just stomped in and out of your house with your head down. You never looked up and therefore, you never said hello.'

She wondered briefly if he knew she was off her head for most of that time, but he still had a soft smile on his face, so she didn't think so. Being pegged as an oddball was fine by her though. She'd been called worse.

'Anyway, this chap on a beautiful old motorcycle pulled up one day and as he was heading towards your house, I called out to him and told him that I'd just seen you leaving. He looked so disappointed,' he shook his head. 'Then he started asking me all these questions, like how often I saw you and if you seemed alright,' he laughed again. 'Sure, how would I know? At first I thought he was a jilted boyfriend or something. I even told him that if you wanted to see him, then you would and that he should leave you alone.'

She smiled at his protective instinct, especially when it came to someone that he didn't know and considered to be an oddball.

'He came every single day for nearly two weeks, but I don't think he ever once actually knocked on your door. In the end he started knocking on mine instead and over the past couple of years, in drips and drabs, he's told me a lot about himself. And about you.' He had a knowing look in his eyes. 'I think that boy had a lot that he wanted to get off his chest. And who better to tell it all to, than a dothery old man who'd probably forget more than he'd remember?' He smiled, but there was no joy in it.

'You think I'd trust a dothery old man with my dog, Terry?' Lindsey half smiled at him. It was true, but she really wanted to go now.

'Lindsey, he told me about Syria. About what you did there.'

She gently pulled her hand away from him.

'You almost lost your life trying to save the life of a child,' the sadness was back in his eyes and his smile was long gone.

'I didn't save anyone's life Mr Hennessey. I got someone killed,' she turned and walked towards his gate.

'It was war that killed that brave boy, Lindsey, just like it was war that changed your life. How many people could say that they could do what you did?'

She didn't turn back and he called after her one more time. 'People like you are essential to this world, Lindsey Ryan. Don't you ever forget that. Now we'll be waiting for you to come back and we'll expect you to-morrow.'

She kept walking and didn't turn around. She didn't want him to see her tears and she didn't want to hear Frank's any more either. He wasn't happy, but he would be, regardless of what happened. The two most important things for him were to feel useful and loved. He would be both of those things with Terry and Irene if Lindsey didn't get back for him. This knowledge at least, eased her mind.

She walked past her house and past her car and continued into town, and even though she wasn't rushing or running tonight, the time that it took to get from her house to her destination passed in a blur. It seemed like one minute she was leaving the Hennessey's house and the next she was standing on the corner of Street's laneway. A laneway that she didn't know the real name of and yet she felt as much a part of it now as Stabber was, and as she stood at the corner, looking down the dark, narrow and soulless street, she could see him sitting in his usual doorway.

She pulled back for a second and leaned against the wall. She thought about Frank. He'd be fine. She thought about Street. He'd be better. She thought about the Centre and the kids. She was replaceable. She thought about the person who hated her enough to dedicate so much of their time to following her around. She imagined that it might be someone in Lenny Jones' family or his circle of friends. In a way, she hoped it was, in which case she might finally make them happy. If not, then whoever it was could go fuck themselves.

That was everything. And everything would be fine. For them. Lindsey had no idea what would become of her after tonight, but what she did know was that it had to be better than this. It couldn't possibly be worse.

She rounded the corner again and walked towards Stabber.

'Well, if it isn't my friend, Lindsey,' he grinned. He was high, but not completely out of it. Maybe he was on his way back to earth for a short visit. 'You lookin' for me?'

She stood looking at him for a minute with her hands in her pockets and for the first time, she envied his oblivion.

'See anything you like?' he held his arms out and looked down at himself.

'What can you get me?'

'How much you got?'

She held a hundred euros towards him, but pulled it back when he went to grab it. 'Not until I get something for it.'

He hauled himself to his feet and nodded, with the same grin on his face. 'Wait here.'

He crossed over and in through the opposite door to the abandoned building that Lindsey had no fond memories of. He was gone just a few minutes when he stuck his head around the door again. 'Hey, in here,' he gestured for her to follow him in.

She stood looking at the door for a second, before following him inside, in spite of her gut instinct which was screaming at her not to.

Stabber walked ahead of her, towards the back corner where she'd found him once before. Clearly, that was his corner. When he got there, he stopped and turned towards her.

'Well?'

'Well,' he smiled broadly.

There was a sudden movement behind her, but before she had the chance to turn, someone's forearm was across her throat, squeezing tightly and the cold blade of a knife pressed against her skin.

'Remember me, bitch?'

She recognised the voice of the scummy, brown-toothed individual she'd punched in the windpipe once. He switched the knife to his left hand, which was attached to the arm that was now crushing her own windpipe, and with his right hand, he reached into her pocket and grabbed the notes that she'd stupidly offered to Stabber. He pulled them out and stuffed them into his own pocket.

'You weren't very nice the last time you were here. Let's see if I can return the favour,' his free hand grabbed her tightly between the legs as he pressed himself against her. 'Trust me, bitch...' his breath on the side of her face was foul, '... you don't want what I got.'

Lindsey may have been on a mission to do damage to herself that night, but she was damned if she was going to give this degenerate the satisfaction of doing it for her. Her only hope was to take advantage of the fact that the blade was now farther away from her neck, because he was still concentrating on choking her, so she grabbed the arm that was across her throat and using his body as leverage she brought her knees up quickly

163

to her chest and then planted the soles of her feet into Stabber's gut. The force of the kick sent Stabber backwards against the wall, but it also caused his friend to lose his balance and stumble backwards. He fell and landed on the ground, with Lindsey on top of him.

She wasted no time scrambling away from him, but he grabbed the back of her jeans before she could get very far and yanked her back. She kicked out again and managed to connect with his face. He'd lost the knife in the fall and she pounced on it as soon as she saw it, before he had a chance to recover. She moved much faster than him and managed to straddle him, pinning his arms to the ground and put the sharp tip of the knife against his carotid artery.

'Stop moving or I will fucking kill you,' she spoke though gritted teeth.

He stopped and looked up at her with pure hatred in his eyes.

'Stabber, unless you wanna be next, you'll give me what I asked for within the next ten seconds.' Stabber, despite his name, was a coward. He was a watcher, not a doer, so she wasn't worried about him.

Four tiny bundles, wrapped in clingfilm, landed on the floor beside her. She left them there while she thought for a second about what to do with the problem beneath her.

'I didn't come here for trouble, but am I gonna have trouble with you?' she asked, pressing the blade against his neck.

He shook his head.

'We don't know each other very well, but here's something that you need to know about me.' Her voice was low and menacing, just like she felt. 'I have almost as little to lose as you do. Do you understand what I'm saying?' she pressed the knife a little harder.

He nodded.

'So know that *if* I decide to show you some undeserved mercy and you were to throw it back in my face…'

'I won't.'

'Why should I believe that? You're a junky. You lie.'

'Because I know now.'

'What do you know?'

'That you're not fucking normal,' he shouted.

She nodded and eased the knife back from his skin. 'Move before I'm gone and we won't have this conversation again.'

It was pure luck that she'd managed to beat this man twice and she had no idea if she'd get away with it a third time. But she was past caring, so she picked up the packages from the ground. It was nowhere near a hundred euros' worth, but it was enough. She got to her feet and walked out. No one followed her.

She left the laneway, headed towards the docks and again walked as far as she could before sitting at the edge with her feet dangling over the evening's high tide. She pulled the packages out of her pocket and held them in her open palm.

Heroin. She had no idea what to do with heroin. She unwrapped one of the packages, which contained a very small amount of brown powder. She brought it closer to her face so that she could smell it and she let it hover there for some time, while she tried to bring herself to snort it. It smelled like a nasty tasting multi-vitamin tablet. She closed her fist around it again and stared into the water. Heroin wouldn't just turn her into someone who was pleasantly oblivious to the world. Heroin would turn her into its degenerate slave, like Stabber and his brown-toothed friend.

She held still for about ten minutes, before finally roaring at the top of her lungs and firing three of the little bundles of oblivion as far as she could, into the deep black river stretched out before her. She still had one clutched in her other hand, but she knew almost for sure that she couldn't do it. And there was no point in considering the high tide again, because she couldn't bring herself to do that either. She was happy to think of Stabber as a coward, but she was just as cowardly as he was, if not more.

'You're not gonna jump, are ya?' came a loud and brash voice from behind her. It intermingled with the click clack of well-worn high heels.

Lindsey turned her head to see a woman, who was clearly a prostitute, hovering well back from her, near the shelter of the quay wall. Despite being at least fifty years old and several stone overweight, she was pouring out of her undersized, black stretchy outfit. Even the tops of her feet bulged over her black, pointy toed shoes, which looked painful and uncomfortable. Lindsey guessed that she'd just disembarked from the fishing trawler that was docked further along the quay wall.

'Not now, girl, OK?'

'It's just that it's bad for business if you go in there. See, I'd have to ring the fire brigade or someone and sure you know the boys in blue will come running then too, and then that's me snookered for the night.'

'Well… you don't have to worry about business. Not on my account,' Lindsey was looking straight ahead of her now, while the woman kept her distance behind her.

'I hate the water meself. That's why I'm standing back here. Come back and keep me company for a bit.'

Lindsey didn't answer. She wished she'd just go away.

'Did you take it?'

Lindsey looked back at the woman, who pointed at the wrapping on the ground beside her.

Lindsey shook her head. Of all the places in Cork that she could have picked to have this particular melt down, she thought that here at least would be a safe bet for some peace and privacy. It seemed she was wrong. Again.

'Good for you. It's no good that stuff. Two of my boys are lost to it.'

Lindsey rolled her eyes and hauled herself to her feet. She felt old all of a sudden.

'That's the girl,' the woman stepped forward and caught Lindsey by the wrist and took a few steps backwards, leading her away from the edge. 'You feel it, don't you?'

'What?' Lindsey didn't need to be led by this woman, but neither did she particularly mind all of a sudden. She was a distraction now. A much needed one. They didn't come to a stop until they were near the wall, under a street light, as far back from the water as they could go for now.

'You know? Like you're in a deep dark hole and no one knows you're there. You feel that.'

Lindsey looked at her now and for the first time, she was focused enough to see the make-up gathered in the wrinkles around the woman's eyes and mouth. The smudged and faded red lipstick, some of which had attached itself to her yellowing teeth. It was the face of a woman who'd had a hard life, but still had the time to talk someone down.

'I've been in that hole too. In fact…' she turned towards the trawler with a half smile, 'I've just come from it.'

Lindsey looked passed her at the fishing boat. It looked filthy; like the last place on earth she'd like to find herself.

'Era would you listen to me?' she snorted. 'They're not that bad. Generally, the fishermen are decent enough chaps. But by fuck, do they smell,' she laughed a deep, throaty laugh that reminded Lindsey of Sheila.

'But there was a time when I did all this…' she gestured again to the boat, '… and still couldn't afford to eat. Every penny I hard fucking earned, pardon the pun, went into the veins of one, or both, of my sons. They robbed me fucking blind. They didn't care that I was in this game for them,' she was becoming more venomous now. 'Michael and Christopher; my first and second born boys. I needed to feed them and keep a roof over them when I was left on my own. I have eight children now and three more in the grave, and those two…' her voice was beginning to shake, but she wasn't about to cry. Lindsey could tell that she wasn't the type of woman who'd let anyone see that. She shook her head and finally cracked an unconvincing smile. 'Christ, listen to me. If you weren't about to jump earlier, you will now.'

Lindsey leaned against the dock wall, while the other woman took out a box of John Players and lit one up.

'What's your name?'

'Depends whose asking,' the woman grinned. 'If you have a few bob and an easy going taste, then I'm Roxanne.'

'And if I have no money and a very specific taste?' Lindsey returned a small smile.

'Then I'm Kathleen.'

Lindsey held out her hand, which the woman looked at for a second, like she was trying to figure it out. 'I'm Lindsey.'

Finally she shook it and smiled again with the cigarette hanging from her lips. 'Don't worry, I'm not gonna ask what landed a nice looking girl like you here, but...'

'My friend got shot in the head in Syria while I was lying, useless on the ground, beside a child that had been blown to pieces. I could have stopped it all, but my brain didn't engage fast enough,' she forcefully tapped the side of her head. 'Now every time I close my eyes, the pair of them are right there,' she held her palm less than an inch from her nose. 'But that's not enough. Someone in this city hates me so much, that they follow me around and photograph me and threaten me, but they won't fucking act, however much I want them to. I'm losing my mind to the point where I don't know what's real and what's not any more and I just bought heroin from two guys, one of whom has tried to... I don't know, attack? Rape? Rob? Kill? Who the fuck knows, but he tried it twice and I let him. And now here I am... talking to you.'

She looked at Kathleen who still had a cigarette hanging from her mouth, but she looked about as shocked as Lindsey felt.

'Sorry...' Lindsey shook her head. 'I don't know where that came from.'

Kathleen finally inhaled deeply on her Johnny Blue and removed it from her mouth. 'Christ girl, no wonder you're looking for an easy way out.'

'Nothing easy about it,' she mumbled in reply.

Catching Lindsey completely off guard, Kathleen grabbed her and hugged her tightly. She smelled of cheap flowery perfume, a hint of body odour, cigarettes and fish, with each scent battling to overpower the other.

'I'm not a natural hugger, love, but by fuck, you could do with one,' she pulled back and smiled. 'But you could also do with a kick in the hole.'

Lindsey tilted her head in question, but couldn't help smiling at the woman's quick turnaround. She preferred it to the hug.

'You're telling me that you survived them fucking lunatics with the tea towels on their heads, but you were willing to give in to a bag of that bastard powder! If I didn't have my good shoes on, I'd bury one in your arse.'

Lindsey glanced down at the pointy toe of her shoe, which was peeling away from the sole. 'Well, thank Christ you wore your good shoes,' she smiled.

'Exactly. Now come and join me for a nice, stiff drink. I think we could both do with one.'

Lindsey reached in her Converse and pulled out another hundred euro. She had no idea how much she'd need for Stabber, so she brought more than enough. 'I think I'll just head home.'

'You sure? Have you someone to go home to?'

Lindsey caught the woman's hand and pressed the money into her palm. 'Why don't you go home too? I think we've both had enough for one night.'

'Hey, I don't want your money, love.' Kathleen tried her best to give it back, but Lindsey shoved her hands deep into her pockets and refused to take it.

'I brought that money to buy drugs with, so you'd be doing me a favour. Plus, I owe you one, Kathleen and I mean that. Thank you.'

Kathleen closed her chubby fist around the money and smiled and this time Lindsey actually thought she might cry. 'I hope I see you again sometime, Lindsey. Somewhere nicer than this, eh?'

Lindsey nodded and walked away and as she passed the trawler again on her way back to the world, her thoughts were no longer on her own problems. Instead, she thought about Kathleen. A lady who should be at home in a pair of slippers with her feet up, was instead standing on a cold quay wall wearing ill-fitting shoes, waiting for the next man to come along and put her on her back.

She sincerely hoped that, for tonight at least, Kathleen went home.

Lindsey walked past Angel's twenty-four-hour adult store, with her hands still buried in her pockets. From this end of the laneway, she'd get to Street's place before having to pass the abandoned doorway, but if Stabber was in his usual spot, then he would see her. It'd be dangerous and very stupid to go back down that lane. She knew this and yet she wasn't afraid. She felt numb towards the two junkies, but somewhere in the back of her mind she did register the fact that she was one of the most stupid people on the planet to have put herself in that position with them once, let alone twice, and not to mention coming back a third time. But she wasn't there for them now. She was there because she was drained. She was completely wiped out and couldn't face the journey home. She was there because she needed a place to sleep and she needed it now.

His spot was empty as she pulled the key out of her jeans pocket and opened the door to Street's, quietly closing and locking it again behind her. She glanced around the gym and just the sight of the heavy bag sapped even more of her energy, so she headed straight for the stairs and went up quietly. She had no idea what time it was, only that it was late, so she opened his door as quietly as she could and let herself in. She tiptoed towards his room to see if he was awake and immediately wished that she hadn't.

There, lying in Street's bed was the man himself, straddled by an extremely busty, naked blonde, who looked nowhere near his own age bracket despite his alleged new criteria.

'Shit… sorry!' Lindsey blocked her eyes and stretched her palm out in front of her, as if to fend off the image, before turning away quickly.

'Who the fuck is she?' the blonde's high pitched voice sounded annoying to Lindsey's ears and she seemed like she was about to throw a tantrum.

'Lindsey?' Street called after her.

'Lindsey?' the blonde repeated. 'Are you fucking married? Tell me who she is right fucking now.'

Against her will, Lindsey glanced back to see the blonde being landed unceremoniously on the other side of the bed, while Street got up and reached for his jeans on the floor.

'He's not married,' Lindsey called back. 'Sorry!'

'Lindsey, hang on,' Street called after her, but she was already closing the door behind her and taking the stairs to the ground floor, two at a time.

Once she got outside and closed the front door, she leaned against it for a minute with her hands covering her mouth. She didn't know whether to laugh or cry, until she remembered where she was and the fact that she had an enemy out here. More than one it seemed.

She pulled up her hood and took off at a jog as far as the end of the street, where she rejoined the main thoroughfare and slowed down. There were taxis queuing in the rank near the bus station, but she'd given Kathleen the last of her money, so she had no choice but to walk the few miles home, even though her legs felt like lead. She buried her hands deep into her pockets again, put her head down and walked.

It was a part of her running route that took no time at all, but she didn't have the energy to run, so tonight's walk seemed to take an age. She felt like she'd never get there and by the time she got to the Commons Road, her body was shutting down. But her brain already had. She was no longer thinking about Syria. She's wasn't thinking about work, or nightmares, or stalkers. She wasn't even thinking about the woman who talked her back from the edge, or even the fact that she was on the edge in the first place. Even the pornographic image of Street and his new friend was forgotten about and her mind was completely blank. Which was why she didn't notice the footsteps behind her and when she opened her front gate and walked up her path, she didn't notice that those footsteps came so close, that she should have almost heard the person breathing. Had she noticed any of those things, then her own baseball bat might not have connected so forcefully with the side of her head and the footpath might not have connected with similar force with the front of her head. But by that time, her blank mind was completely closed to the world and finally, everything was black.

CHAPTER THIRTEEN

'Lindsey, can you hear me?'

The disembodied voice sounded familiar. Someone's hand was on her head and what felt like a knee, rested against her hip, but she couldn't open her eyes.

'Is she alright?' an upset voice called out from somewhere further away.

Then silence again.

She was rocking gently from side to side now. There were vibrations going through her body and a breeze passing over her skin.

'Lindsey?' asked another familiar and slightly panicked voice. 'What the fuck happened? Is she…'

Silence.

'Lindsey? Can you open your eyes for me?'

This voice was calm, but there were lots of other voices now, all barking orders at each other. Through her closed eyelids, she could still make out the brightness of overhead lights, but just for a second. Then it was dark again.

All the movement had stopped now. No voices. No noise. Just one hand on top of hers. The lights were still bright though and when she finally opened her eyes, they gave her an immediate and violent headache.

'Fu...' her throat was dry and the word wouldn't come out, so she brought her free hand to her head.

'Lindsey?' the other person's hand tightened around hers.

She forced her eyes to stay open and she focused them on Street, who was up out of his chair now, still holding her hand.

'My head,' her voice was strangled.

'Hang on, I'll get someone.' Street disappeared and was back a second later with Dr Elaine Cronin, who immediately forced Lindsey's eyelids apart and shone a bright light into her eyes, almost causing her brain to explode.

'Follow the light for me, Lindsey.'

She did it as best she could. 'My head is pounding,' she managed, but talking hurt.

'You have concussion. Take these, they'll help.' She handed her a tiny plastic cup with two white pills in it and Lindsey was in so much pain that she didn't consider what they were. She just knocked them back.

'What happened?'

'We find ourselves back here again,' Elaine half smiled, as she attached a blood pressure machine to Lindsey's arm. 'Here's what we know; you were found outside your house unconscious with two pretty nasty head wounds. One might have been sustained when you fell, but one we think was caused by a baseball bat that was found beside you.'

'*Your* bat,' Street injected.

'You also sustained quite a beating, Lindsey. You have bruising to the ribs and... well, bruising everywhere actually. Amazingly, nothing was broken, but you'll be feeling pretty awful for a while to come.'

'Was anyone else there?'

Elaine shook her head.

'Did you see anyone?' Street asked.

Lindsey shook her head, remembering how switched off she'd been and cursing herself for it.

Elaine went on to ask Lindsey a series of very basic questions, like what was her name. What day of the week it was, which she had to think about. Who the president was. Where she worked. Who was the man sitting in the chair? It went on for a bit and Elaine seemed happy that Lindsey had answered each one correctly. Finally she finished her poking and prodding and as she handed some stuff to the nurse who'd been standing quietly behind her, she spoke one more time. 'The Gardaí are on the way, Lindsey. They've been waiting to speak to you. I'll be back in a while, OK?' Elaine and the nurse left, closing the door quietly behind her.

'I have a room to myself in the CUH? Things must be bad,' she half joked, but couldn't bring herself to smile, or keep her eyes open. The light was killing her.

'Ah sure, you'd get in anywhere,' Street tried to joke back, but even without looking at him, she could tell that his heart wasn't in it.

'Do something about the light, Adam, will ya?'

He got up and turned it off. There was still enough light flooding in through the glass panel above the door to provide sufficient illumination without causing her head to explode.

'Linds, you nearly gave me a heart attack.'

She opened one eye and looked at him. '*You* nearly gave me a bloody heart attack. That girl with the giant knockers was scary,' she managed a fraction of a smile that time. She felt like shit and had pain emanating from every part of her body. She wanted to be alone, but even she knew that she was probably better off with him here. 'I could do without ever seeing that again.'

Finally he laughed quietly. 'She was kinda scary.'

They were quiet for a few minutes and Lindsey thought that she might throw up, but the feeling passed.

'Linds, I need to tell you something.'

'What?' She was suddenly filled with dread. Street wasn't one to break news gently. He was a rip the band aid off, kind of person.

'It's Frank…'

Lindsey bolted up in the bed and her head spun so violently that she threw up almost immediately. She managed to get most of it into the kidney dish that was resting on her legs.

'Jesus Christ, girl,' Street jumped to his feet and shoved the dish up to her chin. 'Calm fucking down and lie back. He's fine.'

'Jesus…' she covered her head with her hands. 'What about him then?'

'He had a heart attack.'

She went to sit up again, but he held her down by the shoulders. 'Street, let me up. Where is he?' It hurt to speak and she'd never experienced such a headache before. But she had to get to her dog.

'The vet has kept him in for a few days. He *thinks* it was a heart attack. They reckon he was trying so ferociously to get to you that he worked himself into a bit of a frenzy and passed out. He nearly gave the poor Hennesseys heart attacks too.'

'I'm gonna kill the fucker who did this,' she mumbled. Her teeth were gritted and she meant it with all her heart in that moment. 'Tell me the truth, Street. Will be he alright?'

'The vet said he would be. I spoke to him about an hour ago and Frank was eating at that stage. He's also crying constantly, but that's probably because he doesn't know what happened to you.'

'Do they know who it was?' she finally asked. She was crying now; for Frank, not for herself.

'No. Linds, I'm so fucking sorry. If you had just stayed at my place…'

'Ah stop feeling sorry for yourself. It doesn't suit you.' She roughly wiped her eyes and grinned. The last thing she wanted was to add to the amount of guilt that she knew her friend already carried.

He was quiet for a while before speaking again. 'Look, I know you keep saying that it's some kid with a grudge, but if it is… you need to think back through all of them. Who has it in them to do this?'

She shook her head. 'Street, I can barely think of my own name tonight, let alone every kid I've worked with.' This was partly true. But she was no longer in any doubt about who did this.

'You know it's not really *tonight* any more? You were out for nearly eighteen hours.'

'Well… that's the most sleep I've had in years. I feel great,' she mumbled sarcastically.

There was a gentle knock and a vaguely familiar face appeared around the door. 'Hey… sorry, am I interrupting?'

Lindsey attempted to sit up.

'No, no, stay as you are,' he held his hand out to stop her, 'you're concussed.' He had a gentle smile on his face, but it was his easy, conversational tone that reminded her of who he was.

'Jason?' it was the paramedic who'd been in the ambulance with her after her unplanned stroll up the Commons Road.

'We have to stop meeting like this,' he smiled.

'Right, I'll be back in a few minutes. Just gonna grab a cuppa.' Street got to his feet. 'Anyone want one?'

'Just had one, thanks,' Jason smiled.

Street left, without waiting for Lindsey's answer, even though she couldn't imagine eating or drinking anything ever again.

'Don't tell me you rescued me again?' She gave a small smile and was suddenly conscious of how she must look. She brought her hand to her head and used her fingers to do God knows what with her hair, but there were bandages in the way, so she soon gave up.

'You're having a run of bad luck alright.'

His smile was bright and very very handsome and she was slightly taken aback when he came and sat in the chair that Street had just vacated. For the first time in a very long time, she wanted a mirror.

'I swear, I'm not normally like this,' she held her hands up in jest.

He nodded. 'I just wanted to see that you're alright.'

'I am. Thanks, Jason.'

He got to his feet again. 'Maybe we can grab a coffee sometime and you can tell me what you *are* normally like?'

She stared blankly at him for what seemed like an age, while the part of her brain that was still functional, begged her to respond.

'Sorry...' he laughed again, 'your boyfriend probably wouldn't be too impressed with that,' he leaned over and whispered, 'And he doesn't look like the type of bloke I should mess with.'

'Adam's not my boyfriend.' She finally managed to string a few words together. 'And coffee would be good.'

He nodded again with the same lovely smile. 'OK... I'll know where to find you,' he gestured to the room around them.

'Hopefully not for much longer though.'

He was still smiling as he left and Street came back in.

They greeted each other the way men do, with some sort of ritualistic nod and a mutter, but as soon as Jason was out of sight, Street's stupid looking, five-year-old boy grin was plastered across his face.

'What?'

He shrugged and sat down.

'Where's the tea?'

'I have tea coming out my ears,' he smiled broadly again. 'The nurses have been looking after me well.'

'Oh well, I'm glad you were taken care of,' she couldn't help a little laugh that time, even though it hurt her ribs and head to do so. 'Is that where you went, to start rounding up phone numbers?'

'I was outside the door, listening to boy wonder trying his luck.'

'Shag off.'

He raised his eyebrows and nodded. 'That wasn't his first visit. Every time they dropped a patient off, which by the way, was very frequently, he stuck his head in.'

'Why?'

'Because he wants to ask your opinion on global fucking warming; why d'ya think?'

'Shit... what do I look like?'

'Like you were hit by a bus.'

'Balls.'

'So, you're going for coffee?'

'You were actually eavesdropping?'

'Just keepin' an eye on things,' he smiled. 'Hey, he's a big step up from that lump of ham you picked up lately, or some bearded bastard you found on the side of a mountain.'

'Hey... don't knock the bearded chap. He was alright.'

'Grizzly bloody Adams?'

'You can talk. Your last tryst was with a blow up doll who speaks. Loudly.'

He laughed out loud, but it faded away when Sinéad and Jim Duggan came through the door in uniform.

'Hey Lindsey,' Sinéad smiled and looked somewhere between relieved and pissed off. 'Adam.'

Adam nodded.

'Hey,' Lindsey struggled into a semi seated position.

'You feel up to a few questions?'

'Sure.'

'Adam, would you mind giving us a few minutes?' Sinéad asked, and Adam got up and left reluctantly.

Lindsey waited for him to close the door before speaking. She didn't want him to hear what she had to say. 'I know who it was.'

Sinéad and Jim both looked surprised and both pulled out their notebooks.

'Directly across from Street's gym, there's a doorway and a guy called Stabber. He's an addict who's almost always there and no, I don't know his real name. Beside Street's, there's an abandoned building. There's another addict in there whose name I don't know either, but I can describe him. In fact, I could find him for you if you like. It was one or both of them who did this. And they gave my fucking dog a heart attack.' She was getting more furious by the second.

'How do you know them and what makes you think that they did this?' Jim asked. 'And the dog's going to be fine. I asked.'

She nodded her appreciation and then gritted her teeth. 'I go there by night, to Street's gym. I run there. Stabber has always been there, but never acknowledged me until recently. One night I turned up and he was missing. It was the first time that he wasn't there, so I went looking for him; to make sure that he was alright,' she shook her head, getting angry at herself. 'I don't know why I did that. But that's when I met the other guy.'

'What happened when you met him?'

'He pulled a knife.'

'Jesus Christ, Lindsey,' Sinéad shook her head.

'Then what?' Jim continued, as if she'd just told him her favourite colour and Lindsey half wished that Sinéad wasn't there. Her reactions were too personal and that was the last thing she needed.

'I punched him in the throat and left.'

'When was this?'

Sinéad rubbed her forehead.

'A few weeks ago.'

'So why would they wait until now to get their own back?'

'I met them again last night.'

Sinéad got up off the bed and walked around the room.

'In what capacity?'

Lindsey rubbed her pained eyes. She didn't have it in her to make something up. 'Look, Jim, Street mentioned you before. He said that you know...' she rolled her hand around, not wanting to have to say the words. 'Well... you might also know that I have PTSD?'

He nodded solemnly, while Sinéad straightened up. She had her back to them, facing the door but was listening intently.

'OK... so I had a bad night.'

He nodded again. 'What happened?'

'I looked for trouble and I found it.'

He paused for a second before putting away his notebook. Then he looked at Sinéad and waited for her to do the same. 'Alright. But I need you to tell me exactly what happened, OK?'

She shook her head. 'Those two have been in the back of my mind ever since he pulled a knife on me. I've been having a particularly shitty few weeks and...' she shrugged. 'I wanted to do some damage,' she looked

179

at him to gauge his reaction. He was stoic. 'While I was talking to Stabber, the other guy grabbed me from behind, around the throat. He pulled the knife again.'

'What did you do?'

'I fought him and I won. He wasn't happy.'

'Did you go straight home from there?'

She shook her head. 'I went for a walk and then called into Street's for a few minutes. Then I went home. I woke up here.'

'So you left the vicinity and then went back there again?'

'Yes. And yes, I know that was stupid.'

Jim took his notebook out again and Lindsey gave a detailed description of Stabber and his friend and after a while, Sinéad and Jim left and Adam came back in.

'You fucking plank.'

'You shouldn't eavesdrop, Street.'

'What were you thinking?'

'You don't really want me to answer that.'

'Are you *trying* to get yourself killed?'

'Of course not,' a half truth that he saw right through.

'Jesus Christ,' he rubbed his head vigorously.

'Don't worry, whatever urge I had has passed.'

'An urge like that doesn't just pass, Linds.'

'In this case it did.' Which was true, as far as she knew. 'Thanks to a hooker called Roxanne,' she smiled.

He looked at her questioningly.

'Never mind. I'm serious though, it was a moment of madness. The Yanks would call it *rock bottom* or something like it. I just lost it for a minute.'

'How do you know it won't happen again?'

'I know,' she replied adamantly. The fact that someone clearly wanted her dead, or badly hurt, was enough to make her certain that she wasn't about to give them the pleasure. Plus, she'd never quit anything in her life. She wasn't about to start now.

Whatever pills Elaine had given her had well and truly kicked in now and she didn't feel much pain any more. Just a dull ache in her ribs and a slight throbbing in her head.

'Now, on another note; what happened to, *I'm sticking within my own age bracket?*'

He looked at her in silence for a minute, before deciding to give in to the change of topic and then he rolled his eyes. 'I might have gone on a Bender too.'

'Ah,' she nodded.

'You wouldn't mind, but I genuinely wasn't looking. And I was in no way interested in her. There I was, happy out sitting at the bar with my Jack and Coke and up she comes, all hyper,' he laughed quietly. 'She bugged the shit out of me actually. I kept pawning her off and she kept coming back. In the end I was so pissed I just thought… fuck it.'

'So you did,' she smiled.

'Well, I started to. Actually, *she* started to. But then you came along.'

'Yeah, sorry about that.'

'You did me a favour. I'm fairly sure she won't be back.'

'So is it my turn to lecture you now, about picking up nutters when apparently, there's so many nicer candidates out there?'

'Lindsey girl, 'tis slim pickings if you're looking for someone who you can actually stand to be around after their clothes go back on.'

'So you're telling me that you haven't been drooling over Sinéad since you met her.'

'Kind of,' he laughed. 'But you've probably warned her off by now.'

'Nah,' she smiled. 'She's one of the good ones though.'

He nodded. 'Anyway, you worry about your hot date with boy wonder and let me worry about my own love life.'

'Hot date?' she guffawed. 'Although, the man *is* smokin'.'

Street stayed at the hospital again that night and he came and went over the next three days and it was only then, on the third day, that he was able to tell her that Frank was back at the Hennessey's house, which prompted Lindsey to leave them with little other choice but to finally let her go home and even then, she had trouble getting Adam to go home too.

Finally he did, and Lindsey wasted no time getting to the Hennessey's house to collect Frank.

'Well by Christ, am I glad to see you, love.' Mr Hennessey opened the door and was nearly blown out of the way by Frank trying to get past him. 'Come in for a minute. Have a cup of tea?'

Lindsey didn't have the heart to say no after all he'd done for her, taking care of Frank, so she stepped inside, with Frank jumping all over her. 'How's he been since he got back?'

'He's fine, love.'

'Mr Hennessey, I'm so sorry. Are you and Irene alright?'

'We're grand,' he smiled. 'He gave us a bit of a scare alright. It wasn't 'til I was carrying him to the car to get him to the vet that I saw all the guards in your garden and the ambulance outside… and you lying on the ground.' He shook his head. 'What an awful night. Of course then I knew what set him off. He was trying to get to you.'

'I'll never be able to thank you enough. You have no idea how important this dog is to me.'

'Oh, but I do,' he nodded. 'And vice versa. He missed you a lot, as you can see.' He was jumping up on her and clinging on for as long as he could, before sliding down her body and going again.

'He's a bit emotional, our Frank,' she laughed, as she kissed and rubbed and scratched him. 'I missed you too, buddy.'

'Come on love. I'll put on the kettle.'

She followed Mr Hennessey to the kitchen and took a seat at his kitchen table, while he worked on making a pot of tea. Their house was similar enough to Lindsey's at the front, but their kitchen was part of a decent sized extension at the back, so it was bigger than hers and the extension also gave them an extra bedroom. Plus they had the attic converted into a third bedroom, though they didn't need it. Theirs was an elderly person's kitchen out and out. Outdated chipboard cupboards in a yellow plastic wrap, under which multicoloured fruit motif tiles adorned the walls as far as the green counter top. She could smell what was probably yesterday's dinner, from a pot that was still half full and would probably make today's dinner too.

'Where's Irene?'

'She's having a snooze.'

'How is she?'

'She's been good actually. This fella makes all the difference when he's himself. Even when he's not, he always seems to know exactly what she needs.'

'Yeah, he has a gift for that.' Frank's head was resting in her lap and his eyes were closed. She couldn't help smiling at him. 'The best dog in the world,' she mumbled.

'How are you feeling, love?'

'Not too bad actually. But then I was always a bit hard headed.' She smiled and tapped the side of her head. 'I'm glad to be home.'

'Did they catch the dirty rotten bastard who did it?'

'They will.'

He sat down with a freshly brewed pot of tea and poured two cups. 'You know, I'm really glad that you have Frank, Lindsey. And Adam. But just so you know, you have me too.'

She smiled affectionately at him.

'See, I'm old,' he smiled a mischievous smile. 'So I'm half deaf. That means people can say whatever they want to me and I only hear the half of it. What's more, I know when to keep my mouth shut.'

She took the cup that was offered and watched him for a minute. He was focused almost entirely on his tea and suddenly, she felt an overwhelming urge, not just to talk, but to spill her guts.

'You mean people could tell you things like...' she pushed the milk jug towards him as he was about to reach for it. 'The fact that they feel responsible for someone's death?'

'Scone?' he lifted a cover off a plate heaped with scones and shoved them towards her. 'I made them myself.'

She'd underestimated little old Mr Hennessey and she could see why Street liked him so much.

'See, I knew that football was an IED. It was straight out of a text book and couldn't have been more obvious, not even if it had a big ticking clock and a load of wires hanging out of it.'

He slurped his tea.

'The APC went past it. It was off the road and partially blocked by a parked car. They didn't see it. I probably wouldn't have either, if it wasn't for that little girl. Beautiful little thing. Massive smile on her face, even though the boys were giving her stick, same way kids do here,' she wrapped her hands around her cup. 'Kids are the same all over the world, aren't they? They don't give a damn about politics, or who owns the land they live on. All they want is to have a bit of fun. The boys wouldn't let her play with them, so she had to make her own fun and whoever planted that IED used a toy as a lure. They didn't care who they killed. I knew though; as soon as I saw it, yet I didn't react. She was skipping towards it; we were still moving forward. By the time I opened my mouth it was too late. She was too close; I couldn't get to her in time.'

Mr Hennessey topped up her untouched cup with some more hot tea.

'See, I did the maths. If I had reacted three seconds sooner, I would have been able to get to her before she got to the ball. Then it wouldn't have exploded. She'd be alive and I wouldn't have been injured. If I hadn't been injured, then Lenny wouldn't have had his back to a sniper, so he'd still be alive too.' She started jabbing her index finger into the table, as if accusing it of something. 'But don't you see? It's not just us. That child's family will never get to see her grow up. Lenny's mother had a nervous breakdown a few months after and he had a younger brother called Brendan, who Lenny always said was the biggest book nerd on the planet. He used to joke that his kid brother would end up working for NASA, while Lenny would still be digging holes to crap in,' she smiled fondly at the memory, but it didn't last. 'Within a year of Lenny's death, Brendan had dropped out of school and was drinking nearly every day. Do you know why?'

Mr Hennessey remained silent.

'Because I was three seconds too slow.'

There was silence for nearly five minutes. Neither of them spoke. Neither of them touched their tea.

'How many lives is that so far?' she mumbled, more to herself than to Mr Hennessey. 'And then there's Damo, Murph, Gordon and Wesley...' she shook her head. 'There was a time when I could tell you what each and every one of them was thinking at any given moment. Now I don't even know where in the world any of them are. Only Street,' she shifted her eyes from the table top to meet his for the first time since she started talking. 'Do you know what he had to do that day?'

He shook his head.

'An improvised explosive can do a lot of damage to a child's body, Mr Hennessey. Both of her arms came off. Her insides were on the outside and he... he tried to hold her all together. Can you imagine what something like that would do to a person? And can you imagine that it was *all* because I was three seconds too slow?'

Five more minutes of silence passed, before Mr Hennessey finally spoke. 'My tea is gone cold,' he picked up both cups and dumped their contents down the sink. Then he refilled them both from the pot.

She smiled at him finally, 'I've probably gone and given you nightmares now too, huh?'

'I sleep fine, love, don't you worry about me. Seems like you have enough people to worry about as it is.'

'I should go,' she got to her feet and Mr Hennessey stood too.

'It occurs to me that in a way, you were all very lucky that you *didn't* continue on up that road,' he mumbled.

'Hmm?'

'That sniper; I'll bet he was waiting for his chance to pick you all off when you were further along the road. But you said that the APC had to come back, so that would have given you lot some cover. Hmm, that scuppered his plans, I'll bet.' He spoke in the tone of someone who was thinking out loud, as opposed to issuing consolations. 'Anyway, hang on a minute and I'll just round up Frank's stuff. I know his rubber chicken is here somewhere and *you* know that he won't be a happy boy if he goes home without it.' He smiled as he started gathering Frank's belongings and putting them in his backpack. 'What do you think of this extension?' he stood up straight and looked around at their kitchen, with a disenchanted look on his face.

'It's great. I wish I had half your space.'

'I preferred it the old way,' he shrugged and continued checking the backpack. 'Didn't have much of a choice but to build it on though.'

'Let me guess, Irene wanted a bigger kitchen?' she smiled.

'Irene burned down the old one,' he replied, without missing a beat and without smiling.

'I'm sorry.'

'No need to be sorry, it was nearly fifteen years ago now. Did I tell you that I used to work at The North Monastery School?'

'You were the principal if I'm not mistaken.'

He nodded. 'Oh she was giving me hell for weeks, my Irene,' he smiled fondly. 'I could do nothing right and I remember this one night we had a blazing row and I slept out in the car. Course we had only the one bedroom then and no one had couches in them days. The next day was a Friday and I went off to work as usual. Now the boys at work, the teachers, they used to go out drinking every Friday night. The single ones mostly. Normally I didn't go with them, but they didn't have to convince me that day. Anything was better than coming home for another old barney.' He shook his head. 'Anyway, by the time I did get home, there wasn't much of a home left.'

Lindsey stayed silent and she could see that he'd been transported to another time now, as he stared off into the distance.

'Irene was alright. She got a fright of course and inhaled a few lung-fulls of smoke, but Paddy Flemming, who used to live in your house, he got her out. Turned out, she'd put the bed sheets in the oven instead of the washing machine and switched it on.'

Once he was satisfied that all of Frank's belongings were accounted for, they walked quietly towards the front door.

'It wasn't 'til years later when I actually thought about all those fights we had back then. One was because she went off into town and left the front door wide open and there was a bag of coal robbed from the hall. And that morning, when I was leaving for work, I went to the fridge to get my lunch. She used to make it every evening for me and put it in the fridge. It was in there alright; right next to a box of washing powder. I'd heard of Alzheimer's of course. Her father had it you see, but it never dawned on me for a second that she was already showing fairly strong signs. In fact, the more I thought about it, the more I realised all of our arguments at that time were down to me, pointing out things that she was doing wrong, or weirdly. She was aware of it herself then and it scared her of course. So we fought.' He sighed heavily with a wistful smile on his face. 'But then they say that hindsight is 20/20, don't they Lindsey?'

She forced a half smile, but couldn't stop her eyes from welling up.

'Come on, Frankie. Let's get home.' Frank trotted out the door and down the path and then he waited by the footpath for her. 'Thanks Mr Hennessey.'

'My kettle's always on,' he smiled. 'And thank you for trusting me.' He went back inside, closing the door quietly behind him.

CHAPTER FOURTEEN

'Thank Christ! Are you back?' Mike was behind the desk when she got to the Centre a few days later and he was buried under a pile of dog-eared files.

'I am,' she smiled. She'd had her first, unmedicated, full night's sleep in God knows how long and she was ready for work.

'Are you alright? How's the head?'

'All good.'

'Have you heard from the guards?'

'I'm expecting to soon. Any other questions?'

'Good. Well pull up a seat. I've been going through these for days and honestly, I could do with a fresh pair of eyes.'

'What are they?'

'All the kids that have been through here since you started.'

'I don't think it was one of the kids, Mike.'

'What makes you so sure?'

'I had a bit of a run in with a couple of lads recently. I'm just waiting for Sinéad to confirm that it was them.'

'What kind of a run in? Ring her now.'

'Someone hit the coffee hard this morning,' she smiled. He was hyper and clearly on a mission. 'Anyway, what's the hurry?' She actually had been glued to her phone, waiting for Sinéad or Jim Duggan to call her, but they hadn't. She wanted to know for sure if it was them. But she didn't want to know if it wasn't, so she was putting off making the call.

'What's the hurry? The hurry is that I want the fucker who did this to be locked up. Linds, they could have bloody killed you.'

'Mike, they didn't have the balls to kill me when they had the chance. Instead they chose to kick me all over while I was unconscious, like the cowards they are.'

'Just ring her, will you?'

'Fine,' she didn't want to look equally cowardly, so she pulled out her phone and called Sinéad.

'Lindsey? Everything alright?'

'Hey… yeah. Just wondering if you managed to track down those two?'

'Yeah, I was going to call round to your place in a while. I just need to check on one more thing before I do.'

'You don't sound convinced, Sinéad.'

She paused. 'Look, give me another hour with this one and I'll call over to see you OK?'

Lindsey had a sinking feeling that she was about to be told something that she didn't want to hear. 'OK. I'm at the Centre, so call here.'

'See you soon.'

'What did she say?'

'She'll be over in an hour. Where is everyone?'

'Watching *The Hunger Games.*'

Lindsey raised her eyebrows. Mike wasn't one to stick kids in front of a telly, no matter how much they begged. 'OK… so what have you got here then?' The files looked like they were split into three bundles, but with the clutter on the desk it was hard to tell.

Mike placed his hand on the bundle to his right. 'These are the least likely candidates, in my opinion.' He moved to the centre pile. 'These exhibited little or no violence while here, but… I could see them possibly making the leap. And this…' he moved to the third pile, 'is a pile of characters that you need to have a closer look at. I'd like you to start with them. Think back, any arguments you might have had, any specific incidents that made you wonder… any gut feelings, Lindsey. Think hard, OK? Start with them and we'll go from there,' he shoved the *pile of characters* towards her and she picked up the one on top.

'Jesus Christ, you're alive!' Sheila barged in with a pot of tea, before she had a chance to get beyond the name on her first file. Ethan Marks.

'You can't kill a bad thing, Sheila,' Lindsey smiled.

Sheila squeezed around her chair, landed the teapot on the desk and grabbed Lindsey's face in her rough hands, which smelled like onions. 'I'm so glad to see you, my love,' she grinned and then planted a wet kiss on Lindsey's forehead. 'I brought an apple tart to the hospital the other day. You were out cold, but I'd bet my life that handsome bastard with the dirty smile ate it all.'

Lindsey laughed. 'That'd be about right.'

'Then again, he can eat my tart any time he likes,' Sheila hacked, coughed and laughed at the same time. When she finally calmed down, she turned her attention to Mike. 'Any news on young Greg?'

'What happened with Greg?' Lindsey asked.

Mike's face turned ashen and he shook his head. 'His mother didn't come home for a few days and he went looking for her. He knew one of her spots and he went there by himself; some flat on the North Main Street. To cut a long story short, he was pinned down by two of his mother's *friends* and injected with heroin. With a used syringe of course.'

'Jesus Christ,' Lindsey jumped to her feet. 'Where is he?'

'Still in CUH. Sit down, there's nothing you can do.'

Eventually she did sit back down, but she felt an urgent need to do something for Greg. Whether it was to hunt down the animals that did it, or go see him at the hospital. Just something.

Sheila had tears pouring down her face. Lindsey rubbed her arm, for lack of anything else to do. 'You OK?'

She shook her head. 'That boy reminds me so much of my Tommy. All brawn and no brain… but a good old heart underneath it all. If that fucking drug gets a hold of him, I swear, I'll hunt down the bastard myself and he'll only wish the guards got to him first.'

Sheila had her first and only child at the age of fifteen. His name was Tommy and he became her life, which was difficult before him and even more so with him. When she finally lost him to heroine at the age of nine-teen, she did her damndest to follow him to the grave. Instead she ended up working at the Centre. Sheila stormed out and slammed the door.

'Will he be OK?'

Mike shrugged. 'He needed an HIV test and those results take forever and a day to come back. They're keeping him in until the drug is out of his system completely, but of course he'll be more susceptible going forward.'

'Fuck sake, wasn't his life hard enough as it was?' she muttered. 'I'll go see him later.'

Mike tapped the pile of folders and she returned her attention to Ethan Marks. She remembered him. He had a history of abusing small animals, but still managed to come across as a really nice kid, which was worrying. He could easily fool people, but she'd had no issues with him at all, so she moved onto the next.

It was a sobering task to read back through the files of kids who'd suf-fered unimaginable abuse and neglect. Some of whom went on to inflict the same upon others. Then there were the kids from perfect, working class families who'd just gone off the rails or gotten caught up in one drug or another or with the wrong crowd. One boy, a straight 'A' student from a trouble-free background, decided one day to beat and sexually assault his little sister. Others wanted nothing more than a little bit of attention. It was all there, in the files piling up around her. Dealing with them one at a time was one thing. Going through them all in one sitting was nothing short of depressing. 'There's nothing here, Mike.' After an hour and a half of reading, she leaned back in her chair and stretched.

'Be certain, Linds. What about him...' he rooted through her pile. 'Kevin James.'

The one who targeted his sister. She shook her head. 'He liked to lord it over smaller kids. He wouldn't take on an adult.'

Mike dropped his head onto the desk.

'Mike, take a break. I'll look through the rest of these myself. You've done enough.'

'Why isn't Sinéad here yet?'

Lindsey looked at her watch, just as there was a knock on their door jam and Sinéad appeared.

'Lindsey, can I have a word?'

'Let me get out and then you'll be able to fit in.' Mike got to his feet and struggled out of the office. 'Should I go?' he asked then, but it was clear that he didn't want to.

'Give us a few minutes, Mike, yeah?' Lindsey asked with an appreciative smile. He didn't have to do the research he had on her behalf and she appreciated it.

He nodded and pulled the door out, while Sinéad made her way around the other side of the desk.

'Well?'

'We found the two lads. They're real names are Dennis O'Leary and Christopher Lawton.'

'And?'

'It wasn't them.'

'How do you know?'

'Because Dennis O'Leary attacked a taxi driver by the bus station at twelve minutes past eleven on Sunday night.'

'Shit. CCTV?'

She nodded.

'That was still early though.'

'We were able to follow him from there, to the back of the bus station, where we lost him for a bit. He was scoring obviously. We picked him up again on his way back.'

'What about Christopher Lawton?'

'He was waiting for him at the corner by Street's place, and they both headed down that laneway. We lost them then, but you were seen about an hour later coming out of that lane and walking towards the bus station. We forwarded on, but no one else came up from that street.'

'They could have gone from the other end. Are there cameras down there?'

'No, but it's doubtful. Dennis O'Leary died of an overdose that night.'

Lindsey rubbed her forehead and thought for a minute. 'Which one was Stabber?'

'That's Christopher.'

'What about him?'

'There was a homeless man who was sleeping in the derelict building that you were telling us about. He raised the alarm. When the ambulance crew arrived, Christopher was beside Dennis. He was alive, but in a bit of a state. We did check all CCTV in the area, Linds, but from what we can tell, Dennis went into that building with Christopher and whatever amount of heroin they managed to score, and it doesn't seem like either of them came back out.'

'Shit.' Lindsey thumped the desk. She should have been somewhat upset to hear that a man she knew had died so tragically, especially knowing what she did about heroin and what it could do to a person. If anything, it made her even angrier at herself for considering taking that road herself. But she couldn't bring herself to care about Dennis O'Leary. Not yet anyway. She was more concerned with the fact that she was back to square one and had no idea who'd been targeting her.

'You OK?'

'You know, I have to question my amazing ability to pick up enemies despite the fact that I have no life,' she shook her head in amazement.

'We have hours and hours of CCTV from the Blackpool area, but you're so much further out that whoever did this, might not even be on them. And even if they are, like I said, it's still far enough away from your house that we couldn't assume that they were anywhere near you. At least not in a way that would stick. Your bat's been sent to Dublin for analysis, but that could take an age to come back. Unfortunately, we're a far cry from CSI here in Ireland. Nothing ever gets solved within the hour,' she half smiled, but Lindsey could sense her frustration.

'OK... let's talk about something else for a while. I need a break and then I'm sure something will come to me,' she slapped the pile of files on the desk.

Sinéad sat up straighter and looked suddenly uncomfortable.

'What?'

'It's the wrong time completely to bring this up, but...'

'But what?'

'I want you to know that I didn't say or do anything to lead him on.'

'Who?'

Sinéad took a deep breath and placed her two hands palm down on the desk. 'Adam rang me yesterday and asked if I wanted to go for a drink.'

Lindsey grinned.

'Lindsey I swear, if you...'

'Sinéad!' Lindsey held her hand up to stop her. 'You don't seem to believe me when I tell you that Adam and I aren't interested in each other that way, but it's true. He's probably the best friend I'll ever have and I love him dearly, but we'll never be a couple. So please, don't ask my permission to go out with him. Actually, I'm amazed that it's taken you both this long to get the finger out,' she smiled.

Sinéad shook her head with a small smile of her own. 'Call me mad, but don't most people spend half their lives looking for the kind of relationship that you two have?'

Lindsey laughed quietly. 'I doubt it. But either way, our relationship is exactly the way it's supposed to be.'

'He said the same. I can't say I understand it, to be honest. You two fight like an old married couple,' she grinned. 'But then I've clearly never had what you two have,' she sat back and looked like she wanted to say more, but was deciding whether or not she should.

'Say it, Sinéad.'

She sighed. 'Lindsey, I know very little, only the snippets of information that I've been hearing lately. But it was like a dark cloud was hanging over Jim's head when we left the hospital the other day. And the way he talks about you and Adam... let's just say, he has a lot of respect for you both. He knows more about the two of you than I do, clearly. Like, that you have PTSD for example.'

She looked pointedly at her and Lindsey nodded. 'It's coming under control,' if one good night's sleep equated to *it's coming under control.*

'When Adam asked me out, I had this same conversation with him; you know the, *But what about you and Lindsey,* confusion? He told me that he'd been to hell and back with you. He also said that if it wasn't for you... he would have given up years ago.'

Lindsey shook her head.

'He didn't tell me what hell you were both in, but if you ever want to tell me about what you've been through, I'm here to listen, Lindsey. But I'll never ask you to.'

So far this week, she'd spilled her guts to Kathleen, aka Roxanne, and in even more detail to poor Mr Hennessey, who she vowed to call upon again and she did genuinely feel better. But that was enough for now. 'Thanks, Sinéad, I appreciate that. But like I said; it's all under control. Now I hope I've put your mind at ease about Adam? He's the best in the world and he really likes you.'

She laughed quietly. 'Yeah... he mentioned that actually.'

'Why's that funny?'

'His exact words were, Look Sinéad, I really like you and I'd love to get to know you better. But if the way things are with me and Lindsey is going to be a problem, then it's probably best if we give it a skip.'

Lindsey laughed out loud. 'Yeah, you'd never guess that he's not actually used to asking women out.'

'I find that hard to believe,' she replied, still laughing.

'Oh, he's used to picking women up. But not actually having to ring someone up that he really likes and ask her out. That's alien to him and he gets a bit gruff when he's nervous.'

'OK then. I'll go for a drink with him,' she was smiling broadly now. 'And if it all goes well, then I'll know I can come to you whenever I need his moods translated.'

'Good. Now go back to work, you. I have somewhere I need to be.'

Sinéad was serious again now. 'Keep on top of those files, Lindsey and if anything jumps out at you, please call me. Otherwise I'm banging my head against a brick wall. We have no witnesses, no footage, no nothing and it's doing my head in.'

'It's someone I know, Sinéad. It has to be, it's too personal. I just need to switch my brain on and narrow it down. Then you'll be the first to know.'

Sinéad ran her hands through her hair, making a mess of her neat ponytail, but rather than fixing it, she just put her cap on over it. 'OK. Talk to me before the day is out, yeah?'

Lindsey got up and went out into the hall, to make it easier for Sinéad to get out and as she did, Sheila shouted from the kitchen.

'Sinéad, I hope someone's looking for that bastard that stuck a dirty, poison filled needle into a child's arm on Monday?'

'They are working on it,' Sinéad answered back, and as they headed down the stairs and towards the front door, she spoke in a lower voice, 'Greg's mother and three other men are in custody.'

Lindsey nodded. It looked like Greg was headed for a group home when he got out of hospital. That wasn't a good scenario, but she had to wonder which was really worse; a group home, or his own home, with a family who seemed determined to get him killed.

After Sinéad left, Lindsey got in her car and headed for the Cork University hospital. Once there, it took another twenty minutes to find Greg, but when she did, her anger towards his mother increased tenfold. He was sitting up in bed, wearing a hospital gown instead of pyjamas. He was staring out the window, looking like someone who'd given up on life. At just sixteen years of age.

Lindsey left again immediately, before he'd even turned to see that she was there. She walked out of the hospital and across the road to the Wilton Shopping Centre, where she stocked up on pyjamas, T-shirts, a tracksuit, socks, underwear, toiletries, magazines, a good stock of fresh fruit and chocolate and a handheld games console that she knew nothing about because she was useless with technology, but it was preloaded with one hundred and one games apparently. Spending her own money on such things would be frowned upon, but she didn't particularly care about that. Here was a sixteen-year-old kid who had the potential to do anything he wanted in life. Someone should care that he didn't have clean clothes and toiletries. Someone should care that he was in hospital and they should most certainly care about how he got there. But those who *should* care were the ones who put him there. This boy was already old and jaded and ready to give up and someone should bloody well care.

When she arrived back, laden with bags, she headed for the lift, knowing now where she was going and determined to get there quickly.

'Lindsey?'

The voice was loud and brash and came from somewhere across the concourse.

She turned and scanned the faces, all moving in different directions, but didn't see anyone that she knew. Not until a hand went up in the air and her name was bellowed again.

A short, heavy woman wearing a long, gypsy style skirt and matching black top was making her way towards her. Had she not spoken, then Lindsey would have passed her in the crowd without ever knowing who she was. No make-up. No big earrings, no flesh on show... 'Kathleen?'

'It is you,' she smiled. 'I was just heading out for a fag when I saw you tearing in, looking like you wanted to kill someone. Everything OK? Why are you in hospital?'

Lindsey was touched by the concern in her voice. She really wanted to get to Greg, but the very least she owed this woman was some of her time. 'I'm just visiting someone, but I'll come with you for that fag.'

'You don't strike me as a smoker.'

'I'm not, but it's good to see you. Come on,' she led the way back towards the front door.

'How've you been, love?' Kathleen asked, as she lit up.

'Much better, thanks to you,' Lindsey smiled. No need to mention what happened after she left Kathleen that night.

'Do you want to tell me what happened here?' she pointed to the gash on the right side of Lindsey's forehead, which was still held together by paper stitches. The gash meant that Lindsey had to decide whether to cover that, or her scar on the other side. It was easier to talk away a fresh cut though.

'I'm a clumsy eejit, is what happened there. How are you? Everything alright?'

What was already a fragile smile vanished completely now and she shook her head. 'My boy is in there.'

'I'm sorry, Kathleen. Will he be alright?'

'I'm begging them to keep him until it's out of his system, but he's causing hell up on the ward,' she started to cry, which surprised Lindsey. It seemed that when she didn't have her war paint on, Kathleen was as soft as anyone else.

'Heroin?' Lindsey asked, guessing that it was one of her two addicted sons. It was only then that she thought about how sheltered her life had been until recently. She'd never so much as heard of heroin, aside from on TV, for most of her life. Now she mentioned the drug at least once most days.

Kathleen nodded. 'A bad batch, they said. The young fella that he was with died.'

Lindsey straightened up. 'Christopher and Michael are your sons, yeah?'

She nodded. 'It's Christopher.'

Christopher Lawton. Stabber. Lindsey's stomach landed on the floor and she could feel her eyes welling up, but she didn't cry. Suddenly though, she no longer looked at Stabber and his brown-toothed friend as the scum of the earth. Suddenly they were sons and brothers. They were boys, like Greg once upon a time. Was there a kind hearted woman like Kathleen, mourning the death of her son, Dennis, today? Or was there a woman like Greg's mother, barely aware that he ever lived, let alone that he had died?

'Kathleen, if there's ever anything that I can do for you…' she pulled a card out of her bag and handed it to the woman, but she instinctively knew that she wasn't the type to ask for help. 'Or I'd love to have a cuppa sometime, when you're not busy.'

Kathleen took the card and looked a bit surprised by it.

'Just call me some time. Let me know how Christopher's doing?'

'Thanks, love. I will. And I hope whoever you're here to see will be alright.'

Lindsey nodded and went back inside.

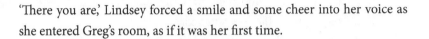

'There you are,' Lindsey forced a smile and some cheer into her voice as she entered Greg's room, as if it was her first time.

He turned to look at her, but turned away towards the window again almost immediately.

'I brought supplies,' she landed the bags on the end of his bed and she could see that he wanted to look through them, but didn't want *her* to know that, so she emptied the contents of one of them onto the bed. The games console and heaps of chocolate spread out around the covers.

Lindsey looked towards the door. 'The nurses will kill me if they see these so close to lunchtime, but a Galaxy Caramel never hurt anyone,' she smiled and threw one of the bars onto his lap. 'Probably beats the food here anyway?'

He shrugged. 'It's not so bad. I got porridge for breakfast today. I never thought I'd like porridge 'cause it looks like someone got sick into a bowl. But it's OK with sugar on it.'

'Ah porridge; the breakfast of champions,' she smiled again to hide her dismay. The child never had porridge before.

He broke a square off the chocolate bar and put it in his mouth, then looked back out the window again. All his fight seemed to have gone.

Lindsey rooted in her bag and pulled out a deck of cards. 'You know how to play forty-five?'

He shook his head.

'Wanna learn?'

He shrugged again and Lindsey dealt.

'Has someone been eating chocolate before their lunch?' asked a smiling young nurse as she came in and wrapped a blood pressure monitor around Greg's arm.

Greg looked at Lindsey who feigned a guilty expression and put her finger to her lips.

'She gave it to me,' he dobbed her in to the nurse with a grin.

'Nice, Greg. Thanks,' Lindsey laughed.

'We'll have to kick her out if she doesn't behave herself,' the nurse joked with Greg and he blushed.

'Don't kick her out yet...' he finally answered. 'I beat her in the last three hands.'

Lindsey rolled her eyes while the nurse laughed.

Despite the chocolate, Greg devoured his lunch when it arrived; a wilted looking salad with four slices of bread. He and Lindsey played cards for another hour and then he tried out his games console while she read some of his magazines. Then they swapped and finally, he no longer cared if she saw his enthusiasm for his new gear and he tore through the bags on the end of his bed. He went and changed into one of his new sets of pyjamas and folded the others, along with his new tracksuit, in the small wardrobe beside his bed. It was only then that she noticed it was getting dark, just as his dinner arrived. It was an unhealthy-looking fry up that made Lindsey's stomach growl with hunger.

'Right, I'd better go rescue Frank from Sheila's kitchen,' she got to her feet and stretched.

Greg put down his fork and suddenly looked awkward. 'Thanks... for all this,' he pulled on his sleeve. 'And for not asking me loads of stupid questions all day.'

She nodded.

'I wrote my number on the inside of that magazine...' she dropped the one that she was pretending to read, on his bedside locker. 'Use it any-time you like. You're the only one who's ever beat me at forty-five and I'm not willing to let that be the end of it,' she grinned.

He lowered his eyes. 'What's going to happen to my Mam?'

Lindsey shook her head. 'I don't know, Greg.'

'What's going to happen to me?'

'In the short term, I don't know that for sure either. But here's what I do know; you're going to be fine.' She leaned on the end of his bed and made him look her in the eye. 'Hear me when I tell you that you're a hell of a lot stronger than you think you are, Greg. You've been dealt a shitty hand and people have made things very tough for you, but *you* can make sure that your adult life is a far cry from this. And we're going to help you, you hear me?'

He lowered his eyes again.

'Do you hear me, Greg?'

He nodded.

'Good. Now I'm going home to practice my forty-five and next time I see you, I'm gonna whip your ass.'

Finally he grinned, 'That's what you think.'

CHAPTER FIFTEEN

By the time Lindsey got back to the Centre it was already dark and Sheila was the only one still there.

'Did you see him? How is he? Will he be alright?' she pounced on Lindsey as soon as she got to the top of the stairs. She'd clearly been waiting anxiously for her to come back.

'Yeah… he's OK, Sheila.'

'I have some of my Tommy's clothes still at home. I'm gonna put them in a bag and bring them in for Greg. That poor boy… and his poor mother.'

Lindsey raised her eyebrows, but didn't say what she was really thinking about Greg's mother. Not to Sheila. It would be too unprofessional.

'Lindsey, I know what you're thinking,' she shook her head and looked incredibly sad. 'And I'm so glad that you don't know firsthand what heroin can do to a person. Even a good, honest, decent person. I know Dennise Patterson. We went to school together. Now don't get me wrong, she's no saint. In fact, she was always a thundering bitch if you ask me. But she did love that boy when he was a baby. Him and his brother… I can't remember his name.' Sheila sat down at one of the tables and lit up a fag. 'The woman did what she had to do to put a roof over them two boys, but I'll tell ya, Lindsey, once that fucking bastard of a drug gets a hold of a person at all, nothing else on this God given earth matters. Not even the family that you love,' she smiled then, as a tear ran down her cheek. 'Tommy had a heart the size of Africa when he was a little boy. Every year on my birthday, he used to make me a card from scratch and steal a few flowers from the neighbour's garden for me, 'cause he never had the money to buy them. I didn't have it to give to him either.' She shook her head, visibly blaming herself once again for everything that went wrong in her son's life. 'Course he had no daddy to keep him on the straight and narrow and God knows I tried. But I had to work all the time, just to keep the wolf from the door.' She brought her shaking, smoking hand up to fiddle with her earlobe; a nervous habit of hers. 'I wish to Christ I'd known then what was coming, because it was so much worse than any fucking wolf at the door. I'd have gone without food. I'd have gone without anything, if it meant that he wouldn't have taken that first drug. If it meant that he'd still be here with me.'

She was full blown crying now and Lindsey moved around the table and hugged her, but she couldn't think of much to say. It was easy for her to condemn the addicts who attacked her and the one who endangered her sixteen-year-old son on a daily basis. But if Kathleen hadn't come along when Lindsey was holding back just enough for her first hit of heroin, who's to say that she wouldn't be headed down that very same road herself?

'I didn't know Tommy, Sheila, but I've known you for a while now and I can say with one hundred per cent conviction, that you were a great mother to him. I see that every day with kids here. They'd be lost without you.'

She pulled back from Lindsey, shaking her head and wiping her nose. 'Greg's going to be fine anyway, that's all that matters.' She pulled herself together again. 'Here, wait 'til I tell ya...' she got up and walked back into the kitchen with Frank on her heels. She was still drying her face.

'Tell me what?' Lindsey followed her.

'Mike went back to Marie.'

'No surprise there then,' Lindsey smiled, happy to let her change the subject.

Sheila rolled her eyes. 'He's just hedging his bets, that fella. Every now and then he leaves her in the hope that you'll finally give him a shot.'

'No he d...'

'Ah shut up! He's a great bit of stuff that Mike, but he's not the one for you,' she wagged her finger at Lindsey, like she knew exactly who *was* the one for her.

'No?' she smiled.

Sheila shook her head. 'Mike needs a woman behind the scenes, to be his support. His backbone if you like. You're no background woman,' she wagged her finger again.

'You know me better than I do, Sheila,' Lindsey smiled. 'You need a lift home?'

'Nah, I look forward to the walk at the end of the day.' She put on her coat and pulled her handbag out of the pot drawer. 'See ya, love.' She rubbed Lindsey on the arm before leaving.

Lindsey stayed for another hour catching up on paperwork and then she took Frank for a walk around the soccer pitch at the back of the Centre, knowing that he'd been cooped up for most of the day watching movies with the kids and for the first time in weeks, she felt somewhere close to her old self. Of course she was acutely aware of the fact that, whoever it was who was watching her, did in fact mean her harm. That much hadn't changed. But what had changed was that she actually cared about whether or not they succeeded now. She no longer felt like jumping into the abyss. She didn't want oblivion, like she had last week, nor was she afraid to go home and close her eyes and she couldn't help wondering how long this could last for. Lindsey didn't believe in therapy but she'd spilled her guts to several people in the past week and technically speaking, all that *talking* was therapy. Maybe it was the fact that none of the people she'd spoken to had tried to give her answers where there weren't any. Who knows, maybe there was something to it after all. Either way, she did feel slightly better.

Of course it was more likely that it was her concussion, which forced her to sleep away long hours over the past number of days, but still, she could feel the fire in her belly reigniting. The fire that made her want to help kids like Greg Patterson in any way she could. The same fire that made her determined not to be gotten the better of by whomever this person was.

That night once again, Lindsey slept for most of the night. That wasn't to say it was a peaceful sleep, but it was sleep none the less. She didn't find herself back in Syria, which was good, but she was somewhere like it. Somewhere barren and war-torn, but she wasn't there with Street and Lenny and the lads. In fact, she wasn't really there at all. She was watching on, as Jamie Cussons sat on a semi inflated football, looking bored. He was using a twig to draw shapes in the dust on the road, until Greg Patterson came along and towered over him. Jamie dropped the twig and squinted up at him with the sun in his eyes. Greg was asking for his ball back. The ball that Lindsey knew could kill them both. But it wasn't the ball that did the damage. Instead Jamie got to his feet and gave Greg the beating of his life, while Greg just took it all. He never returned a punch or even tried to defend himself. He merely curled in a ball on the ground as Jamie kicked him over and over again. Lindsey shouted at him to stop, but neither of them could hear her. By the time the ball exploded, it was morning. The sun was up and it was raining outside.

It was almost six when Frank closed his eyes and Lindsey opened hers and got up. She dressed quietly and headed out for a run. With her hood up she left the house and turned left this time, away from the city. She passed the Hennessey's house, with all its curtains still drawn and she ran along the hard shoulder of the main road, which was still quiet. After forty-five minutes, she turned and headed back. It would have been a boring run if she wasn't preoccupied, as she always was. Greg and Jamie were both on her mind and the subtle changes that seemed to have occurred in both of them, in her dream *and* in real life. Jamie was growing more confident, now that he'd found somewhere where he belonged and he had a goal in life, while Greg was being trodden down one notch at a time and by the time she got home, she'd made up her mind to introduce sport into Greg's life if he'd let her. Running, boxing, hiking, soccer, it didn't matter. They'd all helped Lindsey immeasurably over the years. Sport helped Jamie when he needed it too and who's to say that it couldn't do something, anything, for Greg as well?

It was almost half eight by the time Lindsey got to the Centre that morning and Sheila was already there, as always. So was Mike. He was drinking coffee in the dining room, with the bundle of *characters* spread out in front of him.

'OK, I'm officially taking over this bundle, Mike,' Lindsey smiled as she sat down beside him with a coffee.

'Linds, you don't seem to be taking this seriously. You haven't even looked at these yet. You do realise that someone tried to kill you?'

Mike was stressed. 'If they wanted to kill me, Mike, they had the perfect opportunity while I was unconscious at their feet.'

He threw his hands in the air.

'I assure you, I'm taking this seriously,' she gathered up the bundle and slid the files away from him and towards herself. 'There were just more important things to be dealing with yesterday.'

'What could be more important?'

'Greg.'

He got up and refilled his cup.

'I wanna see if he'll come to Street's place with me.'

'Saint Street, eh?'

Lindsey looked at him waiting for more, but it didn't come, so finally she asked the obvious question. 'Is there a problem?'

He shrugged. 'No problem. If your boyfriend has the answer to everything, then that's great.'

Lindsey furrowed her brow and shook her head. Whatever Mike's problem was, it was *his* problem, so she decided not to take this conversation any further. Instead she turned her attention to Sheila, who'd just joined them. She was also looking at Mike with her, *Get a grip or I'm going to slap you in the head*, expression, but before Lindsey had the chance to speak to her, Mike piped up again.

'You know every time I set foot in your hospital room, I felt like a complete outsider. Like everyone knew something that I didn't.'

Mike sounded like a petulant child now. Lindsey's car crash story was still bothering him and granted, it was her own fault for taking her clothes off with him in the first place, but that didn't make this any less annoying.

She took a breath and did her best to keep her temper in check. 'Mike, I appreciate everything you're doing here,' she placed her hand on the bundle of files and slid them closer. 'And as far as this is concerned, you know as much as I do. Now I think it's you who needs some rest this time, so please, go and get some. Sheila, what time are you here since?' she turned her attention back to Sheila, leaving Mike to calm down from whatever buzz he was on.

'Quarter to six,' she replied sounding tired, as she slurped her tea and lit up a fag with her eyes still fixed on Mike.

'And what time do you leave?'

She shrugged.

'You need help in here.'

'I do not,' she replied adamantly, returning her glare to Lindsey.

'Sheila, you can't keep doing twelve and fourteen-hour days.'

'I get paid for eight hours, same as always.'

'Exactly.'

'Well, kids have to be fed, this place has to be cleaned and it takes as long as it takes.'

Lindsey looked at Mike, who finally seemed to have come back to earth and he was looking at Sheila as if it was the first time he'd ever noticed her. The most taken for granted woman in Cork was sharing a table with them.

'I'm talking to Liam today about getting you a helper.'

Sheila laughed. 'Yeah, good luck with that.'

'Files, Lindsey.' Mike tapped the bundle impatiently and Sheila rolled her eyes and headed back to the kitchen.

'Seriously, Mike. What's up?' Lindsey was half smiling, half exasperated.

'You don't give a shit about this, is what's up,' he raised his voice.

'For the last time; I give a shit. I *am* taking it seriously and this isn't your problem, so what is?'

He brought his hands to his face and finally came round to her side of the table and sat back down beside her on the bench. 'Linds, you don't get it...' his voice was lower now, but still not quite calm. 'You scared the shit out of me the other day. When I got to the hospital and saw you... your face was all swollen, you didn't even know I was there.'

'I didn't know that *I* was there either if that makes you feel any better,' she half smiled.

'It doesn't. Your buddy, Street, was sitting in a chair in the corner and the second I walked into the room he started firing questions at me; it was like he was blaming me or something.'

'I can assure you, he wasn't. If he thought for a second that you knew anything about this, you'd be in no doubt about his feelings.'

He brought his hands to either side of his face again, 'You'll never get it.'

'Get what?' she sounded more impatient now.

'That I love you, Lindsey.'

He said it like he was talking to a four-year-old and Lindsey's only response was to drop her head onto the table, on top of her folded arms.

'See? I can't talk to you,' he got to his feet again.

'Shut up, you are talking to me,' she sat up and swivelled to face him. 'Well?'

'Mike, you don't know me. Certainly not well enough to love me.'

'You mean I don't know you as well as Street does. I've spent almost every day with you for the past year and a half. I've seen you fight tooth and nail for kids that anyone else would come close to giving up on. I've seen you shove yourself into the middle of so many fights, without a second's thought for yourself... I've seen you deal with things in your own life that would reduce a grown man to tears. You can make people laugh when it's the last thing they feel like doing and nothing phases you.' He sat back down the edge of the bench. 'You may not notice me, but I *do* know you, Lindsey.'

She was quiet for a minute, while she tried to think of a response that wouldn't sound harsh, because she genuinely didn't want to hurt him. But she did want to slap him. Mike was someone that she could be good friends with, if he just learned to shut his mouth every once in a while. But he was a man who, outside of work, had no idea what he wanted. 'Fair enough, you know one side of me.'

'I don't know the other side because you won't tell me. You don't seem to trust me with that.'

'I'm not going to keep telling you that I trust you, Mike. Tell me, what's the difference between me and Marie?'

He laughed, exasperated and shook his head. 'Everything!'

'Like what?'

'Like... all the above. Marie gets bored when I talk about the kids here. If she saw a fight break out, she'd ring the guards and run the other way. Actually, she'd find a spot where she could watch to see what happened. Then she'd have something to gossip about with her friends later. She breaks down crying at the slightest little thing. She cries watching *Home and Away* for fuck sake. She has moods that no one could explain, but if she's in bad humour, the whole fucking world has to know about it. Same if she's feeling giddy. Plus... she has no interest in me, physically.'

Again, Lindsey kept quiet for a minute to weigh up her answer, which again, a good slap would have covered where words just weren't enough. But she was making an effort. 'Why have you been together for so long if what you want is the complete opposite of her? Why did you just go back to her the other day? Again.'

He stared at her, like a rabbit caught in the headlights. 'Habit, I guess.'

'That's some habit.'

'I don't mean... it's just...'

'Mike, you're bored. You're sitting on the fence thinking that the grass is greener on the other side. Who knows, maybe it is. But I'm not on the other side of that fence, Mike. In fact, I'm nowhere near it. If you want something different, go have a fling with someone and then go back to your wife like you always do, but for fuck sake, man up. Either leave the woman so that you can both get on with your lives, or go home, talk about something other than work, make her feel like you *are* interested in her, physically and otherwise, and stop banging your head off brick fucking walls.' She genuinely did try not to be harsh, but she couldn't stop the words as they poured from her mouth. 'Last time we had this conversation, you swore it would be the last time. How many more of these do we have to have?'

Mike silently got up and left the dining room and Lindsey dropped her head back and stared up at the ceiling for a bit.

'Good woman,' Sheila whispered, as she returned and sat down.

'Were you eavesdropping?'

'Technically, no. I was peeling spuds, but the bucket is just below the open hatch,' she grinned.

Lindsey smiled, but her heart wasn't in it.

'Christ girl, if I had half your balls when I was a young one, my life would be very different.'

Lindsey shook her head. 'You have balls enough for all of us, Sheila.'

'Not like you. I just took the hand I was dealt and managed to survive. That's nothing. I didn't learn how to tell people where to go until it was far too late.'

'They say it's never too late and I can safely say, you're making up for it.' Lindsey smiled, just as Sheila's smile faded away.

'I've never seen the places or the things that I think you've seen, Lindsey. Things that no one should ever have to see.'

Lindsey didn't respond. She didn't realise that Sheila knew about her past, because the woman never mentioned it and that fact just made Lindsey appreciate her all the more.

She reached out and took Lindsey's hand. 'I know you don't like to talk about the struggles in your life and that's OK. You're a strong woman so I know you'll be alright.' She half smiled and shook her head. 'I never told you this, but sometimes I wish I had a daughter. Not instead of Tommy, but as well as him. I imagine that she'd be like you,' she laughed quietly. 'She probably wouldn't of course, 'cause I would've fucked that up too, but you know… that's what I imagine sometimes.'

Lindsey squeezed the woman's hand and then she got to her feet. 'I'm gonna go talk to Liam about getting you an assistant.'

'I asked him a couple of months ago and got the same old answer,' she picked up her potato peeler and got to her feet again. 'The old, *budget isn't there*, story.'

Lindsey left the dining room with the bundle of files under her arm for fear of setting Mike off on another tangent. She brought them with her to Liam's office. He'd just arrived and was pouring coffee from his flask. For some reason, he always brought his own coffee. He also brought a packed lunch from home and no one knew for sure if it was because he didn't want to eat into their food budget (literally), or if he just hated the mass catered food at the Centre. No one cared really. It just gave them something to speculate about on the rare occasion when nothing more interesting was going on. Liam Walsh was the decision maker. He decided where the funding went and he looked after the day to day running of the Centre. He busied himself with being a manager, delegation was his best friend and they really only ever saw him when something went wrong.

'Hey, can I come in?' Lindsey knocked and stuck her head around his door.

'Lindsey, have a seat,' he smiled a friendly smile. Liam was overweight by about two stone and had a Friar Tuck hair style. He'd been married to a woman called Ann for twenty-five or so years, but Lindsey had never met, or even heard anything about her, aside from her name. He was a genuinely nice man counting down to his retirement, but he was a bean counter through and through. Everything with Liam was about the bottom line. 'I was going to come to see you today.'

'Yeah?'

'Yeah. Are you OK? I heard you had an accident of some sort. Spent a few days in hospital and everything.'

'Yeah, I'm grand now.'

He leaned towards her and lowered his voice, though she didn't know why. His office was far enough from everyone else, that no one would have heard him anyway. 'We don't need to mention it in the salaries. I know you'll catch up in your own time if needed.'

She smiled. 'Thanks, Liam. Actually, what I want to talk to you about is Sheila.'

He sat back. 'What about her?'

'When Sheila started working here, there were about five or six kids who came here regularly. Over the years, that number has increased dramatically. On average, we have between fifteen and twenty kids here most days now, sometimes more and that's not counting volunteers and staff. It's too much work for one person.'

'Has she said something? She's not thinking of leaving, is she?' he sounded almost panicked now and it pleased her to know that he realised how valuable Sheila was.

'No, she hasn't said anything and she probably wouldn't like the fact that I'm here, talking about her either.' He didn't need to know that she'd already discussed it with Sheila. 'I'm just thinking of the Centre. I mean it's probably not legal for someone to work up to fourteen hours a day, nearly every day, for eight hours pay. If anything happened…'

'She doesn't work that many hours,' he guffawed, but looked slightly more worried now.

'Not on paper she doesn't. But in reality, she absolutely does. You need to think about hiring someone to help out. The last thing we'd want is an accident or injury resulting from someone being overworked.'

'But the budget… the funds just aren't there.'

'A part-timer even. For a few hours every morning to help with the food prep, or maybe a cleaner?'

He tutted loudly. 'Ask Sheila if she knows anyone, will you. We could probably get someone for twenty hours a week through the social employment scheme.'

'See? You're good at this,' she smiled. 'Knowing you, Liam, you'd probably be able to come up with a way to increase those hours down the line too.'

He grumbled and stared at his desk, clearly doing the math in his head. 'There might be a way around...' his voice trailed off.

'I'll leave you to mull over the details. I'll go talk to Sheila and get back to work,' she got to her feet and left, quitting while she was ahead.

Still holding the bundle of files under her arm, Lindsey went downstairs to where most of the kids were flinging basketballs at each other. Some of the coaches from Neptune Basketball Club were there to give pointers today and as a bonus, some of the Neptune players had promised to turn up in the afternoon for a game and most of the kids were looking forward to it.

'Lindsey?' Jamie called her, looking excited.

'Hey.'

'Did Adam tell you?'

'Tell me what?'

'What happened to your face?' his excitement vanished suddenly. 'Where've you been for the past few days?'

'Home improvements gone wrong,' she smiled. 'And I took a few days off. Is that OK with you, officer?'

He looked at her suspiciously.

'So what was Adam supposed to tell me?'

'I'm going to be competing in an Irish Amateur Boxing Association's under fourteens tournament in three weeks' time. They call it the IABA for short.'

'A tournament?' Lindsey did her best to sound excited, rather than alarmed at the idea of Jamie being punched around the ring by some unknown boxer.

'I'm ready,' he dropped the basketball and started dancing around, punching the air. 'I can't wait.'

'You're a legend, Jamie, you know that? Well done.' She punched him softly on the arm and went to talk to the coaches, who were about to kick off. They didn't say as much, but it was clear that they'd prefer to work with the kids, without interference from someone who knew nothing at all about basketball, so she left them to it. Mike was in their office and she'd had enough of him for one day, so she headed back to the dining area where she planned to put her head down and focus on the pile of *characters* for at least an hour. But first she had to talk to Street.

'Hey, what's up?'

'You're putting Jamie in a tournament?'

'He's ready, Linds.'

'For competition?'

'More than ready. He's a natural. He really is and you know I wouldn't put him forward unless I thought that.'

'I want to see him in training beforehand.'

'He'll be here this evening, when he's finished at the Centre.'

'Fine. I'll bring him.'

'See you then.'

'Lindsey?' Jamie's voice roared up the stairs from below, as she hung up.

She got up and went to the top of the stairs. 'Yeah?'

'There's some fella here looking for you,' Jamie shouted.

She rolled her eyes and jogged down the stairs. At this rate the morning would disappear before she got anything done. But that thought vanished from her mind when she got to the bottom of the stairs and followed Jamie's outstretched arm and pointed finger towards the door, where Jason the paramedic was standing, with his hands in his pockets, looking like something right out of Lindsey's imagination. The part where the nice things were stored.

'Jason… hi,' once again, she was conscious of how she looked; something that she wasn't used to feeling.

Jamie was looking suspiciously at the pair of them now, so Lindsey

214

invited him upstairs, away from prying eyes.

'Sorry to barge in on you like this, but I never got your number. I asked your friend Adam where I could find you. I hope that's not weird?'

She smiled and could feel herself blushing. Another strange and new occurrence. 'How about that coffee?' she gestured towards the dining area. 'It's not Starbucks, but I've had worse.'

Was that really the best she could come up with? *I've had worse.*

'Couldn't be worse than the stuff at ambulance control,' he smiled and took a seat. 'So, this is where you work?'

'Yeah. It's a bit hectic today. The Neptune basketball team are coming later, so the kids are a bit wound up.'

'That little lad who called you…' he smiled.

'Jamie.'

'Suspicious chap, is he? He asked my name. Why I wanted to speak to you and where I was from, before he agreed to tell you I was here.'

Lindsey laughed. 'He's practicing. Jamie is the future of *An Garda Siochána.*'

'Ah! That makes sense,' he was smiling, as she handed him a cup of coffee and she suddenly found herself picturing him naked. It was a nice picture. But then she thought about how he must be picturing her. Unconscious, semi-lucid, mad maybe… and scarred. He couldn't be picturing her any other way after seeing them.

'So…' she sat down opposite him, suddenly unsure of what to say.

'So… you promised me a coffee,' he raised his cup and took a sip.

'That I did.'

'So now that we've done that; how about dinner?'

'Dinner?'

'Yeah, you know; a few spuds, a lump of meat… dinner. Maybe somewhere else though,' he looked up at Sheila, who disappeared from the hatch as suddenly as she realised that she was caught looking.

She smiled and nodded. 'Yeah… that'd be good.'

'And just so you know, I don't normally scour the city looking for ex-patients.'

'That is good to know.'

'There's just something… I can't put my finger on it.' He maintained his gorgeous smile, while he studied her face, making her blush and curse herself again as he laughed. 'You blush really easily.'

Finally she laughed, despite herself. 'I really don't. I'm a bit thrown by this, is all.'

'You must be used to being pursued, surely.'

She blushed again. What the hell was wrong with her?

He sat back and looked inquisitively at her. 'Do you have any idea what you look like?'

'Oh I know exactly what I look like.'

'You don't wear make-up, you don't do… you know…' he used both hands to make dramatic gestures around his head, 'big, fussy hair…'

She laughed quietly at his dramatics.

'You don't seem like you do the whole, handbags and high heels thing and yet… you're gorgeous.' He picked up his cup and studied its contents, seeming a little embarrassed now too. 'More importantly, you seem quite cool.'

'Can you really say that considering how we met. Twice.'

'I'm sure there's some interesting stories attached to those episodes, which you might feel like telling me sometime down the line. Actually, I think you'd have a lot of very interesting stories to tell, but I'm not sure you're the kind of person who tells stories.'

She smiled awkwardly and drank her cooling coffee.

'Every time I popped in to see you, there were different faces in the room. You have some very interesting friends. Some of them were a little intimidating actually…' he raised his eyebrows, 'but they didn't seem like the kind of people who'd turn up for just anybody.'

Now she was confused. 'Who, you mean Adam, and Mike from here?'

'I didn't meet Mike. But there was a guy called Aaron, a blond chap and a fella called Gordon, who seemed like the brooding type. He didn't talk at all while I was there.'

The only Aaron she knew was Aaron Murphy, better known as

Murph. And Gordon Bennett. She hadn't seen either of them in over three years. They were there and she never got the chance to talk to them?

'I'd like the chance to get to know you.'

'To get to know me, or to quiz me?'

'To get to know you.'

'Well… how about tomorrow night then?'

'Around seven?' he smiled. 'I can pick you up.'

'Pick a place and I'll meet you there,' she pulled a card out of her bag and handed it to him. 'Here's my number… so you don't have to scour again,' she smiled.

He took it with a slightly brighter smile and nodded. 'Well then I'd better let you get back to work before Garda Jamie comes and boots me out.' He got to his feet and held up her card. 'Tomorrow night then.'

She nodded. 'See ya then.'

As soon as he left, a butterfly marathon kicked off in her stomach. She was nervous. It'd been years since she'd been on an actual *date*. What did people even do on those things? What did two strangers talk about over the course of a whole meal?

'Jesus Christ if I was ten years younger I'd make a man out of him,' Sheila barked from behind her, making Lindsey smile.

'I'd say someone already had that pleasure, Sheila.'

'I'll want details. Gory ones!'

'You're getting an assistant.'

'Shag off! Are you serious? Who?'

'He said to ask if you knew anyone,' she swivelled to face Sheila. 'Thing is, I owe someone a massive favour, if you wouldn't mind me giving her first dibs.'

'So long as it's someone I can work with, Lindsey. Don't mind sending me an aul airy fairy princess who's afraid to break a nail.'

Lindsey laughed out loud. 'You're safe as houses.'

CHAPTER SIXTEEN

Lindsey sat anxiously on a bench in Street's gym that evening, watching Jamie in the ring with another kid of roughly the same age. Owen was in there with them, coaching them, and she had to admit that Jamie looked good. He was fast on his feet and well able to duck enough jabs to tire his opponent, while delivering just the right amount of well-placed jabs of his own.

'Well, was I right?' Street came and sat alongside her.

'There's a first time for everything,' she smiled.

'He's good, right?'

'Yeah, he is,' she was still watching Jamie, very impressed by his skills.

'Why don't you gear up and go a few rounds?'

'I don't box.'

He laughed. 'You could've fooled me.'

'That's not boxing. That's fighting. Brawling even,' she smiled at him.

'Well… you haven't brawled in a while. Can I take that as a good sign?'

'I'm good as new. Hey, were Gordon and Murph at the hospital while I was there?'

He nodded. 'Wesley popped in for a minute too. Just long enough to ask if you'd live.' He smiled.

'Fuck. Why didn't anyone wake me?'

'Don't you think we tried?'

'How are they?'

He shrugged. 'They're alright.'

'Do you see them much?'

He shook his head. 'Not really. Every now and then just.' He leaned back with his head against the cool, cinderblock wall. 'Did Florence Nightingale track you down?'

'If you mean Jason, then yes, he did.'

'And?'

'I'm having dinner with him tomorrow night.'

He sat up straight again and smiled at her. 'Lindsey Ryan, going on a date. Well fuck me.'

She didn't answer.

'What?'

'What?' she shrugged.

'You look like you're about to have a tooth yanked out.'

'Forget it.'

He nudged her in the ribs. 'Spit it out woman. What?'

'It's ridiculous.'

He just stared at her, looking annoyingly amused.

'Have you been out with Sinéad yet?'

'Change the subject why don't ya? We went for drinks last night.'

'What did ye talk about?'

He sat back again and laughed quietly, 'Is that what you're worried about?'

'I'm not worried about anything. I'm just asking how your date went.'

'Date; what a ridiculous fucking word. It was just drinks and it went very well, I think. She's pretty cool.'

'Don't you find it awkward? You know, two strangers having to come up with all sorts of conversation topics, when you know that they're dying to ask all about...' her voice trailed off.

His smile faded and for the first time since she'd known him, he looked like he actually felt sorry for her, and she immediately regretted opening her mouth.

'Well... a pub is a little bit easier than dinner I suppose. More background noise, music; more distractions. I think though, being a bloke, I get away a little bit lighter than you on that front.'

She didn't respond.

'And of course I don't have the scars to prompt those questions either.'

'He already saw them. I know he's going to be thinking about them the whole time.'

'That's all in your head, Linds.'

'Wouldn't you be though? He found me in a heap, twice, and I know for a fact that he saw the state of my skin.'

'Hey…' he leaned forward and made her look at him. 'Those scars are there because you put your ass on the line. You should be damn fucking proud of those.'

'Oh I'm sorry; should I be lying on a couch for this? I have them, Street, because I reacted too slow. The same reason everything else went to shit that day.'

'You reacted too slow? I didn't react at all. I didn't even see it until after you started running towards it. None of us did. No one spotted the kid with the rifle either, Linds.' He shook his head. 'I don't know what the fuck happened that day. I was more switched on than ever, nervous even, while we walked along that road. I had a bad feeling in my gut from the minute we set off and I could feel the same tension from everyone else as well. And yet, it all still went to shit.'

Considering that they'd never actually had this conversation, it felt like a strange place to be having it. But maybe it was the perfect place, surrounded by noise and people and the knowledge that they wouldn't get too long to dwell on it. She shook her head and was only half surprised to feel tears rolling down her cheeks, but she still laughed when Street grabbed her face and used the palms of his hands to unceremoniously wipe them away. 'Street, you're rough as sin, you know that? You're giving me whiplash.'

He half smiled as she pulled her head away and nodded, acknowledging that she was fine.

'So here's how I look at it now. Like it or not, we're all going to carry this around for the rest of our lives. I blame myself. You blame yourself. I know for a fact that Damo, Murph, Gordon and Wesley all blame themselves too and if Lenny was still here, he'd be saying that it was his fault. According to Terry Hennessey...' he grinned, '... it's what normal people do. They blame themselves when something goes wrong. So get over it, Linds.'

'I'm over it,' she half smiled and wiped her face with her sleeve.

'Me too,' he lied back.

'How cool is Mr Hennessey though?' She smiled properly this time.

'He makes scones,' Street grinned broadly. 'I call every Tuesday while the wife is at her day care centre, so myself and Terry get to eat scones and have a bit of man time.'

'How strict are you two about *man* time? Those scones are kinda nice.'

'Tuesday around elevenses. We'd be willing to fit you in.'

She nodded.

'Now, back to this dinner date.'

She rolled her eyes. 'You actually felt sorry for me there. How fucking sad am I?'

'Correction; I felt sorry for *him*. The poor fucker had to come around here to find you. I wouldn't give him your number obviously and quizzed him well before I told him where you work...'

She laughed. 'And Jamie quizzed him before letting him into the Centre.'

Street looked at Jamie with an approving grin. He was still dancing around the place, while his opponent looked like he wanted to go home.

'My point is; he seemed like an OK guy. You want some advice?'

'Is it sound?' she grinned.

'I know you, Linds. You're going to be hung up on the fact that he saw your scars and you'll be doing that shit that women do...'

'What shit do women do?'

'You know, Oohh, I wonder what he's thinking... that shit.'

She laughed.

'Rip off the band-aid. Come straight out and tell him.'

She shook her head vigorously.

'Fine. Don't tell him. Instead just sit there and talk about the weather and shit. You know dinner can last for hours? Most fellas want all three courses.'

'That's what I'm worried about.'

'When was the last time you were on a *date*?' the word still sounded ridiculous.

She shrugged. 'The last time I started an actual relationship.'

He looked at the floor, clearly thinking. 'Jesus... was that...? he clicked his fingers as he tried to recall a name. 'The zookeeper fella?'

'He wasn't a zookeeper, he was a vet.'

'But he worked in Fota Wildlife Park?'

'Yeah, him.'

'That was...'

'Six years ago, when I started seeing him. When we went on one of these damn, *let's get to know each other* dates. We broke up a few months before we went to Syria.'

'Jesus. Now I actually do feel sorry for you,' he laughed.

'See?'

'I still say get it out of the way early, but it's up to you.'

'Can you get Jamie home?'

'No problem. I want to run through a few more things with him before I let him go.'

She got to her feet, giving Jamie a thumbs up as their session came to an end. She patted her leg and Frank jumped to his feet and followed her towards the door.

'Hey?'

She turned back to Street as she was about to let herself out.

'Don't forget to shave your legs,' he grinned like a child and she rolled her eyes and left.

On the drive home, she was preoccupied with the imaginary conversation she was planning on having with Jason, covering topics like the health service and all its problems, and the front line work that he did, but as she pulled up outside her house, Jason vanished from her mind and she became conscious of the fact that she was about to walk up her garden path alone in the dark. This was a task that she took far more seriously now and she did it with much more focus than she had in the past.

She parked as close to the house as she could and wedged her car key in her closed fist, with the pointy end protruding through her fingers. The new sensor lights still startled her a little when they came on as she opened the gate and she tightened her grip on the key. Street had the lights installed while she was in hospital and she wasn't overly fond of them, but she was happy for them to stay, for now. Frank trotted ahead of her to the door. He wasn't alarmed or distracted by anything, which meant that Lindsey didn't have to be either, but just before she got to the door, right where she'd been standing when she was hit with her own bat, something in the damp grass glinted in the light. Something silver.

She looked around instinctively to make sure that she was alone, before hunching down to examine the delicate silver chain with a little crucifix on it. She'd seen one exactly like it once before, on the Claragh Mountains in Millstreet and she remembered thinking that it looked like the kind of thing a parent might give to a child when making their first holy communion. She took out her phone and photographed it, while her mind took off in a whole new direction, with no idea where it might end up.

After a few minutes, she called Frank and headed back to her car and back to the Centre, which was of course in darkness. She unset the alarm and reset it again as soon as she was inside, then she made her way to the office and rooted through the files that were piled there.

None of them belonged to a girl called Laura, the only other teenager with the hill walking club that day. So she started with file one, reading everything in it. Family members, any gang affiliates. Anything that mentioned the name of someone, other than the name of whose file she was reading. It took her three hours to get through them all and none of them mentioned anyone by the name of Laura.

She went to the kitchen to find Sheila's secret stash of dog food and she filled a bowl for Frank, along with some water, before returning to the office to sit at the desk and stare at the wall, thinking. What did the girl tell her? She was from Maryborough. Her dad was a solicitor and her mother was a teacher. Did she mention a surname? She shook her head. No. 'Fuck.' Who was she and what was she doing in Lindsey's garden?

The sound of doors rattling open downstairs made her literally jump out of her seat. She'd fallen asleep with her head at such an angle that her neck cried out in pain as files slid off the desk and onto the floor. She'd spent hours staring at the wall, staring at the files, staring at the ceiling, but the only conclusion she'd come to was that she didn't know Laura. Maybe the chain wasn't hers. Maybe it was one just like it and belonged to someone else.

'You're in early,' it was Sheila, of course. 'When's my assistant starting?'

'Hellooo?' the brash voice echoed up from downstairs and Lindsey grinned.

'Soon, hopefully,' she got up and went to the stairs. 'Up here, Kathleen.'

The woman ambled up the stairs and when she got to the top, she and Sheila eyed each other suspiciously. Physically, they were complete opposites; one was skinny, bony and lanky, the other round and small, but both came from the same school of hard knocks where trust was hard earned and right now, neither of them trusted the other.

'Hello,' Kathleen greeted Sheila with an almost uncomfortable grandness.

'Hello,' Sheila responded in kind.

'Kathleen? Come in.' Lindsey gestured towards her office and Sheila made her excuses and headed for the kitchen.

'She hates me,' Kathleen whispered loudly, as Lindsey closed the door and smiled despite her tiredness.

'She doesn't.'

'What's this about, Lindsey?'

'Look, I don't want to put you on the spot or anything, Kathleen, but something came up here and I wanted to run it by you.'

'What is it?'

'Well… we're looking for staff. Someone to help Sheila out around here.'

Kathleen was looking at her, like she genuinely had no clue where this was headed.

'I wondered if you'd be interested.'

'In a job?' she looked confused.

Lindsey shrugged.

'Who'd want to hire me?'

'When was the last time you had a job?'

'I've worked since I was fourteen.'

'Doing what?'

'Same thing I'm doing now.'

Lindsey nodded, feeling in her heart for the woman, but she didn't show it. She was sure that Kathleen wanted sympathy about as much as Lindsey did.

'Well… I don't know how you feel about moving into a new area, but we are hiring someone. It's tough work, preparing up to thirty or forty meals some days, cleaning; keeping this whole place running smoothly.'

Kathleen looked around her, as if for the first time. 'And you'd be my boss?'

Lindsey laughed. 'No. I'm a dogsbody here. The boss is Liam. That's probably him thumping up the stairs now.'

'And you reckon he'd hire me? Lindsey I'm a brasser. Who in their right mind would give me a job?'

'I would. In a heartbeat. Now would you take it, or not?'

She hesitated. Then nodded, still looking confused.

'Well, wait here then. Or better still, go in and get a cuppa. Trust me, you'll like Sheila.'

Lindsey went down the hall to Liam's office, where he'd just arrived himself. She knocked brusquely and followed him in, before he'd even had a chance to put away his lunch box.

'Lindsey... eh, hi. What can I do for you?'

'I have someone for that job.'

'What job?'

'To help Sheila out.'

'Oh! Right... you have someone already.'

'You wanna talk to her?'

'She's here?' Liam sounded alarmed. 'Now?'

Lindsey nodded, struggling to hide her exasperation.

'Has she Garda clearance?'

'She has a character reference from a Garda and one from me.'

'From you?'

'Yes. I vouch for her.'

'And a character reference from the Garda... not Garda clearance? Why not?'

Lindsey wasn't about to tell the man that his new employee couldn't get Garda clearance due to her profession and the number of arrests for same. Nor that she had to beg Sinéad to give a character reference, again based on Lindsey vouching for her. Instead, she gave the answer that she'd prepared earlier. 'Garda clearance can take months to come through and Sheila needs help now. And technically, Kathleen doesn't really need clearance. Most of the cleaning can be done in the evenings, after the kids are gone. She could come in early, at this time, to help out in the kitchen. Generally speaking, the kids don't get here 'til after ten. They're gone by four. Her work would get done outside of those hours.'

He mulled it over for a few minutes. 'And you vouch for her?'

She nodded.

'Give me ten minutes and send her down.'

'Right.' Lindsey left and as she made her way back to the office, Kathleen was sitting in the dining area, drinking tea with Sheila. They were smiling while they talked. That was a good start.

'Kathleen, give Liam a few minutes, time enough for you to finish your cuppa and then head down to him. He'll get you sorted.' Lindsey smiled at the women and then headed back into the office.

'Hey, Lindsey?'

She stuck her head back out.

'Thanks, love.' Kathleen was smiling fondly at her.

Lindsey smiled and nodded, then went inside and closed the door. She opened her diary and scrolled back through the dates until she found the name and number that she was looking for. The phone was answered on the fifth ring.

'Hello?'

'Hi, is that Tim?'

'Speaking.'

'It's Lindsey Ryan calling from the Tús Núa Centre.'

'Hi Lindsey, how're tricks?'

'Not bad. Tim, I want to ask about one of your members. Remember the young girl who was on the hike with you the same day that we came along? Her name was Laura something.'

'I remember two young girls, aside from yourself. One was a blonde...'

'That was Leah. She was one of mine. I'm talking about the other one.'

'I remember her. Was she not one of yours too?'

'No. I thought she might have been a club member? She gave me the impression that she was with your group.'

'Well she explicitly told me that she was with *your* group. I remember she arrived about twenty minutes before you did at the City Hall. She said that she was dropped off early and was waiting for you to get there.'

'Fuck,' she muttered.

'Is there a problem?'

'She didn't happen to tell you her surname, did she?' Or anything else about herself?'

'No, nothing. I only talked to her for a few minutes before you arrived though. I was trying to sort out the bus, but during that time she talked mostly about you to be honest, which is why I'm surprised that you don't know her surname. She seemed to know you pretty well.'

'What did she say?'

'Just that she was looking forward to seeing you because she hadn't seen you in ages. She mentioned that you were a friend of the family and that was about it really. Like I said, I was only talking to her for a minute.'

'Right. Thanks Tim. Listen, if you happen to think of anything else she might have said, would you mind giving me a call back here?'

'No problem.'

As she hung up, Mike came into the office. 'How did you get on with the files?'

'I'm working on it.'

'Lindsey, for Christ sake, tell me you've at least looked at them.'

'Mike, I'm working on it.'

'Fine. Well, here's some more for you to work on,' he landed another, smaller bundle of files on the desk. 'These are very unlikely in my eyes, but if nothing's jumping out at you in that lot, then leave no stone unturned.'

He turned and left without saying any more. He was clearly still pissed off with her, but she couldn't bring herself to care about that today.

She leaned back in her chair and looked at the files. On the top of the pile was Damien Lucey and she rolled her eyes. These weren't going to help.

'Hey?' Kathleen stuck her head in Lindsey's door. She was excited in the same way that a teenager might be when they thought they'd just gotten away with something. 'He gave me the job. I start at half seven in the morning.'

'Brilliant.' Lindsey forced a smile.

'This is my first job,' she was still smiling, but suddenly looked nervous.

'You'll like it here, Kathleen.'

'I won't know what to do with myself… going home in the evening and what? Watching telly?'

Lindsey shrugged. 'Trust me, you'll be knackered by the time you get there.'

'I'm well used to that. You're a decent woman, Lindsey.'

'So are you.'

Kathleen gave a brisk nod and looked like she was about to become emotional, so she promptly left, just as Jamie arrived in her doorway.

'Jamie. Everything alright?'

'I need a word,' he said in a manly tone, which sounded practised.

She gestured towards the empty chair.

'I saw you crying in the gym last night.'

Lindsey sat up straight and switched on. Here was a boy whose toes barely touched the ground when he sat down opposite her, but he was deadly serious.

'Is it because of that fella that was here yesterday? That Jason fella.'

Lindsey smiled. She couldn't help it. 'No, it had nothing to do with Jason.'

'Is he the reason why Adam isn't your boyfriend?'

'Definitely not, no.'

'Did Adam do something?'

'Did you ask him?' she had the feeling that he had.

He nodded.

'And what did he say?'

'He said that if I wanted to know something about someone, then I should ask them myself. He said that you should never trust third hand information.'

'Wise words,' she nodded.

'So? Did he do something?'

Lindsey leaned forward with her hands clasped in front of her. 'Jamie, Adam is my best friend. He could never upset me.'

'Then why were you crying?'

She stayed quiet for a second while she gathered her response. Jamie didn't appreciate being spoken to like a child, or being patronised, so she did her best not to do either. 'Jamie, you've had some horrible things happen in your life.'

'What's that got to do with…?'

'Well, so have I. You don't particularly like to talk about them and neither do I. But every now and then, you don't have a choice. It all comes flooding back, sometimes out of nowhere and there's nothing you can do about it. You have to let it out or eventually you'll blow,' she sat back and replayed those words in her head. It was as if the idea had never occurred to her before.

'What if you never want to talk about it? Ever. Not to anyone.'

She shrugged. 'That's exactly how I've always felt. Then one night, not so long ago…' she shook her head, 'like I said; I didn't have a choice. I just opened my mouth and blurted the whole lot out. To a complete stranger no less!' she half smiled. 'Then before I knew it, I was talking to someone else… a neighbour actually. And to Street,' she guffawed.

'What's so funny?'

'When I say it out loud like that, I've spoken about my life to more people in the past week, than I ever have in my whole life.'

'But what difference does it make? It's not like blabbing about it can make it go away.'

She shook her head again. 'Jamie, last week I would have agreed with you completely. And in theory, you're right. It can't undo what was done. But I'm surprised to say… I feel better.'

He didn't reply. He was thinking.

'I think the trick is to find at least one person who you can trust with anything. You can tell them anything and they won't judge you. You can cry if you need to and they won't see it as a weakness. Or most importantly for me, they won't harp on about it. They'll only talk about it when *you* feel like talking about it. For me, that person is Adam. What about you? Do you have someone like that?'

He shrugged.

'I can think of at least three people.'

'Who?'

'Well, me for one,' she smiled. 'And Adam Street. He always has room for another best friend. And let's not forget Mike.'

He thought about it for a minute and then gave an almost imperceptible nod. 'Can I ask you something?'

'OK.'

'The thing that happened to you…?'

She nodded, hoping that he wouldn't ask her for details. She wanted to answer the boy's questions honestly, but no child needed those details. And she wouldn't give them to him.

'Was it when you were a soldier?'

'It was.'

'Is it why you have a scar on the side of your forehead? You cover it with your hair, but I saw it a couple of times.'

She looked to the ceiling and smiled, before making eye contact with him again. 'Jamie, whatever you decide to do in your life, you're going to be really good at it. You pay more attention to people than anyone else I've met at this centre. And I've met a lot of people here.'

He continued to look evenly at her. He wasn't letting her away with a non-answer.

She took a deep breath. 'Yes Jamie. A lot of people have scars from their past. Mine just happen to be on the outside.'

'But you don't like talking about it?'

'Not particularly.'

'Except with people you trust?'

'When I *need* to talk about it.'

'How do you know that you can trust someone?'

She thought about her answer. 'Because I know them and they know me. They know my flaws, but accept me for who I am. They would have seen me at my worst and still think the best of me. I can talk to them and know that they'll never betray my confidence. People like that, you can trust.'

'They? So it's not just Adam?'

She shrugged her shoulders. 'People like that can be hard to find, Jamie, but they are out there. For me, Adam is one, but there are others. I just don't get to see them much any more.'

'I trust you,' Jamie surprised her with his response. 'I trust Adam too.

I just wanted to make sure that he wasn't the one who upset you.'

She smiled broadly. The kid had a heart of gold. 'He never would.'

'Well, just so you know; you can trust me too.'

'I do, Jamie.'

He got up and left without another word and Lindsey was genuinely touched and impressed by the fact that he didn't come out and ask the questions that he was clearly dying to ask. Like how exactly she got the scars and what she and Street had been through together. In fact Jamie Cussons might have been the most impressive kid she'd ever met, let alone had the pleasure of working with. He was a hell of a lot more grown up than she felt at times.

Thinking about impressive kids, brought Damien Lucey to mind and she idly picked his file up off the top of the new pile. She flicked through it to the most recent entry, which was made in Mike's handwriting. It was an update with last Saturday's date, stating that Damien left Cork, headed for the University of South Wales to study psychology.

She read the update again. And again. And one more time before cursing under her breath. She slammed the file shut, got to her feet and jogged down the stairs.

'Hey, Mike?' Lindsey had to shout to be heard over the noise of the basketball pounding up and down the court, with the chorus of shouts and jeers echoing all around them. After receiving a wealth of pointers from the Neptune team yesterday, suddenly everyone was a professional basketball player in the making. Mike was standing on the sidelines watching with the same keen interest he had in everything that went on around here.

'Hey,' he replied, barely taking his eyes off the game.

'Did you talk to Damien Lucey before he left?'

'Yeah, I brought him to the airport.'

'How was he?'

'Nervous, excited; all the things you'd expect. I'm so happy for that kid. He deserves this.'

'I know; me too. Was he still worried about his family? He was talking about not going a few weeks ago.'

He rolled his eyes and tutted. 'You know, his mother has put so much fucking pressure on his shoulders that he's convinced they won't survive without him.'

'And what about his sister, where's she?'

'She's in St Brendan's, in Mayfield. She's giving them all a run for their money apparently. Greg's being released from hospital tomorrow. He'll be heading for the same group home.'

'How is he?'

He shrugged. 'They say he's fine. Physically at least. I'll be keeping a close eye on him though. Poor fucker. Defend Alison, defend!' he roared.

Lindsey went back to the office and passed the rest of the day with paperwork, but for the first time since starting work here, she was watching the clock for the whole afternoon. When the kids finally left and she and Mike tidied up, Lindsey was out the door as quickly as she could.

St Brendan's was only a short distance from the Centre, but she drove there anyway because she wasn't sure yet what she was going to do once she got there. For now, she and Frank were sitting in her car outside the house, which from the outside, looked like any other end of terrace home, but with an extension on the side and back. Almost half an hour passed before she decided to get out of the car and approach the front door.

She rang the buzzer and waited.

'Hello?'

'Hi, I'm here to see Anne Mayfair? It's Lindsey Ryan from Tús Núa.' Lindsey knew the names of most of people who ran group homes in the area. Anne was particularly nice and also particularly tough.

'Well, you'd better come in if you want to see me.' Lindsey detected a smile in the woman's voice. The buzzer buzzed and the door clicked open.

'Lindsey? How are you girl?'

I'm good, Anne. You?' the women shook hands.

'Ah you know yourself. Never a dull moment in this place. Nine kids and one more arriving tomorrow.'

'Greg Patterson,' Lindsey nodded.

'You know him? Is that a sign of things to come,' she grinned.

'He's a good kid, Anne. Just got a raw deal.'

She nodded. 'Like all of them. Anyway, what can I do for you?'

'I'm really looking for Laura Lucey. Is she here?'

Anne rolled her eyes and blew out a long breath. 'Oh she's here alright. Technically, she's grounded. She likes to push the boundaries that one.'

'Would it be OK if I talk to her for a minute?'

'Anything I need to know about?'

'Not really. I know her brother just left for college. I feel I owe it to him to check in with her.'

'In that case, up the stairs, girl's corridor is on the left and she's the last room on the right.'

'Thanks, Anne.' Lindsey headed up the stairs, while Anne immediately went back to whatever it was she was doing. She was possibly the busiest woman in Cork on any given day.

The carpet on the stairs was brown and well worn, while the wall all the way up was adorned with dozens of photos of kids who'd past through the house. Some as far back as the 80s. Or at least she presumed so, judging by the outfits. At the top of the stairs, the hall went left and right. The boy's side and the girl's side and there were three doors in each hall. There were also motion sensors at the end of each hall and at the top of the stairs. This presumably was to stop any intermingling during the night, or to deter anyone from leaving the house after dark. Lindsey followed Anne's directions to the last room. She knocked and waited but there was no answer, so she knocked again and went inside.

There were two sets of bunk beds in the room, but only one, a top bunk, was occupied. She was wearing the same tracksuit that she'd worn on the hill walk and ear buds in her ears. Lindsey could hear the music from where she was standing in the doorway.

'Laura?'

No answer. The girl hadn't looked up and was seemingly unaware that Lindsey was there.

Lindsey reached out and tapped her on the arm, making her jump and yank the buds out of her ears. Her face was a picture of pure shock at first, before hardening dramatically.

'What're you doing here?'

'You weren't expecting me?'

She was hesitating like most teenagers did when they were trying to come up with a clever answer on the spot. 'No offence, but I don't think I'll be dragging my ass up any more mountains with your old codger friends, if that's what you're wondering.'

Lindsey nodded and sat on the edge of the bottom bunk opposite her. 'That wasn't you though. That was a girl from Maryborough who just looked like you.'

She dropped the pretence and turned immediately hostile. 'Would you want to admit that you were shoved into this fucking shithole?' she roared.

Lindsey didn't flinch. She shrugged her shoulders and looked around the room. It was cramped with the four beds and four old fashioned and cheap pine lockers. A freestanding pine wardrobe stood at either side of the small sash window, which was draped with a net curtain. The window also had a sensor alarm fitted. The furnishings and carpets were old and worn, but the place was clean and well cared for, as were the kids, knowing Anne Mayfair. 'What's so bad about it?'

She guffawed and her face was filled with disgust, as she turned away from Lindsey and stuck her buds back in her ears.

Lindsey reached across and gently pulled the lead, so that the buds popped out again.

'Hey fuck you. What the fuck do you want from me?'

'Nothing. What do you want from me?'

'Why would I want anything from a nosy old bitch like you?'

'Where's your crucifix? The nice silver one that you were wearing on the walk.'

She reached for her neck instinctively, but didn't answer.

Lindsey opened her hand and the chain dropped down. She held it, wrapped around her finger.

Laura's eyes widened. She paused for a second before shouting again. 'You fucking robbed it, you bitch.'

She grabbed for the chain, but Lindsey pulled it back. 'Don't you remember where you lost it?'

'I didn't lose it, you stole it.'

'It was sitting there for days before I found it. You have quite a swing with a baseball bat.'

'What are you talking about? Get the fuck out, I don't have to talk to you. And give me back my chain. My brother gave me that.'

Lindsey shrugged. 'You don't have to talk to me, Laura.' She ignored her claims that her chain had been stolen. 'I'm guessing you didn't see the cameras though, did you?'

There was no response.

'See, someone's been following me for a long time now, taking photos and leaving them for me to find, threatening me. All cowardly stuff really. Clearly it was someone who didn't have the guts to confront me to my face, so I didn't pay it much attention.'

'Sounds like you stuck your nose into the wrong person's business.'

'Anyway, that's why I had the cameras installed,' she bluffed.

'Nothing to do with me what you do.'

'You sure about that? It's just that the guards have been asking and asking for me to get my footage to them, so that they could see for themselves who snuck up and hit me from behind. I think that someone who sneaks around behind someone's back, following them, hiding in bushes, hitting them without giving them a chance to defend themselves; they're either a complete and utter coward, or they're scared. What do you think?'

'I think maybe you're scared. Why else would you be here?'

'Laura, you've been paying close enough attention to me to know that I have a dog called Frank. But I'm not sure if you really know how much

236

he means to me. See, you can knock me out all you want, and yes, I'll be as mad as hell about it. But give my dog a heart attack and you have two choices; make me understand – give me a damn good reason, or you'd better batten down the hatches, girl. So what's it to be?'

Laura laughed out loud. 'You're here because someone gave your fucking mutt a heart attack? That's brilliant. And whoever knocked you out, I wanna shake their hand.' She was smiling, looking genuinely happy. 'But I'm sorry to disappoint you, I never touched you or your bloody dog and I know fuck all about you either, except that you tore my family apart. You really think that I haven't seen more than enough of you for one lifetime? I fucking hate you. Why would I want to waste my time following you around?'

'Why were you on that hill walk then?'

'I wanted to know what by brother saw in you. Plus, it's a free country. I can go wherever I like.'

'Fine. So you're choosing option B, which starts with me handing the film over to the guards.' Of course Lindsey didn't have cameras outside her house and her bluff didn't seem to be working as well as she'd hoped. But now she had no real option but to continue. 'It's in high resolution, so they'll see you quite clearly and soon this place will look pretty good to you when you think back on it.' She got to her feet. 'As I said, that's only where option B starts.'

Laura grinned. 'If you had footage of me doing anything, I'm sure I'd be thrown into some hole by now. I really hope that whoever *is* following you around makes their move soon.'

Lindsey stood quietly looking at her for a minute. She was cold and genuinely didn't seem to care, so either she knew that Lindsey was bluffing about the cameras, or she wasn't worried about getting caught.

'Stop fucking looking at me!' Laura suddenly screeched and jumped down off the bunk. Without warning, she then grabbed her head in her hands and began tearing at her own hair. Then she screamed and started slamming her own head into the wall.

Lindsey grabbed her and wedged her hand between Laura's forehead and the concrete, as Anne came running into the room.

'Not this again, Laura,' she shouted, exasperated, as she ran to the other side of her and helped Lindsey to pull her back. Her head was bleeding. 'Call an ambulance, Lindsey.'

Lindsey let go, but not before they had Laura on the bed with Anne holding her by the shoulders.

Twenty minutes later, Jason and his colleague Jack entered the room. It wasn't until then that she remembered that she was due to have dinner with him that night. In two hours time to be precise.

He and Jack were amazing at what they did. Like they had with her, they chatted to Laura as if they were chatting over coffee, while they worked in perfect rhythm with each other. Checking her vitals, treating the wound on her forehead, asking all three of them what happened and it was only after they had Laura in the ambulance and were about to leave, when Jason asked, 'We still good for later?'

Lindsey nodded, even though the last thing she felt like doing now was having a *get to know each other* dinner with a stranger, no matter how gorgeous he was. Of course if it was a question of skipping dinner and going straight to his place… now *that* she wouldn't mind at all.

CHAPTER SEVENTEEN

She was late arriving of course and looked nothing like she would have planned to, had she actually been planning, and as she walked into the little tapas place that he'd booked, she was grateful for two things. Firstly, tapas were small. Generally speaking, small meals didn't equate to a three hour long affair as far as she knew and secondly, she was grateful for the fact that the place itself was also small and very dimly lit, mostly by candlelight.

Before going to meet Jason, she'd spent another half hour talking to Anne, before going home and spending more time sitting in her armchair thinking about Laura. She was clearly a troubled girl who needed help. But never the less, she'd triggered a lot of shit for Lindsey and that was before she brutally attacked her and worked Frank into a frenzy. It took everything she had to feel sympathy for her. And yet, a part of her did.

'Hey, there you are,' Jason got to his feet as she approached the table. In the restaurant's ambient light, he looked even better than before, wearing a fitted shirt and dark jeans. He caught her by the hand and leaned across to kiss her on the cheek before she sat down, bringing her focus firmly back to him and sending the butterflies into full flight in her stomach.

'Sorry I'm late.'

'No problem. You clearly had work to do. How do you feel about wine?'

'I feel great about wine.' She smiled finally, and he held up his hand to the waitress. There was no further mention of Laura, which made it clear that he took confidentiality as seriously as Lindsey did and she liked him a little bit more for that.

By the time they ordered their second bottle of wine, they'd been through every topic of normal conversation she could think of. They covered the weather first, then the refugee crises, which took a little longer to discuss. Then they moved on to the state of the health service and after having a go off several politicians, she finally couldn't think of anything else to say and was aware once again of how alien this was to her.

'So how's your dog?'

'He's OK. Did you know what happened to him?'

'Yeah, Adam told me. You two are pretty close, huh?'

'Who, me and Frank or me and Adam?' she smiled.

'Frank?'

'My dog.'

'Oh,' he laughed. 'Cool name. Well both, from what I gather.'

'Yeah, I suppose. Up until recently though, I hadn't seen Adam for about three years. But with him…' she shrugged, 'it's pretty easy to pick up where you left off.'

'How come you didn't see him for so long?'

'Life got in the way,' was the answer that she came up with.

'Yip, that can happen.'

They were quiet for a while then and Lindsey found herself obsessing again about whether or not he was thinking about her scars. He seemed awkward all of a sudden and no doubt, she seemed the same to him. Minutes passed like hours and there was still silence.

'Are you wondering about the night we met?' she blurted out.

'Which one?' he smiled.

'That's a yes.'

'I promised you that I wasn't going to quiz you and I won't.'

'Thank you.'

He nodded and returned his attention to his wine. 'Can I tell you something?'

'Please do,' she smiled, glad of the new topic, whatever it may be.

'When I was a kid, my mother and I lived with my grandparents down in Bandon. They had a farm there.'

'Nice.'

He shrugged. 'Nan was what people used to call an eccentric,' he smiled fondly at the memory of her.

'You know, I like eccentric people,' Lindsey smiled and it was true, she did.

'Well in that case, you would have loved my nan.'

'What made her an eccentric?'

'Ah she used to have these… *episodes*, where she'd do something completely random. Like one night, in the middle of the night actually during calving season, she wrestled the vet to the ground. She was shouting all sorts at him and she slapped him over and over again in the face. He hadn't a clue what was going on, but while he was gathering himself, Nan delivered the calf.'

Lindsey laughed quietly. 'I like her already.'

'There was other stuff too. Like one day my granddad was called into Bandon town by the local butcher. Nan was curled in a ball, screaming in the corner of the shop. Of course everyone legged it, thinking she was possessed or something. Granddad was the only one who could calm her down. At that stage, some of the people who used to call her eccentric started calling her barmy instead. Of course this didn't happen every day. She could go months without anything and during that time, she was like any other nan. Well, almost. She still tore around the farm like a legend up until she was in her eighties.'

He stared into his glass of wine, as he twisted the glass idly. Lindsey waited patiently for him to continue.

'They didn't have a name for it then, let alone any form of treatment.'

'A name for what? What was it?'

'Before she met my grandfather, Nan was a nurse in Birmingham in

241

the nineteen forties. She was a midwife actually,' he smiled.

'During the war?' She could see where this was headed, but she still wanted to hear it. She'd never know his nan, but she felt a strange kinship with her.

He nodded, 'You should Google the Birmingham Blitz some time. Nan was in the middle of it at only seventeen years old. Treating men, women and children while trying to stay alive herself.'

'Those nurses were the unsung heroes of World War Two.'

'You said it.'

'Your nan had PTSD,' she mumbled.

'Not in her day. In her day she was eccentric; barmy, gone in the head,' he smiled wryly, though she could tell that it hurt him. He clearly loved his nan.

'A bit like me,' she returned his wry smile.

'She was none of those things and I'm guessing, neither are you.'

'I don't know about that,' she chuffed. 'I know why you're telling me this.'

He shrugged. 'I don't. Not really. It's not something that I normally tell people.'

'But you saw my scars, saw my *episodes* and put two and two together.'

'You don't have to tell me anything. That's not why I brought this up. I just wanted you to know that I understand what a bastard it is. I also understand that it affects some of the strongest people in society and in a lot of cases, they're suffering because they put themselves in a place that most other people would have run a mile from.'

'How come you lived with your nan?' The question was out of her mouth before she could stop it. It was personal and she shouldn't have asked, but she wanted to move on.

He sat back and smiled knowingly and she was thankful for the fact that he moved along with her. 'Well, my dad left when I was six months old or thereabouts. So Nan insisted that we come live with them, so that my mother could still work. Nan took care of me.'

'She clearly meant a lot to you.'

He nodded. 'She was an amazing woman.'

Lindsey asked question after question about Jason's nan and he told one story after another about the woman, who was clearly well ahead of her time, making Lindsey wish that she'd known her. He also told some stories about himself and before they knew it, they were the only ones left in the restaurant and the tired staff were giving them the stink eye.

When they finally left, Jason hailed a taxi and gave the driver both of their addresses and she couldn't help feeling a little bit disappointed that they were about to go their separate ways. But she also knew that she wanted to see him again.

He kept the meter running while he walked her to her door. 'Thank you for tonight, Lindsey. I really enjoyed it.'

'Me too,' she smiled as he leaned in to kiss her. It was long and slow and delicious and left her wanting more. Like the dreaded date itself.

Lindsey sat in her office the next morning with the phone held tightly to her ear.

'Hello?'

'Anne, its Lindsey.'

'Hiya love.'

'How's Laura? Is she back?'

'Yeah, she's here. She's not talking to me, naturally, so I have no idea what yesterday was all about.'

'Has she done anything like that before?'

'She has a history of self-harming, yes.'

'Can I talk to her again today?'

'I don't know, Lindsey. She's quite fragile, even though she goes to extreme lengths to pretend that she's not.'

'I understand that and I promise I'll tread carefully. It's important, Anne. She's about to get herself in some serious trouble. I assure you, I'm trying to help her.'

'What is it? What's she done?'

'Can I talk to her first?'

There was silence for a few seconds, before Anne sighed and said, 'OK. Come around when you're ready. She's not going anywhere today.'

Lindsey had roughly four hours of arts and crafts to get through before she could leave that day. Their volunteer, Liz, was a qualified art therapist in her fifties, though her main job was that of a bored housewife, possibly volunteering to make herself feel better. And maybe to feel useful. One of her conditions was that she would not be left alone with the children. She did use the word *children*, but she always seemed nervous around them. Like she expected one of them to eat her at any moment, which might have had something to do with why she wasn't actually employed as an art therapist.

The only thing that got Lindsey through the day without wanting to pull her hair out, was that Greg Patterson was back. He was quiet, but he was back. What's more, he and Jamie spent the full day working on a model of some Jedi Starfighter together, which was apparently a big deal. For Lindsey, the big deal was this unlikely friendship that seemed to be forming between the two.

When Liz finally finished and they'd cleaned up the enormous mess they'd made, Lindsey offered Greg a lift back to St Brendan's, as she was going there anyway.

'It's good to have you back, Greg,' she started the conversation, not knowing if he'd talk back. He sat in her car and they left the Centre. He chose to sit in the back with Frank. 'It was too quiet without you.'

As she expected, he didn't respond. Instead he stroked Frank's head. Some people would find it amazing that a child who was quite volatile and outspoken could now only be comforted by a dog. But to Lindsey, that was completely understandable. And normal.

'I take it you met Anne last night? She's one of the good ones you know.'

Silence.

'I'm on my way to see her now.'

'I don't want you two talking about me,' he finally spoke adamantly.

'We won't be. Although I did tell her that she'd better take good care of you,' she smiled at him in the rear view mirror. 'But that's it. I need to see her about something else today.'

And that was the end of their almost one-sided conversation, as minutes later they were pulling up outside St Brendan's.

'Hey you two,' Anne opened the door with a smile and she tousled Greg's hair as he passed her into the hall, even though she had to reach up to do it. Greg ignored her and headed straight up the stairs, presumably to his room. 'How is he?' Anne mouthed when he was out of sight.

Lindsey shrugged.

'Poor kid.'

'Is Laura in her room?'

Anne blew out a breath. 'I'm trusting you here, Lindsey. I'm trusting you to tell me anything that I need to know. I'm responsible for that girl and I...'

'And I appreciate that, Anne.'

Anne paused for a minute, before motioning her towards the stairs.

Like yesterday, her first knock went unanswered, so she knocked a second time and walked in.

Laura was in the same position as yesterday only on the lower bunk, sitting with her legs crossed over each other. She raised her head just enough to give Lindsey a filthy look, then lowered her eyes back to the magazine that she was pretending to read.

'How's your head feeling?' Laura had a large white dressing covering her wound.

Like with Greg, she got no answer, but of course that wasn't enough to deter Lindsey, so she took a seat on the bed opposite her again. Thanks to the fact that Jason was apparently a gentleman, Lindsey had the whole night to think about Laura and why it was that she hated Lindsey so much. She could only come up with one possible answer.

'Remember that day on the Claragh Mountain?'

No answer.

Lindsey injected a small smile into her voice. 'I normally love that kinda thing, but I must admit, if it wasn't for you, Leah and Greg, I would have been bored out of my mind.'

Laura rolled her eyes.

'You know, you looked familiar to me that day. It was annoying that I couldn't think where I knew you from. But I remember now.'

Laura glanced at her.

'It was the night that Damien went to hospital.'

The two of them stayed silent for a while now, before Lindsey finally spoke again.

'I was fairly new to this job back then and I suppose like all of us starting off, I thought I could save the world,' she half smiled, though there was nothing pleasant about this. 'At least up until that night I did.'

Laura glanced at her again and Lindsey ran her hands through her hair. 'I'll be honest with you, Laura; that night frightened me,' she looked pointedly at the kid across from her, who was looking at her finally. 'And you were sitting on the stairs looking a hell of a lot braver than I would have been at your age. I saw you. And then I left with your brother.'

'That's right,' she growled. 'You took my brother and left me there.'

'You weren't left there. Your social worker had you.'

'You didn't give a damn, so fuck you and your, *You're so brave* speech. What did you think would happen to me? Or did you even think about that?'

'You went to live with a family called the O'Halloran's.'

Laura looked a little taken aback that Lindsey knew that. For Lindsey's part, she didn't want to admit that the only reason she knew, was because Damien begged her to enquire.

'Damien worried about you and your mother constantly.'

'So why didn't he come for me?'

Lindsey was too slow to answer so Laura continued venomously.

'I'll tell you why; he was too busy sucking up to you to give a damn about what was happening to me.'

Lindsey paused as her thoughts took off in a new direction. One that she didn't like. 'Laura, Damien was only with me... us, because he was court ordered to be. He didn't want to be separated from you. In fact, he still wants to be with you. That's why he almost didn't go to college last week...'

Laura started with a growl that soon became a roar, to shut Lindsey up. After that, they sat in silence for a minute, while Lindsey waited her out.

'Then why did he go?' she shouted finally.

'Because it's the only way that he'll be able to make a life, Laura. He wants to take care of you, but you need an education if you want to take care of anyone. Yourself included.'

'You made him go!'

Lindsey nodded. 'I encouraged him to, yes. Just like I'd wish the same thing for you.'

Laura screeched out a laugh. 'Yeaah! Of course that'll happen. Why don't I just pack my bags now and head off to Harvard.'

'You don't think you could do it?'

'Fuck off.'

'Damien thought you could. He told me that you were the one who used to read him bedtime stories when you were kids, instead of it being the other way round,' she smiled. 'He talked about you a lot actually, how you were the one always making sure that he was OK. He told me once that if you decided that you were going to do something, then hell or high water wouldn't stop you. So what's changed?'

'That's right. I always made sure *he* was OK,' she chose to ignore everything else.

'So what didn't he know, Laura?'

She curled into her seated position again and pretended to read the magazine.

'What happened when you went to the O'Halloran's?'

No answer. Lindsey sat back on the bed and curled her legs under her. She wasn't leaving, but she wasn't going to push her either. The two sat in silence for over twenty minutes, before Laura finally spoke.

'Why are you still here? What difference will it make? We were perfectly fine at home. Me and Damien looked out for each other, no matter what. But then a bunch of nosy busy bodies like you came along and tore us apart. You ruined our fucking lives, just because you thought you had the right.'

'Laura, Damien could have been killed that night. We couldn't walk away and leave you both there.'

'But you did walk away. From me. Damien got to go off and do whatever he wanted, while I was sent away to become a new fucking toy for some fat fuck on the south side.'

Lindsey could feel her chest tightening and her breathing becoming less comfortable. She barely managed to get any words to come out. 'Laura did someone…'

'Yes, someone fucking did!' she screeched. 'That same someone who they said could look after me better than my own mother could,' she laughed sarcastically. 'My mother's a bitch, I know that. But I'd rather be punched in the face by her than have some fat, smelly fuck climbing on top of me whenever he felt like it.'

For the first time in years, Lindsey had no idea what to say. What could she possibly say that would make any difference whatsoever to this girl?

'What, no wise words now?' Laura asked, her voice loaded with sarcasm. 'Why don't you just tell me that it was my own fault and get it over with. Then get the fuck out and leave me alone.'

'Because it wasn't your fault, Laura. The system failed you and nothing I say can change that. Is that why you were following me? You blame me.'

'You keep going on about me following you! If it wasn't for you, Damien would still be here. I'd be with him and not here. I don't ever want to see you. Ever! You know, he used to sneak out to see me every day when we weren't living together, but all of a sudden he was having extra study sessions, or going camping, or meeting with teachers and all because you made him. *You* took him away from me. *You* made him not care what happened to me. Thanks to *you*, if I ever see him again, he'll think he's too good for me.'

'Laura, you could not be more wrong. All Damien could talk about was you and your mother. He's worried sick about you and always has been. He adores you.'

She shook her head and angrily wiped tears from her eyes.

'I won't apologise for helping your brother, but my God, I'm so sorry for what happened to you. Let me help you now?'

She laughed sarcastically again. 'Help me? Aw, do you feel guilty now? Are you feeling sorry for me?'

'You don't need my pity so I'm not giving you that. But you wanna get out of here? You want a different life to the one you have, then let me help you?'

'Leave me the fuck alone,' she spoke slowly and deliberately. The girl was filled with hatred and Lindsey could understand why.

'OK, I'll leave you alone. For now.' Lindsey got to her feet. 'I'm leaving my card on your locker. Call me or come and see me; let me know that you want your life to change and I'll do everything I can to help you. But Laura, keep doing what you've been doing with me and you're shaping your own future into something that won't be much different from your past. You have until tomorrow. If I haven't heard from you by then, I'll be going to the guards.'

Lindsey left the girl's room and closed the door quietly behind her. She stood against the wall for a minute and closed her eyes. She felt sick to her stomach, as she remembered again the phone call from Damien and the scene at their house. But instead of thinking about Damien's smashed and bloodied face, she remembered the fifteen-year-old girl, sitting on the stairs in her pyjamas, crying her heart out. Lindsey barely gave her a thought back then because she wasn't her responsibility. 'You fucking dickhead, Lindsey,' she mumbled to herself.

Finally, she shoved herself off the wall and headed for the stairs, but before going down, she detoured down the boy's hall and knocked on the first door. By luck, it was the right one, as Greg's voice called out, 'What?'

Lindsey stuck her head in. 'Hey, just checking; you still have that magazine?'

'What magazine?'

'The one with my number on it?'

He rolled his eyes and nodded.

'Good. The same rules apply; use it any time.' She smiled even though it was the last thing she felt like doing. 'Otherwise, I'll see you on Monday.'

He nodded with a half smile and she left.

'How is she? There was a bit of screeching going on up there,' Anne asked when she met Lindsey at the end of the stairs.

'I need to talk to her social worker, Anne.'

'Is everything OK?'

Lindsey shrugged. 'They'll be in touch with you.'

Anne nodded, looking a little worried now.

'Do me a favour and keep a close eye on her. You were right; she's more fragile that she lets on. And here's my number,' she handed Anne a card. 'Will you call me if I can do anything?'

Anne nodded and Lindsey left, with the weight of a bowling ball resting on her gut.

Rather than going home, Lindsey went back to the Centre which was locked up and in darkness. She wasn't staying long; just long enough to get some details from Damien's file. More specifically, the name of their social worker. She opened the file to the first page, where Jane McGrath was listed as the main contact. Lindsey vaguely remembered the woman who was at the house that night, but she hadn't spoken to her much, then or since.

It was almost six, but she called the number for child protective services and asked for her by name. Her call was transferred and a woman answered.

'Hello?' she sounded harried.

'Hi, is this Jane McGrath?'

'Yes.'

'My name is Lindsey Ryan. I work at Tús Núa.'

'OK?'

'I worked with Damien Lucey.'

There was silence on the phone. Jane was either trying to recall the person attached to that name, or she had no idea who Lindsey was talking about.

'We met briefly a year and a half ago, on the night that Damien and his sister Laura were taken into emergency care...'

'Look, no offence, Lindsey, but I deal with hundreds of kids. I take dozens into emergency care on a monthly basis. You'll have to be more specific.'

'OK, well let me get straight to the point then.' Lindsey was about to lose her cool with this woman, who couldn't have sounded more disinterested if she tried. But then Lindsey knew the state of their department. She knew the size of the impossible caseloads that each of them carried, which was the only thing keeping her from dragging the woman through the phone and throttling her. 'Are you still placing kids with the O'Halloran's? Larry and Bríd, I think are their names.'

'I can't give you that information.'

'Is that so? Well let me give you some information then; if you currently have kids placed with them, then it would be in your best interests to go there immediately, and I mean this minute, and get them out of there, because I've just been talking to one of their ex-foster kids who I believe may have suffered some form of sexual abuse in that house. But of course if you're too fucking tired to give a shit, then I'll go down there and get them myself.'

'Hang on, what?'

Lindsey could hear a keyboard clicking now.

251

'You heard me. Now are you going down there, or am I?'

'What did you say your name was?'

'Lindsey Ryan. Do they have kids with them now or not?'

'Thanks for getting in touch. I'll take it from here,' Jane's tone changed from weary to official before she hung up the phone.

Lindsey sat there listening to the dial tone for a few seconds, before putting the phone down. Eventually, when she could finally bring herself to move, she drove Frank home and fed him before changing into her running gear. She took the longest possible route to Street's place, though progress was slow with her bruised ribs screaming in pain with each step. Once there, she took the time to strap her hands finally taking Street's advice, and then she threw just two punches at the heavy bag, before dropping to her knees and hugging herself in agony. Once she was able to compose herself again, she moved to the speed bag, which didn't give the same satisfaction. Tonight, she wasn't picturing the faceless rebel fighters that she sometimes pictured, or her own inadequacies that so often took on a life of their own; tonight she pictured a man called Don O'Halloran. Another person who was faceless to her. But a person who'd stolen yet another future.

'Hey, Ryan!' a voice echoed down the stairs from Street's place. It wasn't Adam's voice, but it was a voice that she knew well. One that she hadn't heard in years.

She stopped what she was doing and held the bag to stop it from swinging and she listened carefully, not sure if she'd really heard it.

'Ryan! Get your scrawny ass up here!'

She grinned and unwrapped her hands as she headed for the stairs. She took them two at a time and hugged Damo tightly when she reached him on the top step. He was another Damien, from her old life. Damien Brady, aka Damo. He and Lindsey began their army careers together and in a way, they reached the beginning of the end of their careers together too, in Syria.

'What's this scruff about?' she tugged on his unkempt beard.

'Watch yourself there, Damo. She has a thing for bearded bastards,'

Street jeered.

'Shut up, you,' Lindsey punched him on the arm and followed them both inside.

'How you doing girl? Sorry I didn't come see you, but I fucking hate hospitals.'

Lindsey waved away his concern.

'So what's all this I hear about you having a stalker? You really know how to attract them, don't you?'

'I don't any more,' she looked at Street now.

'They catch him?'

'*Her* actually. It was just a kid, like I said.'

'Did you hand the little psycho over?'

Lindsey shook her head. 'Not yet, Street, and she's not a psycho. Honestly, if I was in her shoes, I'd probably have done the same thing.'

'What shoes are they?'

'It doesn't matter, it's sorted.'

'Lindsey, she could be setting up camp outside your house as we speak, with a fucking machete in her hand for all you know. Why didn't you hand her over?' Street was incredulous.

'She's not. Now will you please trust me to handle it and give it a rest? I haven't seen Damo here in an age.' She smiled as Damo handed around some of Street's beers.

'Tell me about these bearded bastards then?' Damo asked, as he settled back with a familiar cheeky grin on his face.

Lindsey rolled her eyes and took a drink, while Street took great pleasure in filling him in on his own exaggerated version of Lindsey's *moment* on the Comeragh Mountains.

Before she knew it, it was almost two in the morning and it was like no time at all had passed since they'd last seen each other. As was the way with military friends, they had a knack for picking up exactly where they left off and through the whole night, there was no mention of that hellish place called Syria. Instead they talked about their old colleagues. When it came to the ones they hadn't seen in years, at least one of them knew exactly where they were and what they were doing now. They talked about Street's new fangled relationship with Sinéad. They talked about Jason, or Florence Nightingale, as Street insisted on calling him. They talked about the two women that Damo was currently seeing, in two different counties and the three-year-old son that he had in Dublin. Not to mention the mother of said son who, according to Damo, was sent straight out of hell to plague him for the rest of his life. Though he clearly adored his boy. She would gladly have stayed for the night if she didn't have work in the morning and when she got up to leave, they both put up a string of arguments to walk her, or run with her, the five miles home.

She wasn't looking forward to it, now that she'd settled in with several beers, but it'd clear her head and sober her up. Either way, she had no intention of being escorted home.

'Look, if you're not taking me home, then sit the fuck down girl, will ya? I'm not done talking to you yet,' Damo protested, as he opened three more beers.

Lindsey rolled her eyes, but she did sit back down. Truth was, she didn't really want to leave yet, but she knew she'd regret this next beer in the morning.

'So, tell me about these junkies that you've been getting into it with.'

Lindsey got to her feet again. She was out of there.

'What? What did I say?' Damo held his arms out.

'Nothing. I have to get up for work in the morning.'

'Come on, sit down. What, you think I'm going to lecture you about beating up a few junkies? Who am I to lecture anyone? Shur I've been known to answer questions with my fists from time to time too.'

That was true. Damo had started so many fights over nothing in the time that Lindsey had known him, that she'd completely lost count.

'It wasn't like that,' she replied, sitting back down. 'And anyway, one of them is dead now, so it really doesn't matter.'

Street raised his eyebrows, but it was Damo who answered with a grin. 'You fucking killed him?'

'He killed himself. Nothing to do with me, so why are we talking about this?'

'Ah you know yourself, with all the boxing and brawling and every-thing else; it'd be nice for just one of our old gang to maintain their good looks.'

Lindsey looked at Damo with his shaggy beard, his chipped front tooth and his twice broken nose and she laughed out loud. 'Looks like it's too late for us, Damo. Street, it's down to you, my friend.'

Damo leaned forward, still smiling and he brushed Lindsey's hair back from her scar. The one he also knew by heart and he shook his head. 'If anything, it only makes you more beautiful, girl.'

She pulled back slowly and curled her legs under her. Despite the years that had passed, little had changed, though she'd never heard the word *beautiful* from any of them before. Of course they'd slagged her off and used some choice variations of that word over the years, but only be-cause they knew how to wind her up. Plus, they'd never needed to com-pliment each other.

'Christ, Damo, you used to be able to hold your drink,' Street laughed.

Damo shrugged and grinned as he brought the bottle to his lips. 'What I really wanna know is, what makes you so sure that this girl… this kid, is the one who's been following you?'

'It's her.'

'Because?'

'I found something belonging to her in my garden. Right by where I was knocked out.'

'And then she admitted it?'

'She's a teenager. They don't admit to anything.' Lindsey brought her beer to her lips vowing to leave as soon as she'd finished.

'So you don't know for sure?'

'Damo, please shut up,' Lindsey half smiled and shook her head. It was Laura. She was sure of it and she didn't need anyone casting doubt on that. Not tonight.

'Some fucker knocked you out with a baseball bat. You need to be sure, Linds.'

She looked to Street who was watching her intently and she dropped her head onto the back of the chair. 'It'll be settled by tomorrow,' she blew out a long breath and got to her feet again. 'Now I'm going before you actually morph into my mother.' She grinned and roughed up Damo's hair even more than it already was and headed for the door.

On the long walk home, she had the familiar feeling that she was being followed; only it wasn't accompanied by the usual discomfort. That was because, whether she wanted it or not, she was being escorted by a brother. She couldn't see him, but she knew for a fact that he was there. Normally this would annoy her no end, but maybe it was down to one too many beers, because tonight, the presence of this scruffy and rough looking individual, whom she loved dearly, filled her with warmth and reminded her of the fact that, retiring from the army didn't mean that you were no longer a member of the family.

CHAPTER EIGHTEEN

It was the shrill ringing of her phone that woke Lindsey from a restless sleep. She couldn't remember what she'd been dreaming about, but her sheet was balled up under her and her duvet was on the floor. Plus she had a pain behind her eyes, which she knew was the beginning of a hangover.

She felt around blindly for her phone, which seemed to be ringing forever before she got to it. 'Hello?' she finally groaned, while picking up her watch with her other hand and checking the time. Six-forty in the morning.

'Lindsey?' it was Sinéad. 'You up?'

'Hey… yeah, I'm up,' she struggled into a seated position. 'What is it?'

'You called the department yesterday about Don O'Halloran?'

Lindsey's eyes opened and quickly adjusted to the light. She needed to switch on. 'Yeah.'

'I need to you come down to the station.'

'Now? What's happened?'

'There'll be a car outside your house in about five minutes. Can you be ready?'

'Sinéad, what happened?'

'Come down Linds, I'll fill you in.'

As the line went dead, Lindsey pulled back the curtains to see a squad car pull up to the kerb outside. She got up and went to the kitchen to fill Frank's bowls before taking a very quick, cool shower. She got dressed in jeans and a relatively new hoody, just as Frank was finishing up his breakfast and then he came with her to the car. Jim Duggan was behind the wheel.

'Jim,' Lindsey leaned on the passenger window as he lowered it. 'Is it OK if Frank comes with us?'

Jim smiled slightly and pointed to the backseat. Lindsey opened the back door for Frank, then she sat in the front, alongside Jim.

'How's it going, Lindsey?'

'Not bad, thanks. This seems a bit ominous though.'

He returned a half smile, though it was almost automatic. He was clearly very focused on his own thoughts. 'Let's get down to Anglesea Street and we can have a proper conversation, alright?'

'Sure.'

'I hear Damo Brady's back in town?' he asked, by way of small talk.

'For however long he'll stay,' she smiled, though she wanted to pin him down and make him tell her what Don O'Halloran had done and who he'd done it to. But instead, she acted like a normal person and helped continue the small talk. 'Street tells me you were in the army?'

'Twelfth Battalion, Limerick,' he nodded. 'Fifteen years before I took off the green uniform and put on the blue one.'

Lindsey nodded.

'He's a decent bloke, Adam. I hear himself and Sinéad are after getting together.'

'So it seems.' They were nearing Anglesea Street and Lindsey was becoming more anxious and less inclined to wait for an explanation. 'I knew a few people in the twelfth, Jim. None of them were this good at small talk.'

He smiled a proper smile now, but he didn't respond, until finally they were pulling into the garda station car park. He let Frank out his side and they both followed Jim indoors. Sinéad was behind the desk talking to some other guards, but she cut the conversation short as Lindsey and Jim came through the door. She and Jim had a brief, quiet communication and they all headed towards a small interview room. There was a desk with two chairs on one side and one chair on the other. Lindsey sat in one and as always, Frank sat by her side.

'OK, we're here. Can someone please tell me what this is about now?'

Sinéad took the lead. 'Lindsey, you called the department yesterday and spoke to Jane McGrath?'

'That's right.'

What made you call her?'

Lindsey felt slightly torn now. She'd given Laura until today to come to her, before turning her in to the guards. This wasn't enough time. Still, she couldn't hold back anything when it came to Don O'Halloran and her reasons for reporting him.

'I had reason to suspect that he'd been involved in the abuse of a teenager who was once in his care. My priority was to first make sure that if there were any other kids in his care that they were removed immediately and that an investigation would be launched.'

'Who made the complaint, Lindsey?'

She didn't want to give Laura's name without speaking to her first.

'Lindsey, I know you're battling with yourself about whether or not to break a kid's confidence. But it is a kid, I presume? A minor? It is your job to protect them, whether they want you to or not.'

'Sinéad, I know that. Which is why I reported Don O'Halloran and I fully intend to encourage his victim to come forward.'

Sinéad and Jim glanced at each other, before Jim finally spoke.

'Don O'Halloran has been missing since Saturday the twenty-second. The same night that you were attacked.'

'Missing?'

'He was reported missing by his wife, Bríd on the Sunday. He went for a few drinks the night before and never came home.'

Lindsey was staring at them both, but she no longer saw them. Her mind was racing through the possibilities. He went missing on the same night that she was attacked. Could it have been Don O'Halloran who attacked her? But why would he? They'd never even met, as far as she knew.

'Do you have a photo of him? Don O'Halloran.'

'What are you thinking?' Sinéad asked, while Jim thumbed through a file on his lap.

'I'm wondering if I knew him.'

Jim placed an eight by ten inch photo on the desk, of a fat, smiling face. To some his face might seem jolly and kind, but knowing what Lindsey now knew, he looked nothing more than ugly. And she didn't know him. She was certain of it.

She shook her head.

'Where was he last seen?'

'He left home at just after seven on Saturday evening. He was headed for the Turner's Cross Tavern, but according to staff there, he never made it. We checked with all his usual watering holes, but no one reported seeing him that night.'

'You definitely don't know him?' Jim asked.

'No.'

'Do you know of any reason why he might want to attack you?'

She shook her head again. 'No.'

'Think, Lindsey.'

'I don't know him. Plus...'

'What?'

She blew out a long breath. She had to tell them. 'I found a piece of jewellery in my garden, right where I was attacked. It belonged to a girl called Laura Lucey. Her brother, Damien came through our Centre. He's attending university in Wales now. I met Laura on a hill walk...' she looked up at Sinéad. 'She was wearing the piece of jewellery that I found.'

'You think she was the one who was following you?'

'I do. I went to talk to her about it.'

'And?'

'Long story short, I gave her until today to admit to it and explain herself to me...'

Sinéad dropped her pen and slumped back, shaking her head.

Lindsey ignored Sinéad's annoyance. 'Damien got the help that he needed to turn his life around. She didn't. Instead, she was sent to a foster home where she alleges that she was abused by Don O'Halloran.'

Sinéad picked up her pen again and started tapping it against the desk.

'Do you believe her?' Jim asked.

'It doesn't matter whether I believe her or not, an allegation like that has to be investigated. But yes, I believe her. She has every reason to hate the system and everyone in it, me included.'

'But you weren't her social worker. You didn't place her with the O'Halloran's.'

'No. But in her eyes, I'm the reason why her brother left. He thrived with us; he took an interest in his education finally and he got into uni. It just happened to be in another country, away from his sister. As far as she's concerned, she's alone and it's my fault.'

Jim shook his head, looking like he was arguing with himself. 'OK, I can see the rationale in that. But surely it makes more sense for a kid like that to lash out at the person who put her with Don O'Halloran in the first place. If Laura Lucey was going to attack anyone, surely it would have been Jane McGrath.'

'I agree with you. But the mind of a teenager doesn't always make sense. I talked to her. I've seen first hand just how much this girl hates me. She's angry at the whole system, that's for sure, but she openly blames me for taking her brother away from her. They took care of each other when they lived at home. They were close and all of a sudden their lives are going in completely different directions and for that, she blames me.'

Jim shook his head again, but was writing quickly in his notebook. 'So Laura's jewellery was found in your garden?'

Lindsey pulled out her phone and opened the photos that she took of the chain resting where she'd found it. Sinéad took the phone and fiddled with the screen, zooming in and out and scrolling through the rest of the images.

'Did she admit that it was hers?'

'Yes.'

'What was her explanation as to how it got into your garden?'

'She accused me of stealing it.'

'I've just emailed these to myself for our records.'

Jim closed the file. 'OK. I think we need to go talk to Laura.'

Sinéad nodded. 'Linds, you'll just need to write a statement and sign it. Then I'll get someone to drop you home.'

That whole process took another hour and by the time she got to work, Mike had already left with the kids and their two volunteers, both ex-Gardaí turned rugby coaches. They were playing tag rugby up in Mayfield, which left Lindsey to catch up on paperwork and to wait impatiently for a call from either Sinéad or Jim. It was hours later when Kathleen's shrill voice broke through the relative silence in the centre.

'Oh Jesus, Mary and Joseph, don't tell me it's my Christopher?'

Lindsey got to her feet, but before she could get around the other side of the desk to see what was wrong with Kathleen, Sinéad was at her door.

'I'm not here about Christopher, Kathleen,' Sinéad spoke to Kathleen in a reassuring voice. 'I'm here to see Lindsey.'

'Oh… everything alright, love?' Kathleen called in to Lindsey.

Lindsey smiled and nodded, then gestured for Sinéad to come inside and she closed the door.

'Well?'

'OK…' Sinéad took off her cap and sat down. 'It wasn't her.'

'What?'

Sinéad shook her head. 'We have Laura on CCTV up near the Mayfield swimming pool. She and a bunch of her nicest friends were sitting in a shelter there from eleven pm until around two am.'

'Doing what?'

Sinéad shrugged. 'Sniffing glue, drinking… she disappeared around the back of the shelter for about fifteen minutes with one of the boys, then returned for more of the same.'

'OK. So what's to say she didn't come find me then?'

'Because they were busy kicking wing mirrors off cars near St Luke's Cross from about two-thirty until after three and they were next picked up near McCurtain Street at around three-fifteen. She was on a rampage for the night, that's for sure, but she was nowhere near where you were. Plus she was still in St Brendan's around the time that Don O'Halloran went missing. It wasn't her, Linds.'

'Fuck.'

'I need you to go and stay with Adam for a few days.'

Lindsey half smiled, though she wanted Sinéad to go now so that she could think. 'That's not necessary, Sinéad.'

'It is, Lindsey. We think that whoever helped Don O'Halloran to disappear, is the same person who attacked you. It's too much of a coincidence.'

'What if Don didn't need help to disappear? He's a grown man with some big issues. What makes you think that he didn't just leg it. It was only a matter of time before things came back to haunt him. He must have known that.'

'When he left the house he took no belongings with him. Not even a jacket. According to his wife, he had around thirty quid in his wallet and none of his bank cards have been used since. His mobile phone is either switched off or it's gone dead. He had a relatively big win at the bookies last Sunday and he never claimed it, which according to his wife is unheard of for Don.'

'OK,' Lindsey got to her feet. She needed time to herself.

Sinéad stood up. 'Lindsey, think about what I said. You need to be extra careful just now.'

'Just now? Sinéad, you have no idea who this person is and let's face it, you might never find out. What, you want me to move in with Street indefinitely? No. I refuse to let this scummy, cowardly piece of shit alter my life any further.' Her temper was rising and she really needed Sinéad to go.

'Lindsey...'

'Sinéad, I appreciate you coming down here and I hear what you're saying. Thank you.'

'Alright, alright I'll go. But watch your back, OK?'

Lindsey nodded and waited for Sinéad to go, before slamming the door shut.

That night, Lindsey lay on the couch in the television room at the Centre, staring at the ceiling until sometime in the early hours. In fact, the sun was beginning to come up before her eyes finally shut and when they did, the first person she saw was Lenny Jones. He was lying, lifeless on the dusty ground, with Lindsey leaning over him, shaking him by the shoulders. Street and Damo were sitting on the ground beside them, drinking beers and chatting as if nothing had happened. As if their friend wasn't lying dead beside them. Lindsey roared at them and they quietened down momentarily, before they burst out laughing and Damo picked up an old, semi-inflated football and threw it playfully at her. When she looked back to Lenny, his eyes were open and he was laughing too. Then he reached up and slapped her gently on the face and said, 'Wake up girl, will ya.'

She jolted awake and it took her a few seconds to remember where she was. There was a sound coming from the basketball court downstairs; something repetitive, like a clink followed by a little scrape. Frank was snoring softly on the floor beside her. According to the clock on the wall, it was half seven on Sunday morning. There shouldn't be anyone else there. In fact, *she* shouldn't be there, but that meant very little around here. It was probably Mike hiding from his wife again.

She got up quietly and walked around Frank and as she left the room, she pulled the door to behind her and made her way downstairs. The place was still fairly dark with just a beam of morning sunshine coming in through the high windows.

'Mike?' she couldn't see anyone when she got to the bottom of the stairs.

Then she heard the clink and scrape again coming from the corner near the stage. She couldn't see who was there. Just the small flame from the Zippo lighter, before the lid slammed shut on it again.

She glanced around, but everything that she could possibly use as a weapon was packed away, except for a lone tennis racket leaning against the wall. She picked it up and slowly made her way towards the silhouette of a man, sitting on the edge of the stage and as she got closer, it was the renewed flame from the lighter that finally lit up his face.

'Damien?' she lowered the racket, but kept a firm grip on it. 'What are you doing here? Why aren't you at Uni?'

Damien Lucey looked nothing like the lad she knew. The same face that always looked somewhere between mad worried and enthusiastic, now looked menacing and strange. He flicked the lighter three more times, before he finally spoke.

'You know, I'm starting to think that you're even more fucked up than I am.'

Lindsey didn't respond. She just stood, with half the length of the court between them, braced to defend herself, suddenly certain that she'd have to. Though she never imagined that she'd need to defend herself from him.

'Screaming in your sleep. Wandering the streets in the rain in the middle of the night. Mixing with junkies down dark alleyways. Or is all that just because I scare you?' He had a grin on his face that made him look like a complete stranger.

'You don't scare me, Damien.'

'I should. You *should* be scared.'

'Why?' she gripped the racket tighter and wished that she had something more substantial than a flimsy and ancient tennis racket.

'You have no idea what you've done, do you? Of the damage you've caused?'

'Tell me.' What few options she had were flitting through her mind. Her phone was in her jacket pocket, which was flung across the end of the couch upstairs. Even Frank was behind a closed door. It wasn't clicked shut completely, so he might be able to get out. Or he might not and chances were that no one else would come through the front door this morning.

Damien continued clicking open the lighter, igniting it and closing it again. 'Tell you? I seriously need to tell you?'

'Isn't that what you've been trying to do all along? Following me;

leaving messages for me, vandalising my house,' she paused and shook her head. 'Why did you come here in the middle of all that and tell me that you got into uni. Did you? Did you ever intend to go?'

'I did get in. I wanted to see if you cared what it cost me to go.'

'But you didn't go. Instead you stayed here. Why? To try to scare me?'

'How scared do you think my baby sister was, living with that animal?' he shouted. '*Your sister will be fine, you said,*' then he laughed maniacally. 'That was just before you threw me to the ground when your fucking brain exploded or something. You fucking barm pot.'

'Damien...'

His smile vanished as quickly as it appeared, he bounced to his feet and roared again. 'You were wrong! My sister wasn't fucking fine. Not then and she probably never will be again. You took me away from my family.'

'No, Damien. I didn't.'

'Yes, you did!' he roared. 'You made me think that everything was changing for the better. That I just needed to worry about myself and everything else would work out. You took me away from my sister! I wasn't there to protect her from him and that's all your fault.' Spit was flying from his lips as he roared and when he finally stopped, he stood for a minute, breathing hard with the body language of a bull preparing to charge. And then he did.

He was on her before she had a chance to get out of his way and as she hit the ground with him on top of her, the wind was knocked from her lungs and her head hopped violently off the hard floor, reopening the old wound left by the baseball bat.

Damien's hands were around her throat and he was squeezing so hard that Lindsey could feel cartilage crunching under his grip as she struggled to breath. Frank was barking up a storm upstairs, but clearly couldn't get out of the room and she thought briefly about the heart attack he'd had the last time this happened. She cursed herself for pulling the door to, but before she could think about much more, her vision started to blacken around the edges. It was only when Damien made a move to straddle her, presumably to get a better grip, that she was able to bring her knee into contact with his groin and cause him to let go. She managed to roll him and switch positions quickly so that she was on top and she punched him twice, once in the face and once in the throat, but she felt weak and she was sure that her punches did too, so she got to her feet to run, but he grabbed her right ankle and brought her slamming to the floor again. He kept his grip on her leg as he got to his feet and dragged her towards the stage. She kicked as hard as she could, and as he dragged her past the spot where she'd dropped the racket, she managed to grab it again. She swung at him and caught him in the right temple with full force, which felt stronger thanks to the adrenaline which was now charging through her body. He let her go and doubled over with both hands to his head.

Just then, Frank came barrelling down the stairs past Lindsey, and he launched himself at Damien, knocking him to the floor and pinning him there, but it wasn't enough. Damien seemed fearless as he punched Frank in the side of the head. Lindsey grabbed Frank by the collar and pulled him back and though he strained against her, she pulled him away from Damien who was still on the floor, bleeding from the arm now where Frank had gotten a grip.

'Stay down, Damien,' Lindsey shouted over the noise of Frank's barking. Her head was throbbing and she was dizzy and it took everything she had to hold onto Frank. His behaviour now should have been enough to put the fear of God into anyone. He'd never bitten, let alone mauled anyone in his life, but he seemed as crazed as Damien was just now.

Damien hauled himself into a seated position, leaning back against the stage. His grin was gone now and for a second, he looked almost like the boy who'd gone fishing with her.

'You made me forget about her.'

'You never forgot about her. Tell me what you could have done? It wasn't possible for you to be with her when she needed someone.'

'I should have been there!' he roared again, but added to the flying spittle now were tears and snot. 'I should have known that people like us don't get to have the perfect life. I should have known that what I was do-ing was pure fucking stupid. A waste of time, I couldn't leave. How did I think that I could? I listened to you, but what the hell did you know about our lives and what was important to *us*? My sister! She's the only thing that matters to me and you made me walk away from her.'

'Damien...' she struggled to hold onto Frank and reason with Damien at the same time, as he reached for a Coke bottle that was filled with a yellow liquid. She had no idea what was in the bottle, but Damien's expression, which suddenly seemed void of emotion, told her that it was nothing good.

He opened the bottle and poured it over himself and the smell of petrol hit her immediately.

'Damien, stop!' she pleaded with him now. 'Don't do this.' She looked frantically around the court for anything that she could use, before bringing her eyes back to meet his. 'You couldn't have known what would happen to Laura, Damien. No one could. He will never get the chance to do that again...'

Damien laughed quietly. 'You got that right. He won't be touching anyone, ever again.'

'Where is he?'

Damien shrugged. 'Being eaten by the bottom feeders in the Lee somewhere I presume.'

Lindsey held her breath for a second. He'd killed Don O'Halloran, but now wasn't the time to dwell on that. 'Good,' she said instead and Damien looked at her with a hint of surprise. 'You gave him what he deserved, Damien. You did right by your sister. They'll get that, but she needs you now. Laura is strong, she'll get through this, but she needs her brother. You're all she has.'

He half laughed again and shook his head. 'I'm useless to her. I've done the only thing that I could do for her and now there's only one thing left.'

He flicked open the Zippo, lit it and dropped it at his feet, just as Lindsey lunged towards him, but it was too late. The flames shot up too fast and too hot for her to get close. Frank was still barking as she let him go and ran for the table under the window, but Damien's screams were loud enough to drown him out. She jumped onto the table so that she could reach the end of the old curtain on the high window. She pulled it down and ran towards Damien. She covered him with the curtain and with herself, killing the flames, but the heat threatened to cook her from the outside, in. Frank had her shirt between his teeth, trying to pull her back, but she stayed on top of Damien and managed to roll him and smother the flames completely, before she jumped to her feet and ran for the stairs and her phone to call 999. Once the call was made, she slumped to her knees on the floor beside him. He was alive, but so severely burned, especially both of his legs, that there was very little she could do for him bar elevate his legs and move everything away from him. He was in severe shock. His eyes were wide open, staring straight up at the ceiling. Lindsey talked as calmly as she could to him, doing her best to imitate Jason and Jack on the occasions that she's seen them in action, though she felt nowhere near calm on the inside. Damien Lucey was the success story she told herself whenever she had a bad day at work. He was the reason why she kept going, when she felt like the work they did at the Centre didn't seem to make a difference. How the hell could she have gotten it so wrong?

CHAPTER NINETEEN

In the blink of an eye, the day slipped away and darkness enveloped the city that Lindsey loved so much and once again, she was looking at it through a window from a hospital bed. She was fine of course. Just some bruising around the neck, some fresh stitches to the side of her head and some mild burns to both hands. But she was numb and no amount of medication could help with that, even if she chose to take it.

There'd been an endless parade through her room; of medical personnel, *An Garda Siochána*, Department of Social Services, and various other people in suits, since she made the first call that morning with Damien Lucey smouldering beside her. He was in intensive care now with second and third degree burns on sixty percent of his body. Lindsey Ryan's shining success story had become her biggest failure, but that didn't matter. What mattered was that this kid's university education and future career in the field of psychology, all went up in smoke with him. She thought briefly about Don O'Halloran too. About his body being eaten by the bottom feeders of the River Lee, which was being combed by Naval and Garda divers all day. She felt nothing for him. If she could blame anyone, other than herself, she blamed him. He was where he deserved to be as far as she was concerned, but his death was also another nail in Damien's coffin.

'Lindsey?' Sinéad came back into her room, in her civvies this time. Her long and busy shift had ended and she was here as a friend now. In fact, Lindsey's room was busier than she normally would have liked, but none of them expected conversation from her, so she didn't mind any of them being there. In fact, she was happy that they were there. Street, lying across the end of her bed, reading leaflets about breast cancer and living with Alzheimer's. Damo, looking a little bit like a caged animal, but refusing to leave nevertheless. Jason, sitting in the visitor's chair, twiddling his thumbs, in between insisting that people needed tea and coffee and going in search of same. Gordon and Wesley made brief visits throughout the day and insisted that they were never coming to see her in hospital again. Mike came twice and stayed for as long as he could withstand Street's stare each time. And of course, Frank was lying quietly on the floor. Hospital policy normally wouldn't allow dogs, but Street played the *service dog* card with the staff. That and the fact that Lindsey had a room to herself, they allowed him in, but not to stay overnight. Now Sinéad had joined the quiet little group.

Street sat up to make room on the bed for Sinéad to sit down. She was out of uniform, but she looked like she had a lot to say and everyone was looking expectantly at her.

'What is it?' Street caught Sinéad's hand and did his best to encourage her to talk as she looked around the room at the other faces.

'It's alright, Sinéad. Whatever you have to say, you can say in front of these guys.' Lindsey spoke for the first time in hours and to her ears at least, her voice sounded almost robotic.

'I'm not sure if I should really be telling you this now, but...'

'But what?' Street encouraged her again.

'Linds, it looks a bit like Damien was planning an arson attack on your house... maybe with you in it.'

Lindsey continued to look out the window, while Street got to his feet and started pacing.

'Your neighbour, Mr Hennessey, called us at about half five this morning. Someone matching Damien's description was in your garden with a five-gallon drum in his hand. Your sensor lights were on, that's why he went out for a look, but by the time we got there, Damien was gone,' she lowered her head and took a breath. 'There was petrol poured all around the house, over the front door and all of the windows. We think he realised that you weren't inside, which was why he left. While we were there... he

271

was headed to the Centre.'

Lindsey nodded.

'Fucking lunatic,' Damo muttered, hatefully.

'What will happen to him?' Lindsey asked, ignoring Damo.

Sinéad shrugged. 'My guess; Central Mental Hospital. But I really couldn't say.'

'Lads, ye mind if I get some sleep?' Lindsey asked after a few minutes silence. It was time to clear the room, though she had no intentions of sleeping. She couldn't, even if she wanted to.

Damo came and ruffled her hair before remembering that her head hurt. Then he nudged her on the arm instead, but he was clearly relieved to be getting out of there. Sinéad rubbed her arm with a sincere and sympathetic smile and followed Damo out of the room.

Street hugged her tightly and kissed her on the forehead. 'I'll take Frank home and I'll be back tomorrow.'

She nodded. 'I'll be at home by then.'

'Linds…'

'I'll be at home, Street. One way or another, I'm not staying here after tonight.'

'OK… I'll see you tomorrow then,' he nodded to Jason, as he took Frank and left them alone.

'Hey.'

'Hey.' She hadn't really gotten the chance to speak to him all day. 'Look, I'm sorry that you're here again.'

He laughed quietly, though there was no humour in it. 'I'm starting to get used to it. Although I wouldn't mind getting to see you somewhere other than in the back of my ambulance, or in hospital. I much preferred that little tapas place.'

She smiled. 'Me too.'

They sat in silence for a minute, with Lindsey's hand resting in both of his.

'Jason… this is a really bad time for me.'

He squeezed her hand a little tighter.

'I'm going to get away for a while. Get my head together.'

'Where will you go?'

She shrugged.

'Well… do you know when you'll be back?'

She shook her head. She'd just come to the decision that she needed to get out of Cork and she hadn't thought any further ahead than that yet. 'I really like you. And I'd really love the chance to get to know you better, but…'

'But?'

'I don't expect you to hang around.'

He got to his feet and went to the window. 'Just like that?'

'It has to be, I'm afraid. If I don't get myself together; get my head straight, then I'm no use to anyone here. I certainly wouldn't have anything to bring to a new relationship, that's for sure. Maybe when I get back…'

'But you don't know when that'll be?'

She shook her head. It really did hurt to send him away. She hadn't felt this hopeful about starting a relationship in years, if ever. In fact, during the past three years she felt so sure that it could never happen that she'd all but given up trying. And now here it was and she was walking away from it. But she had no choice. She had to leave.

He turned back to her and caught her face in his hands and he rested his forehead against hers for a few seconds, before kissing her deeply and then leaving the room.

The next day, following yet another extremely long night of staring at the ceiling, against doctor's wishes, Lindsey checked herself out of the Cork University Hospital and got a taxi directly to Anglesea Street Garda Station. She asked for Sinéad, but she was out on a call. Jim was there though and Lindsey spent over an hour with him. She was clearing the way for herself to leave Cork indefinitely. They went through her statement again and some new questions he had for her. Also any other details that Jim wanted her to know, which was really nothing new, except that they'd tracked down some other women who had once been in the care of Don O'Halloran and two of them backed up Laura's story, which only made Lindsey feel worse and almost sorry that she hadn't gotten to him before Damien had. Legally, Damien could have come back from the rest, but if he was found guilty of murder then his once bright future looked even bleaker than ever. She left Jim with her mobile number and he kindly agreed to drive her to the Centre.

Unexpectedly, he gave her a piece of paper with the names and numbers of four Gardaí written in clear, capital letters. One was based at the Garda training college in Templemore. One in Dublin city centre, one in Carlow and one in Galway. All ex-soldiers. 'Wherever you find yourself, there's someone not too far away if you need them.'

Lindsey took the paper and held it in her lap, looking at it for a second. She nodded as she held back the tears that came to her eyes. 'Thank you.' She let herself out of the car and went inside.

She stopped just inside the door and looked towards the stage and the scorch marks that were there. The smell of burning flesh still found its way to her, despite the clear efforts that had been made to mask it. Garda crime scene tape was lying loosely on the floor and a lone young guard stood watch over the area, probably waiting patiently to be relieved.

She averted her eyes from the scene that she would never forget and she wiped them roughly with the sleeves of her jumper before finally she headed for the stairs.

'Lindsey?'

Mike was sitting in the office looking as rough as she felt.

'Jesus Christ girl, you'll be the fucking death of me.' Sheila wrapped her in a tight hug and refused to let go until Lindsey gently pulled away. 'Are you alright?'

'I'm fine,' she gave the automatic response that was nowhere near the truth. 'Listen, Mike...'

'You listen, Lindsey. I am so fucking sorry. I don't know how I didn't see this coming... I had no idea he was... I thought he...'

'So did I, Mike. Damien Lucey was the bright star in the sky as far as I was concerned. None of us knew. We couldn't have; he gave no clues. Nor could we have known what was happening with his sister because she was off our radar completely. There's no guilt attached to any of us, for any of this. It's just one of those things that unfortunately can happen in our line of work, which we have little or no control over. It happened. I'm fine. We'll get over it, OK?'

Of course none of this was true. But why should everyone feel the guilt that she felt? Why should everyone be eaten up on the inside over something as horrendous as this? Guilt was like a coat that Lindsey wore and she wore it well. She didn't want anyone else wearing it, but chances are, they would. It was, after all, what decent people did when things went wrong on their watch. At least according to the lovely Mr Hennessey and the man was right about so much.

'Anyway, I'm really sorry, Mike, but I need to leave town for a bit.'

He stood up. 'Where will you go?'

'I have friends up the country. I'll go stay with them.' This was another lie to Mike's face. People like him didn't get those who didn't make plans and she really didn't have it in her to explain herself. *Friends up the country* was vague, but it would have to do.

'Linds, I really think you should be around here, where we can...'

'Keep an eye on me?'

'Well... yes.'

'Thanks, but that's the last thing I need. But I am sorry to leave you in the lurch like this.'

'Don't worry, we'll cope. We always do. Anyway, we're going to be closed for a while until the guards release the scene and then the place will have to be renovated and brought back up to scratch. When will you be back?'

'As soon as I can,' she backed out the door, hoping that that would be the end of the conversation. 'Can you let Liam know and I'll call him in the next few days?'

'OK.' He stood looking mournfully at her as she headed for the stairs. 'He's buried under a pile of paperwork with the department. He's likely to be there a while.

'Well… you can tell him that I'm sorry for that too,' she called back as she went to leave.

'Lindsey, my love, are you OK?' she met Kathleen, hauling herself up the stairs with difficulty.

Lindsey smiled fondly at the woman, who also popped in to see her at the hospital. 'I'm grand.'

'You've been telling me that since the first night I met you… you know where,' she whispered.

'Well, I am this time. Listen, I'll see you in a few weeks, OK?'

'Get some rest love, yeah?' Kathleen hugged her, which was awkward and uncomfortable on the narrow staircase.

Lindsey kissed her on the cheek and left the Centre, looking forward to the walk home. However when she got there, she was greeted by a scene that she didn't expect to see. Not so much Street, who was getting ready to apply a fresh coat of paint to her sash windows, or even Damo, who was busy rooting around inside her shed and hauling pots of paint out onto the grass. What surprised her was Greg Patterson and Jamie Cussons, looking like drowned rats as they took it in turns to power wash the walls of her house.

'What's going on here?' she asked, from the gate.

'Don't ask me,' Greg replied. 'I asked for boxing lessons and I end up here, washing a fucking wall,' he pointed at Street. 'That fella thinks he's Mr Miyagi and I'm the Karate Kid. Next thing you know he'll have me waxing on and waxing the fuck off.'

Lindsey laughed despite herself. 'Well, either way… thanks lads. But you know what? You can all stop what you're doing.'

Jamie and Greg stopped instantly, but Street kept painting.

'I'm heading away for a bit, so I'm sure… whatever's on the walls, will be washed away by the rain by the time I get back.'

Jamie looked sceptically at her, then used his fingers as inverted commas when he spoke, 'Well, *whatever's on the walls* smells like a petrol station.'

Lindsey glanced at Street, who only just turned around now. She wasn't sure how much the boys had been told about what happened.

'Where are you going?' Jamie asked, when no one else spoke.

'To see some friends for a few days.'

'Where do they live?'

'Up the country.'

'Where up the country?'

Lindsey studied the boy for a minute with a small smile on her lips, before reminding herself that she couldn't make a success story out of Jamie. 'Christ, if you want to paint my house so badly, then why didn't you just say so?' she nudged him playfully, before picking up one of the tins of paint that Damo had landed on the path. It was the same colour that she'd only recently painted the place, but if it put a stop to some of Jamie's questions, then she'd gladly paint it again.

And that's what the next few hours were spent doing and by the time they'd finished, the smell of petrol station had been replaced with the smell of fresh paint. They even stopped for tea and scones, courtesy of Mr Hennessey, half way through. He too had a million questions, but true to his nature, he only asked one; if she was OK.

After they packed up that evening, they ate take away pizza in Lindsey's living room. Jamie and Greg did most of the talking, about general teenage stuff. The fact that neither of them wanted to go back to school in a few weeks' time, the five a side soccer tournament that they were in the middle of and some street league that Jim Duggan was trying to get off the ground. Neither of them knew too much about what had happened, only that there was a break in at the Centre, a fire was set and both the guy and Lindsey had been injured. It was almost seven when they got up to leave and as they all piled into Street's car, Jamie decided that he needed the loo. When he came out, Lindsey was waiting in the sitting room for him.

'Good to go?' she asked with a small smile.

He nodded.

'Spit it out, Jamie.' She knew the kid well enough to know when he was about to burst if he couldn't say something.

'I'm thirteen years old. In three months time, I'll be fourteen. I'm not a child, Lindsey.'

She nodded. 'I know that.'

'I know something happened. Something more than just a break in. First someone attacked you in your garden. Then there was a fire at the Centre, you're back in hospital and your house smells like a petrol station.'

She put her hand on his shoulder, but before she had a chance to say anything, Jamie spoke again.

'Someone said that it was an old kid, who used to go there. Like one of us.'

'OK,' she had no intentions of lying to him.

'Why did he come after you?'

'It doesn't matter, Jamie. All you need to know is that it's over now and I'm fine.'

'But you're leaving.'

'Only for a while.'

'Is it because you're afraid?'

'I have nothing to be afraid of. Not any more. What are you worried about?'

'That you won't come back.'

'Hey, I just spent all day painting my house. Why would I do that if I wasn't coming back?'

He nodded solemnly and headed for the door, but he didn't get very far before he stopped again. This time he spoke quietly with his back to her. 'Aside from my Mam, you're the first person who ever...' he shook his head and was clearly searching for the words, 'I don't know... the first person who was normal around me.'

She caught him by the shoulders and turned him around to face her again and she hugged him tightly. 'Thank you, Jamie,' she mumbled into his hair, before releasing him and walking him to Damo's car, where the lads were waiting patiently.

She stood on her doorstep and watched them drive off and stayed for a moment longer to watch the sun setting behind the cityscape. Then she closed her front door and went about filling her backpack. She packed all weather clothing and all of her outdoor gear. Then she packed a smaller pack with enough supplies to take care of Frank for a month at least and then she loaded up her car. Back in her little kitchen, she scribbled a note for Street, the friend who'd been with her through it all. Through all of her training in Ireland and through each of her tours overseas. From Lebanon to Chad and onto Syria and even though she hadn't seen him for three years after that, she was in no doubt about the fact that *he* saw *her*. Street made it his business to check up on each member of his team always and she was lucky enough to be on his team. In her note she asked him not to this time. She gave him every assurance that she would in fact be fine and that she would be back, though she didn't know when. Before leaving, she emptied her pocket of the piece of paper given to her by Jim. She left it on the kitchen table and then tacked Street's note to the front door before she and Frank headed for the car.

As she started driving, she had no idea where she was going, or how long before she'd come back. *If* she came back and as she watched Cork city getting further away in her rear view mirror, she couldn't help wondering what would happen now that, for the first time in a long time, really, nobody would be watching.

About the Author

Michelle Dunne was one of those sporty types growing up, all bony elbows and knees, and as she lived on an island, it stood to reason she'd spend her first couple of decades taking in the salty, seaweedy air at the local rowing club (not the serene looking, posh rowing, but the other kind, undertaken by hardy fishermen).

This was where she learned just about everything she ever needed to know about anything. They brought home the County's, All-Ireland's were won, but the banter on the bus was always the real prize. From there it made sense that she'd leave town and join another club/asylum and found herself wearing a blue helmet somewhere in South Lebanon.

She'd become attached to the UN, but more importantly, to B-Company, the boldest, brightest, bravest the Irish army had to offer. She called them lots of other names too, but only to their faces. As tracer rounds lit up the sky above her and artillery rained down, she learned the words of every patriotic Irish song ever written and how to smile, laugh, and joke about things that would otherwise have you curled in a ball, rocking back and forth in the corner of the room.

Once her eyes had been opened and she returned to Irish soil, Michelle was promoted and following a spell back at college, is now a part of a company providing physiotherapy and staff training in nursing homes and hospitals all over Munster. A slower pace, but still an unruly bunch when they want to be. She's back living on the island of Cobh with her husband Dominic and their daughter Emily and the hundreds of colourful characters waiting to make their way onto a piece of paper.

While Nobody is Watching draws from her military experiences and the types of relationships that form within its ranks.

Folllow her at @NotDunneYet.

CPSIA information can be obtained
at www.ICGtesting.com
Printed in the USA
JSHW042122240421
13923JS00001B/1

9 781951 709396